The Messy Lives of Book People

Also by Phaedra Patrick

The Curious Charms of Arthur Pepper
Rise and Shine, Benedict Stone
The Library of Lost and Found
The Secrets of Love Story Bridge

The
Messy Lives
of
Book
People

Phaedra Patrick

PARK
ROW
BOOKS

PARK
ROW
BOOKS™

Recycling programs
for this product may
not exist in your area.

ISBN-13: 978-0-7783-1200-0

The Messy Lives of Book People

Park Row Books
22 Adelaide St. West, 41st Floor
Toronto, Ontario M5H 4E3, Canada
ParkRowBooks.com
BookClubbish.com

Printed in U.S.A.

To Pat, Dave, Mark and Oliver.

The
Messy Lives
of
Book
People

1

THE APARTMENT IN THE CLOUDS

Liv Green wore her polishing cloth draped over her arm in the same proud way a maître d' might wear a napkin. She'd already cleaned Essie Starling's two bathrooms, each bigger than her own bedroom, polished the white marble kitchen worktops and left uniform vacuum cleaner tracks on the dove gray carpets, just how the bestselling author liked them. She wore one earbud while she worked, listening to the audiobook of Essie's nineteenth novel for the second time and leaving her other ear free in case the author called out any commands.

As Liv carried her cleaning box into the third bedroom, she averted her eyes from the floor-to-ceiling windows. After three years of working here, the panoramic view still made her dizzy. If she were Rapunzel, she'd need a plait thirty-two stories long to reach down to the pavement. Not that many forty-two-year-old mums, wearing bleach-specked jeans and an ancient Rolling Stones T-shirt, ever appeared in fairy tales.

Outside, cars were beeping in the Friday evening traffic. Liv really should be home by now, but there was always something about Essie that made her want to stay.

The apartment's white walls were lined with shelves pop-

ulated with framed photographs and a rainbow of books—
contemporary novels, battered tomes, childhood favorites and
copies of Essie's own novels in forty languages. Liv loved to
gently wipe their covers and admire how various countries
depicted Essie's famous heroine, Georgia Rory.

If she ever told anyone she cleaned for the author, the common reaction was wide eyes and a dropped jaw. "You really
work for *the* Essie Starling?" people would ask. "What is she
like? Why is she so reclusive?" Liv couldn't blame their fascination. She could still hardly believe she worked for her favorite writer, and, out of her three cleaning jobs, she relished this
one the most. In response to eager questions about Essie, she
gave a slight smile and a shrug, adding to the author's enigma.

For the past decade, Essie had refused most interviews and
no longer took part in book tours. Invitations to give talks,
attend literature festivals or go to parties were ignored. She
didn't even take calls from her agent and publisher, contacting them by email or via her latest personal assistant instead.
On the rare occasion Essie left the apartment, Liv never knew
where she disappeared to.

As she straightened up the books on the shelves, Liv spotted a chunk of A4 pages, stained and dog-eared as if handled
many times. It looked like a manuscript and was obviously in
the wrong place. She picked it up to return it to Essie's writing room and recognized the author's indigo scrawl on the
front page.

Book Twenty, it read.

Liv let out a small gasp, her heart dancing in her chest. She
was holding Essie's latest story, the new Georgia Rory adventure.

The series of novels originated in the late eighties. Although literary critics were sniffy about Georgia's clean-cut
character, positivity and verve, readers across the world adored

her. They camped outside bookstores on publication day, and copied Georgia's eclectic outfits of floral tea dresses, school ties, a black blazer and battered biker boots. Young adults and grown-ups alike enjoyed the stories, passing the books on across generations. All the novels became book club favorites, and Liv was happy to label herself as Georgia's biggest fan.

And here, finally in her hands, was a draft of Essie's twentieth book. Other readers would kill for this moment.

Pulling out her earbud, Liv looked over her shoulder toward the closed writing room door. For a moment she wondered if Essie had intentionally left the manuscript for her to find, as she sometimes did with books by other writers. *No, it's not possible*, she told herself. Mere mortals were never allowed to clap eyes on Essie's work before it was published, except for her agent, Marlon, and editor, Meg.

For the first couple of years that Liv worked here, the author had been strictly out of bounds, and her writing door remained closed. But over the last twelve months, things had begun to change. Essie called out to Liv for reminders of plot points, and her characters' likes and dislikes.

"Nobody knows Georgia Rory like you do," Essie once said, making Liv feel like a child wrapped in a hot towel fresh off the radiator.

If she had to find one word to describe it, she'd say Essie was *thawing* toward her.

Warmth spread in Liv's chest, the delicious yearning she felt whenever she held a new book. When she fingered the tatty edges of paper, anticipation shimmied down her spine. Was there any harm in peeking at a page or two?

She nervously glanced at a photo on the shelf of the author. Essie wore a blue evening gown with embroidered birds on the shoulder. Her round glasses had lenses as dark as licorice, and her trademark patterned silk scarf was tied around her sharp black bob. Tangerine orange was her preferred lip color. She once attended all the best parties and award ceremonies, and her fans voted in droves for her to win the global Constellation Writing Prize ten years ago.

And then, on the eve of the Constellation after-party, Essie vanished.

Post-award interviews were canceled, and journalists were left hanging. Speculation raged—was she ill, what had happened, where was she? As the months ticked by, her fans clung to the hope she might emerge from hiding to grace a local bookshop or appear on TV. But Essie hadn't been seen in public for a decade.

Liv always wondered how and why things changed so dramatically for the author. Why would someone with the world at their feet cut themselves off from society? Now *that* would make a great story.

Unable to resist the lure of the manuscript, Liv sat down cross-legged on the carpet and began to read the first chapter. She'd always had a vivid imagination, allowing her to slip into books and become one with the characters. The room and the photographs faded away.

Aware of nothing else but the story, Liv kept on turning the pages.

Georgia swallowed her worries away as she strode into the airport. Old-fashioned fans rattled on the ceiling and did little to circulate the stifling heat. It was a tiny place with a dusty track for a runway and two propeller planes on standby. She gripped the handle of her battered leather suitcase, full of trepidation. She'd traveled the world, and been on many adventures, but this time her throat was scratchy and her anxiety was rising. "I'm not sure where I'm going, or what I need to do," she said aloud. "Is there anyone who can help me?"

"*Olivia.* What on *earth* are you doing?" a woman's voice said. Liv's bookish world snapped away and her cheeks flooded with color. Essie was the only person who used her full name. How long had she been standing in the doorway?

Liv frantically gathered the pages of the manuscript together before realizing they weren't numbered. Questions rumbled in her head about what she'd just read. Where was the warmth and fun in the story? Where was Georgia's usual quick wit and confidence?

Her eyes crept fearfully toward Essie's beige Tory Burch pumps, up her slim black trousers and silk blouse, before reaching the patterned Hermès scarf in her hair and her narrowed eyes. "Essie, I'm *so* sorry," she spluttered. "I started to read and couldn't stop."

Essie's glasses slipped down her nose, so Liv could see her steely gray irises. "My writing room in ten minutes, please," she snapped. She turned on her heels and left the room with the grace of a prima ballerina.

Liv's palms were clammy as she tried to return the manuscript pages to their correct order. Essie employed a revolving door of personal assistants. As one exited, another one showed up. Liv had overheard her firing her last one, Matilda, and was never sure why *she* was the only employee left standing.

She couldn't afford to lose this job. Her husband, Jake, was fighting to stop his family business from going under, and her son Johnny was joining his older brother, Mack, at university this summer. He needed enough stuff to fill a small truck. Liv's wages were on the modest side, but every penny counted in the Green household. If she was going to be dismissed, she hoped it would be quick, like ripping a plaster off a hairy knee.

Returning the manuscript to its shelf, Liv's eyes narrowed when she saw something glinting behind a trophy. She carefully reached up and plucked out a small label-less glass bottle. As she lifted it to her nose, the sweet smell of juniper made her stomach churn.

It was the fifth miniature gin bottle she'd found that week, not to mention the full-size vodka beside Essie's bed. Liv sighed and pushed the bottle into the back pocket of her jeans. Really, where did Essie think they disappeared to when she left them around the place? She wondered if the author had been drinking while reading her own manuscript, and why.

Her pulse performed a quickstep as she padded along the hallway toward the writing room. She said a mental goodbye to the designer side table, books and huge display of lilies.

Before she entered the writing room, Liv clenched her fists. *You've been through worse*, she told herself, trying not to think back to her childhood when she was scared and alone in a strange bedroom clutching her Georgia Rory books for comfort.

Think. What would Georgia do?

Essie's writing room looked like it had been transported from a cottagey holiday home, a contrast to the starkness of the rest of her apartment. Her desk was made of old oak, and there was a wall of dark wooden bookshelves displaying more editions of her books.

"Be seated," Essie said, without looking up from her notepad. Her cut glass English accent had a slight American twang, which made Liv feel very ordinary. Essie was only ten years older than her yet their age difference felt like a generation.

Essie turned and steepled her long, slim fingers. "So?" she said.

Blood thumped in Liv's ears, but she had a touch of Georgia's bravery running through her veins. "I only read a few pages of your manuscript."

Essie's face was still and unreadable. "You know my work is off-limits."

"It wasn't in your writing room, and I couldn't help myself." All of her emotions felt on edge. "Are you going to fire me, or not?"

Essie's mouth twitched into a brief smile, then settled back just as quickly. As she stroked the handle of her vintage teacup, her stare seemed to laser through Liv's skin. "No, I'm not going to dismiss you."

Relief flooded Liv's body. Before she could say anything, Essie continued, "I'd like your opinion on something."

Liv's stomach jittered, and she wasn't sure if it was with fear or excitement. "Oh, okay."

Essie opened her top drawer and took out a magazine, the *Chicago Globe Literary Review*. She tossed it toward Liv and folded her arms. "My agent sent this recent review to me, for *Few and Far Between*," she said. "It's dated April Fools' Day. I assume it's not a hoax."

Liv gulped. She wasn't good with dates, always forgetting birthdays and anniversaries, but the author was highly superstitious about them. She read a section of the critique, for the novel she'd just been listening to. It was a fair summary, albeit with a weary tone of voice.

April 1, 2019

The complexities and delicate emotion of Starling's earlier work are missing in this flat novel. The writing is uncomplicated, and the story unoriginal. Georgia Rory's feistiness has been replaced with a dithering reticence and lack of direction. Once a writer of considerable promise, Ms. Starling continues to let her once considerable talent fly south. It is therefore no surprise she avoids the public eye. Nevertheless, her devoted fans will undoubtedly buy the book in their millions, guaranteeing her yet another bestseller.

Liv quickly considered what she should say. Forget about being caught reading during work hours—saying the wrong thing about the review would surely cost her this job. Did she try to flatter Essie? Should she use a conciliatory tone, or a firm, resolute one? Whatever she said would be judged.

"The truth, please, Olivia." Essie tapped a fingernail on her desk. "And get straight to the point."

Liv ran her tongue around her mouth to get rid of a metallic taste. She tapped into Georgia's mindset once more and tried not to falter. "I think your earlier books had a warm, easy charm, like you really enjoyed writing them. However, if I'm honest, like you're asking me to be—" She hesitated. "I…sometimes feel you've lost your true passion for Georgia."

Essie raised a palm, as if stopping traffic. "And the pages of the manuscript you read?"

Liv lowered her eyes. "Kind of the same thing."

"I see," Essie said through gritted teeth.

"You asked for my opinion…"

"And you gave it to me. Thank you *very* much, Olivia."

Liv fidgeted in her seat, already regretting her frankness. An electronic blast of "Paperback Writer" by The Beatles sounded from her phone, vibrating loudly between her backside and the chair.

Essie's neck stiffened like a cobra. "You should answer that."

"Yes, sorry." Liv tugged the phone out of her pocket and saw Jake was calling. She tucked her chin into her neck. "Hi, yes I'm still at work," she whispered. "I'll be half an hour or so… Okay, I hadn't forgotten… Bye." Liv turned off her phone. "Sorry, my son's bringing a new girlfriend home and I said I'd make a cake for tea. I'll get one from Aldi instead."

"Really? I do recommend Bentley and White. Their patisserie is divine."

"Oh? Thanks." Liv had no intention of visiting the extortionately priced shop. "The window displays are gorgeous."

An awkward silence fell between them.

Liv had an urge to apologize, but Essie waved her hand. "That is all," she said.

Liv's legs shook as she left the room. Thank goodness she still had her job, at least for the moment. She took a few minutes to gather together her cloths and cleaning solutions, then tugged the vacuum cleaner back into the store cupboard. When she'd finished, she pulled on her scuffed yellow Converse. "Have a good evening," she shouted out to Essie.

Strangely, the writing door was wide-open. There was no reply.

Liv padded toward it to say goodbye properly, but Essie's chair was vacant and pushed up to her desk.

"Essie," she called out, frowning as she moved from room to room. She wanted to feel the air was clear between them before she left for the weekend. However, all the rooms were unoccupied. The author was nowhere to be seen.

"Essie?" Liv whispered, as she pirouetted alone in the empty writing room. "Where the hell are you?"

But it was no use. The author was gone.

2

CAKE IN THE BATH

Liv hurriedly bought a cake from Aldi and listened to the end of *Few and Far Between* as she jogged across the city, but her mind was firmly set on Essie. The author had pulled that vanishing trick a few times before. One minute she sat in her writing room scribbling away, and the next she disappeared like a rabbit from a magician's hat. It was at odds with her reclusive behavior, and Liv wondered if she went to visit a neighbor or run an errand. She felt like it wasn't her place to ask.

By the time she reached home her knuckles glowed cherry red from carrying the cake in the chilly late April weather. Liv inhaled a few last seconds of calm before opening her front door.

Entering the Green redbrick terraced house was like wandering into an arcade. Lights were on in every room, screens blaring and music blasting. Johnny was eighteen and attended a local sixth form college, and Mack was twenty and home from university for Easter. They were both six feet tall and bounded rather than walked, making vases wobble and floorboards groan. No matter how many times Liv and Jake tidied up after them, their bedrooms resembled the aftermath of a hurricane.

After the stress of her conversation with Essie, Liv craved normality and a laugh over the lasagna Jake had said he'd make. She hoped Johnny's new girlfriend being present would stave off the constant talk about football around the dinner table.

She called out a quick, "Hi, I'm back," before kicking off her shoes and placing the cake on the radiator shelf. "Bentley and White?" she muttered to herself and laughed. "As if."

Upstairs, she slipped into a shapeless black dress she'd had for years and kept on her socks. She bought them in shades of pink so they didn't get mixed up with the boys' pairs.

She cleaned her teeth and gave her hair a quick ruffle in the bathroom mirror. She'd recently cut it herself to save on salon costs and had taken a slice out of her right eyebrow. Johnny had laughed and called her edgy. Her butterscotch layers were now shaggily uneven, though her contrasting dark roots made her sage eyes appear greener.

Back downstairs, Liv found Johnny slumped at the dining table flicking through one of his dad's film magazines so roughly he almost ripped Keanu Reeves's face. When she squeezed his shoulder to say hi, he grunted without looking up.

Jake stood behind the kitchen island, wearing Liv's pink apron with Keep It Clean printed on the front. The sight of his biceps flexing while he buttered bread could still make her belly flip, though the tawny curly hair she'd fallen in love with over twenty years ago was now cropped and graying. She tried to plant a kiss on his cheek, but they clumsily butted foreheads when he turned to greet her.

"You're here," he said with mock surprise. "I thought you'd been kidnapped."

Liv broke off a piece of bread and popped it in her mouth. "Essie wanted to chat to me about a book review."

"Hmm," Jake said flatly. He wasn't impressed by the kind of books Essie wrote. His family's business, Paperpress, specialized in bookbinding, typesetting and printing textbooks with a particular focus on sports, politics and local history. He preferred to read biographies and journalistic nonfiction over novels. He called Essie's novels *made-up stories*.

That's what fiction is, Liv always wanted to retort, though never said anything back.

An Italian recipe book lay open on the worktop, but there were no pasta sheets or tomatoes next to it. "Aren't we having lasagna?" she said.

"Beans on toast is quicker. Mack's playing football with his mates, so it's just us three eating."

"Oh." Liv tried to mask her disappointment. Jake's girlfriend mustn't be coming anymore. Her shoulders drooped as her vision of a fun, chatty evening evaporated. "Um, three?"

Her husband mouthed, *They broke up*, before nodding toward Johnny.

Before Liv had a chance to ask Johnny if he was okay, Jake plonked down three plates. "Tea's ready," he said, patting his son on the back. "Plenty more fish in the sea, mate. Plus, Man United are on TV tomorrow. Nothing beats that."

Ignoring his dad, Johnny wolfed down his food so fast Liv doubted he tasted it. She stopped herself from comforting her son. The boys used to love her bear hugs when they were young, laughing and pressing their cheeks against hers. Now they winced and shrank away if she tried to show them any affection. Cuddles were in short supply from Jake, too. Most of the romance Liv enjoyed these days came courtesy of Georgia Rory's dashing heroes.

Johnny clattered down his knife and fork. "I'm going upstairs," he said dolefully and pushed his chair under the table. He paused. "Um, I might need a new laptop. It keeps crashing and I can't revise properly."

Jake's and Liv's eyes met briefly. Up until a few months ago, Johnny had a Saturday job at a sports shop, but it had gone out of business. He hadn't been able to find another job to fit around school, and Paperpress couldn't afford an extra pair of hands.

Jake cut his toast slowly. "Okay, mate. We'll see what we can do."

After Johnny left the room, Jake and Liv finished their food in silence.

"Don't worry about money," he said as they washed the pots together. "I'll sort it out."

It was something he'd been promising for some time. Liv hadn't told him the washing machine was on the blink, and there was a hole in their bedroom carpet.

She rubbed his back. "I know you will."

Financial issues at Paperpress meant Jake leaped out of bed in the morning to check his emails and worked at the kitchen table late at night. Now that his parents were retiring, Jake was desperate to keep the business in his family. However, it meant he and his sister, Katrina, had to urgently turn the company's fortunes around. Most of Jake and Liv's modest savings had been sucked into the business, leaving them with zero funds for emergencies and difficulty meeting their household bills.

Jake dipped a plate into the water while deep in thought. "I hate to say this, but…" He hesitated. "Do you really want to clean forever? Isn't it time to try something new?"

"I'm not experienced in anything else, and cleaning fits around the kids." Liv determinedly polished a tap.

"Mack and Johnny are grown up now. You could find something you love doing, and with better pay."

Liv didn't reply. She squeezed out a cloth and wiped all the surfaces in the kitchen. Whenever she felt under pressure, or things were messy in her head, cleaning helped her to create order.

Of course, she'd love to try something new for work, but her embarrassment about her lack of qualifications, after leaving school at the age of sixteen, followed her around like a starving dog looking for scraps. The blood in her veins cooled at the thought of forging a new career in her forties.

"Or, you could have a word with Essie…" he said.

"About what?"

"A pay rise or something. She must be loaded."

After today's events, Liv could hardly do *that*. And she'd never told Jake about the embarrassing way she'd got a job with the author in the first place.

When his phone rang, she welcomed the interruption.

"Can you get that?" He searched for a towel to dry his hands.

Liv gritted her teeth when she saw who was calling. "Hi, Katrina."

"Oh, Liv, it's *you*," Jake's sister said. Her words were as stiff as her copper coiffed hair and the eighties-style power suits she wore. "Is my brother there? It's a *business* call."

Do the grown-ups need to talk? Liv wanted to snap.

Jake took the phone from her and mouthed, *Thanks*. He disappeared into the coat cupboard to take the call. "Oh, Katrina, that's not good news," he said, shutting the door behind him. "How much is that going to cost?"

Upstairs, an Arctic Monkeys bass line thudded out from behind Johnny's closed door. "I'm busy," he called out, when Liv knocked.

"Okay, love, let me know if you need anything," she shouted over the thumping music.

She dusted around her bedroom, even though she'd only done it yesterday. Heaving a sigh, she hung up her jeans and screwed her T-shirt into a ball. Was it normal to feel so adrift in a family of four?

Liv selected her *The River After Midnight* paperback to read for the umpteenth time. It was Essie's third book, a fan favorite that had flown up the bestseller charts when it first published in the UK and US, cementing her stardom. Although she loved reading the latest bestsellers, Liv found it comforting to turn to her old books. Giving them away would be like sending a much-loved pet to a new home.

She ran a bath, got into the water and ate chocolate cake while starting to read. It was only seconds until she imagined herself as Georgia Rory.

Sun sparkled on the azure sea as the motorboat chugged and bobbed on the waves, leaving behind a stream of white foam. Standing at the bow, saltwater specked Georgia's face. The beach ahead shone gold and she couldn't wait to sink her toes into the warm sand and maybe catch a fish or two. She licked her lips and wondered if he'd be there to greet her. Just thinking about him made her body ripple with expectation.

But wait. Georgia squinted at the water. Was that a woman's head bobbing up and down and a hand reaching out? Was that a shark fin circling around? A woman's cry for help split the air. Without a moment's hesitation, Georgia dove into the choppy water and front-crawled toward the woman in danger.

A rap on the door interrupted her reading. "Mum, do you know where my sports bag is?" Johnny said.

"It's in your wardrobe," Liv shouted out.

"I've looked in there."

Liv sighed, irritated. "Look again." She reached over the side of the bath and let the book fall from her fingers. Holding her nose, she sank down until the water covered her face. *Hold on*, she called out in her head to the imaginary woman in trouble. *I'm coming to get you.*

The next day, when Liv woke up and went downstairs, the house was already empty. Jake had left a note stuck to the fridge. "Gone to the park for a kick about x"

The sink overflowed with three sets of used cups, bowls, plates and cutlery. Butter sat on the worktop going soft. Liv put it back in the fridge, unsure if the empty feeling in her stomach was hunger or something else.

She used to look forward to spending Saturdays at the park with Mack and Johnny, before their love of football became competitive and all-consuming. After that, Liv started to meet up with friends instead, but most of them had younger kids. They dragged them along to hip coffee shops where it was tricky to have an adult conversation, and the price of a latte could mean taking out a small loan.

Her spirits lifted when she got a text from her mum.

Hi love. Fancy a coffee in the park café? I'll be there at 10 x

Yes! Liv replied. **Would love that x.**

She took a quick shower, pulled on jeans, Johnny's old Pac-Man T-shirt and a warm coat, then pushed *The River After Midnight* into her handbag before speeding out of the house.

Artisan bakeries, healthy cafés and exclusive boutiques were cropping up around Manningham city center. Situated between Leeds and Manchester, the city in the northwest of England was often viewed as their less glamorous neighbor. But things were changing rapidly. Liv passed a new coffee shop called Launderette and another named The Hub. It was virtually impossible to buy a sandwich made without chutney or sourdough bread these days, and property prices were shooting up. When Liv looked around her, she spotted people driving expensive cars and clasping designer handbags, and felt like she didn't fit in any longer.

In the park, she strolled past the tennis courts toward the three-tiered stone fountain. Her heart pulled when she recalled holding up small versions of Mack and Johnny to toss coins into the water. When they were toddlers she'd fitted her work around them, cleaning in the evenings so she could look after them during the day. She bought them soft fabric books as soon as they were born and read to them throughout their childhood. The three of them spent many happy afternoons wedged on the sofa together, progressing from *Where the Wild Things Are*, to *Diary of a Wimpy Kid*, to *Harry Potter*. She took them to the playground, swimming pool and The Manningham Museum of Writing, and still missed the feel of their small hands in hers. Time had flown by so quickly.

She was delighted Johnny was following Mack to university. He was going to study English literature. Both boys would only be a couple of hours' travel away, yet it felt like an ocean. She and Jake seemed to have less and less in common these days, and she couldn't help wondering if their sons were like scaffolding around a crumbling building that might collapse when the supports were removed.

Liv spotted her mum, Carol, heading toward her. She wore a paisley skirt and a loose purple T-shirt with a diamanté star on the pocket. Her auburn curls framed her round face.

"Hiya, love," she said, her eyes lighting up when she saw Liv. She was a good hugger, using both arms and her body to squash her close. After finding a table inside, Carol set down her bag on a chair and took out an Essie novel.

Liv set hers down, too. "Snap." She laughed. "We've both brought Georgia Rory along for coffee."

Her mum often joked Liv could read before she could walk. At an early age, she had mastered the art of reading and walking at the same time without tripping up. Family picnics were never complete without Liv and her parents bringing along books to complement the food.

After they ordered coffee and a slice of lemon drizzle cake to share, Carol tapped her book. "I've just got to a juicy part. Georgia's heading into the desert with either Mike the rugged aircraft pilot, or James the marine biologist. I don't know who she'll choose."

Liv pretended to zip her lips with her fingers. "I'm not saying anything, except that things get rocky."

"Ooh, love, I don't know how you remember all the stories." Carol shook her head in amazement. "I get them muddled up. I put a tick on the title pages, to remind myself I've already read them."

"I've had lots of practice." Liv had read her first ever Georgia Rory book at twelve years old when she won it in a writing competition at school. Georgia helped to get her through some tough times, and she'd read the full series many times over.

"And how are things with Ms. Starling? Is she still as warm and welcoming as ever?" Carol grinned.

"She's actually getting a bit better," Liv said.

A few weeks ago, the author left her a copy of Stephen King's *On Writing: A Memoir of the Craft*. The yellow sticky note said, "Enriching, enlightening, extraordinary. Read and learn, Olivia." She'd read the book from cover to cover hanging on to every word.

The note was a welcome change to ones Essie used to leave for her. "Olivia, do use an alternative solution to clean my bath. I hate the smell of grapefruit." And, "Olivia, please store your cleaning equipment on the second shelf in the hallway cupboard, not the third."

Liv thought about her conversation with the author yesterday and stirred her coffee too many times. "Actually, I'm a bit worried about my job. Essie caught me reading her new manuscript then asked for my opinion on a review. I think I was too honest."

"Is that possible?"

Liv shrugged. "Maybe I should have flattered her instead. I didn't sleep well last night, thinking about it."

Carol took a fork and dug it into the cake. "Do you remember what your dad's advice would be?"

A rush of warmth mingled with sadness washed over Liv as she thought about him. Grant Cooper had been an English professor who died when she was young, and she could still summon up his smell, of books and musky cologne. Liv smiled. "He'd probably ruffle my hair and say, 'There's no point guessing how a story will end, sweet pea. Keep turning the page until you reach the next chapter.'"

Carol nodded firmly. "He always said it to his students. Worrying never changes anything."

Liv sipped her coffee. She wished she could follow her dad's advice, but it wasn't that easy. "Me and Jake, well…" She looked down at her cup. "We're struggling with our finances a bit."

Carol clicked a tongue behind her teeth. "Sorry about that, love. Is Paperpress still in a pickle?"

Liv nodded. "I'm sure it's just a rough patch." She sat up straighter, wishing she'd kept this to herself. "Everything will be fine. Jake said I should speak to Essie and ask for a pay rise. I suppose I could ask her for more hours…"

"Well, why not? Be brave."

It was something Liv could only manage by pretending to

be Georgia Rory. "It's just that, well, Essie has this *presence*. It makes me feel like a child when I'm near her."

"There's no need to put her on a pedestal." Carol rolled her eyes. "Essie Starling is made of flesh and blood. She's a human being, not a bloody deity."

Her expression made Liv laugh, and she welcomed the light relief. She knew Essie was just a person. So why did she feel like such a mystery?

3

THE FLORAL TEACUP

Liv loved the city when it sparkled at night and also its daytime bustle. She particularly enjoyed when it was blinking to life early on Monday morning, when the people who propped it up emerged from the shadows—the street cleaners who swept up nightclub flyers and last night's pizza crusts, the coffee vendors and the newspaper sellers. She felt a spirit of kinship with this unsung army of field officers. She nipped along back alleys and side streets, avoiding shop windows displaying things she couldn't afford, until she emerged among the shiny office blocks in the heart of the city.

Her first job of the day was for Platinum, a large accountancy firm, where she worked five mornings a week from six thirty, for two hours. While most people were still in bed, Liv and her teammates changed loo rolls, wiped the inside of fridges, disinfected desks and emptied bins. They had to use branded cleaning products purchased by the company, so Liv couldn't make her own natural products. She was careful to wear rubber gloves so the alcohol and bleach didn't make the skin on her hands as dry as papyrus. All Platinum cleaners had to wear a navy tunic emblazoned with the company logo. Liv wondered if the uniforms indicated to the office staff who they could ignore.

The camaraderie of her coworkers almost made up for the horrible things she found in the bins, like holey socks, moldy bread and worse. There were always funny stories flying around about online dating, in-laws, people's holiday plans and silly things their kids had said. She learned which new films were out on Netflix, and updates about celebrity love lives. By 7 a.m., Liv's face and sides ached from laughing so much.

Half an hour later, the cleaning team's conversation filtered away to a hush as the office workers arrived and sat down at their desks, probably thinking the surfaces shone as if by magic, or not noticing them at all. When the cleaners' work was done, they slipped away like melted ice cream down a crack in the pavement.

Liv's next job was for the Cardinal family, a thirty-minute walk away in the wealthy suburbs. She worked for Walter and Hannah five mornings a week also, and did Monday, Thursday and Friday afternoons for Essie.

Walter and Hannah Cardinal schooled their eight-year-old twins, Tarquin and Julietta, from home. What this really meant was Walter, a graphic designer, and Hannah, a beauty vlogger, escaped to their garden offices while the kids sat at the dining table flicking paint at each other. Hannah called it their *artistic freedom time*.

Usually by the time Liv arrived, the kitchen floor resembled a Jackson Pollock painting.

"Hey, Liv, sweetie. Come in," Hannah said, opening the door while she nibbled avocado on toast. She stood barefooted in a khaki linen boiler suit and called back over her shoulder, "Tarkers, Jules, look who's here," as if Liv was a favorite aunt who'd come to babysit.

The kids looked up from their painting. Tarquin had black

circles around his eyes like a panda, and Julietta had painted a red heart on her own white Moschino T-shirt. They smirked at Liv as if silently plotting to hide her sponges and pour her solutions down the sink.

Hannah pulled an apologetic face. "I've got a crucial Zoom at eleven, and Walt's chiropractor is working on his neck. It gets dreadfully tight when he's designing. Could you possibly make an early lunch for the kiddos?" She flashed her puppy-dog eyes. "Pretty please."

Liv tightened her grip on her box of cleaning stuff, thinking how much she needed to keep this job, too. "Sure," she said. "What will they eat?"

"You're a lifesaver, Liv, you really are." Hannah fluttered a hand to her neck. "Just give them something organic and healthy. Oh, except no falafels or hummus for Jules, and Tarkers isn't keen on raspberries. Can you make Walt a little sandwich, too, and take it to his office? There's some gluten-free bagels in the bread bin."

Perhaps you'd like me to stand on my head and play the trumpet to entertain everyone, too, Liv thought to herself. "Sure, I can do that," she said, grimacing as a blot of orange paint landed in her hair.

As she mopped the floor, she listened to an audiobook of *Garden Spells* by Sarah Addison Allen and was transported to a magical garden in North Carolina instead.

After Liv had spent a couple of hours cleaning the house then feeding the family, Hannah appeared again. "Oh, sweetie, just before you go, could you hang out the washing for me? And plant Walt's new shrubs in the garden?"

By the time Liv escaped, she was almost an hour late. Her back ached and the knees of her jeans were grubby with soil. In her rush to leave the Cardinals, she'd left her packed lunch behind. The idea of Walt eating her ham sandwiches by mistake and suffering a gluten rash gave her a tiny thrill.

Above the trees, Essie's apartment block pointed to the sky. Jake once said it looked like it was giving the middle finger to the rest of the city. Even if she might get fired today, Liv hoped Essie had returned after disappearing and was writing at her desk.

In the building's lobby, she admired the huge bronze plant pots that looked like cauldrons and the wall of windows overlooking a Japanese-inspired courtyard. Liv said her usual quick "hi" to a giant golden Buddha statue. The ride up in the lift made her ears pop, and she polished the stainless-steel button panel to distract herself.

Liv had her own access card to the apartment and smiled to herself when she saw the writing room door was open. *Great, Essie's back*, she thought.

Her initial excitement was soon replaced with a pellet of dread as she mused on her honesty about the book review. Once more, she pushed back her shoulders and tried to channel her inner Georgia Rory.

The writing room was empty, and she found the author in the kitchen sitting on a high stool instead. Liv couldn't recall ever seeing her eating in here before. Essie usually skipped lunch or ate at her desk.

The marble worktop was covered with tiny paper plates, displaying triangles of sandwiches and pastel-hued cakes. The sweet smell of vanilla made Liv's stomach growl. There was a china floral teapot and matching cups and saucers. A bottle of champagne sat in a silver wine cooler.

"Ah, Olivia," Essie said, taking a slow sip of her tea. "You've decided to grace me with your presence."

Liv thought this was a bit rich coming from someone who had vanished without saying goodbye to her last time. "Sorry

I'm late," she said, running a hand through her hair and feeling knots of paint. "I got waylaid at another job. I'll wash my hands and get to work."

Essie's eyes followed her around the kitchen as she ran the tap and lathered up soap.

"I'll start with the bathrooms, first," Liv said.

The author wrapped her fingers around her vintage teacup. "Have you lunched already?" she said.

Liv shook her head. "I've not had the chance. I forgot my sandwiches."

Essie pursed her lips together and thought. "You may help yourself to refreshments, if you wish."

Liv froze. Essie offering her food was a *pinch-me* moment. Surely, she wouldn't feed and then fire her? Her first instinct was to politely refuse, but her stomach gave a groan so loud it sounded like thunder. She was also feeling faint after skipping her breakfast.

"There's too much for one person, and I abhor food waste," Essie said. "Your hesitation just wastes my time and yours."

"Well, maybe just a little something," Liv said. She picked up a cream cheese and cucumber sandwich and cupped her hand under it as she ate. The bread was as delicate as rice paper.

"Do use a plate, Olivia." Essie sighed and removed her glasses, nodding toward one. "And sit down. I can't stand people hovering around me like tsetse flies."

As Liv pulled out a stool, Essie poured her a flute of champagne, but left her own glass empty.

"Is this a special occasion?" Liv asked, taking a sip. The bubbles popped against her nose, making her feel like giggling. "Aren't you joining me?"

Essie placed a hand on her stomach. "I'm not very hungry." Her expression didn't alter. "It's the publication day for *Few and Far Between* in the US today. The afternoon tea is a treat from my publisher."'

"Wow, congratulations. That's so special." Liv sighed to herself at how rewarding being a writer must be.

Essie looked around her as if noticing the spread for the first time. "Yes, I suppose it is. They sent things a day late last year. How difficult is it to get a date correct?"

"It looks like the Mad Hatter's tea party, in *Alice in Wonderland*," Liv said.

Essie humphed. "Perhaps, but the Hatter tells Alice he is always having tea because the Queen of Hearts sentenced him to death."

"Yes, because he sang to her, and she claimed he murdered time," Liv added.

Essie's left eyebrow twitched upward, as if both surprised and impressed. She nibbled on a scone and then pushed it away. "Did you inherit your love of books from your family?"

Liv nodded. "I read with my parents all the time. I'd loved to have studied English at uni, but..." She pressed her lips together and glanced away. She'd read somewhere Essie hadn't gone to university either, and liked to think it was something they had in common. "I think I told you my dad was a professor? He taught English at Manningham University."

"Hmm, yes, I think so." Essie looked down and distractedly folded a napkin. She focused on it for a long time.

Liv thought she'd lost her attention until the author looked up again.

"Books must be in your blood," Essie said.

Liv liked the way that sounded. She was too embarrassed to tell Essie that she'd always wanted to write and had a couple of partially finished novels in her bedside cabinet at home that she'd never shown to anyone. Or how she'd secretly taken a creative writing course but had dropped out after a fellow student tore her story to shreds in front of the whole class. The instructor had said she was talented and should stay, but the uninvited criticism ripped Liv's confidence apart.

She wanted Essie to know that cleaning didn't make her leap out of bed in the morning with glee. She had left school when she was sixteen, not because she wasn't motivated, or unintelligent, but because she needed to help out her mum both financially and around the house. Furthering her studies hadn't been an option.

At the same age Essie was popping champagne corks for her debut book deal, Liv was walking down the aisle in a secondhand wedding dress. Mack arrived when she was twenty-two, still young enough to attract disapproving stares on the maternity ward.

As a girl, cleaning was something Liv used to do with her mum. They sang together as they squeezed grapefruits and mixed the juice with salt. Domestic work was the obvious option when Liv needed work. Being able to spot fluff behind a radiator, a dropped piece of Lego, a lost earring or stray biscuit crumbs—in the same way a shark might detect fresh blood—was an art form Liv had mastered.

She didn't say any of this to Essie. "I've always loved reading," Liv said instead. "When I was seven or eight years old, I remember going to the local park. All the other kids were playing on the slide and the swings. They were laughing and having fun and I stood alone, wondering where the word *roundabout* came from. I thought I must be a bit weird."

Essie dabbed her mouth with a napkin. "I can relate to that."

"You can?" Liv said, delighted.

"I always knew I wanted to write, just as some people know they want to be nurses or police officers," Essie said. "You need formal training for those vocations, but with writing you need an idea for a story and the resolve to get on with it. Books don't write themselves."

Liv's neck pinkened at her own incomplete work. "I used to read under the covers using a torch at night, and I studied the acknowledgments in each book, to see who the writer had thanked. All those names of agents and publishers seemed like a secret society I wanted to sneak into."

"I suppose I just see it as work." Essie gazed above Liv's head for a while, her chin tilted as if deciding on something. "Perhaps you could take on some extra tasks for me," she said.

"Yes," Liv said immediately.

Essie fixed her with a bemused stare. "I haven't told you what they are yet. Would you be interested in assisting me with Georgia?"

"Me?" Liv pressed a hand to her chest. She felt her heart beating hard. "How?"

"After reading my review, you observed that Georgia is a little...stuck. I'd like your input."

Liv tried not to nod her head too many times. *Wow*, she thought to herself. Was this really happening? Essie wanted *her* help with her books? She ignored Jake's voice when it dropped into her head urging her to ask for a pay increase. Although she could really use one, it felt cheeky to ask. She had no idea how much extra work Essie wanted her to do, and this was a golden opportunity to get involved with her favorite book series of all time. It was something others could only dream of, and she wasn't going to spoil it by appearing greedy. She reached for a scone and ate it too quickly. "Sure," she said.

"I should clarify, I've never asked *anyone* for this kind of help before," Essie said. "Not even my assistants..." She looked over the top of her glasses, making the task feel even more prodigious.

Liv swallowed nervously. "That's fine. I understand."

"Splendid. I'm going away for a night or two and I shall give it some thought. We can reconvene on Thursday." Essie batted a crumb off her sleeve and put her glasses back on. "Now, we should both get back to work."

Liv wanted to ask Essie where she was going. She hoped it was somewhere nice, perhaps a luxury spa or a retreat. She had been looking rather pale and thin recently and could do with a break. "A writer's work is never done," she quipped, then wished she hadn't.

Essie smiled tightly. "Quite," she said.

Liv returned to her work. She listened to *Garden Spells* again as she mixed together water, lemon juice and a few drops of lavender oil. She cleaned all the windows until they sparkled and sunshine spilled into the rooms. She boxed up the remaining sandwiches so the bread wouldn't curl, and found a container for the cakes. As she waltzed around Essie's bedroom with the vacuum, she noticed a small Louis Vuitton suitcase that she hadn't seen before parked in the corner of the room.

When she finished working, Liv tidied her cleaning stuff away. The writing room door was ajar, and she gave a small rap. Essie sat at her desk staring out of the window. Her right hand rested on a yellow notepad. When she turned, her eyelids looked lilac and heavy.

"I'm leaving now," Liv said. "I've boxed up the afternoon tea for you."

"You may take it with you." Essie waved a hand. "I've finished with it."

"Really? Thank you. The boys will love that. Mack can enjoy a little feast before he returns to university."

Essie tapped a finger on her notepad. "I'll give thought to our conversation and note things down."

Liv felt giddy and warm inside. This could be the start of a beautiful friendship. Essie might even offer to mentor her own writing. She tried not to let her imagination run away with her, but could already picture chatting to Essie about Georgia over a vintage teacup. "I promise to do my best," she said.

"I'm sure you'll try." Essie stared straight at her, eyes full of intent. She paused and parted her lips, as if about to say something important.

As Liv smiled and waited, an expectant tingle ran down her spine.

But then a veil seemed to fall upon Essie's face. Her eyes became slits, and she pursed her lips so they resembled prunes. "That is all, Olivia," she said.

4

THE YELLOW NOTEBOOK

That evening, Liv's stomach fizzed with excitement about Essie's request. She even tried to join in the banter about football around the dining table. Afterward, she, Jake and Johnny gathered in the sitting room to look at laptops on Jake's phone. Johnny pointed to one that was two hundred pounds more expensive than the basic model.

"The cheaper one looks exactly the same," Jake said.

Johnny wrinkled his nose. "I need more internal memory."

"It's fine, get the one you need," Liv said, avoiding Jake's eyes.

"Thanks, Mum."

When Johnny left the room, Jake shook his head. "How will we afford *that*?" he said.

Liv pursed her lips. She didn't want to tell him about Essie's request yet. There was no use getting his hopes up about a pay rise because she wasn't going to ask for one. She wanted to prove herself to Essie before she even thought about recompense. Just a few moments of the author's time, talking to her about books and writing, were worth their weight in gold. Essie's temperament blew hot and cold, so it might only be a short while before her interest in Liv waned. Even so,

Liv couldn't wait to discuss her new duties with the author. Thinking about it got her through the next few days.

When Thursday finally arrived, Liv mopped the Platinum office loos and discovered someone had suffered a stomach mishap in one of the cubicles. As she held her breath and snapped on her rubber gloves, she tried to imagine the vanilla aroma of the tiny cakes she'd eaten at Essie's afternoon tea.

After she'd finished, she was thoroughly washing her hands when a woman wearing a tight cream skirt suit tottered into the bathroom with her ear clamped to her phone. Her stiletto heels left polka-dot circles on the damp floor. She finished her call and looked pointedly ahead, pretending she hadn't seen Liv. Examining her lipstick in the mirror, she pouted her mouth as if air-kissing. When she rooted around in her handbag for her powder compact, a biscuit wrapper drifted to the floor. She glanced down at it, and so did Liv. The woman smoothed a pad around her face and zipped her bag shut. She stepped over her litter and headed out of the bathroom.

Liv felt anger ripple through her. She snatched up the foil and scrunched it in her fist. "Excuse me," she called out.

The woman was halfway through the door. Her face was quizzical as she looked back.

Liv was about to say, *You dropped this*, but then she looked at the woman's smart suit and down at her own uniform. Doubt about her actions clouded over her. "Um, have a good day," she muttered instead, tossing the wrapper into her cleaning cart.

When she arrived at the Cardinal residence, Liv told Hannah she had to leave promptly at noon.

"Oh, sweetie." Hannah's puppy-dog eyes came into play. "I need you to go to the post office and shops. Tarkers has sold his telescope and mineral collection on eBay and it needs mailing out. I've run out of vitamin supplements and teeth whitener."

Liv's stomach skipped when she thought about Essie's yellow

notepad waiting for her. "I really need to get to my next job," she said. "I could go to the post office, and give cleaning the dining room a miss…?"

Hannah glanced at the multicolored splats and handprints that marked the floor like prehistoric cave paintings. She let out the deepest sigh. "Walt and I are supremely busy…"

Liv felt guilt rumble inside her. She ran to the post office with cardboard boxes tucked under her chin, bought bottles of biotin and B12, and wiped paint off the floors at double speed.

Afterward, she sprinted to Essie's apartment and stood panting while she waited for the lift to arrive. As it shot up to the top floor, she recalled a snippet of *The River After Midnight*.

The battered truck dropped Georgia off in the dark of night, in the middle of nowhere. Lights in the closest town twinkled a long way in the distance. Between her and them lay only darkness and the silhouette of trees. Georgia knew she'd have to knock on many doors to find what she was looking for. Life would be a challenge for some time. Even though her stomach churned and her throat was tight, she refused to show any fear. She picked up her suitcase and started walking.

Inside the apartment, Liv took off her Converse in the hallway and neatened the lilies in a vase. She had to constantly wrap sticky tape around her fingers to pick up pollen off the silk table runners. She preferred it when Essie occasionally received extravagant bouquets of white roses, which only left dropped petals. When Liv trimmed the rose stems and arranged them, there was never a message attached. Perhaps a fan or admirer sent them. Or did Essie have a secret lover that no one knew about? When the author vanished, was it to a hush-hush rendezvous in a luxurious hotel room?

When she saw the writing room door was closed, Liv's

heart plunged. She listened for the sound of scribbling before knocking. "Essie, would you like a cup of tea?"

There was no reply. Liv dejectedly mixed a solution of water, lemon juice, baking soda and lavender oil to clean the kitchen. Her excitement about starting her new tasks began to slip away. She resumed listening to *Garden Spells*.

Everywhere looked just how she'd left it on Monday, except Essie's suitcase had gone. There were no miniature bottles around, or notes attached to books, and she recalled a couple of recent favorites.

"To Olivia. An intriguing premise in this sumptuous tale of regret, ambition and forbidden love," had been attached to *The Seven Husbands of Evelyn Hugo* by Taylor Jenkins Reid. "To Olivia. An unconventional heroine has to navigate a brave new world," was adhered to *Eleanor Oliphant Is Completely Fine* by Gail Honeyman. Liv had devoured and loved both books.

After a couple of hours, Liv's fingers were wrinkled and she approached the writing room again. She knocked and quietly inched the door open, pressing an eye to the gap.

Essie's chair was pushed up to her desk. A coiled green Hermès scarf and a bottle of Fracas perfume sat on top of it. The yellow notebook wasn't there.

Liv frowned, her stomach sinking. She hoped Essie hadn't performed a vanishing trick again. Not today.

In the kitchen, she drummed her fingers on the worktop and switched on the fancy coffee machine that looked like a robot. Perhaps Essie was staying at a retreat or spa for longer.

When it was time to go home, she chewed a strip of skin off her bottom lip as she packed away her things. She assured herself Essie would be back the next day.

But on Friday afternoon, Liv found the apartment to be empty again. It had a hollow feeling about it, like a concert hall after the audience had left.

She searched for notes again before glumly making a coffee. As she added extra milk, the landline phone rang on Essie's desk. Liv rushed toward it and snatched up the receiver. *"Essie?"* she said.

The man's voice on the other end was hesitant, as if unsure whether he'd dialed the right number. "Am I speaking to Ms. Olivia Green?"

"Yes, this is Liv."

"My name is Anthony Pentecost," he said. "Are you available to meet me today?"

Liv frowned. "Do I know you?"

"We've not yet had the pleasure." There was a sound of pages being flipped back and forth. "I can see you in Launderette, the coffee place, in forty-five minutes," he said.

"I know it, but—"

"I'll reserve a booth."

Liv nervously touched the scarf sitting on the writing desk. "Is this about Essie?"

"Correct."

"Is she okay? Where is she?"

"I have some information to share with you, Ms. Green," Anthony said. "I shall see you shortly."

Launderette was too trendy for Liv. The front counter was constructed from a row of washing machines, and black coffee cups hung from pegs on a line. The place was full of affluent young mums who sipped lattes while bouncing their babies on their knees. Liv became more aware of the scuffed toes of her Converse.

She smiled briefly at a full-bearded young man behind the counter and asked for the table reserved for Pentecost. He pointed toward the back of the café, where a man was sitting alone in the corner booth. Liv's pulse quickened as she wondered what was going on.

She guessed Anthony was in his early fifties. He sported a cobalt suit, cuff links and a spotted pocket handkerchief. His black hair was slicked back and had a flash of white on the left temple, the size of a baby's palm print. He had a stiff air of legality about him, as if he might sleep with a briefcase at the side of his bed.

As Liv approached the booth, he immediately slid out from his seat. "Ms. Green?" He glanced over her shoulder.

"It's Liv." She held out her hand to shake his. "And don't worry, MI6 haven't followed me."

He managed a tight smile. Although he was smartly dressed, his eyes were rimmed with pink as if he needed a nap. "I'm Essie Starling's solicitor, from Pentecost and Wilde. There was a small flood at my premises this morning, so we couldn't meet there."

"Essie's solicitor?" Liv felt her scalp prickle.

He pointed vaguely toward the counter. "I'll order tea and pastries."

Liv's heart galloped when she sat down. She felt short of breath when she glanced at Anthony's briefcase under the table. It was open, and her eyes widened when she spotted Essie's yellow notebook inside it. Was he going to run through her new work with her? Why wasn't Essie doing it?

Oh, God, has she changed her mind and he's here to fire me?

When he returned, Anthony took a seat and lifted the lid of the teapot. "Earl Grey," he said apologetically.

"I'm not fussy," Liv said. "Just so long as it's hot, wet and brown."

Anthony didn't smile this time. His hand shook as he poured out two cups. "I'm afraid I have some bad news that I wanted to deliver to you in person. There's no easy way for me to tell you..." His words trailed away.

"Tell me *what*?" she prompted.

"Essie Starling has passed away."

He said it so quietly Liv questioned if she'd heard him properly.

"She died on Wednesday evening, May the first. I'm very sorry," he said.

The world seemed to grind to a halt. Liv rubbed the creases between her eyebrows. "No, that can't be right. She was going to a spa or something. I saw her suitcase."

"She went into hospital for an operation. Things didn't go as planned."

A hot tear trickled down Liv's cheek. Her heart felt it might burst out of her body. Why hadn't Essie told her about the op when they had tea together? "N-no," she spluttered. "That *can't* be true."

Anthony shook out his handkerchief and passed it to her. The spots were actually tiny printed bees with gold wings. "After her operation, an infection took hold. The surgeon informed Essie that the outcome was precarious. She left an instruction for you, and I'm here to pass it on."

Liv couldn't see through the tears swimming in her eyes. She hurriedly wiped them with the handkerchief. "Instruction? We were going to talk about her writing."

He bent down and took the yellow notebook out of his case and opened it. He stared at the page for a while as if bewildered. "Her request is brief and it's crucial you follow it precisely. I will read her exact words to you.

"Dear Olivia, if Anthony is speaking to you now, the worst has most likely happened. If you need to take a little time out from this job and your others, you will be paid."

Liv shook her head, unable to comprehend what she was hearing. "Is *that* her request?" she said.

"No, it's a precursor. Her main one is more, ah, unusual."

Liv choked back an unsuitable burst of laughter. How could things get any stranger than this?

Anthony looked down at the notebook and continued.

"If I die, keep my passing a secret for six months. During this period, I want you to complete my latest novel."

"Wh-what?" Liv stammered. She had never experienced vertigo properly before, not even from the heights of Essie's apartment. Her body swooned, as if she was a pheasant shot out of the sky by a hunter. "That can't be right. It must be a plot for one of her books."

"It's the precise message she left for you."

"But why doesn't she want anyone to know? That's crazy. How can something like that be kept quiet? And for six months, too."

Essie had been married twice, in her twenties to Ted Mason, who was twice her age and a big name in the publishing industry, and in her thirties to American crime writer Hank Milligan. *Surely, they'll need to know,* Liv thought.

"What about Essie's fans, and Marlon and Meg?" she said, reaching out for the notebook. "Why on earth would Essie ask *me* to finish her book?"

Anthony moved the notebook away from her. His phone beeped and he took it from his pocket. He stared at it, then at her. "Only you and I can know about this. No one else. We need to abide by Essie's request until the first of November."

"But why?"

He took a moment. "As you know, Essie was a very private person. Whilst her request is unconventional, it is possible. Now, I apologize profusely, but I have an emergency to deal with. May I have your mobile number?"

Liv told it to him. "We need to think about this," she said.

"It's ridiculous, and her book is finished anyway. I saw a draft copy..."

"Please do as Essie instructs." Anthony snapped his briefcase shut. "Take time off, and keep everything confidential."

Liv thought about Jake and the boys, and her mum. How could she hide something like this from them? How could she clean for Platinum and the Cardinals and pretend nothing had happened? "What if I can't do it?" she said.

He fixed her with a sympathetic gaze. "I understand that before she went into hospital, Essie asked for your help with her work?"

She nodded.

"So, you'll keep your employment for six months. Essie also asked me to increase your salary, to recognize your new contribution. I trust doubling your hourly rate is satisfactory?"

Liv swallowed hard and felt a creeping hotness under her skin. The extra money would help to pay for Johnny's laptop, though she'd prefer to have Essie back instead. "What about a funeral?" she asked, her voice cracking.

"Essie has requested a private cremation. I'll deal with the coroner, register her death and make the funeral arrangements. I'll be in touch with more details soon." Anthony stood up. "And there is one other thing..."

Liv folded his handkerchief into the smallest square possible. "What is it?"

"Essie said only you can do this," he said.

5

CHERRY BLOSSOM

At Essie Starling's funeral there would be no magnificent floral displays or limousines waiting to whisk mourners to a local hotel for finger sandwiches and warm brandy; no photographs of her as a child or of her hairstyles throughout the years lining the walls; no friends or family members sharing inspirational stories about her life; no publishing people, press or fans. Just how Essie wanted it.

The service was to take place in Greengate, a tiny, old-fashioned place five miles outside Manningham city center. The village's terraced houses were built from gray stone and the village store still sold tweed hats and carved walking sticks. It was the kind of place where everyone knew each other's name, and the name of their cat, too. If Essie craved privacy, this was the right location.

Liv hunched against the rain and hurried past a small grocery shop with boxes of soggy vegetables outside, toward the address of the crematorium that Anthony had given her. She was glad the day was gray and dull, fitting weather for a farewell.

It had been twelve days since he'd informed her about Essie's death and since then Liv had functioned like a zombie.

She'd told Jake, Johnny and her mum that she had a bad cold and was staying at home so Essie didn't catch it. Keeping the author's death from her family was like a hairball in her throat she longed to cough up.

She left a message advising her cleaning agency she wasn't well enough to work at Platinum, and then rang Hannah to call in sick, affecting a croaky voice.

"Oh, sweetie, I hope you're okay. When will you be back?" she cooed. "I promised Tarkers and Jules you'd help them make a wormery."

Liv felt numb and stayed in bed. She stared at the ceiling in disbelief. Tears waterfalled down her face, wetting her pillow.

What had happened to Essie? Why had she left such strange demands, and why specify secrecy for six months? None of it seemed real.

She heard Jake downstairs on the phone with Katrina, pacing around the kitchen and slamming cupboard doors as he talked about their parents' pensions and the cost of new printing equipment. But Liv felt curiously blank, as if Essie's death had stolen her worries about Paperpress away.

Johnny occasionally appeared in the doorway of her bedroom, whispering to ask if she knew where his football socks and shorts were. Liv pulled the bedcovers up around her shoulders and read Essie's debut novel *The Moon on the Water*, never growing bored of the book that had been so important to her growing up. When she finished it, she reached for *Olive Kitteridge* by Elizabeth Strout and found comfort in the familiar prickliness of the main character.

After a few days of lying in bed, Liv forced herself to get up. Her skin cried out for Jake's strong arms to wrap around her. Not being able to tell anyone about Essie or the huge task she'd left behind made her feel like a prisoner in solitary confinement.

She cleaned her house from top to bottom until it smelled of grapefruit and lavender. She made packed lunches and matched up socks, but all the time she could see Essie in her head, typing in her writing room with her back to the world. When Liv sat with Jake on the sofa in the evening, their bodies sank against each other like bags of treacle. They stared vacantly at the TV. He was too exhausted from his dealings with Katrina to talk, and she was still in shock.

In order to make sense of the author's bizarre request, Liv tried to view it as her last wish. Perhaps she'd been woozy after the anesthetic, or even smuggled a bottle of gin into the hospital, so wasn't coherent when she wrote in her notebook. Hopefully, Anthony would realize she hadn't meant what she'd written. After all, Essie *was* a storyteller.

When Anthony phoned her with the funeral details, Liv had furtively taken the call inside the coat cupboard.

"It will take place on May the fifteenth, at Greengate Crematorium. Four thirty in the afternoon, the last service of the day," he said.

Liv wrote the date on her hand. She'd once gone to a friend's birthday party a day early, and another time missed one of Johnny's important football matches.

"Ah, she also made another request," Anthony added.

Liv flopped her head against the coats with a sigh. "Really? Was this written in her notebook, too?"

"It's something she told me personally." He cleared his throat. "In her own words, she doesn't want any 'fussing or faffing' at her funeral. There should be no hymns, flowers or eulogy. You and I may attend but no one else."

Liv didn't know whether to laugh or cry. "Will a minister be there?" she said.

"Actually, no." His voice expressed little emotion.

Liv felt like she was sinking into mud, and she replied more sharply than she meant to. "This is just weird. Why doesn't she want to be remembered properly? If she asked you to jump off a cliff would you do it?"

"As Essie's solicitor and the executor named in her will, it's my legal responsibility to carry out her terms," he said. "Insisting that no one else attends her funeral is the most straightforward of her requests."

Liv found the smallest smile at his comment, and the shared strangeness of their situation. He did the same, and for a moment she felt like a fine strand of silk connected them together somehow.

When Liv pushed the huge oak crematorium door open, she shivered as she stepped inside. The main room was spacious and light with a large window looking out onto a garden with a rockery and waterfalls.

She couldn't help memories of her dad's service creeping into her head. She'd been so distraught her teeth chattered and her whole body shook. Afterward, Liv tried to blank out the agony and memories of that heartbreaking time. The anticipation of attending a funeral could still bring a knot to her throat and her emotions bubbling to the surface.

As she made her way past rows of wooden benches, she couldn't stop tears from rolling down her cheeks and dropping off her nose. Inside her head, she heard Essie's voice, heavy with exasperation. *"You're not crying are you, Olivia? Please use a handkerchief."*

Liv had washed the bee-printed one Anthony had given her, and wiped it across her face, soaking it again. Her insides tangled with feelings—sadness mixed with disbelief, and a flash of anger that Essie had vanished from her life, just as they were getting to know each other. Her death felt like a stab to her heart that would always leave a jagged scar.

The thought of never reading a new Georgia Rory novel

made her feel like she was tumbling down a hill, unable to stop. She'd never again experience the joy of carrying a copy home from the bookstore in a small, shiny bag, or sinking into a fresh story.

Liv could also imagine the earthquake of shock that would hit Essie's fans when they found out the terrible news five and a half months from now. She was sure they'd experience her same feelings of disbelief and loss.

Not feeling ready to say goodbye, she selected a bench and sat down with a stiff back. A few folded pieces of paper for Essie's service lay around, and she picked one up.

In Memory of Elsbeth Smart...

For a second, Liv thought she'd stepped into the wrong service until she saw the black-and-white shot of Essie. It was one she hadn't seen before. *Essie Starling must be her pen name,* she realized.

If Essie's death was registered under a different name, she supposed others wouldn't recognize it. Maybe the hospital staff hadn't even known they were operating on a bestselling author.

When Liv heard someone else enter the room, she glanced up to see Anthony appear at her side. His lips were tight and his eyes were watery. She wondered if solicitors usually got this emotionally attached to their clients.

"Hi," she said, as he sat down next to her.

"Hello, again."

She handed him a service sheet. "I didn't know Essie's real name, did you? Elsbeth is so pretty."

"Yes, I created the document."

Liv paused at this. Wouldn't the funeral service people usually do that? It was beautifully done, maybe part of Anthony's mission to keep things private.

A man whose moustache and skin matched the gray of his

sharply pressed suit walked along the aisle toward them. "I'm the funeral director. I'm sorry for your loss," he said, looking around him. "Um, are you expecting more guests?"

Liv shook her head. "It's just us." She eyed the unoccupied seats, too. "It's pretty dead in here." When she realized what she'd said, she clamped a hand to her mouth.

He smiled at her kindly. "I understand this is a private ceremony, so please take your time. I'll leave you in peace. Mr. Pentecost, may I have a word?" he added.

Anthony slipped out of his seat and the two men talked together for a while. Liv noticed how the funeral director placed a comforting hand on Anthony's arm, as if he'd lost a close relative. She wondered just how well the solicitor had known Essie.

As she waited for him to return, she had a sudden urge to do *something*. She couldn't stand this feeling of no one else knowing Essie was gone. There should be wailing, shuffling and hymns sung off-key, followed by sniffling and hushed condolences.

Liv felt like frogs were jumping in her stomach, the same sensation she experienced when she'd arrived at Essie's apartment block for her job interview, three years ago. She could clearly remember standing on the pavement with one hand pressed to her belly and the other clutching the confirmation email she'd printed out. She kept checking the time, date and location, not quite able to believe she was about to meet Essie Starling, the reclusive creator of her favorite books ever. The author hadn't been seen in years and Liv was *here*.

Essie's assistant at the time was called Jane. She met Liv outside and escorted her up to the apartment. "So, you're here for a job with Essie?" Jane said stiffly.

"Yes, I'm a cleaner," Liv said.

Jane's demeanor warmed a little. "Oh, right. I thought you were another assistant."

"Does she have a few?"

"One at a time, but we don't last for long."

Liv felt her legs go shaky. "Why's that?"

"You'll see." Jane let her inside and opened the writing room door. "Olivia Green is here. I'll bring tea," she announced before darting away.

Essie didn't turn around. She continued typing and Liv wondered if she was hard of hearing. After several moments of awkward silence, Liv cleared her throat and smiled. "Excuse me, Mrs. Starling. I'm Liv, here about the cleaning job."

Essie spun around suddenly, staring Liv directly in her eyes. "I *know* who you are."

Liv's smile stiffened. She was in the presence of a goddess and the paper in her hand stuck to her sweaty palm. "And I know who you are, too," she joked. "Everyone does."

Essie's gaze swept over her so intensely Liv felt like fingers were prodding her skin. "You remind me of someone," the author said.

"Someone nice I hope." Liv gulped.

Essie tossed her head. "Be seated," she said. "References?"

Liv sat down. She took a few sheets out of her bag, glad she'd thought to bring them along.

Essie scrutinized them and her expression gave nothing away. "Why should I hire you? And don't waffle on."

Liv swallowed. "Because I'm hardworking, do a great job and make my own cleaning solutions."

Essie pressed her hand to a yawn.

Liv tried to think quickly. She and Jake needed every penny, and Essie was her heroine. What could she say that wasn't sycophantic or dull? "In addition to that, I'm discreet and quiet," she said. "You'll probably be working while I'm here, and I'll be sensitive to that. When I was growing up, Georgia Rory was very important to me, helped me through some tough times in my childhood. I try to emulate her tenacity and attention to detail."

Essie's lips twitched ever so slightly. "Quite." She handed the references back to Liv, and turned back to her laptop. She started to type again. "That is all."

Liv sat there for a while not knowing what to do. Eventually she stood up and said, "Um, thank you."

Jane met her by the front door. "How did it go?" she said.

Liv shook her head, puzzled. "I really have no idea."

But that evening, the offer of a job had arrived in her inbox.

Even now, Liv was still astonished by Essie's offer of employment.

When Anthony rejoined her on the bench, Liv snapped back to the present. "What happens now?" she asked him.

"We take a little time to pay our respects to Essie, then leave."

She crumpled her brow. "But someone has got to say a few words."

"Her instructions were clear, no fuss or faffing."

"But that's wrong. We can't just let her go like *this*." Liv had brought along her copy of *The Moon on the Water*, which she took from her bag. She'd bookmarked a favorite passage and leafed to it.

"What are you doing?" Anthony said, touching her wrist.

She shook his hand away and squeezed past him off the bench, not meeting his eyes. "I'm saying goodbye. Someone's got to do it properly." As she walked to the front of the room, she spoke to herself under her breath. "You didn't say anything about banning prose, Essie."

Taking a deep breath, Liv faced the rows of empty benches and visualized Essie at the back of the room, her dark lenses like bluebottle eyes, tossing her bobbed hair as if reluctantly granting her permission. Liv cleared her throat and started to read.

"The wind shook the cherry blossom trees so petals danced around Georgia's body like a flurry of snowflakes. She took a deep breath, stuck out her chest and batted them off her shoulders and from her hair. Her heart pitter-pattered when she thought about her next step into the unknown. The journey might be long, and the terrain would certainly be rocky, but she told herself that wherever she went there would always be flowers. She refused to be scared about whatever lay ahead..."

Liv's voice wobbled as it echoed around the room. Afterward, she hurriedly pushed the book back into her bag. Her legs quaked as she walked toward the polished wooden casket at the front. A sob rose in her chest when she thought about Essie lying inside, and she frantically plucked out her own image of the writer instead, wearing her blue embroidered dress and proudly clasping her crystal Constellation star.

"Sleep tight, Essie," Liv whispered. "Sweet dreams."

She stood there for a while, until Anthony appeared at her side.

"I'd like to say goodbye, too," he said. "Alone."

Liv obliged and stumbled outside. She stood on the doorstep for a while, taking gulps of the damp air. The rain had dispersed, and the sky had lightened from gray to the palest blue, weak sunshine winking through the clouds.

She peered around her, fearful that word of Essie's death had got out somehow, and that she was to blame. She imagined photographers, inconsolable fans dressed as Georgia Rory, and chic people from the literary industry milling around, pretending to look at gravestones with their cameras and phones hidden under their scarves. But there was only a family of mourners at the far end of the yard, and her breathing grew easier.

More than ten minutes passed before Anthony joined her.

Liv thought he might apologize for keeping her waiting, but he was quiet and his eyes were downcast.

As they walked toward the gates together, the sound of their feet on the gravel path was as loud as pistol shots.

When Liv closed the gates behind her, she shivered, feeling numb. "What should we do now?" she said. "Find a pub and raise a glass to Essie?"

Anthony's face was ashen, and he checked his watch. "I need to get back to work."

"Oh, okay." The ending to the funeral didn't feel right, a full stop when it should be a comma. Liv waited, hoping he'd reconsidered Essie's very strange request and was going to admit it *was* ridiculous.

Instead, he took out his phone. "I'll call you a taxi," he said. "We'll speak about your new role soon."

He returned to his own car and Liv stamped her feet to warm them up.

As Anthony drove away, she saw him dab his nose with his handkerchief and questions ricocheted inside her head.

Why wouldn't Essie want more for herself than this?

Why did she choose me?

6

CANDY FLOSS CLOUDS

After the funeral Liv returned to Essie's building to wash her face before she went home and had to pretend everything was normal to Jake and Johnny. Not wanting to face any strangers in the lift, she headed for the stairwell instead. As she trekked her way toward the top of the thirty-two flights, she regretted her choice. By the time she unlocked the apartment door, she struggled to catch her breath and her legs wobbled.

Inside the hallway, Liv held her sides and immediately noticed the brown shriveled heads of lilies strewn on the tabletop. She hadn't returned to the apartment since Anthony told her about Essie's death, and a layer of dust coated everything. Liv felt guilty as she picked up the flower heads. She vacuumed and wiped all the surfaces, before finally splashing her cheeks with water. It felt wrong to be commemorating Essie by cleaning.

There was a void in the pit of her stomach when she thought about the lack of a wake or memorial service. To hold her own toast to Essie, Liv found a bottle of Moët & Chandon in a kitchen cupboard and didn't care if it was tepid.

Her bottom lip quivered as she glanced out of the writing

room window at the viaduct and orange-topped market stalls below. People in the streets were as small as speech marks. She slid a copy of *Few and Far Between* off a bookshelf and stood it on the desk to display the author photo inside.

Liv crashed down into Essie's writing chair with a resounding creak that filled the apartment. She half expected to hear Essie's voice demand, "What on *earth* are you doing in my seat, Olivia?" But there was only the sound of a ticking clock.

Liv popped the cork, poured herself a large glass of champagne and held it aloft. "You were prickly and complicated, Essie, but you were also amazing and…you gave Georgia Rory to me, and to the world. You have no idea how she helped me to be stronger." Her voice broke. "You'd started to show faith in me that I don't have in myself…"

Unable to say anything else, Liv gulped the bubbly liquid and found some music on her phone. To stop herself from crying, she waltzed around the room, spraying Fracas onto her neck and wrists. As she sashayed, she picked up Essie's green scarf and tied it into her hair. Dancing did little to stop all her questions rearing up again and they crawled in Liv's head like wasps swarming out of their nest. She couldn't understand why Essie had asked her to complete Book Twenty, especially as they'd only just started talking together properly, and there was a draft copy of the manuscript sitting on a bookshelf. Why keep Essie's death a secret until the first of November? How was Liv going to *do* this?

She carried the champagne bottle and glass into the award room. Picking up the manuscript once more she flicked through it, her eyes skimming the pages.

Essie's writing became messier as her work progressed, and Liv peered closer, trying to make out some of the more indecipherable words. There were lots of sentences crossed out and scrawled notes in the margins.

When she reached the last page, Liv frowned and her mouth dried. The end chapter was numbered thirty-two, but that couldn't possibly be right. Each Georgia Rory novel was forty chapters long. She pulled a few of Essie's other books off the shelf and checked their length to confirm she was correct. When it became apparent the last eight chapters of the manuscript were missing, Liv slumped a shoulder against the wall.

The author's novels always followed the same structure. In their last fifth, Georgia found herself in increasing amounts of trouble, until all seemed lost and she was on the verge of defeat. That's when she dug deep and found reserves of pluckiness and skill. She teamed up with a love interest to turn the tables on the bad guys. Georgia won a battle against the odds, and had some kind of epiphany, before riding off into the sunset with the man of her dreams. She gave young girls a role model to aspire to, and adult readers a global adventure their own nine-to-five lives didn't allow. Georgia was brave and ballsy, a writer and intrepid adventurer who lived and loved with abandon. Liv wished she had half her bravery.

Liv drank another glass of champagne and shook her head. Trying to complete Essie's book was a stupid impossibility, especially with a big chunk of it missing.

With an urge to find out if the absent chapters existed, she began to hunt around the apartment, sliding books off shelves, opening drawers and cupboard doors. She always cleaned thoroughly and didn't recall seeing another chunk of paper anywhere. Could the missing work be in Essie's yellow notebook?

After circling the apartment twice, Liv huffed and carried the champagne bottle into Essie's bedroom. Setting it down on the bedside table, she lifted the pillows as a last resort.

When she saw a small green leather box sitting under one of them, she momentarily held her breath. The box hadn't been there when she last changed the bed linen. Essie must have placed it there before she went into hospital. It had gold embossed lettering on the top and Liv recognized the name of the posh city center jewelry shop, Longley Jones. It sold ten-thousand-pound wedding rings, and the staff looked like models.

Liv flipped it open to find a pair of men's cuff links. They were gold, intricately cast and shaped like bees. "Hmm." She stared at them for a while, remembering the tiny bees on Anthony's handkerchief. Could they possibly belong to him?

Liv gnawed her lip, wondering whether to contact the solicitor or not.

If she told Anthony she couldn't finish Essie's book, she'd be making herself redundant. She'd lose six months' double pay, and the thought of trawling the internet for more work, or queuing up at the recruitment office made her queasy. Her pay rise would be useful for Paperpress and her boys' university costs. It had always been her dream to be a writer, though never in this way.

After yet another glass of champagne, Liv sat down on Essie's bed and took out her mobile phone. "Hey," she said tipsily when Anthony answered.

"Sorry, who is this?" he said.

"It's Liv. I'm having a toast to Essie. On *my own*," she said. When she closed her eyes, her head suddenly felt floppy. Her heart dipped when she pictured Essie's polished wooden casket. Georgia's bravery in her system trickled away, replaced by worry. "I'm not sure I can do this, Anthony. I only clean for her... I vacuum and dust and mop. I know you've promised me extra money, but..." She let out a long sigh.

He was quiet for a while and she could hear his breathing. Eventually, he said, "Essie must have identified *something* in you."

She shook her head. "I don't know what it is, and you seem to know her *much* better than I do."

"I'm her solicitor," he said firmly.

Liv looked down at the cuff links in her hand. It seemed the wrong time to ask if he shared Essie's bed, too. "The end to her book is missing and I'm trying to find out if it exists or not. Perhaps there are some missing chapters in her yellow notebook. It was on her desk when I last saw her."

"She used it to write down her instructions for us. That's all."

Us, Liv thought, thinking the word sounded strange. She wondered what else the author might have asked Anthony to do.

"Oh, right," she said and flopped back on the bed with her mind careening around. She hoped there was a more complete version of the manuscript somewhere, something typed up. Perhaps Matilda, Essie's last assistant, would know. When she closed her eyes, the room started to spin. "Essie only died two weeks ago. How can I possibly keep her secret for another five and a half more months?" she murmured.

"I'm sure you'll think of something," Anthony said gently.

"But it means keeping up a charade that Essie's still alive," Liv said, aware her words sounded slurred.

"Let's not discuss all this now," Anthony cut in. "Let's converse again when you're more composed. It's been a long day, for both of us."

Liv glanced at the empty champagne bottle and noticed it was growing darker outside. Lights sparkled from the bars and restaurants in the streets below, and she felt like a skydiver on the verge of jumping out of a plane. She started to hiccup. "When can we meet again?" she said, feeling drained.

He was silent for a while. "Next week, Wednesday at the Museum of Writing," he said. "Does 10 a.m. work for you?"

Liv had hoped it would be sooner, but she could hang on for seven days. "Sure, I'll see you then."

After hanging up, she stood and traipsed into the kitchen where she found a bottle of Merlot. She carried it into Essie's writing room and slumped at the desk. When her phone pinged, she saw the message was from Jake.

Where are you? he said.

She sighed. Didn't he trust her?

I'm fire, don't wossy, she replied, only realizing her misspellings after she'd sent her reply. **Be home soon x.**

He rang her back, but Liv didn't pick up. She closed her eyes until "Paperback Writer" stopped playing. Not wanting to speak to him or anyone else right now, she switched off her phone and dropped it into her bag. She giggled at how inebriated she felt, which made her feel guilty, so she started to cry. Tears streamed down her face and her nose grew snotty.

Exhausted, Liv circled her arms on top of the desk and let her head drop forward. The varnished oak felt cool and smooth against her skin and her eyelids grew heavy. She drifted off into a woozy sleep.

When she woke up, she had a floor-to-ceiling view of an ethereal peach sky and candy floss clouds. It was beautiful but also made her feel light-headed. She limply raised her wrist to look at the time.

4:27 a.m.

Liv sat bolt upright. She snatched up her bag and knocked her glass off the desk. Drops of wine sprinkled the carpet and she gave them a quick rub with her socked toe. With no time to worry about stains, she tugged on her shoes in the hallway and scrambled out of the apartment.

Once she was out in the street, she attempted to sprint across the city. The thump of her feet against the pavement made her brain bounce painfully. The park gates were locked and the windows of all the cafés wore metal shutters. Figures moved stealthily in dimly lit office buildings, and she recognized the movements of the cleaners.

When she reached her house, the street was silent apart from her panting. Liv gritted her teeth as she unlocked the front door. She pulled off her shoes and crept upstairs. Each stair groaned as if telling tales on her.

She left her clothes on the floor before slipping into bed. For a few seconds she thought she'd gotten away without waking Jake. But then he sat up.

"Where've you been?" he hissed. "What time is it?"

Liv's mind jumped around, trying to think of an excuse. She was pretty certain she'd never lied to him properly before, unless knocking fifteen pounds off the true cost of a dress counted. "I was at Essie's place and...um, I felt ill, really dizzy," she whispered. "I lay down and must have dropped off."

"You told me you were fine." He was quiet for a moment. "Did Essie find you asleep? Why didn't she wake you up and call for a taxi?"

"She was...working away." Liv half expected a lightning bolt to strike her between the eyes. She had a desperate urge to tell him everything and let the events of the last fortnight come gushing out. She dug her fingernails into her palms to stop herself.

"I was worried." Jake reached out and stabbed the button on the alarm clock, letting out a groan when 5:18 a.m. projected in red digits on the ceiling. "Johnny wanted your help with an essay."

"Sorry," she said and meant it. The mattress felt like it was sucking her down, and her head contained an orchestra of tom-tom players. She wondered if Essie felt this way after drinking her gin.

"Well, I might as well get up," Jake said, slapping his hand on the duvet.

"What, *now*?"

"I promised I'd call Katrina. I was going to see her last night," he said rigidly. "But you weren't here."

Liv frowned in the darkness. They'd been leaving the boys on their own in the house since Mack was fifteen. "You could have gone—"

"I was too busy worrying about you," he said. "Go back to sleep, I'll try to be quiet."

Jake's side of the duvet landed on her and he got out of the bed. She heard the bedroom door open and his footsteps on the stairs.

Liv pulled the covers over her head and her eyelashes brushed against the cotton. She plumped up her pillow and tossed and turned for a while, trying to summon up a Georgia Rory story to imagine herself in. She was the custodian of Essie's last ever book, and the satisfaction of millions of readers sat firmly on her shoulders. The responsibility made her feel like she was lying in an open grave with soil being shoveled on top of her.

Tugging Essie's scarf out of her hair and scrunching it in her fist, Liv only managed to drift off to sleep when she breathed in the scent of Fracas.

7

THE PLASTIC SLIDE

Liv eyes pinged wide open when she woke midmorning. She was supposed to be back at work for Platinum today and hated leaving her teammates in the lurch by not turning up. Her head throbbed when she called Hannah Cardinal and arranged to work extra time on a different day instead. Scrubbing herself in the shower did little to alleviate her hangover.

She was glad Jake had already left for work, so she wouldn't have to face more of his questions. Her brain felt swollen and her tongue was as dry as sandpaper. But the manuscript and her monumental task to complete it were crystal clear in her head. Matilda was the longest serving of Essie's assistants, having lasted seven months on the job. She might know if any missing chapters existed. If Liv had to keep up the pretense Essie was still alive, the PA could tell her more about the author's day-to-day life. She might know something about Anthony, too.

Matilda could be as difficult as Essie, so Liv texted apprehensively to ask if they could meet to discuss Essie's work.

Why would I want to help Medusa? Matilda fired back. **What did she ever do for me?**

It's for me, not her, Liv replied. **Please. I really need this.**

Matilda's response took a while to arrive. **Okay. Meet me at Alchemy at 2 today.**

Alchemy was a huge white block on an industrial estate on the outskirts of the city, where lots of creative businesses had their headquarters. Liv grabbed the dog-eared manuscript from Essie's apartment on the way and carried it in a tote bag. It was so heavy the bag straps cut into her shoulder, leaving a red weal.

Her mouth fell open when she stepped inside the Alchemy foyer. The floor was covered with emerald green fake grass, and there was a small crazy golf pitch, a large sand pit and a turquoise plastic slide curved down from the mezzanine to the ground floor. The place looked more like a youth center for overprivileged kids.

Liv tried not to stare at a heavily tattooed man who rode a scooter across the floor. A woman with a shaved head wore so many rings through her nose, ears and eyebrows you could hang curtains on them. Liv felt very boring in her retro Coca-Cola T-shirt and jeans. She had always envied people who did things their own way. They might dye their hair flamingo pink, or wear tartan trousers when they weren't Scottish. She wondered how it would feel to walk into a room and to be *seen*.

She took a photo of the golf course and WhatsApped it to her mum. **My meeting place for the day!**

Very fancy, Carol replied. **Hope you've brought your golf club. Come over for cake soon x.**

Liv replied, **If it's Victoria sponge, I'm in x.**

She saw Matilda heading toward her with the flounce of a catwalk model. She wore a red tiger-print dress, and pink sandals with huge wedged soles. Her lips were overplump and she had marker pen eyebrows.

"Liv, you didn't have to dress up," she said, smirking at Liv's jeans.

Liv consciously ran a hand down her T-shirt. "You look glam, as always."

"I'm temping here for a while, getting myself noticed." Matilda waved a hand as if she was royalty. "Follow me. We'll grab a smoothie and you can tell me what *Medusa* wants."

She led the way across the grass and up a spiral staircase to the next floor. There was a juice bar and a man's blond spiky hair bobbed above the fruit-filled baskets on the counter. Liv took out her purse.

Matilda shot out a hand and pushed it away. "Don't *pay*," she snorted. "It's a perk."

The list of smoothies was bewildering and contained ingredients Liv wouldn't normally associate with drinks, like turmeric, kale and cucumber. "The Swampalicious sounds interesting," she said.

"Make it two," Matilda said to the spiky-haired man.

"Please," Liv added on her behalf.

They sat down on low pink stools that had cow udders underneath.

"So, what's this about?" Matilda said.

Liv sipped the khaki concoction and picked out something stringy from between her teeth. "Essie wants me to do some of her admin work, and I don't know where to start," she said vaguely.

Matilda tossed her hair. "Well, hello, can't *Medusa* tell you that?"

Liv wished she wouldn't use that name for Essie. "She's working away," she said, thinking the excuse sounded more plausible each time she used it.

"*Really?* She hardly ever leaves that apartment. When she does, it's like some kind of top-secret mission. Have you noticed she vanishes? It's pretty obvious why." Matilda tipped a pretend glass to her lips.

Redness mottled Liv's cheeks. "Do you know where she goes to?"

"I didn't have the chance to find out before..." Matilda sliced a finger across her own neck. "If you want my advice, make sure you leave work on time, before she hits the gin. I stayed late one night and *Medusa* started droning on about the only man she ever loved. She claimed she couldn't finish writing her book without him. Totally pitiful."

"Who is he?" Liv said, intrigued.

"Don't know, don't care." Matilda performed a fake yawn and fanned her mouth. "Have you seen those huge bouquets of white roses she gets? What man would be crazy enough to send them to her?"

"Did she ever mention the name Anthony?"

"No." Matilda frowned. "Who?"

Liv pursed her lips, not wanting to mention Essie had a solicitor. It would be nice to think she had someone special in her life, to hold her hand in her final hours.

"Did you know *Medusa* wouldn't read my boyfriend's manuscript and give him feedback?" Matilda carried on. "He worked on it for two whole years."

"Reading a book takes me around eight hours," Liv said, her mind still on Essie's mystery man. "It's a big commitment."

Matilda gave her a withering look. "She owns all these gorgeous designer clothes, yet wouldn't lend me anything to wear to a wedding. And she *refused* to give me a reference when I left."

"What kind of things did you do for her?" Liv prompted.

Matilda eyed her for a while. "Promise me a reference from her, if I tell you."

"I *can't* do that..."

Matilda tossed her head and folded her arms.

Liv's temples began to pound. She was sure yesterday's champagne was still running in her bloodstream. "Okay, okay," she relented.

Setting down her smoothie glass, Matilda counted on her fingers. "I did *everything*. I answered her fan correspondence, and fought off all the requests for free books. Most readers are darlings, so sweet, but there's always some scroungers..." She sighed dramatically. "And there's this guy who mails her weird things. Watch out for him."

Liv shivered. "What things?"

"Strange poems, and he once made her a blanket out of his cat's hair."

"That sounds...warm."

Matilda continued. "I handled her Facebook, Twitter and Insta. She actually made me *write* the instructions down in a file. Totally Neanderthal.

"Then, there's all the stuff she gets asked to do. Can she open a school fete, or run a writing workshop, or present certificates to students, or sit on a literature festival writing panel? All in exchange for a cup of tea and a Kit Kat.

"Publishers and other authors always want her to read their books and write blurbs. You know, 'This is masterful storytelling' kind of stuff, and I ended up doing it. I handled some of her financial admin, too, like trade subscriptions and expenses. And I sometimes wrote her answers to interview questions. It was so embarrassing to keep making excuses when she refused to do them."

Perspiration pooled in Liv's collarbone at what covering up Essie's death might entail. She hadn't expected all this and she shifted in her seat. "You *pretended* to be her?"

Matilda tapped her nose. "*Some* big authors use ghostwriters, you know?"

Liv smiled knowingly to herself. Essie said she never asked for help with Georgia, and she felt a trickle of pride that the author had chosen *her*. Picking up her bag, she put it on her knee. "Did Essie tell you anything about her latest book?"

"A little. I know she was struggling with it. It's her twentieth one, a totally big deal for her publisher. She missed her deadline several times and Peregrine were totally miffed. I think they gave her extra time to finish it."

"When is it due?"

Matilda thought for a while. "I think Essie mentioned November 1. She wanted to finish it by then."

When Liv tugged the manuscript out of her bag, the pages looked even more battered. "I found this copy. Do you know if there's another version anywhere? The last eight chapters are missing."

Matilda scoffed. "I'm surprised she's even got that far with it. Does she know you've got that? She guards her work like Cerberus."

"Perhaps she typed it up?"

"Please." Matilda batted a hand. "I did all that stuff, inputting hours of handwritten Georgia Rory for her last book, before Essie edited it all. I didn't do anything on her latest one."

Liv didn't speak. Her stomach lurched when she realized she was holding the latest, unfinished and only version of the manuscript. She carefully put it back in her bag, its existence to her more precious than ever.

"Why's she asked *you* to do her work anyway?" Matilda narrowed her eyes. "You're a cleaner, not a PA."

Liv bristled. The faith Essie had shown in leaving her a last wish made her feel unusually defiant. "I'm sure I'm more than capable," she said.

"So, you're experienced in communication *and* organization *and* diary keeping *and* administration?"

Liv straightened her back. "I'm a mum to two teenage sons, so I'm an expert in all those things, and more."

"Well, just be careful." Matilda sniffed. "When Essie's nice to you it's like being on the sunny side of the street. Then you turn the corner and an icy wind smacks you in the face."

Liv had heard enough and finished her smoothie. She wanted to get back to the peace and solitude of the apartment and think what to do next.

Matilda glanced at Liv. "*Medusa* had the world at her feet and messed it up. Sure, readers still love her books, but somewhere things went very wrong for her."

But why? Liv thought, agreeing with Matilda for the first time today. She felt something akin to frost creeping across her skin. Just what had happened to Essie ten years ago?

"Take a look at her last interview, for the *Book Ahead Blog*, and see what you're dealing with," Matilda said. "So bitter."

"I thought she refused to do them."

"*Book Ahead* are big influencers and her publisher insisted on it. Essie made sure they don't make the same mistake twice." Matilda took a pink lipstick from her purse and wound it up. "Right, gotta go. I've got a Zoom to prep for."

Liv didn't bother much with social media. She had no interest in uploading photos of her morning muesli, or her bare ankles on a sun lounger. She used a dictionary more often than she googled, but now she wondered what other information was out there. It might give her a clue why Essie vanished ten years ago. "Thanks for meeting me," she said and stood up.

"Good luck, you'll need it. And don't forget my reference."

Liv carried their empty glasses back to the juice bar counter. The man serving raised his eyebrow. "You're the first person to do that," he said. "I usually have to collect them myself."

Liv could well imagine. She might not share Matilda's experience, but surely being polite, hardworking and resourceful were a good start. She headed back toward the spiral staircase.

"Take the slide, it's quicker," the man called after her.

When she reached the turquoise plastic, Liv lugged her bag across her body and sat down with her legs outstretched. After pushing off, she laughed as she whooshed down and jumped off the end.

Matilda stared down from above and shook her head.

Liv waved, smoothed down her T-shirt and strode toward the front door.

Later that afternoon, when she arrived back at Essie's apartment, she sat at the writing desk and reluctantly typed out a reference on Essie's headed notepaper.

I, Essie Starling, am writing this letter as a personal reference for Matilda Hennessy. She is a most excellent worker and I recommend her wholeheartedly...

Liv sat back and read what she'd written. Pretending to be the author hadn't been as difficult as she'd thought. Reaching down, she adjusted the height of the chair and repositioned the backrest so she felt more comfortable. If she could channel even more of her inner Georgia, perhaps she could do this after all.

She searched online for the blog Matilda mentioned, to look for clues about where things went wrong for Essie.

THE BOOK AHEAD BLOG

Let's say a big Book Ahead hello to book queen Essie Starling! Since hitting the bestseller lists in her twenties, über-writer Essie has scribed nineteen novels featuring her have-a-go heroine Georgia Rory. Let's find out what makes her tick.

Q. Readers everywhere can't wait for Georgia's twentieth outing. Is it difficult to keep writing new, fresh adventures for her?

A. Georgia says what people are thinking and does what they're afraid to do, so her readers expect more of the same. She's more popular than I ever expected, maybe even outgrown me, but we both keep on going.

Q. Do you base your characters on anyone in your life? How can we find our own writing inspo?

A. I'm no different from other writers who draw upon their own lives for their work. I find inspiration from everywhere, including people I know. It's not that difficult.

Q. Your characters are often emotionally damaged with hidden secrets in their past. Is there a particular reason you write about them?

A. My characters sometimes make big mistakes that shape their lives. They have to live with their guilt and try to make amends. Calling them "emotionally damaged" is unhelpful and insensitive.

Q. What's a typical day in your life?

A. I get up, I write. Repeat.

Q. You've not been seen in public since winning the Constellation a decade ago. Are you planning to step back into the spotlight for your new release?

A. My job is to write the book, and my publisher's role is to print and market it. I have no desire to tell everyone what wine I drink, or where I purchase my bed linen. My privacy and personal life are of no relevance to my work.

Q. If you had a time machine, where would you go and why?

A. The late eighties, to make different decisions.

Q. If you could give your younger self any advice what would it be?

A. Life is too short to answer inane questions.

8

GREEN PARAKEETS

After the weekend, Liv headed to Essie's apartment and noticed the May sky had brightened as if Photoshopped. She even spotted green parakeets flying around the park. She bought a macchiato from the park café, rather than a flat white from a cheap coffee stand, and a new notebook and pen from a stationery shop.

She opened all the internal doors and window blinds in the apartment, to let light flood into the cavernous space. Sitting down at Essie's desk, Liv took the manuscript from her bag. She wanted to spend the entire day reading it properly and making notes, and had warned Jake and Johnny she might be home late for dinner.

As she sipped her coffee, Liv considered the importance of the story in front of her. This was Essie's legacy, and she couldn't disappoint millions of Georgia Rory fans by making a hash of the author's last ever book. Her cheeks burned when she thought about her tipsy call to Anthony. When they met at the museum, she wanted to prove to him that Essie hadn't made a big mistake leaving her the novel to complete.

The pages of the manuscript curled like autumn leaves, and

she smoothed a hand across the paper. Liv felt a familiar leap of excitement as she started to read, even if she needed the Rosetta stone to interpret Essie's handwriting. Sentences trailed off to nowhere, and there were holes in the pages where the author had scrubbed out words. The notes she'd scribbled to herself in the margins were tiny, written at angles and even upside down. For now, Liv ignored them to concentrate on the story.

She found Essie's twentieth book to have the bones of a good tale. Her pulse sped when the tension ratcheted up, though not as much as usual. Tears didn't spring to her eyes during the emotional scenes. Her heart radiated hope the story would come together as she kept turning the pages, but there was something terribly wrong. Liv sucked on the end of her pen and realized she couldn't *see* herself in the book. She couldn't *become* Georgia in the story.

The heroine's usual sweet but determined persona had a weary bitterness about it, and her jovial, whip smart banter was tired and tetchy. Georgia had always been teetotal, to appeal to her teenage audience as well as adults, so Liv raised a disappointed eyebrow when she reached for a whiskey bottle to drown her sorrows. She spent lots of time alone rather than throwing herself into new adventures.

Hmm, rather like Essie, Liv mused.

The author and her heroine seemed to have become intertwined on the page, and not in a good way. Georgia only sprang off the page when she harked back to the love of her life.

"I was a fool to try to change you," Georgia said. She tossed her hair and her copper curls bounced around her face. She tried to disguise the pain and longing in her eyes, at seeing the only man she'd ever truly loved again. It was a moment she'd re-

played in her head many times over. She often felt she couldn't live without him.

He reached out for her hand. "I can offer you my mind but never my heart," he said.

Every molecule of Georgia's body cried out for him to kiss her. "Please," she said. "If we try hard enough, I know we can make it work…"

Liv heaved a sigh at the melodrama. She usually loved the old-school feel of Essie's books, but the author seemed to be going through the motions with this one. Readers everywhere, like her mum and herself, deserved more for Georgia's final adventure and the end of the series.

Essie might claim to base her characters on people in her life, but Liv couldn't imagine Anthony as inspiration for a dashing hero. He seemed more the steady, studious type. So, who had provided the inspiration for Georgia's nameless and faceless love?

Liv mused upon the heroes in Essie's novels and made a list of them in her notebook. There were several contenders for Georgia's greatest love that appeared throughout the series. So, why didn't Essie name him in Book Twenty?

The author appeared to have the same quandary. She'd written in a margin.

Who is the love of Georgia's life?

What does she do next?

How should her story end?

Liv usually turned the last page of Essie's books feeling full of glee. Today she crashed back in her chair, frustrated and confused. She'd almost filled her notebook with observations and comments, and her mouth twisted. Who was she to question Essie's work?

Perhaps she'd got it wrong. After all, she'd felt emotionally rocky since Essie's death. But when Liv read through all her notes, the evidence was clear. As well as the missing ending, the entire manuscript needed reshaping.

As she dolefully stacked the pages back together, she caught sight of a doodle of a small blue heart on the back of a page. Essie had written next to it,

I wish I could be more like Georgia again.

Liv pressed her hand to her chest. The nine words packed more emotion and longing than anything she'd read in the manuscript. They sounded heartfelt and so unlike the thorny version of Essie she knew. Georgia Rory had lost her way, and Liv pictured Essie reading her own manuscript while swigging gin. What, or who, had been on her mind? And how could Liv conjure up a happy ending for Georgia, when Essie appeared to have given up on her heroine, and her own life?

Stretching her legs and taking a break, Liv meandered into the award room and looked to the photographs on the shelves for inspiration for Georgia's hero. She thought how Essie's two ex-husbands were like chalk and cheese.

Ted Mason was a behemoth in the publishing world, the CEO of Lioncorp, a top global publishing house. He looked like a distinguished grandfather, with his flock of paper-white hair and a custom-tailored suit. Liv supposed there were many raised eyebrows when the divorced father of three walked down the aisle with Essie, his young protégé.

Hank Milligan was much younger with smoldering good looks, a slick smile, and tanned pecs beneath his denim shirt. He wore chunky gold chains around his neck and wrists. Known as the bad boy of crime fiction for his serial killer novels, he didn't seem like the perfect match for Essie either.

Liv also examined any men standing next to Essie in her

photos, looking for a sparkle in their eyes, a knowing smile or a hand around her waist.

She noted how Anthony didn't appear in any of the shots. If the solicitor had been close to Essie, Liv wondered why he was absent.

She picked up a photo of Hank and swept away a speck of dust off the glass with her finger. The glass shifted, moving the photo with it. It revealed another shot underneath. Wondering what it was, Liv unfastened the clips and opened the back of the frame.

The hidden photo was of a handsome blond man with longish hair and a beard. His arm was wrapped protectively around Essie's shoulder. Tattoos peeked out from the cuffs of his shirt like blue lace. There was a large rose inked on the back of his hand. With his Viking-like looks, Liv could imagine Essie falling into his arms, and she questioned why he'd been relegated to the back of the photo frame.

She wondered if any of these men sent the big bouquets of white roses to Essie.

Finally, her eyes settled on her favorite photo of Essie at the Constellation ceremony. The author's tangerine lips beamed as she held her crystal star aloft. She looked so vivid, strong and alive.

Liv again wondered what went so wrong after that night. Did any of Essie's men know why she disappeared?

She sighed as she imagined herself wearing a fancy silk dress, too. She and Jake hadn't been to a wedding reception or proper party for years. Paperpress hosted its annual staff awards to recognize the contribution of its small team of employees. She got to dress up a little and style her hair for a night, but it wasn't as glamorous as the events Essie used to attend. Liv couldn't help feeling a touch envious.

When she'd met Jake for the first time, twenty-three years

ago, she had been wet and bedraggled. Rain bounced off the pavements on the dark gloomy evening.

The Picturehouse was a local family-run cinema. *84 Charing Cross Road* was a film Liv wanted to see, about an American lady heading to London to visit a bookshop specializing in out-of-print books.

The cinema was quiet, and she meandered around the foyer looking at the film posters alongside one other person, a man with curly hair. They approached the popcorn stand at the same time and there was only enough left for one person.

"You take it." He paid and handed the popcorn tub to her.

"No, it's yours."

"We could share it," he said with a smile. "I'm Jake, by the way."

"Hi, I'm Liv."

They were the only two people in the screening, and they sat next to each other in the back row. Liv tried to eat her popcorn quietly. She liked how Jake concentrated on the film, without chatting all the way through it, like her last date had done.

Afterward they went to a pub for a glass of wine and chatted about the film. Liv didn't usually kiss anyone on a first date, but when Jake told her that his family business typeset and printed books, her heart melted a little.

"Paperpress binds books, too," he said. "I fold paper into sections called signatures and sew them together using waxed linen thread to create a text block, then adhere end papers to the spine edge and shape it with a hammer. The cover is glued to the end papers, forming the hollow you see between the cover and pages."

Liv felt like he was reading her a bedtime story. They kissed in the doorway of the pub.

He was eight years older than her, like a strong, solid oak

tree, while she still felt like a sapling. While her friends were out dancing in nightclubs and doing the walk of shame home in the early morning, she curled up on the sofa, reading books or watching movies with Jake. She didn't tell him about her dream of being a writer, feeling too foolish to share it.

In the award room, Liv tore herself away from Essie's photos. When she returned to the writing room, the manuscript felt like a massive undertaking. She wasn't sure where to start and she tried to tap into Georgia's spirit once more. However, the story had left her feeling flat and uninspired. When Liv leafed through her notes, her lungs felt heavy and fear tightened her throat. She couldn't possibly fit all this work around Platinum and the Cardinals, and she wondered if the deadline to complete the book was movable. Why did it have to be within six months?

Feeling very alone, Liv had an urge to reach out to someone who loved Georgia as much as she did. Neither Anthony nor Jake fitted the bill, so she found herself googling Essie's agent, Marlon.

She found that Marlon had worked as a car mechanic for many years before returning to university as a mature student. After gaining his English degree he worked for a large London literary agency before setting up The Marlon Austin Literary Agency. His image showed a plump, bald man with an auburn goatee and mischievous smile. He dressed with dapper rebellion in a tweed waistcoat teamed with a leather biker jacket. Other than Essie, his client list consisted of only nine little-known authors, and Liv wondered how this quirky-looking fellow had attracted Essie to his agency.

She nibbled her thumbnail until she summoned up the bravado to call him. She told the agency receptionist she was Essie Starling's assistant and needed to speak to Marlon.

As she waited for him to answer, Liv practiced refining

her accent and grammar. She'd once read the success rate of a writer getting a literary agent was six thousand to one. They were an elusive breed, and she was nervous about speaking to one in real life. It was something she'd dreamed of, but never in this way.

"Matilda? Is that you? Are you alright?" Marlon said in a booming voice, not the posh one Liv expected. He had a Birmingham accent so his pronunciation of vowels made the word *right* sound like *roit*, and *you* sound like *yow*.

"Sorry, it's actually Liv... Essie's new assistant," she said.

"*Another* one?" he said. "I thought I was speaking to... Oh, never mind. Where's Essie been hiding, Timbuktu? Is that why she doesn't answer my emails?"

Liv laughed politely. "I'm calling about her deadline."

"Oh, really? Fantastic. Hit me with it, Liv. When will I see her latest masterpiece?"

Liv ran her tongue around her teeth, considering how much she could tell him. "It's still at the handwritten stage, so I need to type it up," she said. "Then Essie has lots of editing to do. She still has to write the last eight chapters."

The silence that followed sounded deafening. "Seriously?" Marlon said. "Are you trying to give me a heart attack?"

Liv shifted in her chair. "I understand Essie has until November the first to fin—"

"That's over five months away," Marlon interrupted. "It was due eons ago. Meg's literally pulling her hair out. The schedule is planned, and her team is working on marketing. She wants a big hoo-ha around this one."

"And that's why I'm calling you." Liv swallowed. "Essie's finding writing really tough right now."

"If it was that easy, everyone would do it."

Liv's stomach shrank. "But what if she needs more time?"

Marlon let out a low rumbling noise. "You and I need to be

a team, Liv, pulling together. With all these delays, I'm expecting something brilliant. Unplug Essie's phone, lock her door, buy her a horse's nose bag so she can eat while she's writing, whatever you need to do for her to finish this book. I don't want to ask Meg for more time until we absolutely need it. It'll push her over the edge. Call me anytime for a bit of support. You okay with that?"

Liv wrapped her fingers tightly around the phone. The pages of the manuscript were furling again, and she flattened them down with her elbow. The quietness in the apartment made her feel suddenly isolated. The feeling reminded her of trembling under the bedcovers reading *The Moon on the Water* by torchlight, after losing her dad.

She'd always imagined becoming a writer was like an invisible path stretching out in front of her, waiting for her to start her journey. It looked like she had to stamp on nettles and jump over potholes to walk along it. Just like Georgia Rory. "Yes, that's okay." Liv screwed her eyes shut. "I'm sure Essie can get it done."

"Good stuff," Marlon said. "I'll take that as your guarantee."

As she hung up, Liv's dad's voice appeared in her head. *"Just keep turning the page until you reach the next chapter, sweet pea,"* Grant Cooper said.

"Okay, Dad, I'm going to try," she whispered.

9

SHAKESPEARE

The night before meeting Anthony, Liv dreamed she was surrounded by book pages swirling around her. They stuck to her body and coated her face until she couldn't breathe. Essie had died three weeks ago, but it felt like only yesterday.

"Stop wriggling," Jake huffed and pulled the bedcovers around him. "You're keeping me awake."

Liv couldn't stop moving, twitching and staring into the darkness. She was determined to carry out Essie's last wish to the best of her abilities, but the worry of hoodwinking millions of Georgia Rory fans crept over her skin like soldier ants.

She tried telling herself that author James Patterson openly employed cowriters to help craft his many bestsellers, writing outlines that others then drafted out. Was it so bad if she worked on Essie's novel and no one knew about it? Authors Stieg Larsson, Robert Ludlum and Agatha Christie had all had their characters and stories passed onto new authors, to continue telling them posthumously. Though, unlike the Essie situation, it was done candidly.

Liv's self-assurances did little to quell her concerns.

She dressed in black trousers and a white blouse for her

meeting with Anthony. She didn't usually bother wearing makeup to work and made the effort with pink lip gloss and mascara. She called at the apartment on the way to the Museum of Writing, where she added Essie's green scarf around her neck for a splash of color. The sun was out again, so she took a pair of Dior sunglasses off a bookshelf, popping them on before adding a squirt of Fracas to her collarbone.

As she passed the hallway mirror, Liv caught sight of herself and did a double take. Her Sheryl Crow vibe now had a touch of Emily Blunt classiness, and she liked it.

When she reached the lobby, she noticed a woman meandering on the pavement outside as if waiting for someone. She wore jeans so tight they looked sprayed on, and her long glossy hair was at least four shades of caramel. She looked like the kind of woman who'd sit on her kitchen worktop for *OK! magazine*, grinning over a slice of watermelon.

As Liv walked through the door, the woman darted inside and flashed her a megawatt smile. "Thanks, hon. Forgot my key."

Liv smiled back. It was only afterward she remembered entry was via an electronic fob, not a key. The thought was probably nothing, but it played on her mind as she walked to the museum.

The ornate orange brick building was wedged between the library and a discount clothes store, so was often missed by shoppers. A portly man dressed as William Shakespeare, resplendent in black knickerbockers and a frilled collar, opened the door for her.

Liv wandered around looking at the exhibits while waiting for Anthony to arrive. She admired notes by Charles Dodgson for *Alice's Adventures Under Ground*, and a copy of the book when it was later published as *Alice's Adventures in Wonderland*, under his pen name Lewis Carroll. There was Tennessee Williams's pen, and one of Evelyn Waugh's diaries.

There weren't many other visitors around and Shakespeare kept looking over at her, so Liv moved into a different room to escape his attention. She learned that Mary Shelley started to write *Frankenstein* when she was only eighteen years old, and that J.R.R. Tolkien worked at the *Oxford English Dictionary* for two years. Her favorite piece of information was that Sir Arthur Conan Doyle and Houdini were once friends.

When Anthony showed up, he was dressed in jeans and a blue linen shirt with a worn leather satchel across his body. There was a bee-shaped pin on the lapel of his jacket. He didn't look entirely comfortable in casual clothes and still had a formal air about him. Liv wasn't sure whether to shake his hand or not, so improvised with a smile and a hello.

As they walked around the museum together, Anthony's nostrils flared. "Ah, you smell like Ess—" he said before stopping himself.

Liv side-glanced at him, wondering how he knew. She had to remind Jake of her own favorite fragrance each time he asked for birthday ideas. She didn't want to tell Anthony she'd used Essie's perfume that morning. "I borrowed her scarf," she said. "Her scent's probably still on it."

She was about to ask him how long he'd known the author, but Anthony started to explain how Pentecost and Wilde sponsored the museum financially and that he sat on the governing board. His manner was assured, polite and a little tense. Liv could see why Essie entrusted him with her instructions, but found it tricky to imagine any romance between them. Could the cuff links she'd found under Essie's pillow really belong to him? At this moment, it felt too forward to ask.

When she looked around the museum for anything to do with Essie, she was disappointed to find it lacking.

Anthony seemed to read her mind. "There are hundreds of thousands of writers in the world, so the museum can't possibly feature them all," he said. "The board has discussed implementing a contemporary writers' room for some time. Securing funding is the issue."

Liv turned around on the spot. "I'd love to see Jojo Moyes's notes, or a photo of Marian Keyes's writing desk. I'm sure others would, too."

"Correct, though I suppose Shakespeare offers better costume opportunities." His smile had a hint of warmth.

They found a blue velvet sofa in front of a portrait of Lord Byron. When Liv looked up at the painting, it felt strange to be sitting here with a man who wasn't her husband.

When she and Jake had first started dating, they used to love spending their weekends hanging out at museums and art galleries, perusing the exhibitions and sharing cake in the café. When Mack and Johnny arrived, they moved into the children's zone instead where they all donned wigs to dress like Charles Dickens, or made up limericks.

She loved the adult versions of Mack and Johnny with all her heart, but there was something special about having small children. All the shoelace tying, and nose wiping, and remembering to carry snacks had been exhausting, yet she missed the feeling of being the center of someone else's world.

"My wife, Harriet, is a little in love with this portrait of Byron," Anthony said. "I suppose I should be jealous."

So, Anthony's married and unlikely to be romantically involved with Essie, Liv thought to herself. It made things even more confusing. She wrinkled her nose at the flamboyant poet. "I prefer Neil Gaiman, or Khaled Hosseini."

Shakespeare appeared and handed pencils and sheets of blank paper to them. "For you to scribe sonnets," he said.

Liv took the opportunity to move along her conversation

with Anthony. "I still don't know exactly what happened to Essie," she said. "Why did she go into hospital?"

Anthony pressed a finger against the point of his pencil and thought for a moment. "Are you aware she'd had chronic pancreatitis, for some time?" he said.

Liv shook her head. "I'm not sure what it is."

"It's when the pancreas becomes inflamed and permanently damaged, meaning it stops working properly. It can be terribly unpleasant, causing weight loss, and severe abdominal pain."

Liv felt a flush circle her neck. She wished she'd asked Essie about her weight loss, or mentioned the hidden gin bottles, even if the author might have accused her of prying.

Liv searched on her phone for the condition, and read her findings aloud. "'The most common cause of pancreatitis is by drinking excessive amounts of alcohol over the years. It can cause repeated episodes of acute pancreatitis which results in increasing damage to the organ, so surgery might be needed...'" She stopped and considered her findings. Maybe Essie's condition was yet another reason why she shut herself away in her writing room.

"It can be a risky operation. Afterward, the doctor was honest and told her things could go either way," Anthony said, toying with his pin badge. "Essie called me that night, groggy and worried about the outcome. When I visited her the next day, she'd taken a turn for the worse."

Liv pressed her lips together. "What happened?" she said.

"She'd developed an infection that was spreading throughout her body. The doctor said nothing could be done. They'd try to keep her comfortable, but..." Anthony shook his head in disbelief. "Essie managed to write a few things down in her notebook, before..."

Liv's stomach knotted as she thought about Essie being given this terrible news. She held a hand to her throat. "Were you with her when...?"

"Yes." His jaw clenched.

"What about a partner, or boyfriend?" Liv said, thinking about the bouquets of white roses again. "Essie's ex-PA Matilda said she was in love with someone."

Something imperceptible fell across Anthony's face. He adjusted his jacket. "Then Matilda must know more than I do," he said. "Let's not turn Essie's passing into one of her romance novels."

"I wasn't trying to. And her books are adventures." She wondered if Anthony had even read any of them. "I just think someone should tell this guy. He'll wonder where Essie is and we can't just leave him hanging. Are you sure there's nothing else in her yellow notebook?"

Anthony's mouth became a straight line, and he didn't speak.

The air had tensed between them so Liv focused on her blank piece of paper and attempted to write a sonnet. She made it about a writer and her mystery lover, to connect Essie with someone on paper, if not in person.

Anthony did the same and sighed at his own writing efforts. "It's rather a huge task she left you," he said eventually. "How long did you work for Essie? Three years?"

Liv heard suspicion in his voice. She supposed a bestselling author thinking of her cleaner on her deathbed *was* unusual. "I met her twice before then," she said.

"Ah, really. Twice?"

Liv folded her arms. Anthony obviously didn't know that she and Essie shared some kind of connection they were only beginning to explore. If she told him about their afternoon tea, or the notes Essie left for her, it probably still wouldn't convince him. She swallowed away the lump in her throat that swelled when she thought about her first ever encounter with Essie, and felt obliged to share it with him.

"When I was twelve, I went through a really tough time," she said. "Me and my mum had to go to live with her sister, my aunt Peggy, on the other side of the country for several months. I had to attend a new school, too, and it felt like I'd been sent to the moon." She shrugged a shoulder, as if it didn't really matter, when it actually had felt like her entire life had been upended. She could still feel her new classmates' fingers drilling into her back and pulling her hair.

"Why did you have to move?" Anthony said.

"Several reasons." Liv scratched the back of her neck, hating her memories of those days. There were some things she didn't want to share with him. "One day, Essie came into my class on a publicity tour for her debut novel *The Moon on the Water*. All the pupils had to write a poem, and she chose mine as her winner. I was so chuffed. She gave me a copy of the book and wrote inside it, 'To Olivia, keep writing. Best wishes, Essie Starling.'" Liv grinned. "I read it over and over and imagined I was Georgia Rory, trekking across the desert or snowy terrain on my way to school. It helped me to cope with being away from home.

"After that, I became a big fan and bought all Essie's next books, too. I queued outside bookstores on publication day, and swooned over photos of her in LA, wearing her gorgeous gowns with Hank Milligan. I voted for the Constellation Prize, and when Essie won it I actually cheered at the TV. I hoped she might do a publicity tour, or at least an interview. Instead, she seemed to vanish off the face of the earth." Liv shook her head. "I thought it was really odd. She kept on writing, though, even if the quality, um…tapered off."

"When was the next time you met her?" Anthony said.

"Around three years ago. I was feeling listless about what to do next in my life. I often turn to *The Moon on the Water* for comfort and, when I reread Essie's message, I had an urge to tell her how much Georgia Rory meant to me." She stopped and her cheeks reddened. "So, I wrote a letter and sent it to her publishing house.

"I suppose I rambled on a bit, reminding her how she selected my poem. I told her I'd always felt guilty not writing much else, especially because my dad was an English professor. I admitted I was struggling to find meaning in my cleaning work."

Liv had also revealed to Essie that she longed to be a writer, too, but she didn't divulge this to Anthony.

"You *asked* her for a *job*?" the solicitor said, raising an eyebrow.

Liv shook her head vigorously. "No, I certainly didn't mean it that way. It was a fan letter, that's all. I poured out stuff because it was cathartic. I felt really embarrassed after sending it. Essie must receive loads of letters and I didn't expect a response. But then a signed copy of her sixteenth book *When Midnight Beckons* arrived for me. There was a small note from her PA asking me to get in touch about a job. I had no idea Essie only lived a couple of miles away from me."

"It sounds very serendipitous," Anthony said. "But I'm not sure it explains everything."

"What do you mean?" Liv frowned at him.

"About why she left this wish for *you*."

Liv kept asking herself the same thing.

Anthony toyed with his pencil for a while, as if wondering whether to tell her something. "You should know Essie also left something for you in her will," he said.

Liv's jaw dropped. Was he kidding her? "That's so amazing of her, and kind," she said. Curiosity rumbled inside her and she stole a side-glance at him. "Do you know what it is?"

Anthony's left eye twitched. "Applying for probate and dealing with Essie's estate could take a long time. There's lots to do, notifying various organizations and authorities."

"Won't they recognize her name?"

"Everything will be done under Essie's real name," he said. "I'll share the contents of her will with you as soon as I can. Hopefully before you finish writing her book."

"Oh, right." Liv bit her lip. She felt dreadful speculating what Essie might have left her, but a sum of money could really help out her and Jake's finances. "Did she have any close relatives?"

"No. She must have thought a great deal of you."

Liv caught something strange in the tone of his voice, perhaps bewilderment, or even jealousy. "Well it's a nice surprise," she said.

"Yes, I thought so, too," he replied coolly.

Liv fidgeted with her pencil. She'd told Anthony things she'd never even revealed to Jake and now he was acting all judgmental. "How did *you* know her?" she said.

He cleared his throat. "A client recommended me to Essie, ah, several years ago."

Liv thought how he'd personally produced the funeral service sheets and how sympathetically the funeral director had consoled him. She couldn't help thinking about his bee handkerchief and pin badge, and how they matched the cuff links under Essie's pillow. "You must have heard of her, before then?" she prompted.

"I think I read her first book, a long time ago."

Before Liv could point out that he knew Essie well enough to recognize her perfume, Anthony peered over her shoulder and read her sonnet. "That's rather accomplished," he said.

Liv looked up as a woman wearing a bonnet approached

them. "My name is Emily Brontë. Accepting your questions would be my pleasure," she said.

Liv gripped her handbag. It was strange enough dealing with the Essie situation, without striking up conversation with pretend-deceased authors. She shook her head and Emily Brontë bustled away.

"I have something for you," Anthony said. He delved into his satchel and handed a thick brown envelope to her.

Liv opened it and gasped at the wad of money inside. "What's *this* for?"

"It's your expenses, anything you need to complete Essie's task. Six months of spending shouldn't come out of your own pocket. I've also set up your pay increase. You'll see it in your next wage."

Wow, Liv thought to herself. She imagined showing her bank statement to Jake and seeing his eyes light up. She also thought about her conversation with Marlon about the deadline for delivering Essie's book. "I really can't accept this."

"Take it." Anthony smiled. "It may prove useful."

Liv met his eyes. She took a moment to think how Georgia Rory would handle things. "I actually need more," she said.

The solicitor frowned and his mouth parted. *"More?"*

Liv swallowed. "I've read Essie's manuscript and there's lots of work to do, more than I imagined. I *want* to do this for her, but I can't squeeze it around my other cleaning jobs, and I can't afford to give them up. A raise is great, but I only work for Essie three afternoons a week and I'm in…" She trailed off her words, not wanting to say *dire straits*.

"Are you telling me you need to work on this full-time?" Anthony said.

Liv nodded. "Essie's agent won't extend the deadline."

His eyes flashed briefly. "You've conversed with Marlon?"

"Don't worry. I didn't say anything about the Essie situation. I wanted to see if there was more time available to write."

Anthony pursed his lips and thought for a while. "Please talk to me in future," he said.

"But I feel like I'm bothering you." She didn't say that *he* made her feel that way.

"I'll make the necessary arrangements for a full-time salary, on your new pay rate. It may take me a few days to set up a contract."

"Thank you," Liv said. "I need time to let my other clients know anyway."

"Let's keep in touch." Anthony stood up and shook her hand.

As he walked away, he chatted to Shakespeare for a while before leaving. Liv watched him and felt a rush of emotions catching her off guard—worry, panic and pure excitement. Also, a growing sense of fascination about Anthony she couldn't ignore. Why did he claim his relationship with Essie was purely businesslike, when several things indicated otherwise?

More than anything, Liv felt rather proud of her new go-getting attitude and felt like blowing on her fingernails and polishing them on her blouse.

She was actually going to be a full-time writer. Whether she'd be able to finish Essie's last ever book was a different matter. But she was going to damn well try.

10

HANDPRINTS

While waiting for Anthony to sort out her new contract, Liv continued to empty bins for Platinum and make sandwiches for Tarkers and Jules for the next few days. She didn't want to jump the gun by giving up these jobs, or telling Jake about her new role, until she had something in writing. She dug out her cleaning agency contract and groaned when she saw her notice period at Platinum was one month. She wanted to do things by the book, and didn't want to leave the Cardinals without a cleaner either.

While she cleaned, dusted and scrubbed, Liv listened to *Big Little Lies* by Liane Moriarty. She devoted every moment she could to typing up Essie's manuscript. As she tapped away, she finally felt like she had a mission in life. She wanted to show Anthony, and herself, that she could do this.

Fortunately, Liv wasn't a complete novice when it came to using computers. She'd taken IT lessons at school, and an evening course to help Mack and Johnny with their homework. She could use Word and type, even if she only used two fingers.

Many of Essie's sentences and paragraphs were messy and disjointed, but Liv loved seeing the book slowly taking shape on screen. She couldn't wait to finish inputting and start to work on the story itself.

However, the thought of summoning up her own words felt like a huge step in the dark. She worried her prose would be more like *The Very Hungry Caterpillar* rather than Essie Starling. She wondered why Essie hadn't passed her task on to someone more experienced. The author had only ever read her childhood poem, hardly enough to instill a sense of confidence in Liv's abilities. So, what *had* Essie seen in her?

Wanting to see and feel close to the author again, Liv looked up the Constellation Prize footage on YouTube. There were several videos of Essie's acceptance speech and Liv clicked on one of them. Might she glimpse Anthony in the audience, too?

Essie stood on stage, her face illuminated by spotlights. Her eyes swam with tears and she hugged the crystal star to her chest. "I'd like to thank everyone who voted for this award. You have no idea what it means to me. I want to keep taking Georgia Rory on adventures for as long as you want me to. I'd like to say a huge thanks to Hank, and Ted, Meg at Peregrine, and…" She reeled off many more names Liv had seen in the acknowledgments in her books.

"Finally," Essie said, "I'd like to thank someone very special who helped me to write. He encouraged me to live and to love, and this award is for him."

Liv's ears pricked. She moved her face closer to the screen.

The camera panned to Hank grinning proudly in the audience, and Ted standing there with a stern expression. There was a brief shot of the bearded, tattooed man she'd seen in the hidden photograph.

Essie was about to speak again, but a tear trickled down her cheek. "Thank you. That is all." She performed a small curtsy then swept off the stage.

While watching, Liv's body flooded with pride, too. Her

cheeks glowed and she realized her own eyes were wet. The version of Essie in the video was so unlike the guarded figure she knew. The Constellation was a real pinnacle in the author's career. Was her illness really enough for her to walk away from it all?

In the video, Essie stopped to pose for photographs in front of a banner.

Liv noticed the date of the awards was printed on it, November 1. She frowned and drummed her fingernails on the desk for a while. It was the same date as the Book Twenty deadline Essie requested, and the fictitious date of her death. Was it just a coincidence?

Liv searched around some more.

There was only one video taken at the Constellation after-party. It was jerky and dark, made by someone wandering around the room with a low-resolution phone or camera. It lasted an hour and Liv yawned, stopping the film after ten minutes. No wonder only a few people had watched and liked it.

When she started to type again her heart still swelled at seeing Essie in her prime.

Liv didn't really believe in guardian angels, but she could still sense the author's presence in the apartment, like how a headmistress can make pupils straighten their ties simply by walking down a corridor. It was a sensation that gave her comfort and also a shot of fear.

A memory of Essie dropped into her thoughts, as if the writer planted it there.

Around a year ago, she'd been dusting the shelves in the writing room when the author had lifted her chin. "If you had to describe the art of writing, Olivia, what would you say?" Essie said.

Liv froze with her cloth in her hand at this unexpected query. They'd never really had a proper conversation before, other than discussing Essie's cleaning preferences. Why would the author ask *her*? Was it some kind of trick question?

Anything sensible flew out of Liv's head and she garbled the first thing she thought of. "I'd say it's a bit like wading through mud without wearing Wellington boots," she said.

Essie tilted her head and considered this for a while.

Liv wished she could take it back. She was horrified Essie might take her silly comment seriously.

"I agree, somewhat," Essie said. "Personally, I think it's more like being on board a small yacht on the ocean, looking over the side and glimpsing something shiny on the seabed. It shimmers and then vanishes again, so you don't know if it's a precious ring, or just the tab pulled off a drink can.

"Others around you might tell you it's a piece of rubbish and to ignore it. But you can't stop thinking what it might be. You drop into the water and kick your feet to stay afloat. Touching and holding the shiny thing takes precedence over anything else.

"You dive down until your fingertips brush against it, pushing it farther away. Wet sand blooms and obscures your view. You rush back to the surface spluttering for breath with salt water running down the back of your throat. Yet, you keep on diving until you finally wrap your fingers around the shiny thing. It's finally yours, and you clench it in your fist and hold it to your heart."

Liv had never heard Essie talk so much before and her cheeks felt fiery at her own flippant answer. She'd had a unique opportunity to impress Essie and had messed it up. "So, are you holding something precious, or is it just rubbish?" she asked.

Essie smiled enigmatically. "I have no idea. And that's the thing, Olivia. You never know if the thing glinting on the seabed is something special or not, until you force yourself under water and hold it in your hand. And *that's* what writing is like."

Liv had no idea what to say. She clutched her cleaning cloth and when her words didn't emerge, Essie turned away. The moment was lost between them.

As she relived her own disappointment in herself, Liv's backbone stiffened. If she had the opportunity to answer the question again, she would say something smarter to Essie. "Writing is like a life belt keeping me afloat right now, when everything else seems to be pulling me under. I don't want to dive and search around on the bottom of the sea bed. I want to swim to a beautiful shore."

This time she pictured the author smiling and nodding.

And if Essie believed in her, Liv had to find belief in herself, too.

But she wondered why and when Essie had stopped diving for her own treasure.

A week after meeting Anthony in the museum, Liv's new contract arrived in her inbox. She surreptitiously opened the email as she trundled her cleaning cart through the Platinum office. A suited man passed her and mumbled, "The ladies' loos need cleaning."

Someone had been sick in a sink and Liv gritted her teeth while tugging on her rubber gloves. She pledged to hand in her notice right after this shift.

After she finished wiping the basin, the door to the bathroom swung open and the woman in the cream skirt suit tottered up to the mirror again. She averted her eyes from Liv and searched in her bag for something. A sweet wrapper and a crumpled receipt fell to the floor. The woman opened a mirrored compact and powder sprinkled into the sink Liv had just cleaned. The woman swept aside her litter with the side of her foot and reapplied her lipstick.

Liv felt something switch inside her, as if someone had turned the power back on after a blackout. As the woman turned on her heels and made to exit the room, Liv snatched up her rubbish from the floor. "Excuse me," she called out.

The woman looked back, her eyes sweeping over Liv before settling on the embroidered logo on her chest.

"You forgot something." Liv strode toward her and held out the wrapper and receipt.

The woman eyed them, as if they were dog dirt in the middle of her lawn. "It's not mine," she said.

The something inside Liv started to boil over. "You need an optician. Clearly there's something wrong with your eyesight."

The woman smirked. "I don't think so."

Liv spotted her handbag wasn't fully zipped up. She shot out a hand, pushed the litter into the gap then zipped it. "In case you need them," she said with a smile.

"Don't you dare touch me." The woman shrank back, her top lip curling. "It's your *job* to pick things up. I'm going to report this. What's your name?"

Liv glared at her defiantly. The spirit of Georgia Rory felt alive within her. She made a show of peeling off her tunic before slinging it over one of the cubicle doors. Her notice period had just ended super early. "My name is Liv Green," she said. "And in the future, don't judge a book by its cover."

At the Cardinals' house, Hannah had covered the dining table with cosmetics and set up a ring light and tripod for her iPhone. She studied her own face reflected on the screen. Liv noticed her cheeks were bright pink, as if she'd fallen asleep in the sun.

"Hey, Liv, sweetie," she said. "The electricity in my shed isn't working. I have to vlog in here today." She pointed both index fingers at her face. "I have to gush about dermaplaning while suffering from a migraine." She said it as if she had to address the United Nations about world peace and had lost her voice.

"What's dermaplaning?" Liv said.

"It's a beauty treatment. A dermatologist uses a scalpel to scrape away the top layer of skin and the peach fuzz. It helps to..." Hannah stopped and fixed her eyes on Liv's complexion. "Oh, it doesn't matter. It's kind of a premium treatment."

Liv's head felt floaty from the insult. She wanted to tell Hannah she was leaving but the woman was busy swallowing down herbal headache tablets with a glass of San Pellegrino. "Do you want me to clean today, or look after your children?" she said stiffly.

"Just do both, okay, sweetie. Walt and I will be busy bees all day."

Liv glowered as she cleaned the dual black marble sinks and heated mirrors in the bathroom. In their bedroom, Tarkers and Jules had pulled out a suitcase full of old clothes and played a game, mimicking their parents.

"Walt, sweetie," Jules said, wearing a Victoria Beckham dress with her hand on her hip. "I said dark chocolate with an eighty percent cocoa content, not fifty."

Liv pressed her lips together and tried not to laugh. She sprayed the shower tiles and wiped them down.

"Sorry, darling," Tarkers said. "It's not my mistake, I was busy with my therapist."

"Well, who got it wrong?" Jules let out a shuddering sigh. "Probably Liv. She knows nothing about quality. I should take it out of her wages."

"No, you can't do that. How will she afford her abominable T-shirts?"

Liv gripped her cleaning cloth. She swallowed away a sour taste that appeared at the back of her mouth. The children were probably only repeating what they'd heard from their parents. She shoved all her cleaning things back in their box, dumped it in the bath and headed into their bedroom.

"Hey, Tarkers, Jules. Your mummy and daddy are busy all day. Again. Why don't you give them a nice surprise?" she said.

The kids looked at each other. Jules peeled off the VB dress and kicked it off the end of her foot.

Liv smiled and left it lying on the floor. "I'm sure I overheard your mother saying she'd love some of your super handprints decorating her bedroom wall."

Jules folded her arms and her rosebud mouth pouted. "We're not allowed to do *that*."

Tarkers dug her in the waist with his elbow. "It's artistic freedom," he said solemnly, but had a wicked glint in his eye.

"The paint is in the cupboard," Liv said. She picked up her handbag, and took out her packed lunch. "I'm leaving, so you can share my sandwiches, crisps and chocolate bar if you like? Sorry, they're not that healthy, or organic."

The children's eyes widened with delight.

"Are you going to the post office?" Jules said. "I got a Barbie for my birthday and Mummy says I have to sell it because it objectifies women."

"No, I'm not going. Not any longer." Liv pressed her hand briefly to the young girl's cheek, and performed a fist bump with Tarkers. "I'm sorry, but I probably won't see you two again. I need my artistic freedom, too."

11

WATERFALL

Trying to untangle Essie's manuscript was like unknotting a huge ball of wet wool. Liv was glad it was now her only job, although she still felt like an imposter working at Essie's desk. It was four weeks since the author died and Liv half expected her ghost to appear and say, "What on earth are you doing in my chair, Olivia?"

Liv soon developed a squint from staring at the laptop screen for too long and a painful crick in her neck from trying to interpret and type up Essie's writing. Did that word say *octopus* or *audacious*? Did the author mean *progress* or *process*? A place name beginning with *M* and a squiggle could be Mississippi, Massachusetts or Michigan.

Liv took a stab, inserting words at random and underlining them. When she reread her paragraphs, many of them didn't make sense.

Georgia raced across the city torrential the railway station, darting around cars and bluffing into strangers. The mango train was about to leave and she had to get on board, or else she'd never see him again. The train wheels scattered as they began to turn. "Miss, it's already left," a guard shouted. But Georgia ran on, sensually running alongside it. She managed to grab a *handful*, and hoisted herself inside through an open door.

Liv looked to Essie's other novels for guidance, even copying and rewriting a few sentences, anything to keep things moving. It wasn't proper writing, but she wasn't a proper writer.

Georgia's ultimate hero remained frustratingly out of reach, even when Liv studied the photos of Ted, Hank and the tattooed blond man again. She opened the green cuff link box and set it down in front of her, but no inspiration came through.

She tried to work on the manuscript at home in the evening, too, but there was always some kind of backing track going on. Johnny's music thumped and Jake's voice droned from the coat cupboard as he discussed the costs of a new printing press with Katrina. Liv couldn't seem to find the right moment to tell him about her new role.

Each morning, when she arrived at Essie's apartment, she opened the front door and stood in the hallway. Liv closed her eyes and breathed in the silence. The serenity of the space felt like cool water trickling over her skin during a heatwave. It smelled of lemon rather than men's socks and toast. With Tarker's comments about her abominable dress sense still ringing in her ears, she wore trousers and a white blouse instead of her jeans and T-shirt.

When Liv finished typing up the manuscript, there was still so much work to do it scared her, especially writing anything herself, but it was satisfying seeing everything on screen in black and white. On her way home, she bought a chocolate cake from Bentley and White to celebrate.

Jake rattled around in the kitchen, wearing her pink apron again. A bag of dried pasta and a can of tomatoes sat on the worktop. "Hey," he said wearily. His eyes narrowed when he saw the cake in its cellophane topped box. "Is that for us? How much did *that* cost?"

"Don't ask," Liv joked, still shaken by the price.

Jake's lips thinned. "I mean it." He pointed to the ceiling where water trickled down the wall. "I think we've got a burst pipe in the bathroom."

"Oh, God." Liv looked up. "It's like Niagara Falls. Thank goodness we're insured."

A necklace of red circled Jake's neck and he fixed his eyes on the ceiling. "Um, I don't think I renewed it this time."

Liv frowned at him, unsure if she'd heard him correctly. She slid the cake onto the worktop.

"Plumbing insurance is expensive, and we never used it." Jake's cheek twitched.

"We'll have to call for an emergency plumber." She plunged a hand into her handbag to find her phone.

"No way, it'll cost a bloody fortune. I'll try to patch it up myself. I need to eat something first, though, I'm starving."

It was the third time he'd cooked pasta that week, and Liv longed for something different. She felt the chunk of cash in her bag, having carried it around since Anthony gave it to her. She wasn't sure when her new full-time pay would land in their joint bank account.

Liv glanced up at the streaming water again, and at Jake gnawing his lip. The weight of keeping Essie's death a secret from her family felt like shackles around her ankles. She took out the envelope and felt like a drug dealer when she slipped it into his hands. It was open, revealing the money inside.

Jake's eyes shot open. "Where the hell did that come from?" He gasped. "Have you robbed a bank or something?"

"I'm helping Essie with her work," Liv said, her cheeks flushing. "It's my expenses."

"When did cleaning pay *that* much?"

"There's something I've been meaning to tell you..." She swallowed away the temptation to tell him about the author's death. "Essie's asked me to be her personal assistant."

"You?" he said. "Why?"

Although Liv constantly asked herself the same thing, his questioning stung.

"She knows I'm interested in her books and I know her characters inside out. In fact—". she hesitated for a moment, considering how much she could say "—she wants me to work for her full-time, in the new role."

He nodded at the cash. "So, that's your pay raise? Wow."

"Not really, this is more for..." She couldn't think how best to explain it. She certainly couldn't tell Jake she was completing Essie's book. "I've packed in my other two cleaning jobs."

Jake raised an eyebrow. He turned a dial on the oven and took the pasta off the hob. "When did all this happen?"

"Hmm, a while ago."

"And you're only telling me now? Didn't you want to discuss it first?"

"You've been busy with Paperpress," she said. She'd hoped for a nice family meal with posh cake, not having to justify herself. "Congratulations might be nice."

Jake shook his head as if stunned. "Yeah, sure, well done." He rubbed her arm absentmindedly before flicking through the money in the envelope. "This is brilliant. We can pay for the plumbing, and an electricity bill has just arrived. We're a bit short on the Paperpress wages this week."

"Hold on a minute," Liv said, snatching it back. "The leak is an emergency, and we'll have to pay the cash back."

Jake scratched the back of his neck. "Why?"

"This money is for things I might have to do for Essie. We'll just borrow it for a short while until I receive the extra pay in my salary. And we don't want to spend it all on bills anyway. What about a nice meal out, or a weekend away? We've not done that for ages."

He nodded at her. "Okay, let's think about it," he said. "Writing nonsense sure pays well for Essie."

Liv felt her body rock. Jake's comment felt like a spear through her gut. "What did you just say?" she said.

Pink tinged Jake's cheeks. "Nothing. I just mean that she churns out her wild stories and gets paid a fortune, while the rest of us work proper jobs."

When Liv thought about all Essie's handwritten pages, her throat shrank so tightly she could hardly speak. She'd typed up seventy thousand words and now had to stitch them together like an intricate embroidery, plus add more of her own. How dare Jake call it nonsense. "So, in your opinion, gluing pages and leather covers together is more creative?" she said. "It's certainly not more lucrative."

"Most of the pages are hand stitched," Jake muttered, his face red at overstepping the mark. "It's a skilled trade."

"And so is writing books, no matter what kind they are. Why should a book on politics be more highly regarded than a novel that entertains millions of readers? Without writers you wouldn't even have any pages to assemble." Liv stuffed the cash back into her bag. She realized with a jolt that usually she wouldn't have said anything.

Jake's shoulders slumped and he held out a hand. "I'm sorry. I'm under a lot of pressure right now."

"You and me both," she said.

He took her into his arms and she reluctantly let him. "I *am* really proud of you," he said, kissing the top of her head. "The cake looks delicious and it's great Essie is recognizing your skills. It's been a long time coming. I knew you could do more than cleaning."

Liv wanted to tell him that cleaning was an art form, too, but she was tired, and it had been a while since she'd felt the warmth of his body against hers. She inhaled the smell of ink on the neck of his shirt and within seconds imagined she was Georgia Rory in the arms of her mysterious hero.

"Why don't you go and get changed?" Jake said gently, pulling away. "The pasta will be ready in ten minutes."

In the bedroom, Liv's cheeks were still fiery from his comments. She tugged off her clothes and pulled on fresh ones. She found her hairbrush in her bedside drawer and dragged it through her hair. As she placed it back inside, she saw the corner of a photo poking out. She picked it up and sank down onto her bed to study it.

Liv was around ten years old, standing between her parents and holding their hands. Her dad wore a black suit and striped tie, just as she always remembered him. He had a flock of wavy hair with the tips of his ears peeping through, and looked so formal compared to Jake. Carol was neat and tidy as always in a pencil skirt and tight sweater. Liv wore a cardigan with glass buttons, and a paisley tiered skirt. The three of them grinned for the camera.

They'd been such a happy family, the house full of laughter and books. Just how she, Jake, Mack and Johnny used to be.

Liv had been a carefree, if studious, girl back then. She loved the simple things in life, reading novels in bed, and eating crisps in the park, just like her dad.

Grant Cooper didn't care for the trimmings that came with university life, the end-of-term drinks that lasted all afternoon, the glitzy proms and the glamour of big-name authors who visited his lecture theater. His eyes shone brightest when he taught his students about character journeys, story goals and plot twists, and when Liv got great marks for her creative writing at school.

Liv's heart ached as she remembered the day Peggy had been waiting for her at school, sitting in the headmistress's office and wringing a handkerchief in her hands. As soon as Liv arrived, the headmistress closed the door quickly, her face drawn, and stood behind her desk.

"Your mum's at the hospital, lovey," Peggy said.

Liv stood with her arms glued to her sides. She could hear pupils chatting and laughing in the corridor. "Is she okay?"

Peggy didn't nod or shake her head either. "There's been an accident." She took hold of Liv's hand, something she'd never done before.

"Where's Dad?" Liv said, her voice weak and raspy.

Peggy swallowed and clasped her handbag. "Let's get you home and I'll make us a nice hot drink. I'll tell you everything then."

Liv felt queasy as she followed her aunt through the playground and out of the school gates. She felt like the ground was quaking beneath her feet. Something deep inside told her that her dad wasn't waiting for her in the house. And her instinct was right.

Peggy burst into tears as soon as the front door closed behind them. "Your dad was on his way to meet your mum. He was rushing past a building site when a wall collapsed. He pushed a stranger out of the way, to safety."

"But, where is he?"

Peggy's face crumpled. "Gone," she said, her voice filled with pain. "He took the brunt of the accident. I'm so sorry, love."

Liv fell to the floor, so shocked she couldn't even cry.

Here, in the bedroom, her tears welled at the photograph. She gently touched her dad's face. He was a real hero. Whenever she thought about him, her emotions were tainted with sadness, but she also felt his pride running through her veins.

"I'm finally writing," she whispered to the photo. "I wish you were here to see me, Dad."

Liv knew he'd be supportive of her new role. She could help her family out more financially, especially if Essie proved to be generous in her will. So why did Jake make her work for the author feel like a frivolity?

12

WHITE ROSES

The plumbing work proved to be more extensive than Liv and Jake imagined, wiping out her new salary for this month and the next, so she couldn't afford to buy new clothes yet. The house became like a scrapyard full of pipes, rolled-up carpets and loose floorboards. Liv embraced her escape to the peacefulness of Essie's apartment even more.

She attempted to rewrite Essie's first few chapters several times over, never quite pleased with the results. Her progress felt slow, as if there was a roadblock in her head stopping her words from flowing. Spraying Fracas and wearing the green Hermès scarf didn't help.

After spending yet another morning reworking just a couple of paragraphs, Liv stopped to study a red dint in her stomach. Her trouser button cut into her belly, and she entered Essie's bedroom to see if she could find something more comfortable to wear.

Liv's own wardrobe at home was a secondhand oak monstrosity with more clothes thrown in the bottom than hanging up. Essie's was an entire room, with rows of spotlights and an illuminated full-length mirror. There were sections for blouses, skirts, trousers, and a huge space for long and short dresses. Each pair of shoes had their own transparent box with a Polaroid photo taped to the front.

Liv recognized things Essie wore in the award room photographs. Her fingers lingered on the beautiful blue Constellation dress with birds on the shoulders. The author had looked so beautiful and composed at the ceremony.

She took the dress out and held it up to her chin, imagining wearing it, too. She could almost feel the heat of spotlights on her skin and hear the applause of the crowd. What story could the dress tell about the night of Essie's disappearance from the public eye? It was disappointing the YouTube footage hadn't revealed any clues.

Liv noticed something had fallen to the floor, a striped burgundy-and-mustard necktie. It looked old with a yellowing label on the back. The fabric was frayed as if handled or tied many times, and it smelled a little musty when she picked it up. She tied it around her neck anyway, wondering who it belonged to.

She browsed through Essie's clothes again, discovering a floral summer dress and a black blazer. She changed into them and laughed when she saw Georgia Rory looking back at her in the mirror. She'd have loved to own these clothes when she was twelve years old, and they were much comfier than her trousers.

When she returned to the laptop, Liv adjusted the knot in her tie and sat upright. Somehow, dressing like Georgia made her feel more attuned to the heroine. As she started to write again, her words tumbled out more easily. She intermittently stood up, acting out hunching against falling rocks and swimming for her life. Pulling her face, she mimicked surprise, anger and fear, observing her expressions in a hand mirror before adding them to the story.

By the time the afternoon arrived, Liv had managed to re-draft the first chapter. The main sticking point was the identity of Georgia's great love.

With a shot of renewed confidence, she decided to reach out to Anthony again. Almost seven weeks had passed since Essie died, so it felt appropriate to ask him how he really knew the author. He might even provide a touch of inspiration for Georgia's hero.

The ringtone sounded for a while before a voice mail message kicked in. "This is Anthony Pentecost of Pentecost and Wilde Solicitors. I am now out of the office for an extended period of time and may be unable to reply to your message. If your query is urgent, please contact my associate..."

Liv huffed and frowned at her phone. Why hadn't he told her he was going away? Was he on holiday, or working away? His message sounded a little ominous and she spoke after the beep. "Hi, it's Liv Green. Can we talk when you get back? I'd like to know how you met Essie," she said.

Her mood slipped a little at not reaching him, but she stroked her striped tie. *What would Georgia do now?* she thought.

Her eyes settled on the small green box, and she pushed the bee cuff links into her pocket. Liv saved her work, closed the laptop and exited the apartment.

Several years ago, she'd visited the Longley Jones jewelry shop to buy a birthday present for her mum. As she perused the store she felt the shop assistants' eyes following her around. Liv's mouth dried at the prices of necklaces in the display counters. She meandered around a little more to save face, before dipping her head and scurrying out of the shop.

Today, she strode inside and headed straight toward a man with greased back blond hair and an aquiline nose.

His eyes ran quickly over her blazer, dress and tie. "How may I help you?" he said, as if she was looking for directions to somewhere else.

Liv placed the cuff link box on the counter and flipped open the lid. "I wonder if you can tell me more about these?"

The man hitched an eyebrow. "Oh, how interesting. May I?" When Liv nodded, he found his eyeglass and peered more closely at the bees. "Are you looking to sell them?"

She shook her head. "I'd just like to know more about them. Are they new?"

He tilted them this way and that. "They look more like vintage pieces. May I take them to show my colleague? He's one of the store owners."

Liv nodded. She browsed the showroom while waiting for him to return. As she studied bracelets that cost the equivalent of her annual mortgage, she could never understand the appeal of wearing such expensive trinkets. What if you lost an earring while swimming, or a ring while out shopping? Her own wedding ring was a thin gold band with the tiniest diamond. She'd always loved wearing it, and the sentiment behind it was more important than the materials.

The man returned with the box. "They're certainly exquisite," he said. "My colleague says the cuff links are a one-off commission piece originating from the late eighties."

"How can he tell?"

The man smiled. "Because he made them."

"Oh." She smiled back.

"He keeps a record of everything he makes." The man passed her a slip of paper.

Receipt. Elsbeth Smart. £995

Liv nostrils flared. "That was a lot of money back then."

"I suppose it was. And they're worth three or four times that amount today."

Liv gulped. She wondered who Essie had commissioned

them for. She'd have only been in her early twenties when she bought them. It was a lot of money for a young woman to spend. Had she bought them for Anthony, or someone else? And why had she pushed them under her pillow before going into hospital?

"They're very special," the man said. "If you ever consider selling them, please do think of us first."

"I will do, thanks." Liv placed the box in her pocket, keeping her fingers wrapped around it. This time, she left the shop with her chin held high.

When she returned to the writing desk again, more new feelings raced inside her. Acting like Georgia had given her a thirst for adventure. It was the same feeling she got when she read books, except she was no longer pretending to be a heroine in a story. She was acting like one in real life.

Essie seemed to have left her the task to complete in true Georgia Rory fashion, with a mystery, an impossible task and a ticking clock. A random ghostwriter or editor couldn't deliver it like she could, and she replayed Anthony's words in her head, "Essie said only you could do this." And perhaps he was right. But what plot twists and turns lay ahead in the story?

Liv worked on redrafting yet another chapter. Her work was a little disjointed and she stumbled over words, but she kept pressing on, looking forward with her writing and not back.

She was checking over her work when a knock on the apartment door startled her. She'd never known Essie to receive a visitor before, and she wondered why the person hadn't used the intercom system to call first. Liv hunched her shoulders and stayed very still. She planned not to answer, but the pounding came again.

Liv padded along the hallway to look through the spyhole in the door. With her imagination still inhabiting a fictitious world, she imagined Georgia's lost love, or Essie's mystery man, standing on the other side of it. Instead, she saw the woman with the caramel hair and tight jeans, who'd nipped past her into the building a few weeks ago. She held a huge bouquet of white roses in her arms.

Liv frowned as she tentatively opened the door and peered through the gap. "Yes?"

The woman flashed Liv a toothy smile, as if they'd been friends since childhood. "Hi, hon. These flowers arrived for Essie Starling. The delivery guy asked me to bring them up," she said.

Liv relaxed a little. "It looks like someone's bought the entire shop." She opened the door farther and reached out to take the bouquet. But the woman kept a firm hold of it.

"Yeah, I'm thinking I should give them to her in person," she said.

Liv noticed a tag on the flowers and tried to glimpse who'd sent them, but it was turned over. The woman didn't look like a stalker, or the type to make blankets out of cat hair, but she still felt a prickle of unease. "I'm sorry, she's not here," she said.

"You sure about that, hon?" The woman raised herself on her toes and looked over Liv's head, in the direction of the writing room. "I can see her laptop's on. I'll just pop in and pass these to her. Only take a min." She stepped a pointed snakeskin shoe over the threshold.

Liv's heart rate shot up. She pressed a hand to the doorframe and blocked her entry. "Excuse me. Who are you?"

The women sucked in a breath before holding out a slim hand with tapered lilac nails. "Chloe Anderton, *Sheen* magazine."

Blood rushed to Liv's brain, making her light-headed. "You're a *journalist*?"

"Hey, don't say it like that. I'm one of the good guys. *Sheen* is a new mag. Imagine *Vanity Fair* meets *The Times*, with a focus on media. We have a great online presence, too. I'm a *huge* fan of Ms. Starling, and I'm writing a feature about—"

"I'm *very* sorry, she's not here," Liv interrupted. "The laptop is mine. Ms. Starling is working away at the moment. She's not contactable and she doesn't give interviews." She tried to close the door but the journalist's foot stopped her.

"I see." Chloe puckered her lips and stepped back. "It'll be a classy piece, published ahead of her twentieth masterpiece. My working title is, 'The Enigma of Being Essie.'"

Liv performed a slow blink of disbelief.

"Are you her PA?" Chloe said. "What's it like working for a bestselling recluse? I'll be discreet and *Sheen* will pay for your time."

Trying to emulate one of Essie's steely glares, Liv narrowed her eyes. "I'd prefer to pull out my own teeth."

Chloe's face set like concrete. "No worries, hon. I'll find out what I need from my other sources," she said with a sniff. "Ted Mason's already agreed to meet me." She said Essie's ex-husband's name as if it was a shiny coin on the pavement for Liv to pounce on.

Liv pretended to think for a while, biding her time. She fixed Chloe with a disarming smile. "Ted Mason? Wow. Well, I suppose if he's going to—" As the journalist hung on to her words, Liv shot out a hand and grabbed the roses, pulling them inside the apartment. "I'll make sure Essie gets them," she said. "There will be no interview."

She slammed the door shut and double locked it. Her heart pounded wildly as she returned to the writing room. The roses left a trail of white petals along the hallway.

The bouquet was from Bloom and Dale florists, but the sender's name was missing. Liv wondered if Chloe had bought them herself and engineered the delivery. Or had she hijacked a gift from Essie's man?

"Hey." Chloe rapped on the door. "I'm only asking what everyone wants to know. What happened to Essie Starling? And why are you dressed like Georgia Rory?"

Liv heard the journalist moving around outside for a while. She considered phoning the building concierge to complain about an intruder, but then saw the gray shadow beneath the door disappear. After a few minutes, Liv slowly opened it. She circled the landing area before blowing all the air from her lungs.

The thought of Chloe digging around for information about Essie made Liv grind her teeth. What if Chloe discovered the author was not only missing, but dead? She shuddered when she remembered allowing Chloe to dart into the building. How had the journalist known Essie's address? Had she been loitering outside the apartment block to try to get a story? And if she was tracking down people from Essie's past, how much longer would it be before she uncovered the truth of Essie's death? What might Chloe discover if she took the meeting with Ted?

Liv adjusted her necktie. Georgia Rory wouldn't stand for such a thing, and neither would she.

Chloe mentioned having a meeting scheduled with Ted Mason, a name Liv had read in many author acknowledgments. He'd accompanied Essie at the start of her journey, and also down the aisle. This could be Liv's chance to speak with him and learn more about Essie's past and what made her withdraw from society, clues that might help Liv with reshaping her novel and writing the missing chapters.

Liv had to get to him before Chloe did. But how?

First, she phoned Bloom and Dale to see who'd ordered the bouquet of white roses. The young woman who answered was new in her role. She spoke to the shop owner before returning the call. "Sorry, it's confidential information. We value our customers' privacy."

Liv ran her tongue over her front teeth at reaching a dead end. After hanging up, she googled the phone number for Lioncorp and dialed it. She managed to reach a chatty young intern called Rex.

Liv explained that Chloe Anderton had a meeting lined up with Ted Mason, and that she'd been given the task of rearranging it. "Sorry, I don't know the date and time. I'm an intern, too."

"No worries, I get it," Rex said. "Bottom of the pile and no one tells us a thing."

Liv laughed nervously.

"Right, well the meeting is for next Tuesday, something about discussing key players in the publishing industry. Is that the one?"

"Oh, yes." Liv toyed with a pen, thinking that next week seemed too far away.

"Okay, that one's now canceled. Hmm, Mr. Mason doesn't have much availability in his diary. He's got a cancelation, tomorrow at 4 p.m. Is that too short notice?"

"I'll take it," Liv said, smacking the desk. "I mean, I'm sure that will work for Chloe."

"Okay. I've made that change. Does she still require picking up?"

Liv's rib cage tightened. She no idea what logistical arrangements Chloe had made, or what discussion she might have already had with Ted. All she could do was channel Georgia again and brazen things out.

"Yes, please," she said, and gave him Essie's address.

13

THE DUCK POND

The next day, Liv tried on several things from Essie's wardrobe for her meeting with Ted, finally settling on a powder blue silk blouse and gray pencil skirt. If she was supposedly a journalist from a glossy magazine, she had to look the part.

Essie took shoes a size larger than hers, and Liv's feet slid around in a pair of black stilettoes. On the top shelf she found a new navy Coach handbag that was smaller than her supermarket branded one, so she couldn't fit all her things inside it.

The cracked eyeshadow palettes and dried out pencils she'd brought along didn't compare to the treasure trove of new cosmetics Essie had set in lines in the drawer of her dressing table. The packaging felt shiny and luxurious.

Liv applied a touch of shimmery beige to her eyelids and a slick of coral lipstick. When she saw her reflection, she took a sharp intake of breath. Somewhere, buried deep inside, had lived this prettier, more polished version of herself. It was strange to finally meet her in person. But she didn't feel as comfortable as when she dressed as Georgia. Before she left the apartment, she pushed the striped tie into her bag.

As she paced up and down the pavement outside waiting

for Ted, Liv tried not to bite her nails. Was she doing the right thing, meeting the man who married Essie and helped her to become a megastar? Would Ted see through Liv's makeup and expensive clothes to the cleaner hiding beneath them?

She had to hold her nerve. If she wanted to find out more about Essie, while stopping Chloe from digging around, she *had* to do this.

The vintage Rolls-Royce Phantom that glided up outside the building was the color of chianti and shiny as a mirror. The silver lady mascot on the bonnet flung back her arms as wind rippled her dress. Every centimeter of the car exclaimed, *Look at me, I've made it!* It was the opposite to the battered family Fiesta that Jake and Liv affectionately called "the rust bucket."

A peak-capped, besuited driver got out, nodded courteously toward Liv and opened the back door for her.

She always cringed when people did things for her that she could do herself, like pulling out a chair at a restaurant, or draping a napkin across her lap. She always overtipped waiting staff to overcompensate for her awkwardness at being served by others.

Ted Mason sat on the back seat with the perfect posture that came from being supremely confident, overly wealthy, or both. Looking much older than in Essie's photographs, his white hair was combed back, displaying a speckle of age spots on his forehead. His burgundy cashmere scarf matched the car and featured an embroidered gold lion. "Ted Andrew Mason," he said, holding out a knobbly hand.

She gave it a small shake. "Liv Louise Green," she said, cursing herself for matching his full name. Her nerves were making her feel nauseous. "I'm afraid Chloe Anderton can't make the meeting today."

Ted's irises were so pale they looked almost supernatural.

She felt them boring into her. "We rearranged this meeting to suit *her*," he said sharply.

"I'm sorry, it couldn't be helped," she blurted. "I'm sure we'll get along if we try."

He twitched the smallest smile as if amused. "I thought we could take a drive," he said. "I'm squeezing you in between meetings."

"Of course," she said, as if it was something she did all the time.

As the car glided along, Liv couldn't feel any bumps on the road. The car made a soothing shushing sound, and the cream leather seats were so soft she wanted to stroke them. When she side-glanced at Ted, she couldn't imagine him and Essie ever eating breakfast together or reading or kissing. He seemed a very manicured choice for the author.

"So, you're writing an article about the publishing industry?" he prompted.

"Um, yes." She stumbled a little. "I understand no one knows it like you do." She thought her flattery might please him, but he gazed out of the window as if bored.

Ted tapped the gold sovereign ring on his middle finger against the glass. "Have you seen all the bloody buildings going up around here?" he said wearily. "The entire city is a construction site. There are too many new apartments, too many cars on the roads and even too many books these days. Or do I sound like an old man?"

"Is there such a thing as too many books?" Liv said.

"Possibly so. Did you know 180,000 books are published in the UK alone each year? How can debut authors hope to have their work seen?"

Liv nodded. "The average person reads a book a month," she said. "I'm more of a one-a-week person. It's a bit of an addiction."

He twitched an eyebrow. "And your favorite writer?"

She couldn't lie. "Essie Starling."

"Ah," he said, his face not giving anything away. "I see."

As they continued their drive around the outskirts of the city, Ted began to open up, telling Liv about his worries for the closure of libraries and bookstores, and the rise of reading on smartphones and iPads. He was an interesting man, speaking for fifteen minutes before he halted and stared at her. "Don't you want to write any of this down?" he said.

Liv was so in awe of him she'd forgotten she was supposed to be conducting an interview. Her heart tripped, and she fumbled in her bag. Her fingers ran over a lipstick and a packet of chewing gum before she realized she'd left her pad and pen in her other bag. She only calmed a little when she felt the striped tie. "Please carry on," she said firmly. "I have a very good memory."

He studied her for too long, his eyes glinting. The tendons in his neck stretched like latex. "You're not actually a journalist, are you?" he snapped. "I've met enough of them in my time to realize that."

Liv's throat tightened. She felt like she'd tripped at the top of a steep hill and was trying to keep her footing. "I...um..."

"Please don't insult me by lying. Or shall I stop the car right here?"

Liv glanced out of the window and had no idea where she was. There was wasteland on one side and a brewery on the other. She began to gabble against her own will, unable to keep her words inside. "I'm not from *Sheen* magazine and wanted to reach you before Chloe Anderton did, so I hijacked her meeting," she said. "I'm Liv Green and I work as a cleaner and assistant for Essie. I'm not writing an article but wanted to speak to you about her." She gripped her seat, expecting the car to screech to a halt, and for her body to launch forward.

Ted's top lip curved to display creamy fangs. Liv thought he was going to call for his driver to stop.

Instead he threw back his head and laughed. "That is the

craziest story I've heard in a long time. You should write a book. Essie's cleaner, rearranging a meeting I had set up with a journalist, because she wants to talk to me about my ex-wife? You've certainly got some chutzpah. I wondered why you asked to be picked up from Essie's apartment building." He focused his gaze on her. "What do you want from me?"

"A couple of things," she said, trying to keep her voice steady. "Chloe from *Sheen* is writing an article about Essie. She's digging around and I'm trying to protect Essie's best interests. She won't want her private life laid bare to the world."

Ted nodded. "Hmm, you're right. Essie will hate that. I can certainly put out a message to the Lioncorp team, asking them not to collaborate on anything. And the other thing?"

Liv gulped. This was it. The moment Ted flung open the car door while they were still moving, and she rolled out into the middle of the road and oncoming traffic. Why couldn't she have come up with a different plan? "Essie is brilliant. I love her books and I've worked for her for three years, and yet I feel like I don't know her at all. What drives her? Why should she shut herself away?" she said. "I'd love to know how you and she met."

Ted's jaw hinged. "That's another thing she won't like," he said. Surprisingly, his eyes sparkled impishly. "After your bizarre little story, I suppose I should tell you mine."

His thoughts drifted away, taking him to a different place and time. "I was at a party, some stuffy affair in the grounds of a country house." He circled a finger. "Women in ball gowns, men in tuxedos, all talking about who's hot and who's not in the publishing world. And do you know where I first saw Essie?" He raised a bemused eyebrow.

Liv shook her head.

"She was sitting at the edge of a duck pond with her feet dangling in the water. Her dress was scrunched up around her thighs. One of my colleagues was most perturbed about the tone she was setting and asked me to speak to her. I carried my glass over and asked what she was doing. She looked up at me with those gray eyes of hers and said, 'My feet are hot and the water's cool.'" Ted laughed.

That's so very Essie, Liv thought.

"I wasn't impressed by her attitude and I went to find a towel. When I returned to pass it to her, she reached out and pulled on my shoelace, untying the bow. I was furious and about to give her a piece of my mind, but she lifted my foot and took off my shoe. I was so astonished, I just let it happen.

"She was much younger than me, twenty years and more. I had three daughters at university, and my wife and I were on the verge of divorce." He smiled and shook his head, as if reliving the surprising experience. "There are few moments in life when the earth seems to stop spinning, and you have a split second to decide to walk away or take a leap into the unknown. I'm usually a man of strategy and routine. I polish my shoes each night and have dedicated suits for each day of the week. Yet there was something about Essie that made me take off my other shoe, too. I tossed my socks onto the lawn, hitched up my trouser legs and sat down beside her. We sipped champagne from the same glass and Essie told me I should publish her next book."

Liv smiled to herself at this bold, playful version of Essie. Where had it disappeared to?

She couldn't help feeling envious, too. When she was a similar age, she had been busy washing baby sick out of her hair. Mack had a habit of projectile vomiting if he drank too much milk. If she ever received an invitation to a party, it was at a soft play center with lukewarm sandwiches made with ham so thin you could see through it.

"Didn't she already have a publisher?" she said.

"Yes, but the success of *The Moon on the Water* was far greater than originally expected. Essie was like a piece of sea glass on the beach among all the gray pebbles. She just needed a little polish to shine like a jewel. Soon after the party, and to my great surprise and delight, we became a couple. I advised her on how to fit into the literary world better, and introduced her to people who could help her career."

"And you also decided to get married?"

He broke into a surprised cough. "Yes, that, too. One night we went to dinner and Essie claimed I was impolite to a waiter. She never could stand people who looked down on others. She was right, of course, and I apologized...and somehow I found myself proposing." He stared out of the window and thought for a long time. "I think I knew, even then, that she didn't love me. Not in the way I loved her. She admired the writers I published, my age and experience, living with me in London. But it wasn't enough. There was always a part of her locked away that I couldn't reach. I wondered if there was someone else." His eyes glinted with sadness. "We drifted apart and divorced on our sixth anniversary. Essie claimed I stifled her. We had differing ideas about the direction of her career."

"About Georgia Rory?"

"Ah, yes, Ms. Rory," he said with a sniff. "Essie was more than capable of pushing her boundaries as a writer but refused to expand her horizons. She said readers saw themselves in Georgia, and she did, too. I admit it was something I kept pressing her to reconsider. One day I arrived home and she'd gone." He pursed his lips and looked out of the window again before continuing. "She always had a strange habit of vanishing, and this time it was for good."

She did it even back then? Liv thought. *Where did she go to?*

"When Essie makes up her mind to pursue something there's no going back," Ted said. "I hoped we could keep our professional relationship going, but then she signed up with an agent and Peregrine. At the time, I thought she was extremely ungrateful. Our relationship was difficult for a long time afterward. She didn't appreciate that without me there would be no Essie Starling."

The car hit a bump in the road and Liv's teeth clanked together.

Up until his last sentence, she had been warming to Ted. He was a little pompous and stilted, but taking the credit for Essie's work wasn't fair. Liv couldn't keep her feelings to herself, no matter who he was. "Essie got her first publishing deal without you," she said fiercely. "Her talent shone through. You said it yourself. You tried to stop her writing what she loved."

Ted looked rather shocked. He resettled himself in his seat, took off his scarf and folded it. "I suppose you're right," he said eventually. "Essie has always been her own woman, and that's why I adored her. If she wants something she goes for it and no one can stop her. It's been ten years since we last spoke and I miss her greatly. I often wonder how she is."

Liv hadn't imagined the great Ted Mason could appear so vulnerable. When the news about Essie's death eventually reached him, she could tell it would hit him hard. She pursed her lips at having to keep it from him.

"I'll never meet anyone again with her spirit and impetuousness, not in my lifetime. If Essie's part of your life, make sure you cherish and learn from her, not try to shape her, like I did," he said. When he jerked his head away, he suddenly looked incredibly old.

"I have a couple more questions..." Liv said cautiously. "Did Essie ever buy you cuff links, shaped like bees?"

"No," he said with weariness in his voice. "Next?"

Liv spoke hurriedly, sensing she was about to be ejected from the car. "Do you know what happened to Essie at the Constellation Prize after-party? I saw footage of you at the ceremony."

Ted sniffed. "I was delighted she won. It was well deserved.

I stood in line to shake her hand. We were pleasant to each other, and I left."

"And that's all?" Liv felt a slide of disappointment. She'd hoped he could tell her something more revelatory.

"I'm afraid so. Now, please give your address to my driver and we'll take you home."

Liv stared ahead. She told the driver where she lived and set her jaw. If she wanted to know more about Essie's past it looked like she'd have to speak to others, too. Perhaps she could somehow track down Hank to see what he knew, or even the bearded blond man with the rose tattooed hand. She hoped Chloe wasn't on their trails, too.

When the Rolls-Royce stopped outside her house, Liv saw a curtain twitching and a glimpse of Jake behind it.

"I'm sorry again for stealing your meeting," Liv said, as she unfastened her seat belt.

Ted smiled tightly. "It's exactly the kind of thing Essie would have done," he said. "Don't let anyone stifle your spirit, Liv. It's a rare thing."

There was something in his words that made Liv think of her dad. If he were still alive, he'd be a similar age to Ted. Perhaps she *had* squashed her spirit into a little box when he died. Now it was emerging the longer she worked on Essie's manuscript and connected with Georgia. She held back the sting of tears as she reached out and slipped her hand into his. "Thank you."

Ted looked taken aback before giving it a squeeze. "You're more than welcome. Please pass on my well-wishes to Essie."

Liv opened the car door before looking back over her shoulder. "One last question," she said.

He let out a mock sigh. "Shoot," he said.

"Do you ever send white roses to Essie?"

He shook his head. "I suspect she'd throw them away."

"Do you know anyone else who might send them?"

"Most people might send nettles instead." He raised an eyebrow. "Anything else?"

Liv paused for a moment. She was here with Ted and might never have this opportunity again. "Just that... I've always wanted to be a writer, too," she said, wondering if it sounded pathetic. After keeping her dream locked inside her for so long it felt freeing to release it.

He took time to consider her words. "In that case, you may find an old article Essie wrote to be of interest. I'll ask my assistant to send it to you. Please get in touch with your email address."

Liv nodded. "Thanks for everything."

When she stepped out of the car, Liv felt somehow taller and wiser for spending an hour with him. She also felt she knew Essie a little better, though she still remained an enigma.

As soon as she stepped foot in the hallway, Jake appeared. "What were you doing in that posh car?" he said.

"Essie's ex-publisher offered me a lift home," Liv said, avoiding using the words *ex-husband* in case it raised more questions.

He squinted at her. "Are you wearing a new blouse?" he said. "It looks expensive."

"Yes." Liv touched the fabric and smiled, expecting he might compliment her outfit and makeup.

Instead he folded his arms and raised a wry eyebrow. "You're mixing in high circles recently," he said. "You'll be too grand to be seen with me soon."

Liv forced a smile. "Never." She touched his arm.

However, as she went upstairs to change her clothes, she wondered if her husband actually meant what he said. And if her reply was strictly true.

Ted Mason was true to his word. The following day, an article from *Writer's World* magazine landed in Liv's inbox.

HOW I WRITE

by Essie Starling
Writer's World Magazine

I place myself in my characters' heads and think of their goals and motivations for the scene, so I can draft out the action. It's like putting skeleton bones and vital organs in place. I can then flesh out the dialogue and sentences, forming the muscles and veins. Other than that, I don't plot. I let the story take me on a journey.

My first draft will be a Frankenstein's monster of a thing. My story might have the equivalent of a head and torso, and also three legs and one arm. I keep operating to bring the book to life. The finer details, the equivalent of the eyelashes, fingernails and birthmarks take much longer to appear. I delve deep into my own experiences to breathe life into my characters. They allow me to say sorry when I can't do it, and to be brave when I'm not. I know what it's like to nurse a broken heart and live with regrets.

Many writers produce a terrible first draft where anything goes. It's getting words down on a page that counts. You can't edit something that doesn't exist.

Do I have any advice for budding authors? No book is going to write itself. No one will wave a magic wand to grant you more talent or time. It all boils down to having a good idea, some writing ability, a strong work ethic and determination. The first step is often the scariest. Find writers you enjoy, read their work and learn from them. Write a sentence, write another one and keep going. Perseverance is key. If I can do it, perhaps you can, too.

14

PINK ENVELOPE

Liv read the article over and over. She passed on her thanks to Ted, via Rex the intern, for sending it to her. Over the next few days, whenever she felt a dip in confidence with Essie's manuscript, she reached out for the piece again and hung on to the author's words. "Perseverance is key. If I can do it, perhaps you can, too," she repeated to herself.

She tackled her own writing in the same way she did her cleaning, making sure she had all her tools to hand. Instead of bottles, lemon, salt and cloths, she had paper, pens, the laptop and a vintage teacup. She wore the black blazer, floral dress and old striped tie. The peacefulness of Essie's apartment, and even her bittersweet tussle with Book Twenty, gave her an escape from the noise at home, especially now that Mack had returned home for the summer from university.

Liv worked methodically and patiently, polishing Essie's words and adding her own. Sometimes they poured out of her, and at other times they choked and spluttered, kicking their heels and refusing to hang out together. Her worries about Chloe still hung around like an overly keen childhood boyfriend.

She found herself living for the kissing-on-a-beach and rolling-in-the-hay scenes. Liv imagined she was the one scrambling her way out of raging rivers and clinging to crumbling rock faces. Creating her own paragraphs gave her a heady rush.

To tackle the emotional scenes, Liv forced herself to revisit the wrench of losing her dad, until tears streamed down her face and she could hardly see the laptop screen. And she grabbed hold of these feelings and gave them to Georgia so she could experience them, too.

However, Georgia's true love still remained out of reach. Liv kept studying the list of existing heroes she'd noted down. She made comments to herself in the margins of the manuscript, just as Essie did. Their thoughts aligned often.

What happened in Georgia's past that makes her who she is today?
Which lover defines her?
Who is worthy of her love?

Liv chewed her pen and still didn't know. She crossed heroes off her list that reminded her of Ted Mason.

After rewriting a scene where Georgia finds her old family home burned to the ground, Liv felt as emotionally drained as the heroine herself. She took a break to make a cup of tea.

When she saw a pink envelope lying on the hallway carpet, she felt a coolness rush over her body. Essie's mail was usually left in the lobby mailbox for her to collect.

Her name was written on the front of the envelope in neat capital letters, and she opened it up.

Hi Liv
So, I find my meeting with Ted Mason was canceled and no one will answer my queries at Lioncorp. Anything to do with you or Essie? I felt like an idiot waiting for him to show up. You're just making Essie's story even more intriguing.
I'm only doing my job. (Looks like we're both strong women

working for strong women.) In fact, my editor now wants me to write a longer piece, and has given me more time. I've always wanted to switch up from the gossip columns, so you've done me a huge favor, hon.

I admire Essie and what she's achieved. Nineteen books and an amazing penthouse? Wow! I bet her readers are crying out to know more about her. Is it so bad to give it to them? If I don't write her story, someone else will. So why not make things easier for us both? I think you're the woman with all the answers.

Let's do coffee sometime.

Chloe x

Liv screwed the letter into a ball. She scratched her neck and wondered how Chloe had got into the building again. And how did she know Liv's name? She felt like she was being watched.

She had a gut feeling the journalist might try to contact Hank Milligan next, and she carried out her own research online.

She discovered Hank had recently opened several crime-themed bars in the US. He hoped to bring Hank's Bar to the UK soon. A photo showed him holding a bottle of beer against a lined wall, as if part of a criminal lineup. He still lived in Los Angeles and had never spoken publicly about his divorce from Essie, so he'd be unlikely to grant an interview to Chloe. Liv breathed a small sigh of relief.

When she recalled all the photos of Hank and Essie draped over each other, in front of their luxury houses and cars, they looked so in love. What had gone so wrong for them? She hoped Chloe wasn't in the process of finding out.

Liv looked up Hank's PR company. She sent an email asking if they could put her in touch with him. She didn't really expect them to do it, or for him to reply, but there was little else she could do.

When she left the apartment that evening, Liv triple-checked she locked the front door properly. As she broke into a jog away from the building, a shiver ran down her spine.

Each time Liv wrote, she couldn't help thinking about Chloe nosing around. So, she jumped out of her skin when the desk phone rang. "Hello, Marlon," she said, with her pulse racing.

"How do you know it's me?" he boomed.

She rolled her eyes. "Because everyone else knows never to call Essie."

"Ha, yes, got me there. Look, Meg's been on my case again, asking when those golden pages are going to land. So, go on, hit me with it, Liv. Give me an update and please don't say the first of November."

Liv glanced at her work on-screen and the amount of notes she'd written to herself that morning. She noticed the date on the computer was July 1, exactly two months after Essie died. "She's got her head down and is working hard," she said. "If you're lucky, you may get it on Halloween."

"Ha, very funny," Marlon said. "Remember our partnership, Liv. You keep cajoling Essie, and I'll try to keep Meg out of her hair. When you get a chance, ask her about Dubfest. It's in one month's time and Meg's desperate for her to go. We don't need to be psychic to predict her answer."

Liv quickly googled Dubfest. It was the Dubrovnik Book Festival, three days of literary events on the Croatian coast, taking place August 1–3. Photos on the festival website showed hundreds of publisher display stands and bookshelves. Goose bumps rose on her forearms when she saw all the rows of books and authors she'd heard of. It looked like her idea of heaven.

"Tell Essie if she goes, you can accompany her," Marlon said.

Liv took a sharp intake of breath. She pressed a hand to her chest. "Me? Why?"

"You're her assistant, aren't you?"

"Well, yes."

"Meg's willing to pay, and Essie can fly business class. Work your magic on her, Liv. Tell her we'll keep things nice and low-key. It's a business event rather than a public appearance. We don't want hordes of fans showing up and scaring her off."

Liv wondered if he could hear her heart pounding. "What will she do there?" she said.

"Meet and greets, going to dinner with publishers. All the things she hates."

"You make it sound so tempting."

"It's actually an amazing experience. I believe she used to go every couple of years. And then she stopped."

Liv touched her tie. "Stopped? Why?"

Marlon made a rumbling sound. "I only know what Meg told me. I didn't represent Essie back then."

"How did you and Essie actually meet?" she said. The author and her agent weren't an obvious fit.

"She read an article I wrote for a magazine, about my career. She gave me a call, one of the few times she actually talked to me." He laughed.

As Marlon started to talk about deadlines again, Liv searched for his article online and read it.

Years ago, I was down on my luck, relying on bottles of vodka to get me through the day. A close friend had died and drink helped with my pain. One day, I woke up under a bush and found a copy of The Alchemist *by Paulo Coelho left on a park bench. It felt like a message and after reading it I knew I had to change and follow my dreams. I took night classes and begged anyone in the literary world for experience, often working for free. I eventually opened my agency.*

Liv found a lump in her throat. She realized she hadn't caught the last thing Marlon said to her and she cleared her throat to speak. "You should know a journalist has been in touch with me. Her name's Chloe," she said. "She's writing a piece about Essie."

"Humph," Marlon replied.

"You don't sound too concerned."

"Nope. Essie won't collaborate. Meg only managed to get her to do one interview in ten years. Others have tried writing about Essie's life, and the last decade will sound extremely dull. Unless this Chloe person finds a new angle..."

Like the fact Essie died two months ago, Liv thought to herself.

She said a quick goodbye to Marlon and hung up. When she looked at the Dubfest website again she felt the strongest pull toward the festival. But how could she possibly accompany a dead author to Croatia?

She browsed the conferences, seminars and awards with a seed of excitement growing in her stomach. It reminded her of when she was little and her dad used to usher her into his lecture theater. She sat at the back of the class ignoring the inquisitive glances from his students, and attempted the exercises he set on crafting character journeys, motivation and flaws. He marked her work, too. *A+ Excellent attempt.*

Liv clicked on the webpage labeled "History" and read the festival had been running since 1980. It broke for the Croatian War of Independence in the nineties, before resuming again in 2000. There were lots of photos from over the years, and Liv spotted a face she recognized.

A much younger version of Essie walked along an aisle, alongside a tall handsome man. He was speaking into her ear, his face pressed close to hers. Essie laughed and smiled up at him. It looked like they were holding hands.

When Liv saw a patch of light in his hair she thought it

was a flash from a camera. But then she frowned. Surely it couldn't be... Anthony?

The solicitor's hair was shorter and unrulier. It had the distinctive daub of white on the side.

Liv traced her fingers down her neck. Anthony had given her the impression he'd only worked for Essie for a few years. In the image, they looked more than just good friends.

Had she just found the real love of Essie's life, and he'd been hiding in plain sight all along? Why would Essie drink too much and tell Matilda she couldn't write without him, when Anthony was there on her doorstep? Maybe because he was now married to Harriet?

There seemed to be more to Anthony than met the eye.

It had been a couple of weeks since she left a message on Anthony's voice mail, and she gave him a call. This time he picked up.

"Liv," he said, his voice barely a whisper. "How are you?"

"I'm fine. Have you been on holiday?"

"I'm in Bologna with Harriet."

"That sounds lush."

"Ah, not really. Her father had a heart attack and we traveled out to look after him. He's just sleeping. Hold on, I'll move to a different room."

Liv felt guilty for calling. "Oh, gosh. I'm so sorry... Is he okay?"

"Things have been precarious but are looking a little brighter. I've arranged to work out here remotely until he improves some more. My colleagues will be looking after some of my other clients." He let out a small sigh. "How are you? Is everything going okay?"

"It doesn't really matter..."

"It's fine, go ahead. It's nice to talk to someone other than doctors."

It didn't feel right to ask him about Dubfest up front. "Well, I've been working hard on Essie's novel. Things are going okay, but I'm stuck on Georgia's hero." As Liv said it, she wondered how on earth the solicitor could help with her writing, but he responded kindly.

"I took note of something Essie told me once," he said. "If you meet something insurmountable, don't try and fight it. It will only leave you with bruises. The trick is to outsmart it and do something it wouldn't expect."

Liv jotted it down. It was as if Anthony hung on to Essie's words. She had no idea how to relate them to Book Twenty.

"They've proved helpful throughout my career," Anthony added.

"It sounds like you've known her for a long time," she said.

He didn't speak for a while. "Ah, yes, I got your question on my voice mail asking how we met. Essie and I *were* friends once, a long time ago. We kept in touch sporadically over the years, and I eventually became her solicitor."

Liv looked at the Dubfest photo again. Was she really looking at two close friends, or lovers? "Did you ever go to Croatia with Essie?" she said.

Anthony's breathing grew shallower. "Not that I can recall," he said a little curtly.

She opened her mouth to push back, but then thought about his poorly father-in-law. It didn't seem the right time to quiz him further. "Oh, okay. No worries," she said reluctantly.

"Anything else?"

Liv swallowed. She wanted to ask him about the bee-shaped cuff links, too, but didn't want to needle him. She approached her next words softly. "Yes, a journalist called Chloe Anderton came to Essie's apartment, asking questions," she said. "She's writing a magazine article. I know it's not the best time to tell you, but I thought you'd want to know."

"Did you talk to her?" Anthony said.

"Not about Essie. But she got in touch with Ted Mason and seems determined."

"Nothing must come out about Essie's death," Anthony said, sounding like a headmaster. "Not before November 1. She was very firm about that date."

"I know. Chloe won't hear anything from me."

"Good. You have Essie's will to think of. Actually, she... ah, inserted a proviso."

Liv frowned at the word. She knew what it meant but had no use for it before. "For me?" she said.

"Yes. Everything must be kept private, or you won't receive your inheritance."

A knot in Liv's belly pulled tight. Any money Essie left her could help out her family, and maybe even turn her fortunes around. "I'm committed to this," she said. "Why would Ess—"

"Sorry, I've got to go," Anthony said quickly. "Harriet is calling me."

The phone went dead and Liv pressed it to her lips. She hadn't meant to irritate him. It wasn't her fault Chloe was being a nuisance. Perhaps she shouldn't have mentioned Dubfest when Anthony was under a lot of stress.

She sent him a quick text to try to clear the air. **I have everything under control. Nothing to worry about. I hope your father-in-law is okay.**

He didn't reply.

And, after a few more days without a response, Liv couldn't help thinking Anthony was keeping something from her, and she wondered what it was.

15

FILM NIGHT

Liv started to work on Saturdays while Jake and the boys played football. She stayed later into the afternoon, relishing her time at the apartment rather than the park. As she wrote, she looked down at all the people milling around the market stalls in the streets below. Many of them were likely to be Georgia Rory fans.

She imagined dropped jaws, hands pressed to mouths and sobbing when the news emerged that Essie Starling had died. She knew she'd also relive it again, and she channeled her heightened feelings into her work. Her desire to craft the perfect ending to Georgia's book, and ultimately the series, pushed her on through the next couple of weeks. Time was ticking away.

One Saturday, she arrived home and felt stripped of energy. She had never thought writing could be so physically and mentally draining. She'd acted out more scenes, cried, laughed, and developed a stiff neck and even sore knees from sitting at the desk. She longed to flop on the sofa and zone out in front of the TV. Each Saturday night, the Green family got together to watch a film and she wondered whose turn it was to choose.

Liv liked comedies the most. Jake was a thriller kind of guy and Johnny enjoyed action movies. Mack had developed a worrying taste for killer clowns that no one else shared. Now he was home from university for the summer, Liv worried they'd all have to sit through blood, gore and greasepaint.

As she took off her shoes and shrugged off her blazer in the hallway, she froze and wondered if she'd entered the wrong house. This one had no music blaring, or shouting going on. "Um, hello?" she called out and stuck her head around the living room door.

Jake sat on the sofa alone. The TV was on low volume and all the cushions were placed neatly on the sofa, instead of lying on the floor where the boys usually left them. "Had a good day?" he said.

She arched an eyebrow at how tidy the room looked. "Is everything okay?" she said.

"Yep, all's fine. You shouldn't be working at the weekend, though." He patted the seat next to him. "Fancy a sit down? The boys have gone out."

"Both of them?"

Jake grinned. "I may have bribed them with pizza vouchers. They were free in a newspaper."

It was then Liv noticed the scented candle flickering on the coffee table, even though it was bright outside. Rather than his weekend jeans and T-shirt, Jake wore trousers and a smart blue sweater, his date night attire. Usually she'd feel a gush of tenderness toward him, but she was so tired her bones felt like they'd been replaced with mashed potato.

"I thought we could watch a film together," he said. "Just you and me."

Upstairs, Liv took off her floral dress and tie, and put on her black dress and pink socks instead.

When she slumped next to Jake on the sofa, he took hold of her hand and stroked it, as if it was a pet gerbil.

"I thought we could watch something, um…" He gave her a coy shrug. "Romantic."

Something inside Liv slid like an avalanche. All she wanted to do was stare at the TV screen. "Sure," she said blankly.

"We've both been working so hard. We could do with relaxing and forgetting everything else for a while."

It was something she'd been imploring him to do over the years, and which he'd ignored. There were many things they could be doing instead right now, talking about the mounting bills on their worktop, Johnny's forthcoming student accommodation and the Paperpress finances. But he was right, they both needed this little oasis of time together.

Jake reached an arm around her shoulder. The brush of his biceps against her neck made her stomach ripple unexpectedly. A trickle of heat slowly radiated throughout her body, overtaking the tiredness. She had grown used to summoning up the feeling at will when she wrote about Georgia, but hadn't experienced it with Jake for quite some time.

Her muscle memory kicked in, and she remembered the sensation of how her bare skin felt next to his. When Jake leaned over to kiss her, his lips were soft and tasted of cinnamon. Liv found herself sinking into him, becoming a little giddier as she imagined their evening together.

"Shall we watch *Titanic*?" he said, which made her feel even more attracted to him.

She curled her legs on top of his. When the movie started they cuddled even closer, and Jake ran his thumb along her thigh and back again. They kept glancing shyly at each other, sharing smiles and small kisses.

As Kate Winslet stood at the bow of the ship with outstretched arms and the wind in her hair, Jake's phone buzzed on the coffee table. Katrina's name lit up the screen.

Liv thought about kicking it out of sight. "Don't answer it," she whispered as Leonardo DiCaprio sang into Kate's ear, and they entwined fingers. "Call her back later."

Jake stared at the TV. His phone stopped vibrating and he held his palm to his chest.

Liv was proud of his resistance. She took hold of his other hand and kissed his fingertips, one by one. "Perhaps it's time for an interval," she said seductively.

Jake grinned. "I don't think we have any ice cream."

"We don't need it." Liv climbed onto his lap. She brushed a hand over the face she'd loved for over twenty years and their eyes met greedily. She pressed her mouth against his and pushed a hand under his sweater. She imagined she was Georgia.

Behind her, Jake's phone buzzed again. He pulled away from Liv to look over her shoulder.

"Just leave it," she whispered, her words more threatening than sexy.

He bit his lip, running a hand through her hair and kissing the tip of her nose. "I can't. It might be important," he said, pausing the film.

"*Jake.*"

He leaned forward and shot out a hand for his phone. Liv toppled sideways and banged her head on a small table next to the sofa with a yelp. Tears stung her eyes and she rubbed the plum-sized bump rising on her temple.

He patted her shoulder. "Oops, sorry. You carry on watching." He stood up and answered the call, clicking the play button on the remote control. "Hey, Katrina. No, it's fine. We were only watching an old film."

As he padded off toward the coat cupboard, Liv glared at

him. She cracked her knuckles as his muffled voice sounded over the film for fifteen minutes.

When Jake returned, he plonked himself down next to her. "Give me a recap." He nodded at the TV. "What just happened?"

Liv felt the pressure of the last two and a half months rise inside her like mercury in a greenhouse thermometer. How could he interrupt their first romantic moment in ages to take a call from his sister? During the most iconic moment of the film, too. "Bloody hell," was all she could manage to say.

Jake's eyes widened. "What?"

"We were watching it together. We were...you know."

"It was only a little break."

"Well, what couldn't wait?" Liv demanded. "What was *so* important you had to interrupt *things*?"

"Just business," he said. "Tricky to understand..."

She shot him a death stare.

"Tricky for *anyone* to understand," he added.

"Try me." She folded her arms. "I might have ideas, too."

The smirk he performed was so brief, she almost missed it. She flinched and hutched away from him. "I'm forty-two, Jake, not nineteen any longer. I think you forget that." She picked up a cushion and hugged it.

Jake set his jaw. "It's my gut instinct to look after you," he said.

"I don't need protecting."

"You did once." He sounded rueful.

The pause that followed between them was loaded with two decades' worth of tiny resentments that spread like spots of mold on a bathroom wall.

Liv had always thought that couples fell into one of two camps when their kids got older. Group A reverted to their pre-children days, relishing afternoon trips to the cinema together and lazy lie-ins without kids jumping on the bed.

Group B lost their individual identities and could only function as part of a family. When the children left home there were long silences that couldn't be filled, and the hollowness of empty bedrooms.

She'd always thought she and Jake would slot into Group A. Increasingly, she wasn't sure which way they'd swing. She wondered if they'd ever hold hands and wander around art galleries ever again.

"We've both been really busy, haven't we?" Jake said wearily. "Not talking enough."

"We have to actually be in the same room to do that."

"I'm sorry I took the call."

Even though he sounded truly apologetic Liv's jaw was tense and the lump on her head throbbed.

"When things settle down, let's do something nice," he said.

"Like what?"

"A family holiday. Let's book a break away, like you mentioned." When he slipped his arm around her shoulder again, Liv felt her anger seep away a little. They hadn't been away for a couple of years and she loved the thought of sunshine heating her skin. "Maybe we could go abroad, somewhere cheap and cheerful," she said.

"Sure. Or, I was thinking of a nice little B and B in England. Or, camping is always fun. Then we'll still have some money to spend on the house."

Liv froze. She had a vision of herself cooking sausage and eggs on a tiny outdoor stove for breakfast in the rain. Even if Jake did it instead, it still wouldn't feel like a holiday. The unreliability of the British weather meant taking a whole car full of stuff, from sandals to hats and gloves. It was weird how you could go on holiday with three suitcases of things, and return with six cases' worth of laundry. Her blood simmered at the thought of Jake allocating all their money to bills, repairs, his business and the boys. The only treat Liv had given herself was better coffee. Even the Bentley and White cake she'd bought was for the family.

She suddenly wasn't sure if she wanted to holiday with them all.

You could get some sunshine, on your own, a voice cooed in her head. *A working break, of course.*

Liv ran a tongue over her top teeth and let the tempting thought take root. It seemed to grow at an alarming rate, swelling in her lungs and chest, pushing her to let it out. The more she tried to quell it, the more it rebelled. "Essie's asked me to accompany her to Croatia," she blurted.

Jake frowned at her. "Why?"

"Because I'm her assistant."

"And who'd pay for *that*?"

"Her publisher, of course."

"What about the boys?" he said, wearing the expression of someone watching their shoes being swept out to sea.

Liv eyeballed him. "What about them?"

"Well, what if they need you?"

"They're adults, and they have *two* parents."

Jake bristled. "Well, it sounds very odd to me. What would you do out there?"

Liv didn't even know. She shook her head, wishing she hadn't mentioned it. "I've been doing some writing for Essie and—"

"Writing? I see..." Jake interrupted. He nodded several times, in the same way he did when Johnny swore blind he didn't know how biscuit wrappers got under his bed.

"What's wrong with that?" She glowered at him.

"Nothing. It's not going to be *real* writing, is it?" He picked up the remote control. "As if Essie would ask you to do *that*."

Liv's face blotched. She knew tiredness and stress might be fueling her anger, but her words spewed out anyway. "Essie trusts me more than *you'll* ever know."

His eyes became surprised circles. "What's brought this on?"

She hadn't eaten anything since a brownie at lunchtime and her blood sugar was flatlining. She was aware of how childish she sounded, but couldn't stop herself. "You have. All you think about is football, work and your sister. You make more effort arranging raisins in your muesli than you do with me."

"Raisins?" Jake said.

"You don't even know that Essie is dea—" Liv clamped her teeth together, horrified she'd almost let this slip out.

"Essie is *what*?"

Liv's pulse jumped. She fought against revealing the truth. "Um, that Essie is *ded*icated to helping me realize my talents more."

Jake switched off the TV and set the remote control down on the coffee table. He leaned back and regarded her. "I didn't know I did *that* with the raisins."

"You set them out in a circle before eating them, and it's weird." Why was she even bringing this up? It was the least of her worries. "*And* you never send me roses," she added.

"Well, you ate chocolate cake in the bath and dropped crumbs. I thought there were insects on the plastic," he said, then paused. "I *have* been keeping stuff about Paperpress from you. It's because I didn't want to worry you."

Liv heard the weariness in his voice, and she felt it, too. Her body was as heavy as an anvil. She flopped her head back and stared at a mark on the ceiling, wondering what would work best to clean it off. She wriggled a shoulder to release the tension knotted there, and Jake reached out and gave it a rub.

"Can we watch the rest of the film, please?" he said. "I shouldn't have answered the phone. All I want to do is sit next to you."

She gave him nonchalant shrug.

"There's a pizza in the fridge," he said. "I'll put the oven on."

When Jake returned, he stretched out his arm and Liv hesitated before nudging under it again. It felt both heavy and secure at the same time.

"Margherita in fifteen minutes," he said, dipping his head to catch her eye. "Sorry again about Katrina, and the raisins."

They resumed watching the film and Liv hugged a cushion to her chest. Although they'd argued and made up, her body still felt as stiff as corrugated cardboard. At this moment in time, when she glanced at the gray bristles on his chin and ones that had sprung up in his ears, she didn't know if she wanted to wake up with him for the rest of her life.

Words circled around in her head a few times before she released them out loud. "I think I'm going to go to Croatia with Essie," she said. "She needs me."

Jake didn't answer. He stared ahead without blinking.

Not that it mattered anyway. Because now Liv had set those words free, there was no going back.

16

GRAND PIANO

"Is it essential that you go?" Jake asked Liv as he pulled onto the car park of Manningham Airport. "Can't Essie go to Croatia on her own? Where are you meeting her?"

"Yes, no, and in the departure lounge," Liv said, as patiently as she could. "Please don't fuss."

Since she'd told him she was going to Dubrovnik, Jake fired questions at her like a round of pellets from a BB gun. She detected a tang of jealousy in his concern. It caused her to toss and turn in bed, questioning herself, too. How could she pull this off? Was she being resourceful or deceptive or both?

It was all too late anyway. She had fire in her belly and Georgia's sense of adventure running in her veins, urging her to try new things. Liv wanted to get to know the heroine even better, learning how she might act and feel, so she could really capture her character for Book Twenty.

She was halfway toward Essie's death being formally announced to the world, but hadn't yet reached the midpoint of reshaping the manuscript. The missing eight chapters loomed large in her head. She hoped an escape to Croatia would give her some much-needed material for the novel. It was also a unique opportunity to be part of Essie's world and to discover more about the author, too. The trip might give Liv some of the answers she was looking for.

"Mum'll be fine," Johnny chipped in from the back of the car.

Jake turned and fixed him with a stare.

"It's only a short flight," Liv assured him. "There'll be lots of other people at the book festival."

"Croatia's supposed to be very hot in early August." He stretched out his neck. "Ring me when you get there."

"I will."

After switching off the engine, Jake got out and Liv joined him behind the car. "I'll carry your luggage," he said.

"I can do it."

They both reached for the handle at the same time. Liv got there first and heaved it out of the boot. It thudded onto the pavement. She'd packed two versions of the manuscript in her case, Essie's handwritten original, and printed sheets of the work she'd done so far. They took up just as much space as her clothes.

"What have you got in there?" Jake said, letting his hand drop to his side. "Bricks?"

They studied each other for a while, as if reading each other's thoughts and choosing to ignore them. Liv couldn't deny she had a flutter in her stomach that was part excitement and part fear. "Well, this is it," she said.

"It's not too late to—" Jake started. His words were interrupted by the back window of the car winding down.

"Bring back sweets," Johnny called out.

"Chewy ones," Mack yelled.

They sounded like young boys again, and she walked around the car and spoke through the window. "I'll do my best. Keep your rooms tidy."

"Yeah, right," Mack said.

Liv gulped away a lump in her throat, unable to remember the last time she'd gone away without them. A strong pull reared inside her, ordering her to get back into the car.

Don't go, Liv.

Even her own thoughts were taking Jake's side.

She gripped the handle of her suitcase and looked toward the airport terminal. People were filing in and out, arriving and leaving. Jake's eyes were full of hope that she'd change her mind. She kissed him on the cheek. "I'll be back before you know it," she said.

Wheeling her suitcase toward the building, she turned back to wave. As she stepped through the glass doors, her heart soared with excitement and her mind spun with worry at the same time. After checking in her luggage, she headed toward a bookstore and browsed all the novels, to restore a little calm.

When she touched down at Dubrovnik Airport, Liv was greatly impressed by its cleanliness. The frayed navy fabric of her suitcase looked tatty against the shiny white marble floor.

After going through customs, Liv spotted a man dressed in a smart black suit and a peaked cap. His sign read Starling and Green, and he insisted on carrying her suitcase to the shiny black car that awaited. She informed him she'd be his only passenger.

He opened the rear door for her. "Welcome to my beautiful country, Ms. Starling," he said.

Liv didn't correct him.

The thirty-minute drive along the coastal road felt like they were gliding. The car rose up high in the mountains, giving her a magnificent view of tiny white houses and the glistening turquoise sea below. The scenery was so otherworldly it belonged in the pages of fiction.

When they arrived at the hotel, Liv navigated the revolving

doors into the lobby while still wearing her sunglasses. She kept her head low and peeped over the top of them.

The winding grand staircase looked like it had been transported from a Hollywood movie, and a pink marble fountain had coins shining in the water. A woman in a black sequined dress tinkled a tune on a grand piano. Liv became aware that her mouth had dropped open, and she clamped it shut again.

A small group of girls loitered in a corner, straining their necks to look at Liv. They were dressed as Georgia Rory in blazers and floral dresses with big black boots. They looked away again, their faces etched with disappointment. Even if Meg and Marlon had kept things quiet about Essie's attendance, it looked like word had filtered out to fans somehow.

The driver spoke to the man behind the reception desk and deposited Liv's suitcase. He touched his cap and said goodbye to her.

The receptionist tapped on his keyboard. "Welcome to Croatia, Ms. Starling. I hope you had a pleasant journey." Tap, tap, tap. "May I have your passport please?"

Liv shifted uncomfortably. She'd not thought to bring Essie's passport along and only had her own. Her hand shook as she fumbled in her handbag and handed it to him.

The man opened it up and frowned. "Madam?" he questioned, turning it around to show her the photograph. "This appears to be the wrong one. This is for Olivia Green."

Liv stared at it and didn't blink. "Yes, I'm Ms. Starling's assistant," she said, affecting a posher accent. "Her passport will be in her suitcase. I'm seeing her shortly."

"Hmm." He raised an eyebrow. "The driver said you were Ms. Starling. Perhaps a silly mistake, yes?"

Liv nodded. "Must be. May I also check in for Ms. Starling, please? I'll pass the room card on to her."

The man hesitated for the longest time. "That is absolutely

fine," he said eventually. "My fiancée is a huge fan of Ms. Starling's books. Please bring her passport to me when you can. I'm pleased to upgrade her room to our honeymoon suite."

Liv shoved the passport back into her bag. "Splendid," she said. After he handed both room cards to her, she hurried toward the staircase.

"Ms. Green," the man called after her. "Your suitcase…"

Liv looked down at her empty hands and clenched them into fists. She performed a shuffle, not sure whether to move backward or forward. "Oh, yes. Sorry."

"No problem," he said. "I'll have it brought up to your room."

When Liv reached her own bedroom, it was compact and gorgeous with a view of the gardens from the window. By some miracle her suitcase was already waiting for her, and she carried it up two flights of stairs to look at Essie's honeymoon suite. *Wow*, Liv thought as she opened the door.

The floor space was as big as all three of her bedrooms at home combined. It came with a lounge area and small kitchen. She whooped as she bounced up and down on the squishy leather sofa and gazed through the sliding doors that lead to a terrace with a sea view. The bathroom housed a jacuzzi with steps leading up to it, a bidet and two marble sinks.

After Liv and Jake's wedding, they'd spent a couple of nights at a country hotel for their honeymoon. She'd thought the bathrobes, fluffy slippers and croissants on the breakfast table were the height of luxury, but they didn't compare to this.

Thinking this might be her only chance to stay somewhere so luxurious, Liv nipped back downstairs and hung a Do Not Disturb sign on the door to her own room. She didn't want hotel staff to notice no one was using it.

Back in Essie's suite, guilt tainted her mood about enjoying this experience alone, so she texted Jake and the boys to let them know she'd arrived.

Have fun! Jake messaged back, though she assumed he didn't really mean it.

Liv hitched herself up onto the bed and let herself fall backward. Jake liked to lie on a hard surface, insisting it was better for his back. Some mornings, she felt like she'd been sleeping on the streets. This mattress hugged her body and she grinned up at the ceiling, not quite believing her luck.

Maybe Essie would have invited me anyway, she thought. *If she leaves me anything substantial in her will, I can take the boys somewhere like this.* All she had to do was keep the author's secret for another three months. She was already halfway there.

After a while, she heard footsteps and saw a shadow shift across the gap underneath the door. When a note swished along the carpet into the room, she padded over to pick it up.

Hello Essie
I'm pleased you've arrived safely. Let's catch up in the lobby for
a drink at 7:00 p.m. Looking forward to meeting you in person.
Best,
Marlon

Liv stared at the note and a sword of doubt thrust inside her. Marlon's words confirmed her deception, and she smoothed her hand across the Egyptian cotton sheets, pressing down imaginary creases.

For the next couple of hours, she wanted some peace and quiet, and not think about her meeting with the agent that evening.

What on earth was she going to tell him about Essie?

Liv tried not to stumble as she descended the grand staircase. Her gourmet lunch on the plane had been several hours ago, and she felt shaky from hunger.

Wanting to be punctual, she arrived in the lobby fifteen

minutes early. To kill some time, she headed into a room she thought was a bathroom. As her eyes adjusted to the darkness, she made out the silhouettes of several long tables piled high with books. There was a box of bookplates and lines of name badges in front of her. Several featured author names she recognized and her eyes shone at the thought of spotting some of her favorite writers in person.

She picked up the badge for Essie, pinned it to the lapel of her jacket and performed a pretend handshake to see how it felt being a real writer. "Hi, I'm Essie Starling. Pleased to meet you..." She stopped herself and furled her hand into a fist, embarrassed by her own action.

There was a drift of citrus aftershave and a door opened and shut behind her. A cool hand brushed the top of her arm and she spun around. Liv recognized the man immediately.

Marlon wore a tweed waistcoat, a pink tie and a gold hoop through his ear. His auburn beard looked more orange in real life. "Oh," he said. "Sorry, I thought you were someone else for a moment."

Liv smiled. "Essie Starling? You're supposed to be meeting her."

"Yes," he said. "How do you—"

"I'm Liv." She held out her hand.

As he shook it, Marlon's eyes flicked to her lapel. "Marvelous. Great to meet you."

Liv deftly unpinned the badge and slipped it back onto the table. "Just making sure it fastens properly," she said. "Essie likes me to test these things."

"I bet she does. How was your journey?"

"Fabulous, thanks. On time, and very smooth. And they served hot nuts with the ice cream in business class." She had been dying to tell someone about *that* extravagance.

"I love airplane food, too. Can't get enough of those tiny

toothpastes. I have a full collection of eye masks." Marlon smiled at her for a few beats too long. "So, is Essie around?" he said.

Liv pulled a sympathetic face and hoped it wasn't too dramatic. "She's not feeling too well. I'm afraid we won't see her tonight."

Marlon frowned. "Oh, that's bad news. What's wrong?"

Liv hadn't planned what excuse to make. She rubbed between her eyebrows.

"A migraine?" he deciphered and stroked his beard. "How awful. I have some little aromatherapy samples that might help. I could pop up to see her…"

"*No,*" Liv blurted.

Marlon's eyes widened.

"She needs to rest."

"Yes, of course you're right. We need her bright-eyed and bushy-tailed for tomorrow. The book festival's always hectic. Remind her to be on the stand at 10:30 a.m., will you? Meg wants her to meet some bigwig overseas publishers. And then there's the big dinner."

"Dinner?" Liv said, as if the other things weren't enough. "*Big?*"

"It's a fancy annual thing. Essie will be the guest of honor. She's turned down invitations for the past umpteen years, so everyone's excited she's joining us."

Liv's legs felt even weaker.

Marlon placed a hand on her forearm. "You're doing a great job, coaxing her out of her cave. Whatever magic you're casting, it's working wonders."

She mumbled that it was nothing.

"Shall we grab a beer together? Have you eaten?" he said.

Although she was starving, Liv wanted to get back to the

safety of the suite. Gilding the truth was proving exhausting. "No, sorry," she said. "Essie has things she wants me to do."

"Well, tell your boss I said hi. I hope she feels better soon. Are you heading back to the lobby?"

"I'd like to stay and look at the books, if that's okay?"

"Sure. They look great, don't they? Piles of pure joy. I'll see you on the stand tomorrow. Nighty night."

"Night," she said, and waited for him to leave the room.

When the door swung shut, Liv exhaled. Every tendon in her body grew looser. She helped herself to a wedge of the bookplates and a Sharpie pen and tucked them into her handbag before switching off the light. She stared straight ahead as she strode across the lobby, not wanting to catch the eye of the receptionist.

Outside the door of Essie's suite, she gaped at the things piled there: a teddy bear, Dubrovnik guidebook, a tote bag, box of chocolates and a small bouquet of white roses. There were a few envelopes with Essie's name on the front and she opened a card. "Dear Essie. You are the most talented writer, ever. We can't wait for Georgia's 20th story. With love from your biggest fans ever xxx"

The note was signed with lots of names.

Liv gathered up the gifts, struggling to hold them in her arms. When a group of girls dressed as Georgia Rory suddenly appeared around the corner, she quickly opened the suite door and heaved the presents onto the bed. Chattering sounded outside the room for a while, and she ignored the knocks sounding on the door.

"Esssiiiiieeee," someone shrieked. "Is Georgia in there?"

Liv kept quiet. Did they actually think the character was real?

The talking died away after a few minutes. When Liv's phone vibrated, she was pleased to see Jake had messaged her and she sat down on the bed to read it.

Do you know where Johnny's long blue sports socks are?

Liv gritted her teeth and tried to remember. Perhaps they were in the bottom of his PE bag, or still in the laundry basket. The boys had a habit of asking her before looking for themselves. She was about to reply with suggestions when her gaze fell upon the roses. Could Essie's mystery man be here in Dubrovnik?

She lifted and smelled them. If her family could see her now, in her luxury suite, perhaps they wouldn't take her for granted so much. Was it such a big deal if Johnny had to find his own socks, or borrow some off Mack?

I'm enjoying myself, thanks for asking, she replied. **Missing you all x.**

Her stomach rumbled as if congratulating her. Navigating Essie's world had made her ravenous, and she called for room service.

When the food arrived, Liv sat on the end of her bed. She ate her burger and fries with silver-plated cutlery and drank a large glass of Merlot, then watched a Croatian DIY program on TV while waiting for the jacuzzi to run. There was no loud music, banging or floorboards groaning. Only the gentle sound of bubbling water, and it was blissful.

17

BOOKPLATES

Liv woke to sunlight dappling on the ceiling and the faint smell of cooked bacon and eggs. At first, she thought she was still at home until she saw the sea glistening through a gap in the curtains. The beautiful view made her heart race, beating harder as she thought about what today held in store. She sat up in bed and used the Sharpie to fashion Essie's signature on the bookplates.

After a quick shower, she dressed in a cream linen dress, tan wedged sandals, and added one of Essie's blue scarves around her neck to match the Coach handbag. She pushed the striped tie into her pocket, to add a touch of Georgia, too. She placed both versions of the manuscript in the tote bag and heaved it onto her shoulder, planning to work on them if she was at a loose end.

When she stood at the top of the staircase, the activity in the lobby below made her skin feel clammy. People were already bustling around, and she felt like it was her first day in her new school. She reached up and rubbed her back, where elbows had once drilled into her ribs. Too nervous to eat breakfast, she headed directly to the exhibition area where she registered at the desk and received her own name badge.

Liv's right shoulder hung low from her bag as she entered the football pitch–sized room. The ceiling was high and arched with colorful banners hanging down. There were rows of stands for publishers and literary agencies, and her eyes skirted around in wonderment. She was so busy looking at all the books that she didn't notice Marlon heading toward her.

"Morning, Liv. All set for today?" he blasted. "How's Essie?" Liv smiled faintly.

"Oh, no, a migraine still? Awful things. Has she taken anything for it?"

"I guess so."

"Don't forget she's due on the Peregrine stand in an hour. Meg can give you a copy of her agenda." He paused and his eyes fixed somewhere behind Liv.

She followed his gaze to see a tall gray-bearded man who she recognized from somewhere. He held his phone to his ear, and when Liv spotted the rose tattoo on the back of his hand, she caught her breath. "Who's that?" she whispered to Marlon, remembering the hidden photo she'd found in Essie's award room. The man looked older now. Had he left the white roses outside Essie's suite?

Marlon nervously stroked his goatee. "It's Essie's ex-agent, Sven."

"You don't seem pleased to see him."

"He's still sore Essie moved to my agency. She was with him for many years."

Liv stole another look. "Why did she leave him?"

"They had a big row. She can tell you more about it. I believe it was awkward."

Or I could just ask him myself, Liv thought to herself. She wondered if her next question might sound odd to Marlon. "Were Sven and Essie ever romantically involved?"

"What?" Marlon said, his brow furrowing. "I mean, I

wouldn't know for sure. They worked together for a long time. Why would you ask *that*?"

"I'm not sure." Liv flushed.

"Look, have a wander around, check if Essie's okay. I'll see you both on stand B52," he said.

Liv eyed Sven again. He must have been a big part of Essie's life once. She meandered toward him, pretending to look at a few books on the way. How on earth could she approach an important literary agent and quiz him about his ex-client?

She was racking her brains when she overheard him wrapping up his conversation. "So, I will see you in Bar Boca in the city, tomorrow at 9 a.m., yes?" Sven said in a Scandinavian accent.

As he walked away, Liv wanted to speed after him and tap him on the shoulder. Instead, she wrote down the meeting details on her hand, plotting to catch him the next day.

When she made her way along the middle of the aisles, exploring the festival, Liv couldn't help grinning to herself. There were so many new books around her, they looked like postage stamps. The twelve-year-old girl inside her wanted to run around and stroke all the covers. The forty-two-year-old version felt pretty much the same way.

Liv pictured Essie and Anthony holding hands and walking together in the photo on the Dubfest website. In her head, they looked very much in love.

She felt guilty about interrupting his time with his family in Italy but wished he'd reply to her message. She wanted to feel everything was okay between them.

When she saw a large banner featuring a peregrine falcon, Liv steeled herself and headed toward the publisher's stand. Rows of Essie's novels, English and foreign editions, lined the shelves. Marlon sat on a stool talking to a woman with short chestnut curls and huge diamante clustered earrings.

The woman stood and flung her arms open. "Livvy, darling. Marlon's told me all about you. I'm Meg, Meg Stuart. So wonderful to make your acquaintance."

Liv felt sticky lip gloss press against each of her cheeks.

"Marlon says your understanding of Essie's creative temperament is akin to a sixth sense," Meg gushed.

"Thanks," Liv replied, not entirely sure what this meant.

"I simply can't wait to read her latest work. Has Essie allowed you the pleasure?"

"Yes, it's been…eye-opening," Liv said.

"You must spill your thoughts over dinner." Meg looked around her. "Now, where is the lady herself?"

"She's got a migraine," Marlon chipped in.

"Oh, poor thing," Meg cooed.

When 10:25 a.m. arrived, Liv, Marlon and Meg sat around a tall red table. Marlon kept eating sweets from a bowl, and Meg fiddled with her earrings. "Do you think Essie's on her way?" she asked Liv. "I want her to sign some books as a little giveaway for our visitors."

"It doesn't look like she's joining us," Liv said. She took the signed bookplates out of her handbag. "She asked me to bring these along, just in case."

Meg pressed a hand to her neck. "Gosh, that woman is *so* selfless, thinking of others."

Liv smiled to herself. "I could start sticking them into the books…"

"Would you, darling?" Meg gave a resigned smile.

As Meg drifted away, Marlon leaned in. "I'm really worried about Essie," he said. "I should go up and check if she's okay."

Liv's hand froze. She looked up from the bookplates and swallowed hard. "Please don't do that."

"I've brought my aromatherapy oils along."

"She might be asleep…"

"I get migraines, too. Believe me, they make sleeping impossible. I'll only be a few minutes."

"*No,*" Liv said, more aggressively than she meant to.

Marlon shrank back.

Liv's eyes darted as she thought of something to waylay him. She bent down and wrestled the printed manuscript out of her tote bag. She leafed through the pages and held out the first three chapters she'd worked on. "Essie gave these to me, this morning. Would you like to read them?"

Marlon eyed them with wonder. "Has she finished the book?"

"No, but these will give you a good flavor."

He took the pages off her and held them gently, as if they were ancient parchment that might disintegrate. "Are you sure she won't kill you? I'd love to read them."

Liv tried not to worry about how unprofessional her own writing might be. Anything to stop Marlon from trying to see Essie. "Let's not disturb her."

He held the pages protectively to his chest. "You know her best, Liv."

When she returned to the stand, Meg was shaking hands with two men and presenting them with copies of Essie's sixth novel, *The Silent Touch.* She opened the covers to show off the signed plates inside.

"Any luck reaching Essie, darling?" Meg said. "I'm meeting an important French publisher next, La Plume. They'd *love* to meet her. They've published her before and are undecided which book to choose next. They want to grow her readership in France."

Liv smiled apologetically. "I don't think we'll be seeing her."

"This is truly unfortunate." Meg tapped her pen on the table and mused for a moment. "Perhaps you can step in for her..."

"*Me?*" Liv said. "Oh, I don't think I can—"

"But you're literally her spokesperson." Meg placed a hand on Liv's arm. "Oh, here they are now, Stéphane and Brigitte."

The two publishers walked over and shook hands with Meg, who spoke to them in fluent French. The trio laughed and took their seats. Brigitte had the glossiest long brown hair Liv had ever seen, and Stéphane's magnificent curls looked like a lion's mane.

Liv remained standing. She had a pulsing sound in her ears. Somewhere across the hall she saw Ted Mason, and sat down quickly on a stool. "Um, *bonjour*," she said.

Meg reverted to talking in English and held up a couple of Essie's books. Liv was so anxious she didn't take in any of her words. She felt like she was watching the meeting from a soundproof glass booth. She smiled until her jaw ached and became aware that Meg, Brigitte and Stéphane were looking at her.

"I *said*, don't you think *The River After Midnight* would be a good choice for La Plume?" Meg nodded at her.

Stéphane and Brigitte looked at her expectantly, too.

The book wasn't one of Liv's favorites. It featured a condescending hero and fewer action sequences than usual. "What are you looking for?" she asked.

Brigitte thought for a moment. "Something with depth and heart. Our readers want to feel every emotion."

Liv ran through all nineteen novels in her head. One stood out for her, but it wasn't one of Essie's biggest bestsellers. "I'd suggest *The Daylight Stream* instead," she said.

Meg flashed her a stare. *"Really?"*

Liv nodded. "It's Essie's eighth book and makes me cry the most. Georgia uncovers lots of secrets and reconnects with the daughter of someone she thought was dead. It's incredibly moving."

Stéphane's eyes met with Brigitte's. *"Très intéressant,"* he said. "I have not read this one."

Liv scanned the shelves and picked up two copies of the book. She opened the covers and adhered a signed bookplate into each.

Stéphane nodded as he read the blurb on the back.

"Merci." Brigitte smiled and shook Liv's hand. "This sounds perfect. We shall discuss, and you may expect our offer soon."

Meg stared after them, her face etched with surprise. "Well done, Livvy," she said from the corner of her mouth. "Do you fancy meeting the Italians next?"

Throughout the course of the day, Liv joined Meg for several more meetings. At first, her shoulders were rounded, and her blood pressure shot up if anyone spoke to her. But by midafternoon she felt more confident in displaying her vast knowledge of Essie's work. Perhaps she was the best person to tackle the author's manuscript after all.

People treated her very differently from the Platinum office staff, who had pretended she wasn't there as she cleaned, or Hannah Cardinal, who had made her run errands. Liv wondered if it was all their fault, or if she'd allowed them to treat her that way. What might have happened if she'd stood up for herself more? She was going to do things differently from now on.

Editors sat opposite her with their pens poised, nodding and hanging on to her words. Liv sat at the high table, smiling and speaking with ease and authority. At first, she thought people held her in higher regard because she was Essie's assistant, and they were interested in the author's work. Slowly, Liv realized *she* was the one holding their attention, and pride warmed her chest.

When the festival came to an end for the day, Meg took a

call as she and Liv left the exhibition space together. An offer had come in from the Italian publishing house.

"This is super. Well done, Livvy," Meg said, after hanging up.

Liv hutched her tote bag up her shoulder and found a spring in her step despite the weight of the two manuscripts. She wondered if everyone could see her cheeks blooming with color. When they reached the hotel lobby, she kissed Meg on both cheeks and arranged to meet her later for the big dinner.

As she made her way back up to her suite, Liv wrapped the striped tie around her hand and held it tightly. "Thanks, Georgia," she whispered.

18

ANIMAL HEADS

Liv put on one of Essie's long black silk dresses for the dinner. Her whole body felt like it was shaking, but when she looked in the mirror she appeared still. And she also felt beautiful. Not in a film star way, with flawless skin and perfect makeup, but for a forty-two-year-old cleaner who'd stepped into a different universe, she felt as if she was glowing. She unpacked things from her tote bag and transferred a few bits into one of Essie's sequined clutch bags. There was just enough room to squeeze in the striped tie, too.

When Liv got engaged to Jake, Carol insisted she wanted to buy the wedding dress. The two women had gone shopping for it together.

Liv gazed at rows of gorgeous gowns in several boutiques before her eyes were drawn to a silk dress with tiny glass beads and lace on the bodice. As soon as she held it up to her chin, it felt like *her* dress and her excitement blossomed. But then she saw its price tag of seven hundred pounds.

"Oh, love. It's absolutely stunning," Carol said.

"It costs a fortune," Liv whispered.

"Don't worry about that." Carol ushered her into a changing room. "Try it on and give me a twirl."

When Liv zipped herself into the dress, it was a perfect fit and made her feel like a princess. As she stepped out from behind the curtain, tears sprang to Carol's eyes. "You've found *the one*," she gasped.

Liv smoothed a hand over the ivory silk. She loved it so much, but knew her mum couldn't afford the dress, and neither could she and Jake. "I'm not so sure," she mused, trying to find fault with it. "Maybe it's a little tight on the waist."

"Are you sure? It looks perfect to me."

Liv looked longingly at her reflection in a mirror. "I'll try a few more dresses on first, to help me decide."

As they continued to browse other stores, Liv spotted a simple white sheath dress in a charity shop window. It was pretty and elegant, though didn't light up her senses. The price tag said forty-five pounds. "That one is lovely," she said, tapping the glass.

Carol stared at it for a while. "It is…but it's secondhand, love."

"There's nothing wrong with that," Liv said firmly. "And it's crazy to pay a lot for something I'll only wear for a day. I'll go inside and try it on."

The dress was a little too large on her shoulders. Liv didn't feel the same love toward it, but it was a practical choice. She stepped out of the changing room to show her mum. "I really like it," she said.

Carol smiled. "It does look very nice. But don't let the cost sway you. Choose the one that's right for you."

Liv tugged down the skirt and put her hands on her hips. "This is the one. Mission accomplished."

At home, she adjusted the shoulder seams so the dress fitted better, and she got it dry-cleaned. However, as she walked down the aisle with Jake, Liv couldn't help yearning for the dress she didn't buy.

In the hotel suite, Liv ran her hand down Essie's luxurious dress and she turned around in front of the mirror. This time, she was wearing something beautiful that she truly loved, and she felt like she could float. She held on to her clutch bag and took a deep breath as she left the room.

The dining room was decorated with black-and-gold-striped wallpaper and large gilt animal heads on the walls, including a lion baring its teeth. Liv thought all the overseas publishers might display the same expression when they found out Essie wouldn't be attending.

Marlon appeared at her side. He looked dapper in a tweed three-piece suit and a tie with piano keys running down it. "No Essie?" he said, in a voice that was quiet by his standards.

She shook her head. "So sorry."

"I *really* need a word with you," Marlon said and took hold of her elbow. He led her to the corner of the room.

Liv pressed a hand to the wall to steady herself. The urgency in his voice made her think her pretenses had been discovered. "Um, yes?"

He lowered his voice even further. "I've read Essie's first chapters and I'm confused," he said. "Her writing is…different."

Liv felt her earlier confidence ebbing away and found it tricky to meet his eyes. "Essie wrote them very quickly," she said, thinking how feeble it sounded.

"It's fresher."

"What?" Liv lifted her chin. "It is?"

Marlon nodded. "It reminds me of Essie's first couple of books. She was good but still finding her way as a writer. Her work had raw edges but shone. These chapters read like she's falling in love with Georgia again."

Liv could see how Georgia's decline had been mirrored by Essie's own. She was helping both women back onto their feet, and could feel Georgia's personality shining through, in the manuscript and within herself. "I actually think she's doing that," she said.

"Will you tell her what I said? Spur her on?" Marlon said. "Come on, let's eat."

When Liv followed him to the dining table, she wore a Cheshire cat grin, feeling her work had his stamp of approval.

Laughter tinkled around the huge table and Liv heard several accents she couldn't place. Marlon waved a hand to announce their presence, and fifteen pairs of eyes pivoted toward them.

"I'm afraid Essie can't join us tonight," Marlon boomed. "However, we're blessed with the company of her delightful assistant, Liv."

Several smiles around the table stiffened.

She stood helplessly until Meg circled a finger in the air. "Livvy, do join me."

Liv gratefully sank into a chair next to her.

"Poor Essie. Don't let it spoil your fun," Meg said. "You did tremendously well today. We won't need you or Essie on the stand tomorrow, so you can have a little rest."

Waiters began to glide into the room, carrying plates at shoulder level. The maître d' announced each course as if he was an esteemed Lord Mayor making a decree.

An entrée looked like a small egg set on a spoon, but passionfruit exploded on Liv's tongue when she bit into it. *Wow*, she thought. She chased a tiny pink ball around her plate with a fork. A culinary meal with Jake and the boys was a Five Guys hot dog and fries. She stared at her rows of knives and forks and had no idea which ones to use.

"I'm *so* excited for Book Twenty," Meg said, as she poured

Liv a glass of champagne. "I'm intrigued to know your thoughts about it, darling, as a beta reader."

Liv remembered that her honesty about Essie's book review hadn't gone down well. She hoped Meg wouldn't react the same way. She placed her clutch bag on her knee and glimpsed the striped tie through a gap.

When she started to speak, it was like a small crack appeared in a dam and her passion took over. She had lived and breathed Essie's manuscript for three months and hadn't been able to share it properly with anyone until today. Her words trickled out at first, before turning into a gush.

"The story's taking shape," she said. "Personally, I think Georgia's grown too staid over the last few books. She's lost her spirit of adventure. Sure, she still travels around and falls in love, but she acts like it's a weight on her shoulders. Readers want to feel her excitement and energy, not think she's resentful, or miserable. She needs to change and I think that's happening in this book."

Meg nodded for a while. "You've hit the nail on the head, Livvy. I've said similar things to Essie. I worked with her on edits, but..." She let her words drift. "I don't wish to be indiscreet. It sounds like you're getting both Essie and Georgia back on the right track. Well done."

Liv sipped her champagne gratefully. "Essie's struggling with the love of Georgia's life. She hasn't decided who it is yet, and I'm trying to help her. The end of the story is proving evasive."

"Love of her life?" Meg mused. "I always had a soft spot for architect Dean Andrews in *The River After Midnight*. He's very dashing and spontaneous. Essie should choose wisely. Her readers need someone memorable and to feel Georgia's longing for him."

Liv's plate was whisked away and replaced with something

tiny and cut into thin slices. The maître d' announced it as *truffle supreme*, and it was so delicate she wanted to sigh after each bite.

"Now, when am I going to read this book, darling?" Meg said. "It's vastly overdue."

"Essie says the first of November."

Meg chortled as if Liv had told her a joke, until her face eventually straightened. "Oh, darling. I told Marlon I *must* have the manuscript before then."

"That's not possible."

"But we're already working on strategy. We're planning our marketing campaign."

"There's still heaps to do."

Meg wet her lips. She lowered her voice. "I must tell you, we have interest from a major film studio in this book, Livvy. They love Georgia, but have been waiting for the *right* story. The last few books haven't been it, and I think Essie knows that, too. She's always refused adaptations of her work, not wanting anyone to mess with her characters, and we're all hoping she'll change her mind."

"Films shouldn't be a marker of success for books," Liv said. "Books allow you to tap into your imagination and conjure up your own pictures, not lay everything out on-screen."

"Well, I see your point, darling." Meg shifted in her chair. "We still need conflict and romance, a battle against the odds, and heaps of emotion. Do you think this novel will deliver it?"

Liv closed her eyes briefly. She pushed a hand into her bag and touched the tie. The old version of her would simply agree, putting everyone else's needs above her own. Trying to complete the book more quickly would compromise its quality. "Yes, it will deliver," she said firmly. "But only if Essie has enough time to finish it properly. She's insistent on a November the first deadline and Marlon knows that, too..."

At the mention of his name, Marlon appeared and gave a small cough. "May I steal Liv? I'd like to introduce her to Milo and Giuseppe from Antelope."

"Fabulous idea. Then do come back and keep me company." Meg air-kissed Liv and twinkled a wave. "You do drive a hard bargain, darling."

Liv staggered a little as she followed Marlon around to the other side of the table. "Meg asked for the manuscript earlier, but I said no," she said, still surprised by her own boldness.

Marlon's cheeks colored. "I've been waiting to warn Essie about it in person."

"Well, it's all settled now. Essie will be taking three more months. And even that will be tight."

When Liv thought about everything she had to deliver, it felt like the Sword of Damocles hanging over her head. One false move and it might fall and slice her jugular. She had to find Georgia's man, edit the complete book, and write the eight missing chapters in thirteen weeks. A ticking clock sounded loudly in her head.

She hoped speaking to Sven tomorrow would help bring much-needed answers.

When Marlon introduced her to the Antelope team Liv couldn't concentrate properly. When she returned to her original seat, tiny unidentifiable things continued to arrive on plates. Next to her, Marlon and Meg soon fell deep into conversation. Their foreheads almost touched as they nodded and made notes. She wondered if they were talking about her and Essie, and the weight on her shoulders felt even heavier.

After eating dessert, Marlon spoke to Liv. "Slip away and see how Essie is," he said. "The dinner will go on for at least another hour."

She nodded gratefully. She said good-night to everyone before leaving the room.

As she walked through reception in a haze, the man behind the desk beckoned to her. "I still need to register Ms. Starling's passport," he called out.

Liv fixed her eyes on the staircase and pretended not to hear him. When she reached the top step, she halted when she spied a gaggle of people hanging around on Essie's floor. They clutched Georgia Rory books and seemed to be waiting for the author. "I think Essie Starling went that way," she pointed back down the stairs.

A man let out an excited yelp, and Liv waited for them all to disappear before she returned to the suite.

Outside, the scene now resembled a shrine. There were photos and notes pinned to the wall, a bottle of champagne and another basket of fruit. Messages exclaimed admiration, undying love and get well soon wishes for Essie. Liv bristled at how people knew. She scooped up the goodies and took three turns to heave them all into the room.

It was a little after eleven and Liv knew her adrenaline wouldn't allow her to sleep for some time. She listened to an audiobook of *The Accidental Tourist* by Anne Tyler and ran the jacuzzi. Before slipping into the water, she blinked at herself in the bathroom mirror, not really recognizing the person who stared back at her. It was someone she wanted to get to know better, someone who'd lost her direction in life and was now emerging from the shadows. But was it as Liv, or as Georgia Rory?

19

TATTOOED HAND

On her last morning in Croatia, Liv woke at 5:30 a.m., too early to phone home. The last couple of days had taken their toll, and her head lolled with tiredness as she packed her belongings into her suitcase.

After showering, she slathered on sun cream and dressed in a floral dress and comfy sandals, adding the striped tie loosely around her neck. It was a beautiful day, and she wanted to wander the streets of Dubrovnik before she tried to speak to Sven, after his meeting.

Holidays for Liv usually meant six weeks of planning for one week in the sun. It was a thankless task buying sun lotion that didn't irritate Jake's skin and shorts with zips so the boys' mobile phones didn't fall out. It was freeing not having to lug anyone else's sunglasses or reading material around. She left the two manuscripts behind on the bed and took the empty tote bag.

She bade *"Dobro jutro"* to a lady on the reception desk and wandered outside into the sunshine. The morning was already hot, and Liv bought bread from a baker's shop for breakfast, tearing off pieces to eat while she waited at the bus stop.

During the twenty-minute journey into the city, she listened to Euro disco playing on the bus radio and realized she'd left her mobile phone back at the hotel.

After a few moments of panic, she knew it was too late to go back. She gazed out of the window and decided to embrace the rare freedom of being uncontactable.

The bus arrived at the Pile Gate, the main entrance to the city walls, and Liv hopped off. A woman dressed all in black and wearing a white headdress sat on a low stool making lace. She had a pile of postcards at her feet for sale and Liv picked up a few and handed over some kuna.

She made her way across a beautiful old stone bridge that was once a drawbridge. The Stradun stretched before her, a long square with shiny limestone paving stones and a statuesque white clock tower. Liv walked along it with her chin raised, taking in the wooden-shuttered windows, arched doorways and a majestic domed cathedral. She felt like Alice stepping into Wonderland.

It felt strange not having to chastise Jake for walking one meter in front of her, or to referee Mack and Johnny's squabbling. She could turn corners and slip down streets without prior negotiation of who wanted to do what.

Most of the shops were still closed, and there weren't many people around yet. Liv meandered, looking in windows at handcrafted leather handbags, and chocolate truffles with curls of coconut on top. On one of the side streets, a man stood in a doorway and held out a plate full of crystallized orange slices and caramelized almonds. "You try." He gestured.

"*Hvala*," Liv said and crunched into the sugary orange. "Delicious." She bought three small bags and asked him how to find Bar Boca.

He pointed toward a narrow street. "Look for the gap in the wall."

As she walked, a small truck trundled past her with crates of Coca-Cola rattling on the back. Liv glanced after it, her throat suddenly dry. She soon found herself in a tangle of streets with stone walls so tall it was like being in a maze. The paths crossed, and she relied on her instinct to take her in the right direction.

After a while, she saw a person-sized slit in the wall revealing a vertical slice of sparkling teal sea. A small piece of wood read Bar Boca in crude letters.

Liv squeezed through the gap and saw hundreds of tiny steps carved into the rock face, curving down to a paved plateau set out with tables and chairs. Beyond that was a sheer drop where waves crashed against the rocks below.

On a table overlooking the sea, Sven sat talking to another man.

Liv held out her arms for balance and made her way down the steps. She sat at the bar on a stool made out of a beer barrel, ordered fresh orange juice and glanced over at Sven.

He was the epitome of the word *chilled*, wearing a gray linen suit with battered sandals that displayed his tanned ankles. Liv could see the bluey patterns of his tattoos through his white cotton shirt. He sipped coffee from a tiny cup and silver rings on his fingers flashed in the sunshine.

She'd heard of his agency before. It was famous for representing dark Swedish thrillers featuring feisty tattooed heroines, and also for losing Essie as a client. She'd found out the beginning of Essie's story from Ted, but how did it pan out from there? Could Sven tell her anything about the night Essie disappeared? Was he possibly her mystery love?

She waited until Sven's colleague left.

Liv had met many people at the book festival and couldn't remember all their faces and names. She assumed it would be the same for Sven, too.

She ordered a coffee and carried the cup over, setting it down on his table. "Sven, isn't it? I'm Liv Green. I saw you at the festival, yesterday." She extended her hand, congratulating herself on her acting.

His eyes flickered, with no idea who she was. "Oh, yes," he said, in his lyrical accent. "How are you?"

"Good," she said. She sat down opposite him, without waiting for an invitation. "I didn't get a chance to tell you I work with Essie Starling. I'm passing on my regards."

"Oh," he said, followed by a long pause. His rings clinked against his coffee cup. "That is good. I heard that she's here in Dubrovnik. I hoped I might see her."

"Unfortunately, she's been otherwise engaged."

"I am sorry to hear that."

Liv paused a beat. "You wanted to see her?" she said. "Is there anything I can help you with?"

He smiled and stirred his coffee. "That is kind of you, but no. It was something between Essie and me."

"Something...from the past?" Liv said.

Sven eyed her. "Why do you say that?"

"Marlon mentioned something happened between you and Essie." She wondered if she'd moved on their conversation too speedily.

His eyes flashed before calming just as quickly. "Ha, Marlon. He has nothing to worry about. Essie chose him instead of me. All is good."

Liv waited to see if he'd add anything else. When he didn't, she jumped in. "Actually, may I ask you a few things about Essie?" she said. "I'm doing a little writing for her and would like to understand her better."

He laughed. "This sounds like you want to interview me."

"Oh, no, I'm not a journalist." She rolled her eyes for effect.

"Good. I heard from one only last week, asking me questions about Essie."

Liv controlled her breathing. "Was her name Chloe Anderton, from *Sheen* magazine?" she said nonchalantly.

"Yes, you know of her?"

"She's writing an article about Essie."

"So, I learned. I told her I was not interested in talking about my ex-client. What is it you want to know?"

"I believe Essie bases her characters on real people. Did you inspire any of her heroes?"

"This question!" He tipped his head back and laughed. "Me? I doubt that very much."

"Didn't Essie sign with you after splitting up with Ted? That's what he told me."

"Sure." Sven twisted a ring around his thumb. Her mentioning Ted's name seemed to assure him it was okay to talk. "After her divorce, Essie was flying high. She wanted to start over and sign with a literary agency, to get her the best deals. The trouble was, everyone wanted her."

"How did you woo her?"

"I like this word, *woo*." He laughed again. "With someone like Essie, it is mostly about the mind. You have to pique her interest, challenge her or equal her. I knew flowers and flattery would not do the trick."

Liv thought how Sven was unlikely to send Essie white roses.

"We had a terrible first meeting. I spilled a little coffee on her dress, and asked which author's career she would most like to have. She stared at me as if I was an imbecile. 'My own, of course,' was her reply." Sven made his fingers into a gun and mimed shooting into the air, and his hand fluttering down. "Pow. I thought it was over. I mean, it was bad."

"How did you win her around?"

"I didn't try. I gave her space. She met other agents and called me after a couple of months, sick of everyone sucking up to her. We were like a married couple straightaway, bickering and annoying the hell out of each other. Our wordplay together was a little like foreplay."

Liv blushed.

"Ted wanted her to be some literary darling, but I said she should be herself. If you're good at something, why not stick with it? She wasn't super original, but she was driven and readers loved her work. I told her she was a golden goose that should keep on laying."

Liv cringed inwardly. "Didn't she mind?" she said.

"She thought it was funny. I remember at our first Dubfest together we sat in a bar like this one at midnight, talking about her books. The sea was black, stretching before us. The moon was out, and the stars twinkled. I asked Essie what she wanted from life. And she held out a palm and said, 'All this, for a start.' She enjoyed the attention, and the awards and the clothes, and the men. She was always looking for *something*, and people flocked to her."

Liv wondered how *that* would feel. Essie had wanted so much from life and then turned her back on it all. But why? "Were the two of you ever romantically involved?" she said.

"Definitely not," he said.

"Oh...okay." Liv found the photo on her phone of Essie and Anthony. "Do you know this man?"

"Who is he, a lover?" he said, pinching his lips together. "I thought Essie and I shared the same taste in men."

"I'm not sure."

"Well, I do not know him. Men usually kept Essie entertained for one night, maybe two, and then..." He snapped his fingers. "I remember her dancing once at a party and everyone's eyes were upon her. She told me there was only ever one man who could hold her attention, who she really loved. Then, a few weeks later, she announced she was moving to LA with Hank Milligan." He raised both eyebrows.

"Was he *the* man?" Liv said.

"I don't know. Hank is a super fun guy to be around. Maybe a little *too* fun. He has lots of energy, you know? And a pre-dilection for serial killers." Sven stopped talking and finished his coffee. "What I thought would be a fling turned into a ten-year marriage.

"Hank was gorgeous, a real party guy," he continued. "He took Essie to some great parties. They both loved the lifestyle in the sun, you know, the cars, and the houses. I stayed with them sometimes…"

Liv heard a downturn in his words. "What happened?" she said.

Sven let out a sigh. "Hank drank a lot. And Essie joined him more and more. It began to affect her work. Writing Georgia Rory became a necessity, you know, a chore. I sus-pected there were things going on in her personal life that I didn't know about."

Liv wondered what they were. She was about to ask Sven when he waved for more coffee.

He waited until a waiter brought over their cups before he spoke again. "When Essie sobered up, her writing picked up and she won the Constellation. Hank was by her side. And then, after that night…" He gave an exaggerated shrug and did his shooting motion again. "Pow. Nothing. I don't know what happened, but she would no longer meet me. She turned down invitations to festivals. I thought I had done something wrong. It went on for several years."

"Until she left you for Marlon?" Liv said.

He nodded. "One day I spoke to Essie on the phone. I re-minded her she was a golden goose. Except, this time, she went crazy, calling me names. I think I hit a nerve. And then I heard she signed with Marlon." He looked down at the table. "It was like a divorce, and it stung."

Liv had always thought writing was a glamorous career. But for all Essie's parties and clothes, cars, houses and fancy hotel rooms, had the author felt like a commodity in the publishing world? Moving to Marlon appeared to give Essie a little more freedom.

She finished her coffee and looked out to sea.

"Did you tell me what your job is?" Sven said. "I can't remember."

"I'm Essie's assistant," Liv said. "She thinks I might be able to write, too."

"She wouldn't say that if you weren't any good." He smiled.

"I'm not qualified at all. Not that it stopped Essie doing so well..."

He placed a hand on the back of hers. "Don't believe everything you read. Essie went to university. Being self-taught was a little myth her original PR team cooked up. They thought readers would relate to her more."

"Oh." Liv's shoulders fell. She felt like she'd been hoodwinked somehow. Not having a higher education was something she had thought she and Essie shared.

"It does not matter. If you want to write, you must do it. Essie has seen something in you," he said. "Do you enjoy working with her?"

"It's a bit like an obstacle course."

"Yes. I found this also. Yet, we still want to take part, even if we can never win." Sven stood up and shook Liv's hand. "It was good meeting you again, Liv. Please say hello to Essie for me."

Liv ordered a sandwich for lunch and sat thinking about Essie for a while. No one could tell her what happened the night of the Constellation Prize. At least she had found out that Sven wasn't Essie's mystery man.

After eating, Liv looked at her watch and realized more time had passed than she thought. She whispered a quick farewell to the waves, before climbing the steps and squeezing back through the gap in the wall. She panted as she jogged to the bus stop and waved at the driver who was already pulling away. The brakes of the bus screeched and the doors hissed open. *"Hvala,"* she croaked breathlessly and sunk into a spare seat.

The bus set off again and she flicked on the air-conditioning above her seat, letting the cool breeze lift her hair.

Back at the hotel, Liv wanted to make sure Marlon wouldn't be around to notice Essie's absence when she came to leave. She explained to the man on reception that Ms. Starling would like her car to arrive thirty minutes earlier than planned.

He clicked a few buttons on his keyboard. "Ms. Starling would like this, or Ms. Green?" he said, fixing her with a stare. "It's very strange because Ms. Green's hotel room hasn't been slept in whereas Ms. Starling's suite has been used. My fiancée asked me to get her autograph, but I haven't seen her once. She is like the Invisible Woman."

"Some writers like to maintain an air of mystery," Liv said.

"Hmm," he said quietly. "Do you have Ms. Starling's passport for me yet?"

Liv held his gaze, guessing he knew of her ruse. Usually, she'd try to bumble out an excuse or apology. Instead she shook her head. "If she is the Invisible Woman, you wouldn't be able to check her photograph anyway."

"This is true." He shrugged.

Liv tapped the desk. "Let me ask Ms. Starling for a signed bookplate for your fiancée. And perhaps a special edition of one of her books, to prove that she really does exist."

They shared a glance and he found a smile. "Thank you," he said. "I'm sure I'll be able to sort out her passport details."

Liv packed up the rest of her things. She cleaned her teeth and shoved her phone into her bag without checking it. She stuffed as many of the gifts as possible into her case, leaving the flowers and fruit behind.

In the lobby, she passed a signed copy of *The River After Midnight* to the man on reception then positioned herself under the staircase so no one would see her. When the car pulled up outside, Liv hurried out of the hotel and slipped into the back seat, sinking down out of sight.

It was only when she arrived at the airport and checked her phone that she saw the flurry of missed phone calls and messages from Jake.

Liv. Phone home. Urgent.

20

NIGHT CREAM

Liv tried to call Jake back, but her phone battery was dead. At Dubrovnik Airport, she found a pay phone but couldn't reach him. She left a voice message explaining her situation and advised him her flight was on time.

She spent the entire return journey home willing the airplane to fly faster. The worried lump in her throat meant she couldn't eat or drink any refreshments during the flight.

When she landed back at Manningham, Liv grabbed her luggage off the conveyor belt and jogged through customs.

Jake and the boys stood waiting with sorrowful faces.

"Are you okay?" Jake sped toward her.

Liv's eyes alighted on the navy fabric encasing Johnny's arm and holding it across his torso. His fingers poked out of the end, pale and limp. "What happened?" she gasped.

"Didn't you get my calls and texts?" Jake said. "I asked the hotel to push a note under your door. Johnny's broken his arm."

Liv's face felt hot with guilt. She hadn't checked her own bedroom when she left the hotel, only Essie's suite. "I didn't get the message," she said.

"We should complain. I specifically told them to—"

"It doesn't matter. I'm here now."

"I slipped on some mud," Johnny said dolefully.

Mack stared at him. "You said you broke it playing footie."

"The ground was muddy."

"Okay, lads," Jake said. "Let your mum catch her breath. She's only just landed." He took hold of Liv's suitcase and frowned at its weight, testing it with his hand. "What have you got in there, more bricks?" he said.

Liv smiled weakly. The four of them walked toward the exit.

"How was your break?" Jake asked her, and she wasn't sure if he was being sarcastic or not.

She wanted to gush how the sea was the bluest she'd ever seen, how she'd given a stellar performance at the book festival, and how Marlon thought her writing was fresh. She felt like showing him photos of her hotel suite, and insisting they buy a softer mattress. But, she kept it all to herself. Instead she said, "It was fine. Tell me what happened to Johnny."

"I got a call from one of his mates yesterday, saying he'd had an accident," Jake said. "I drove over to the park and Johnny was lying on the ground clutching his arm. I took him straight to the hospital and they did an X-ray. He's fractured it just below his right shoulder."

Liv flinched as she imagined his pain. Guilt churned in her stomach at not being there to accompany him to hospital, and she couldn't help wondering if the accident wouldn't have happened if she hadn't gone away. The bright skies of Croatia dimmed in her head, as if clouds drifted in front of the sun. Her overseas escape suddenly felt like several weeks ago, rather than mere hours. When they reached the car, she slid into the passenger seat in a daze.

"It's a nasty break, the worst kind," Johnny announced.

"The doctor said so. It frigging well hurt. My shoulder was all swollen, like the Hulk. I don't need a cast because my arm hangs in this sling and the weight of it pulls the bones back into place. It's gross."

Liv winced.

"He might need screws or a metal plate putting in," Jake murmured as he turned the key in the ignition.

When they arrived home, Liv saw hospital documentation on the kitchen table and a spare sling. There were piles of pots in the sink making her feel even more guilty for not being here to help out.

Jake put the kettle on, Mack disappeared upstairs and Johnny loitered as Liv sat on the dining room floor, unzipping her suitcase. She threw her used clothes onto separate piles, and he scanned over her stuff.

"Did you get me anything?" he said. "I need cheering up."

Liv smiled at all the gifts hiding under layers of clothes. "Maybe a few bits and pieces."

Johnny kicked his toe against her case. "Dad was really worried about you."

"No need to be. How long will you be out of action?" she said.

"Dunno."

Jake reappeared and set down a cup of tea on the dining table for her. "He won't be arm wrestling for a while, that's for sure." He looked her over. "You've caught the sun on your nose." His tone was flat, as if disappointed.

"Thanks." Liv took Essie's black silk dress out of her case and carefully draped it over a chair.

Jake stared at it.

"It's Essie's," she said, avoiding his gaze. "I said I'd get it dry-cleaned for her."

"Just how much did you spend on souvenirs?" he said, after

she'd unpacked the teddy bear, guidebook, and the almonds and orange slices she'd bought.

"Nothing, they were gifts."

He looked at her, as if she was speaking in a foreign language. "When you're finished unpacking, I've got a couple of things to ask you."

Liv didn't feel like talking, or listening. Part of her brain was still in the sunshine, and not drinking anything on the plane had left her feeling dehydrated and a little dizzy. "I need to sit down with my drink first."

Jake passed her the tea. He looked at her expectantly.

"What's so urgent?" she said with a sigh.

"It's Katrina's big 5-0 in September. She wants to go to a spa."

Liv gaped at him, wondering why this couldn't wait. "That's next month, it's weeks away."

"She's booking a pamper day at Hampton Hall for friends and family," he continued. "There's a pool, sauna, massages, facials, that kind of stuff."

Jake once told Liv he'd rather be ridden over by a horse than pay someone to rub his skin. She could tell from his expression that they were all expected to go. It was bad enough going to a party with all his relatives, without seeing them half-naked.

"The ladies are going to have treatments, and the men can use the pool and sauna. Johnny's broken arm means he'll have to sit some things out. We can all meet up for lunch afterward."

Liv leaned down to pick up a bra. "Hampton Hall is really expensive. Is Katrina paying for everyone?"

"Um," Jake said, which she deciphered as a *no*. "We have to confirm today. And we'll need to get her a birthday present, too."

Liv ignored the word *we*. Jake always left his gift buying

until the last minute, so she had to step in to do it. "Why do you always bend over backward for your sister? When she clicks her fingers, you come running."

He was quiet for a while, as if considering telling her something and deciding otherwise. "It's her special birthday," he muttered.

Liv sipped her tea, not impressed. "Did you say there's something else?"

Jake rubbed the back of his neck. "It'll wait," he said. "You get settled and we'll talk later."

For the rest of the day, Liv tidied her things away and carried out her laundry. She admired her tanned arms each time she stuffed the washing machine. Her hairs were bleached blond, and she wished she'd taken more photographs to prove the last three days had actually happened. She wasn't entirely sure if she'd dreamed them or not.

As she hung her clothes on the washing line outside, she pictured herself wandering the sun-soaked streets of Dubrovnik. She'd spent so many years cleaning and not having the confidence to try anything else. A voice had nagged in her head for years. *Will you get another job? Are you good enough? Isn't it a bit late to move on?* Now she'd managed to shoot all her own concerns down in flames.

As she was discovering more about Essie, Liv was finding things out about herself, too. She'd masterminded a meeting with Ted, been resourceful talking to Sven, proved knowledgeable about Essie's books, and Marlon had admired her writing. She felt like a very different person to the one who sat timidly with Essie nibbling tiny cakes in the kitchen.

Before Liv went to bed that night, she found the hotel room card in her bag. She'd been in too much of a rush to hand it in to reception.

She entered the bedroom to find Jake hurriedly stuffing something under his pillow. "What's that?" she said.

His eyes flitted. "That? Oh, nothing."

"There's some paper poking out." She caught sight of words and figures.

He pushed it farther under. "It's just a few notes."

Liv wasn't in the mood to question him further. She slipped her room card under her own pillow and unscrewed a jar of night cream. Johnny and Mack called out good-night and turned off their lights. "What's this other thing you mentioned?" she asked Jake.

He lay back on his pillow. "Can you ask Essie for time off work?" he said.

She dotted cream around her eyes. "Me? Why?"

"Johnny's got hospital appointments, a checkup and an X-ray. They're going to assess if he needs surgery. I've got a heavy few weeks at work, so he'll be in the house on his own. Remember when Mack broke his arm and couldn't do anything for himself?"

Liv thought back to when Mack was ten, holding his wrist and blinking back tears. He'd fallen off his bike and his classmates covered his plaster cast with rude words and *Minecraft* stickers. He wasn't able to wash his hair, butter toast or get dressed on his own for weeks. Liv had to promise to shut her eyes when she helped him in and out of the bath.

"Johnny's a lot older than Mack was. He'll be okay on his own," she said.

She thought of how Jake's job was always the static one, whereas hers was expected to bend and shape, and stop and start around their family. A calendar appeared in her head with the three months she had left to complete Essie's novel, ripping off and flying away. She needed every minute she could to write. "Perhaps Mack can help out, since he's home for the summer."

"His mate Ned's invited him to his parents' caravan in Blackpool for a couple of weeks. Plus, one of us will need to go with Johnny to the hospital, to see what they say," he said.

"Hmm, you're right."

"Plus, cleaning Essie's place is hardly a matter of life or death," Jake added.

Liv shot him a glare. Her tiredness after traveling had taken its hold. She set her cream jar down on her bedside table with a thud. "I told you I'm helping with her writing. What if *that's* a matter of life and death?"

He eyed her for a while. "What do you mean?"

A compulsion swelled inside her, making her want to spill everything that had been going on in her life. She tried hard to swallow it back. When she was with Jake, she felt like she was on a boat with no paddles being swept farther and farther out to sea. Sharks were beginning to circle. Meanwhile Jake was on the shore not even noticing she was drifting away.

At this moment in time, Liv wished she could reveal how Essie had entrusted her with a huge last wish, and how she was delivering it and thriving. Yet she couldn't say a thing, or else she'd risk losing her inheritance.

"Nothing," she muttered. "I'll take Johnny for his appointments."

"Good. Thank you." He squeezed her leg. "Perhaps he can go to Essie's place with you some days. Give you both some company."

Liv thought about trying to write while her teenage son lounged around on the cream leather sofa. "Can't he go into Paperpress with you and help out?"

"He's not much use with one arm."

Johnny called through from his room. "I can hear *everything*. Go to sleep."

Liv lay down and roughly pulled the covers around her, already missing the fine Egyptian cotton. She thought about how Ted had tried to shape Essie to fit his ideal version of a wife and a writer, and how Sven had wanted her to keep producing the same work over and over. She understood the author a little more with each day that passed, and wanted to keep peeling back the layers of her life.

Jake's hand crept to her shoulder, making a small circle with his finger. Liv froze before shrugging it away. "I'm really tired."

His hand thumped onto the mattress. "Okay. Night."

As Liv settled down to sleep, she could still feel the glare of the sun on her neck and hear Euro disco thrumming in her ears. And she thought how much she preferred living Essie's life to her own.

21

PAPER PLANES

For the next few days, Liv tried writing at home. When she sat at the dining table, Johnny constantly drifted in and out of the kitchen, slamming the fridge door and cupboards. He munched cereal straight from the packet and glugged milk from the bottle, even though Liv told him not to. His answer to everything was, "I've only got one arm."

When she changed the bedcovers, Liv found three sheets of Paperpress headed paper under Jake's pillow. Items written in abbreviations had rows of scribbled figures set against them. Some of the amounts were alarmingly large but she couldn't work out what they were for.

Liv scribbled edits onto her own printed manuscript pages as if she were possessed. She wrote while waiting for her bath to run, in bed before she went to sleep and even as she walked to Essie's apartment. All that existed in her head was crafting Georgia's last story. It became like an addiction she had to feed, and she was ever more aware of the countdown toward the deadline. She relied on dressing in the blazer, floral dress and striped tie to help her to work.

Georgia pressed her hands flat against the glass box. The water was filling up inside rapidly, reaching her knees and then her thighs. It would take only seconds to reach her neck, then her mouth. She shivered but didn't thrash her legs and arms, knowing panic wouldn't solve anything. If she screamed, no one would hear her. She had to breathe calmly, keep focused, and think what to do next. She'd been in many dangerous situations before and had always managed to escape.

When Liv accompanied Johnny for a checkup at the hospital, she felt twitchy at leaving her writing behind for a while. She scrunched her head into her neck as she walked along the corridors with her son. She'd hated the place since childhood, after finding her mum waiting for her with tears streaming down her face.

"I'm so sorry, love. Your dad's gone," Carol had said. "They tried their best but couldn't save him…"

The two of them clung together and Liv could still sense her mum's heart palpitating against her cheek.

When the doctor pointed to Johnny's X-ray on a computer screen, Liv was grateful for her thoughts to jump back to the present.

"I'm very pleased with your recovery, young man," he said. "Your bones have aligned nicely and are healing well."

Liv felt overcome with relief. "Will he need any surgery?"

The doctor shook his head. "I don't think so. He should rest his arm up for a few weeks more, and then we'll book him in for some physiotherapy."

Johnny moved his fingers a little. "What will they do to me?"

"Nothing too tortuous. You'll start with a few gentle exercises to get your arm moving again. With this kind of break your movement might be more restricted from now on."

Liv swallowed. "By how much?"

"He might struggle to reach books on top shelves."

Johnny shrugged. "I'm not bothered by *that*."

Liv shook her head slowly at him.

Afterward, they caught a bus back to the city center where Liv picked up some dry cleaning. She draped Essie's black silk dress over the crook of her arm. "We'll go to Essie's flat to drop this off. I need to do some work."

"Cool," Johnny said. "She lives in that tall building, right? I think Daz Milan does, too."

"Who?"

He fixed her with an incredulous stare. "Footballer, millionaire, playboy."

She shook her head. She supposed the apartment block must be awash with the successful, rich and famous. "Just promise me you won't touch anything."

"Okay," he sighed.

When Johnny looked up at the luxurious lobby, his face became a little boy's again. Liv recalled his same expression when she took him to see the holiday light displays in the local shopping center at Christmas.

"This place is awesome," he said. "You need to be loaded to live here."

"I know."

When the glass lift door opened, his mouth dropped. "It's see-through," he said. "When I'm older I'm going to live here."

"Start saving now," Liv laughed. "You might get a mortgage when you're eight hundred years old."

Johnny unfastened his laces in Essie's hallway. He cocked his head, looking and listening. "Isn't she home?"

"She's working away," Liv said, the lie now rolling off her tongue like dice from a gambler's fingers.

When he stepped inside the living room, Johnny pretended to stagger backward. "It's like being in heaven," he said. "Why can't we live somewhere like this?"

"Because I'm not a bestselling author." Liv put her hands on her hips and looked around her. As the sun sparkled on the glass and the city stretched out before her, she couldn't help feeling like the apartment was hers, somehow. She was the only one who used it. Might Essie have left it to her in her will, or things from inside it? Or was that crazy thinking? It would mean she could carry on writing as her job.

She just had to keep focused and not invoke the proviso Anthony had mentioned in Essie's will.

It was the first time she'd thought about the solicitor for a few days, and she wondered if he was still in Bologna. "What are you going to do while I'm working?" she asked Jake.

He shrugged a shoulder and settled down on the sofa. "Go on my phone?" He raised it.

"You're not doing that all day. Essie's got lots of books you can look at."

"Maybe later," he said, clicking around the screen with one finger. "Hey, have you seen the memes about Essie on Instagram?"

"What are those?"

"People put together photos and quotes, and post them online." He held out his phone for Liv to see.

I've given up on boyfriends and husbands. I have affairs with my characters instead. I can tell them what to do and they don't cheat on me.

I always hoped to have children one day. I try to see my books as my offspring and my readers as my family instead.

If you meet something insurmountable, don't try and fight it. It will only leave you with bruises. The trick is to outsmart it and do something it wouldn't expect.

If you're not enjoying a book, there's a solution for that. Close it up and move on. It's not the end of the world.

I'm drawn to books with happy endings. Who wants to spend time reading a story where things don't work out?

It would be splendid to be remembered for my books. However, I'd prefer to be remembered kindly.

"She must have said those things a long time ago," Liv said. "She refuses to do interviews these days." The last quote struck her as particularly poignant. She would always remember Essie's kindness.

She took some blank sheets of paper from the printer and looked in Essie's desk drawer for a pen. There was a mass of elastic bands, staples, pencils, erasers and scraps of torn paper. Among all the stuff she found Anthony's business card. Written on the back was.

Call me anytime, day or night. A xxx

Liv recognized his handwriting from his attempt to write a sonnet. She assumed the solicitor didn't offer this personal touch to all his clients. It had been five weeks since they'd last spoken, and she assumed he must have been busy juggling his family and work. She decided to call him.

After passing a copy of *The Moon on the Water* to Johnny, she closed the kitchen door to keep her conversation private.

"Liv? Hello," Anthony said, sounding pleased to hear from her.

"Hi. Are you still in Bologna? Is your father-in-law okay?"

"He's feeling slightly better, thank you. I'm still working remotely in Italy but hope to be back home at the beginning of September. Shall we meet then?" he said. "You can update me on Essie's novel. Have you heard anything more from the journalist?"

"Not personally, but she's been speaking to people who know Essie. I've just got back from Dubfest in Croatia."

"You went *there*?" he said.

"Yes. I had work to do."

"Hmm," he said, leaving a long pause. "Perhaps you should come over to my office, to talk? I'll look at my diary when I get back to the UK."

Liv pursed her lips. It sounded official and she wondered what Anthony had to tell her. Maybe it was something to do with Essie's will. "Great," she said, thinking she could finally show him the bee-shaped cuff links. "I look forward to it."

When she returned to the sitting room, Johnny was sitting stiffly on the sofa. His lips were a fine line as he stared at his phone. He'd attempted to make a few paper planes and they were strewn around the floor.

"Are you okay?" she said. "What are you doing?"

"Stuff."

"Do you fancy a brew? Essie has this posh coffee maker. It looks like a robot and takes capsules. Sometimes it spits at you."

He shook his head and didn't look at her.

She sat down on the other end of the sofa. "Is anything wrong?"

"Nope."

Something was ruminating in his head. Liv took hold of his ankle and pulled his socked foot onto her lap. "Come on. What's the matter?"

He worked his mouth as if plucking up the courage to say

something. He glanced at her and back down again. "Are you and Dad splitting up?" he said quietly.

His question made Liv feel like she was cartwheeling and couldn't stop. "Oh, my God," she gasped. "No. What made you think *that*?"

He stretched his neck. "You closed the kitchen door to talk to someone. Dad's always in the coat cupboard on the phone…"

"I was talking to Essie's solicitor. Dad talks to Katrina."

"You went on holiday on your own, and keep coming home late from work and at weekend, too. You and Dad argue. I wondered if, you know…" He left a long silence. "There was someone—"

"What, like an *affair*?" Liv interjected.

When Johnny dipped his head, it felt like a skewer through her heart. She squeezed his toes, trying to hide her horror. "I'm busy, that's all. I'm not seeing anyone else. Honestly. I wouldn't do that. Me and your dad, we're…" She struggled to find the right word. "We're…solid." Even as she said it, it sounded hollow to her.

Johnny rubbed his nose and was quiet for a while. "My mate saw his dad with this other woman. His dad swore it was nothing. Then he left home and moved in with her." He shrugged. "His parents are splitting up."

Liv's skin felt sore, as if pricked by a thousand needles. She felt sure there must be blood specks on her dress, but the fabric was clean. "You, your dad and Mack are all I've ever wanted…" she said, letting her words fall away. When had she started to want so much more? Maybe when she got the job with Essie?

"Will you both be okay when I go to uni?" Johnny said.

"We'll be fine," Liv said, muffling her own concerns. "We've been married for over twenty years. There's nothing to worry about. We're both busy with work at the moment. It's a rough patch, but not between us. It's other things in our lives." She smiled at him, and knew it didn't reach her eyes.

She'd only been nineteen when she met Jake. At the time she didn't give it a second thought. Now it seemed so young. If Johnny told her he was settling down with someone, at his age, she'd think it was foolish at worst and optimistic at best. She'd ask him what the rush was and tell him to take his time.

She remembered for their third or fourth date, Jake had taken her to Paperpress before they went out to dinner. His face lit up as he told her about the printing presses and showed off his bookbinding tools. He'd made her a leather-bound notebook and demonstrated how to apply gold leaf to her name on the cover. When he'd finished, he handed it to her on his palms, as if it was a cushion displaying the crown jewels.

"Gosh, thank you, it's so beautiful. What should I write in it?" Liv said. It seemed too precious to use. No one had ever done anything like this for her before.

"Whatever you like. Shopping lists, reminders...the names of our children."

He said it jokingly, but they caught each other's eye, both knowing there was something special between them.

If Liv could go back, in the time machine mentioned in Essie's *Book Ahead* interview, she might whisper in her own ear, "Slow down a bit, Liv. You've only just met him. Are you sure he doesn't do this for his other dates, too? Do you want to settle down with the first guy who shows you any interest?" But she was so wrapped up in him, she doubted she'd have listened.

As time passed, she and Jake chose Mack and Johnny's names out of a baby book while watching TV. The little leather notebook still sat in her bedside drawer at home, waiting for her to use it.

Liv focused her attention back on her son. "I liked that your dad was older than me. He seemed so clever and mature, not like anyone I'd met before," she told him.

Johnny slid his foot off her knee. "I'm never getting married. It's weird promising to stay with one person forever."

When he said it like that, it sounded true.

"It's like a partnership," Liv said. "Someone is there for you during the good times and bad, to support and love you. And you're there for them. Of course, sometimes they drive you nuts..." She took a moment to consider her relationship with Jake. If she could score a line onto a wall for each argument they'd had recently, or the times he drove her crazy, the count would be much higher than the smiles and hugs column.

She supposed it wasn't inconceivable that Johnny suspected an affair, on either her side or Jake's. She currently devoted more time to Essie than she did to her husband, and Paperpress had felt like a mistress to him for a long time.

The trouble was, Liv was feeling more alive than she had done for years. Jake's attention and affection toward her had been dwindling for a while, and she'd found an exciting replacement, with Essie, and her new role.

After she'd had Mack and Johnny, Liv had been full of happy hormones, like she was floating on a cloud when she pushed their prams. After that came the flurry of nursery runs, grazed knees, ironing small clothes, rushing off to work and back again. She'd enjoyed the hectic whirl of life, until it was gradually replaced with a creeping sensation of losing her identity and direction, as she neared her forties.

And now, she was embracing changes she'd always shied away from. Uncovering new confidence. Worries she'd had about trying new things were falling away from her, as if she was shedding heavy armor. Her body felt freer and lighter. It was something she didn't want to stop. But she would have to be more careful.

Sometimes you had to make decisions and build them on whatever foundations you had closest to you. Even if you couldn't tell if they were made of sand or concrete.

She turned and fixed her son with a reassuring smile. "Really, you've got nothing to worry about," she said. "Me and your dad are doing just fine."

22

STRAWBERRY TART

Liv and her mum met every so often on Sundays, at a local café or Italian chain restaurant.

Sorrento's, a new upscale eatery, had opened on the outskirts of the city, and Liv booked a table for two. It was the kind of place Essie might have dined at once. Liv had been writing hard since returning from Croatia a couple of weeks ago, and welcomed the break from her work. She'd just been paid and wanted to do something nice with her mum before the money got swallowed up by bills and Paperpress again.

She took a taxi to her mum's house and asked the driver to wait outside. She had her own door key and let herself inside the bungalow.

Her mum's hallway always looked nice and homey. The carpet was patterned and worn and a purple glass vase with a silk flower display had sat on a slim table for years. Carol's shoes and slippers were set in a line against the wall.

When Liv's dad died, her mum had entered a state of shock, unable to think or function properly. Liv had to cook and clean for weeks, battling against her own landslide of emotions and with her mind playing tricks on her. Sometimes, she could swear that her dad was still at home before she remembered he was gone, and that she'd never see him ever again.

Extremely worried about both Carol and Liv, Peggy had invited them to stay with her. Her house was a couple of hundred miles away and, at first, Liv was glad for the change. Her mum needed her sister, and she knew whispers would be rattling around school about her dad, just as they did when another pupil had lost a parent.

Carol lay in Peggy's spare bedroom in the dark, refusing to eat. The doctor said she was suffering from a deep depression. Their stay with Peggy lasted for so long Liv had to join a new school. The kids pounced on the chance to torment a bereaved new girl, and Liv's only consolation was Essie's visit and winning her signed copy of *The Moon on the Water*.

When Carol and Liv eventually returned home to their bungalow, almost a year had passed. They both tried to blank out the date and event of Grant's death, choosing to focus on positive aspects of his life instead, such as looking at his favorite books together.

When Liv rejoined her old school, she had grown by two inches and cut her hair short. Different friendship groups had formed, so fitting back in proved difficult.

In the evening, while other kids were hanging out on the local field, sneaking cigarettes and first kisses, Liv stayed at home and read library books with her mum, feeling responsible for her health and happiness. They both liked Maeve Binchy, Rosamunde Pilcher and Essie Starling. The stories slowly helped Carol to find her smile again.

Nevertheless, Liv felt like she'd lost a chunk of herself, of her education and concentration, that could never be recovered. She felt like she'd been climbing a ladder and had slid back down the bottom rung, skinning her shins on the way.

She wished her dad was here to stroke her hair and tell her things would be okay.

When Liv turned sixteen, she heard her classmates chattering excitedly about joining the sixth form, or a local college. Liv just wanted to leave school. She struggled to focus on her exams and knew extra money would help out at home. Carol had a couple of cleaning jobs, and Liv thought it was something she could do, too.

In the bungalow, she called out to her mum. "Hiya. Are you ready for lunch?"

"I'm starving, love," Carol said as she appeared in the hallway. She picked up a box off the hallway table and put it in her handbag. "I could eat a moldy muffin."

Liv laughed. "Me, too."

Liv would never usually eat somewhere like Sorrento's. She'd become aware of every bobble on her sweater, or shiny ironing mark on her skirt, and the prices would give her palpitations. She felt a bit guilty spending money on herself, but her mum deserved a treat.

Topiary peacocks guarded the tall smoked glass doors, and there was a menu on a lectern outside. Carol eyed the alabaster Roman statues flanking the entrance. "This place looks very posh, love. Do you think they'll let us in?"

Liv was glad she was suitably attired in a dress and blazer rather than her jeans. Carol wore a pretty turquoise dress with a necklace of oversize white beads.

Liv assured her mum, but when they stepped inside a bow-tied waiter swept past without giving them a second glance. She squirmed when she saw a waistcoated waiter placing a linen napkin on a customer's lap. About to suggest they try somewhere else, a waitress with a high ponytail headed toward them.

"*Signoras*, I'm afraid we're fully booked," she said.

Liv felt a vein pulse in her neck. She didn't like how the woman looked at her mum, and she took hold of the striped tie in her pocket. "I have a reservation for two people." She fixed the waitress with a stare. "Under the name of Essie Starling."

The waitress twitched her lips. She checked a computer screen and picked up two menus. "*Certamente*, please follow me." She seated them on a window table with a view of the whole restaurant.

Carol waited until she moved away. She leaned in toward Liv. "Why did you use Essie's name?" she whispered.

"Strangely, when I used my own there were no tables available."

"Won't she mind?"

Liv batted a hand. "I'm sure it's fine."

They were presented with menus so stupidly large they had to peer around them, like theater actors checking out the size of an audience before going onstage.

"Have you seen the prices, love?" Carol hissed. "It's twelve pounds for a bowl of minestrone. Do they sprinkle parmesan in it, or diamond dust?"

"Shhh," Liv laughed, worried the waitress might hear. She'd already noticed a bowl of spaghetti bolognese cost more than she usually spent on a blouse. "Don't worry, I'm paying. Order whatever you want."

They both skipped having a starter and ordered fettucine with sundried tomato and olive sauce for their main course. When Liv requested a bottle of Chardonnay that cost over sixty pounds, her mum's eyes almost popped out of their sockets. Before she could protest, Liv quickly handed their menus back to the waitress.

Carol settled herself into her chair, as if it was a throne. "My friend Maureen has invited me to Benidorm," she said. "I'm not sure I fancy it."

"What? All those hot Spanish men and paella? You should go." Liv couldn't remember the last time her mum had been abroad. She'd usually went on coach trips in the UK, with three-course dinners each night and singers impersonating George Michael or Elvis.

"I'm not confident booking somewhere abroad, and there's all that traveling, too," Carol said.

"You could always fly first class and get extra legroom," Liv said, without thinking.

Her mum stared at her. "Who do you think I am, Paul McCartney's love child? I don't have a money tree."

"You don't want to be uncomfortable..."

"I think I'll stay at home, thank you very much. There's nothing wrong with Blackpool and it's cheaper. Are you and Jake going on hols this year?"

Liv shook her head. "I doubt it. He's too wrapped up in the business. Sending Johnny off to uni is costing a fortune, too."

"I bet you'll miss him, love. But you and Jake will get more time together."

Liv pictured her husband talking to his sister in the coat cupboard while she lay in the bath reading on her own. "I'm not sure that's a good thing," she said.

"Oh," Carol said softly. "Things not too good?"

Liv sighed. "Everything else in his life comes first, before *us*. Jake's got his agenda and I've got mine. They don't seem to meet in the middle, or even meet at all."

"You've been married a long time. It's not all hearts and flowers."

"It was for you and Dad. I'd love a relationship like yours."

Carol ran a finger around the rim of her glass, thinking for a while. "Me and your dad had our issues, too," she said. "You shouldn't think everything was perfect."

Whenever Liv thought back to her childhood, before her

dad's accident, the sun sparkled, flowers blossomed and birds sang. "Everything felt that way to me," she said.

Carol was about to speak but their main courses arrived. She dug into her fettucine.

"How is it?" Liv said.

"Lovely, but I'm not sure it's worth twenty pounds. You can buy a handbag in the sales for that."

"Hmm, I think you're right."

"What I was saying before, love," Carol said. "Marriage is like a marathon. You start it full of energy and enthusiasm, and you might enjoy the scenery and challenge of the first few miles. It's still a test of endurance, though. There might be times when you're lagging and feel like giving up."

"But you never felt like that, right?"

Carol smiled wryly, then went quiet for a while. "I've been sorting through some of your dad's things, photos and mementoes. I thought they'd be something nice to look at over dessert."

"Sure," Liv said. She glanced down at the box sticking out of her mum's handbag and wondered what it might have to do with her parents' marriage.

Carol sipped her wine. "I'm proud of you, love. It's good to see you doing so well. Jetting off abroad, dressing up all smart and eating in these fancy places. You're turning into a different woman."

Liv felt the same way, too. Who needed fiction when you could live the real thing?

"How's Essie's new book going?" Carol said. "I can't wait to read it."

"She's got two and a half months left to finish it, and there's still lots to do."

"Well, I hope it's a goodie. Don't tell her, but the last few have been a bit…" She made a rocking motion with her hand.

"You think so?"

"Hmm. She's been writing the same series for a long time. It must be easy to get stuck in a rut."

"I know what you mean." Liv browsed around the restaurant and caught the eye of a man dining alone. He was a decade younger than her with twinkling blue eyes and a stubbly chin. When he tilted his glass of wine toward her, Liv blushed. "I hope you'll love this last ever one," she said distractedly.

"*Last* one?" Carol frowned. "Isn't she writing any more?"

Liv flipped her attention away from the man, and realized what she'd just said. "Oh, yes," she backtracked. "I'm just guessing Essie will want a break from writing for a while."

After finishing their pasta, they ordered homemade strawberry tarts with Chantilly cream.

"Ooh, very posh." Carol broke off a bit of pastry and popped it in her mouth.

"You've got a dessert fork there, Mum," Liv laughed.

"At these prices, I'm going to enjoy every little nibble." Carol snapped off another piece of tart and closed her eyes as if in ecstasy. She turned eating slivers of strawberry into a ceremony.

Liv noticed that other diners were daintily holding their knives and forks to eat the tiniest morsels of food. A couple of them side-eyed Carol and a red-haired woman whispered behind her hand to her friend.

Liv bristled. The snobbish vibe of the restaurant wasn't her thing at all. What had she been thinking coming here?

Feeling protective of her mum, she set down her own cake fork. She picked a strawberry off her tart and made a great show of licking cream off each of her fingers. "Hmm-mmm," Liv said, while staring at the red-haired woman. "Shall we take a look at your photos, Mum?"

Carol set the box down on top of the table and took off the lid.

Liv took out a stack of photos and leafed through them. She'd seen some of them before, but not others. One was of her mum and dad holding candy floss. In another, Liv stood patting a donkey. There was one of her dad feeding pigeons, and another showed him sitting in the park reading.

She came across a pair of theater tickets with the stubs still attached. "You didn't use them?" she said.

"Oh, I've not seen those for ages. They must have been hiding," Carol said. She took them out of Liv's hand before she could look at them properly. "*West Side Story*, the matinee performance. I really wanted to see it and your dad treated me." Her eyes became misty and she lowered the tickets, staring at them for a long time.

"Mum?" Liv said, as she watched a tear trickle down her mum's cheek. "Are you okay?"

Carol nodded slightly, then sniffed. "We'd agreed to meet at the park gates, to walk to the theater together," she said, her voice quavering. "We'd been having a few arguments and your dad bought me the tickets to say sorry.

"He was late and I stood there waiting for him, for well over half an hour. I was annoyed at him but worried, too. When he didn't arrive, I set off on my own."

Liv frowned. It didn't sound like her dad to leave her mum waiting. "What had you been arguing about?" she said.

"The amount of time he spent at work." Carol sighed. "He always gave his students his full attention, nurturing their talent. Some were needier than others. He thought I was fine at home. I had cleaning jobs, I had you, I belonged to a book club. But I felt neglected by him, unfulfilled somehow, and I told him so. Several times. Things changed for a little while, then slipped again. I felt like I might be losing him…"

Liv knew how that felt. Jake seemed to be drifting away from her, too. "What happened?" she said.

"I tried to shock him, I suppose. I gave him an ultimatum, even mentioned divorce. I made an appointment to see a solicitor. I didn't mean it of course, just wanted him to listen and notice me again. Take things seriously. And it worked. He apologized, said he hadn't been thinking clearly. He was under a lot of strain at work. He still wanted me, and our family, just as it was. He bought me the theater tickets and things got much better."

"So, why did he leave you waiting?"

Carol chewed the inside of her cheek. "To this day, I don't know, love. I reached the theater and hung around outside. The time grew closer to the start of the performance and he still didn't arrive. I didn't want to sit on my own and watch the show, so I went home instead. There was a call from the hospital, saying your dad had been admitted. When I got there, it was too late…" Carol started to cry properly now. Diners looked over at her. "I should have waited for him at the park gates," she wept.

Liv moved her chair around the table. She put her arm around her mum and passed her a napkin to use as a tissue. "I'm so sorry, Mum. It wasn't your fault. It was purely an accident."

The two women sat hunched together until Carol let her breath go. She patted the back of Liv's hand. "If things are rocky between you and Jake, try to sort them out eh, love? But don't rely on him for your happiness. You have to find your own path, too."

"I will do." Liv gathered the photos and tickets together and put them back in the box. She put on the lid. "Can I take this to look at another time?"

"Of course. That's why I brought it," Carol said, dabbing the corner of her eye. "I could do with a strong coffee."

Liv looked around at all the chrome and glass. "Shall we go someplace else?"

"Let's stay here. I can show all the other diners I'm okay. I can feel them looking at me."

They ordered coffee and laughed at the size of the tiny cups.

"Deary me, it's like a thimble," Carol said, her eyes still pink.

Liv grinned, too, glad her mum felt better. Even so, she couldn't help thinking about why her dad had left her waiting.

When the bill arrived, Carol whipped it off the plate.

"Mum, I'm paying," Liv said, trying to grab it.

Carol held it out of reach. As she unfolded the paper, the color drained from her face. "Oh, my," she gasped. "We'll have to do the washing up."

Liv took it from her and felt like her rib cage was shrinking. Their lunch had cost a fortune, plus had a 15 percent service charge. She hadn't expected it to be so much.

"Blimey," Carol said.

Liv reached down for her handbag and missed the handle. "Don't worry. Essie's been very generous recently," she said, her voice almost a squeak.

"Well, I've got to contribute something." Carol pushed a ten-pound note into her hand. "Get Essie a little bunch of flowers, to say thanks for the table."

After Liv called a taxi and made sure her mum was safely inside, she needed to walk around and get some fresh air. She hated to think there had been some kind of discord between her parents when her dad died.

She wandered around the area, until she got disorientated. When she saw a blue florist sign that said Bloom and Dale, Liv recognized it from the tag on the bouquet of white roses Chloe brought to the apartment. She still had her mum's money in her fist and headed into the shop.

A young woman with tight black curls stood arranging carnations in a bucket. Her name badge said Sam. "Can I help?" she said.

"I'm looking for a small bunch of flowers." Liv looked blankly around the shop, at bunches of red roses, and heart-shaped balloons, thinking she couldn't actually give any of them to Essie.

"I've just made up a few summertime sprays, white roses, carnations and gypsophila They're really cute and only cost nine pounds."

"Perfect. I'll take one."

Sam wrapped patterned paper around the stems and added tape. "Anything else?"

"Actually, yes," Liv said, recalling phoning the florist and how they wouldn't share who'd sent flowers to Essie. She had to think of another way to glean the information. "I believe Bloom and Dale sometimes deliver white roses to the author Essie Starling, but her most recent bouquet didn't come with a message. I'm her assistant and she's asked me to send a thank-you note to the sender."

"Oh." Sam hesitated. "I'm not sure. I'll ask Belle, she's the owner."

At the mention of her name, a woman appeared, clutching a bunch of sunflowers. A multitude of grips pinned up her unruly auburn hair to display her large hooped earrings. "We're really not supposed to give out—" she started.

"I completely understand," Liv said. "But I believe Ms. Starling is a long-standing, valued customer, and she's really keen to say thanks. I can call her, if you like." She gestured to take her phone out of her bag.

Belle paused before holding up a hand. "Please don't bother

her. I'm sure we can make an exception. We're big fans in this shop, absolutely love Essie's books." She took out her order book. "Let's see... Essie Starling. Yes, she usually has white lilies, delivered each week and yes, white roses, twice a year."

Liv sucked in a breath and held it in her chest. Was this finally the moment she discovered the identity of Essie's mystery man?

Belle's laugh tinkled around the shop. "You won't need a postage stamp for the thank-you card," she said.

Liv tilted her head. "What do you mean? Who sends them?"

"Essie orders them for herself."

"Oh." Liv felt redness flourish from her neck, up to the roots of her hair. Damn it, she shouldn't have lied about the thank-you note. She mumbled thanks and turned toward the door.

"Shall I carry on sending them?" Belle called after her.

Liv glanced back over her shoulder. "Um, yes please." She reached out for the doorknob.

"On the same dates?"

Liv stopped with her hand extended. She thought for a moment. Was there any significance to when Essie bought which flowers? Why did she choose roses instead of her usual lilies?" She affected a nonchalant tone. "Can I just check what those dates are?"

"Of course," Belle said. "Here we are, November the first, and a bouquet on June the seventeenth."

The June date must be when Chloe showed up with the flowers, Liv thought to herself. Perhaps she *had* intercepted a deliveryman, to bring them up to the apartment for Essie. Unusually, she had a slight inkling that June might be Essie's birthday month and she checked it out on her phone. Wikipedia confirmed her suspicion, it was listed as June 17. Liv had never heard Essie mention her birthday before or seen cards displayed in her apartment.

"I read somewhere Essie's debut novel was published in November, and she still celebrates it with flowers each year," Belle said.

Liv had a vague recollection of reading the same thing. It was something she'd forgotten about. A small chime went off in her head, telling her the date was significant for her, too. It was the date the manuscript was due, and that Essie requested for her death. And it seemed to be stalking her. Something cold tingled down her spine.

But, too embarrassed to stay any longer, she closed the door behind her and hurried away from the shop.

23

LILAC FINGERNAIL

The next morning, Liv brought her mum's box of photos to Essie's apartment. She put them on the bookshelf, intending to look through them properly when she got the chance. Working on Book Twenty took priority. When she pressed her nose close to the laptop screen, she entered a dreamlike state where time didn't exist. She wasn't aware of Johnny lounging around on the sofa, throwing paper planes around the sitting room while she worked.

At home, she didn't really listen to Jake's chatter about the annual Paperpress staff awards. She absentmindedly promised to be there as usual, but didn't make a note of the date.

She reached two-thirds of her way through the manuscript and was hurtling toward the eight missing chapters. The security of reshaping Essie's existing work was getting ever closer to ending. Meg's words about a film studio waiting for *the one* crunched in her head.

As Liv worked, she pictured the Georgia Rory fans in Croatia folding their arms, waiting and staring at her expectantly.

Georgia felt hundreds of eyes upon her as she stood on her own in the middle of the arena. She heard the gates rattling as bulls jostled together, waiting to charge into the ring. A red cloak rippled, and the crowd roared with expectation. Were they willing her to succeed, or urging her to fail?

The ultimate hero she was developing for Georgia had become a mishmash in Liv's head and she struggled to set him down in words. He was polite and reserved like Anthony, with Sven's good looks, and Ted's wealth and confidence. She gave him a touch of Hank's swagger, even though she hadn't experienced it for herself. Liv also looked to Essie's old characters, Mike the rugged aircraft pilot and James the marine biologist. They each had their appeal, but Liv knew Georgia wouldn't choose them as her greatest love. She crossed their names off her list.

As the deadline crept closer, Liv grew tetchier at her dwindling shortlist. "You're only characters," she hissed at them. "Play ball."

As more time passed by, the end of August arrived and the weather heated up even more. Liv arrived at work with a clammy back and armpits.

By now, her one-a-week paperback habit had dwindled to one a month. She felt nostalgic for the gossipy chatter of her Platinum cleaning friends, and even wiping away Tarker's and Jules's handprints. Life seemed much easier back then. Writing had been a dream rather than a job.

Johnny's start date at university was also creeping closer. He'd soon fly the nest, leaving her and Jake alone in the house. She worried about it almost as much as the deadline to complete Essie's book.

One day, Liv hit a complete mind block and turned to Essie's bookshelf for inspiration. When she spied the edge of a yellow note in a book, she grabbed and opened it. Was it a divine message from the author to spur her on? She opened it and saw Essie had underlined some text on a page.

He was the sentence to her paragraph, the full stop to her words. Without him there could be no story.

Liv loved how the words sounded. This was the passion and loveliness she was searching for. But who did they relate to?

"When are we having lunch, Mum?" Johnny called through from Essie's sitting room, interrupting her thoughts. "I'm starving."

Liv hoped taking a break and eating would give her a shot of energy. She found her son lying on the sofa reading a book. He'd never been a big reader, grumbling when he had to study Shakespeare and Dickens for his English literature exams. "What are you reading?" she said.

He semi-closed it so she could see the cover. "*The Moon on the Water.* Are you proud of me?"

Liv laughed. "It's more constructive than trying to make paper planes."

"I can't stop turning the pages."

"What do you think of the hero?"

Johnny pulled his face. "Dunno," he said. "He's a bit obvious. Handsome, brave and strong. Like a cardboard cutout."

"Isn't that what readers want?"

"I'd pick someone cool, not the usual kind of guy. Shake things up a bit."

Liv decided to give it some thought.

The sun was beating down outside, so she took off her blazer and striped tie before heading out of the apartment to buy lunch.

Her eyes shone when she saw a new bookshop had opened in the city. The Bookshop on the Square had three rooms full of packed shelves, reaching from the floor to the ceiling. Worn velvet armchairs invited readers to sit and read, and there was a coffee shop at the back. She'd have stayed longer if she didn't have a hungry teenager and an unfinished book to write waiting for her.

Five of Essie's books sat in the fiction section and Liv thought they should be displayed more prominently. She slid them off the shelves and looked around her. When she was sure the shop assistants were busy, she gave three of the books new positions on tables, and placed two in the window display. She swallowed a giggle as she left the store.

In a delicatessen, she bought ham and mustard sandwiches, apples, and flapjacks, and clasped the paper bags to her chest. Georgia's hero was still on her mind when she returned to the apartment. In the hallway, she shouted out to Johnny, "Hi, I'm back."

Immediately, her eyes fell upon a curved lilac thing lying on the carpet. She was sure it hadn't been there when she went out.

Holding her lunch under her chin, Liv reached down and picked it up. It was a false nail with a thick white tip. Her body cooled as if her blood had been drained and replaced with mercury. She ordered herself to stay calm.

She entered the sitting room as if in a trance and passed Johnny his lunch. "Did anyone call here while I was out?" she said.

He took out his sandwich, wrinkling his nose at the seeded bread. "Just the estate agent lady," he said.

Liv's throat tightened. An uneasy sensation flooded over her. "*What* estate agent lady?"

Johnny chewed and shrugged a shoulder. "She had this long blond hair and wore jeans and high heels." He eyed his mum. "Don't worry, she took them off in the hallway."

"What *exactly* did she say to you?"

"Just that Essie's selling the apartment and she needed to take photos for the website."

Liv sank down heavily on the sofa. She knew Anthony wouldn't have sent anyone here without telling her first. She was sure the lilac nail belonged to Chloe. An apple rolled out of her bag onto the carpet and she didn't pick it up. Johnny reached down and tossed it to her. It landed in her lap.

Liv imagined Chloe standing behind Buddha in the lobby, watching as she and Johnny arrived, and then Liv leaving on her own at lunchtime. She pictured the journalist smiling smugly to herself and drumming her fingernails in the lift on her way up to the thirty-second floor. She had sweet-talked a teenager with a broken arm into letting her into Essie's apartment.

The more Liv thought about it, the more she seethed. She felt her eyes might fire out sparks. When she grabbed the arm of the sofa and heaved herself back to her feet, the apple bounced onto the floor again.

"*Mum.*" Johnny huffed at her.

"Which rooms did she go into?" Liv said.

"All of them. She said she wouldn't be long." His eyes swept over her. "Is there anything wrong?"

Liv tried to keep an edge out of her voice even though she wanted to scream. "I just wasn't expecting her, that's all. If she calls again, don't let her in. Essie might have some precious things lying around," she added.

"Oh, right. Sorry."

"Hey, it's fine. If she has any questions, I need to be here to answer them."

Liv walked around the apartment with her heart booming in her ears. She tried to see the place through Chloe's eyes.

Liv's old handbag sat in the corner of Essie's bedroom, and

her name was written on the dry-cleaning bags. Her jeans and T-shirt were folded up on the side of the bath. Her son was hanging out on the sofa and his paper planes littered the carpet. Any journalist worth their salt would have spotted all these things and more.

Essie's laptop had a screensaver of floating books, and was also password protected, so there was no way Chloe could access it. Even so, the original handwritten manuscript lay on top of the writing table, and Liv's typed up version sat next to it. It was covered in her handwriting. She ground her teeth as she rejoined Johnny.

"Did the woman go into Essie's writing room?" she said lightly.

"Dunno. Why, what's wrong?"

"Oh, nothing," she said, feeling like she could kill Chloe.

Liv sat down next to Johnny again and tried to eat her sandwich. The bread stuck in her throat and made her cough.

"I nearly forgot," Johnny said. "She asked me to give you a message."

Liv sucked in her breath. "What is it?"

"Um, why didn't Essie show at the book festival? Or something like that. Does that make sense?"

Liv stormed back to the writing room. Her eyes bore into the screen. She kept hearing imaginary sounds and jerked around to see what they were. How had Chloe known Essie was supposed to be attending Dubfest? What else did she know?

She looked around for the striped tie, only to find it had gone. She frantically searched under the desk and around the room. Liv touched her collarbone and pictured Chloe stuffing the tie into the back pocket of her jeans. Did she recognize it from somewhere, or was she trying to mess with her head?

She felt naked without it, as if a piece of Georgia Rory had been snatched from her.

Had Chloe discovered enough pieces of the puzzle to pull a full picture together? How long would it take her to realize Essie hadn't been in the apartment for months? And what would the journalist do with this information? Perhaps the photos in Essie's award room had given her new contacts to approach.

Liv felt so helpless. The apartment was her haven, somewhere she felt safe. And now it had been invaded. Her skin crawled and she wanted to scratch it raw.

Would Chloe dig her talons into Hank next?

Liv googled him once more, looking for information the journalist might have missed. She patiently scrolled through page after page until she found a link to a PR company. Buried among the information, she read,

Hank's Bar.
VIP private opening. Invitation only.
Thursday, September 5.

Bingo.

It was only a week away and she congratulated herself for finding it.

Liv felt like she'd discovered a twenty-pound note in an old handbag. She smiled to herself and noted the date down so she wouldn't forget it.

However, when she tried to work on Book Twenty again, words stuck in her head and refused to come out. It felt like Chloe had broken some kind of spell.

24

MARKET STALLS

When Anthony finally arrived back from Bologna, he messaged Liv, asking to meet her at the Pentecost and Wilde offices. Liv arrived too early and meandered around outside the cream stone building for a while. There was an engraved brass plaque on the wall and three besuited men talked together in the reception area. It all looked very stuffy. Anthony had been gone for two and a half months and she wondered if he'd be pleased to see her or not.

Liv kept glancing at her watch and struggled to breathe in the early September heat. After Chloe's intrusion, she couldn't bear the thought of being hemmed into a small meeting room. She fingered the scarf she wore around her neck. It belonged to Essie and its tag made her itch.

Market stalls stretched along the road in front of the building. She could smell watermelon-scented soap, and glass beads glittered as they hung down from an umbrella. A busker played something by Arcade Fire on his guitar, with a terrier at his feet. People sat in striped deck chairs to listen to him and tossed pieces of bread to the dog.

Liv wiped her forehead with her hand and texted Anthony.

Can we meet in the market instead? I'll be near the hot dog stand.

I'll be there in 10, he replied.

Liv's stomach growled when she saw people carrying hot dogs striped with ketchup and mustard, but her nerves meant she couldn't face eating one. She sat down in a deck chair and soon glimpsed a cobalt jacket weaving through the crowds toward her.

"Gosh, it's hot," Anthony said.

"I know. I needed some fresh air," she said. "Is your father-in-law okay? And Harriet?"

"He's doing well." His eyes flicked away.

And your wife? Liv wanted to ask, but didn't.

"How are you getting along?" he said.

She attempted a smile. "Oh, you know, the usual. Frantic, confused, working hard, lying to my family..."

He smiled sympathetically. "I do know that feeling, and I'm sure you're coping admirably."

"I'm trying," she said. "But I'm running out of time...for everything."

"There are two months left." He loosened his tie. "Will you complete the book?"

"I'm determined to. For Essie's sake, and all her readers. And because I'll lose my inheritance if I don't." She eyed him for a reaction, but his face was expressionless. "It's strange that Essie gave me something, and also threatened to snatch it away..."

Anthony didn't speak. He tilted his face toward sunshine.

She wished she could twist a key in his back to make him more animated. "Time's moving on," she said, making a ticking motion with her arm. "What happens when the deadline is up?"

It was a question that made her toss and turn in bed at night. When the news of Essie's death was set free, would she have to return to the recruitment office, or beg the Cardinals for her job back? Essie's book would be complete, and no one would know about her huge contribution. Like Cinderella at the stroke of midnight, would her new world turn back to rags?

"I'll probably be in a position to share the contents of Essie's will with you before her death is announced," Anthony said. "I'll work on her obituary, too."

Liv recalled his attempt to write a sonnet and pursed her lips. "It sounds like you've thought of everything. Will there be any kind of service, or a celebration of her life?"

"No. She wouldn't have wanted that," he said. "Now, tell me about this journalist. Is she still snooping around?"

Liv pictured the lilac acrylic fingernail lying on Essie's hallway carpet and Chloe prowling around the apartment. "Everything's fine," she said, not meeting his eyes. "Nothing to worry about."

"Good. Well done for sorting it out," he said.

Liv's face felt hot, as if sunburnt. "Do you remember I mentioned Dubfest to you, the book festival in Croatia?" she said.

"Ah, yes. That."

When he didn't admit to attending, Liv took the phone from her bag. "I found a photo on the website of you and Essie." She acted breezily, showing it to him.

Anthony took the phone. He stared at it for a long time until his jaw cricked.

"How did you really know her?" she said. "This was taken a long time ago. You both look very *friendly*. I also found these..." She took the green leather cuff link box from her pocket and opened the lid.

Anthony's face glowered when he saw the gold bees. Liv thought steam might puff from his nose.

"Are they yours?" she said.

"No. They are definitely *not* mine," he said brusquely. "You're as persistent as Georgia Rory."

"Thank you. But how would you know?" Liv raised an eyebrow and pushed the cuff links back in her pocket. "You said you'd only read one of Essie's books. You didn't seem to remember it very well."

Anthony blinked up at the sky. Eventually he rattled a laugh. "You're right," he said. "I did say that."

"You're still not sure why Essie chose me, are you?"

"I'm getting to *see* why. You have a very good eye for detail."

"Shark blood senses." She nodded. "When Essie left the task for me, I could tell you were suspicious. Perhaps I wanted to know why she trusted *you*, too."

"I understand that now."

"So, how did you really know her?"

Anthony wiped his brow and took a few moments to gather his thoughts. "I can still remember the precise moment I first saw Elsbeth," he said, glancing at Liv. "We met at university. I hadn't been studying law long when I walked past a group of girls. They sat on the grass eating sandwiches. Elsbeth's hair was black, cut into a sharp bob. It was rather old-fashioned and somehow modern at the same time. She had bright orange lips, and there was just something very different about her. She…sparkled.

"One of her friends caught me staring and tossed a slice of tomato at me. It skimmed my shirt and left pips on the shoulder." He rolled his eyes, not impressed. "Elsbeth ran over and apologized. She promised to buy me a drink, if we ever met again. Then, a couple of days later, I saw her in a student bar and we got talking. Her eyes were full of passion and determination. She had such a clear vision about what she wanted from life, to bring stories to people. When she said she was writing a book, I knew it would be a success."

Liv detected longing in his words. "So...you did love her," she said.

Anthony nodded. "Very much so. I fell deeply," he said. "We were both eighteen. We sat on her bed together at night and played records until we fell asleep. She loved The Cure and New Order. I'd wake in the morning and find her scribbling beside me. She read everything she wrote aloud to me. I encouraged her submission letters and consoled her through many rejections. She said I was her rock, the most dependable person she knew."

His description reminded Liv of the early days of her relationship with Jake, when they couldn't get enough of each other.

"I remember her shrieking with delight when her book offer came through and we danced together on the bed. By then, we were in our third year at uni. We were very much a couple...and then we weren't."

"What do you mean?" Liv said, finding it difficult to imagine Anthony acting with such enthusiasm. "What happened?"

He shrugged. "It's all ancient history."

"I'd still like to know."

He cast her a look. "I thought you were a cleaner, not an archaeologist."

"I'm a good multitasker."

Anthony closed his eyes, thinking back in time again. "Things changed between me and Elsbeth over the last few months we were together. She became more furtive and distant, said she was changing her name to Essie Starling. She started to hang out with other writers. They wore biker jackets and drank too much, not my kind of people. I thought I saw her with someone else. They were standing close together under a tree, I'm not completely sure. I tried hard to save *us*.

"She invited me to her publication party for *The Moon on*

the Water, but I could tell it was out of habit, maybe even duty. I decided not to go.

"I think she was in love with someone else by then, but wouldn't tell me who it was. After university we went our separate ways for several years. We kept in touch sporadically, more due to my effort than hers. I followed her career from afar and was astonished when she married Ted Mason. How can you know someone so well, then feel like they're a stranger? Ted was much older and more experienced than me. I wondered if he was the other guy…"

"I've met Ted. I don't think he's the love of Essie's life."

He smiled, as if grateful. "Essie and I got back in touch after her divorce. We became friends again. I hoped in time we might, ah…" He sighed to himself. "But she married Hank Milligan next. And I met Harriet."

His voice slipped when he said his wife's name.

"I told you the truth, about working for Essie," he added. "She contacted me out of the blue, a few years ago. She asked me to be her solicitor and I agreed. We had a purely business relationship. I was one of the few people she trusted. It was disconcerting to see how much she'd changed. But there were still flashes of Elsbeth…" He smiled to himself.

Something fluttered in Liv's stomach. "You were *still* in love with her?"

He opened his mouth to deny it before letting his shoulders fall. "Yes," he said. "I was."

Liv felt like a tight flower bud had opened, revealing its petals.

"I'm getting divorced," Anthony said. "It's something Harriet and I have been discussing for some time. I supported her through her father's heart scare, and hoped we might get back together. But her mind is made up. I tried to hide my feelings for Essie and obviously did a poor job. Harriet called it an *emotional affair*. She's probably right."

Liv thought for a while. Lots of things made more sense now, Anthony's evasiveness when she first met him, and how he wanted to say goodbye to Essie on his own.

Matilda said Essie drank too much and yearned for the only man she ever loved. Had the author been full of regret about how she treated Anthony? Was he out of reach because he was married to Harriet? Perhaps Liv had finally found Essie's mystery love, even if the solicitor wasn't a perfect template for Georgia Rory's hero.

"I'm glad Essie was with someone she loved at the end," she said.

Anthony placed his hand on hers. It felt warm and protective, two people connected in a moment rather than anything romantic. And Liv welcomed it. At that moment in time, she felt closer to Anthony than she did to Jake.

"I'd love to think that, too," he said. "But I'd only be lying to you, and to myself. Essie hadn't loved me for a long time. Not in that way. It was a one-sided affair, if you can even call it that. I was never enough for her, and I've always wondered who really captured her heart."

As Liv sat with his hand still touching hers, she felt a vein pulsing in his wrist and asked herself the same thing. Did it mean Hank Milligan was the only contender left for the title of Essie's greatest love? He was married to her for ten years, and by her side the night she won the Constellation Prize. Would he know why she dropped out of the public eye? In order to finally tie up the loose ends of the mystery, and to write the end to Georgia's story, Liv needed to speak to him. He just might be the missing link to it all.

25

PINE TREES

That night, Liv lay in bed listening to Jake snoring gently beside her. She marveled at how soundly he could sleep, whereas her thoughts wouldn't settle. When she closed her eyes, faceless figures chased her through mazes, up never-ending spiral staircases. She slept intermittently, sometimes not knowing if she was awake or not. When she buried her head in the pillow, different scenarios scuttled around in her mind.

What if Anthony didn't announce Essie's death at all? Did anyone actually need to know the author was dead? It would only distress and disappoint her fans. Could they both keep silent about the author's death forever? Perhaps Liv could continue to do Essie's admin and also write her books. There could be a Book Twenty-one and Twenty-two, and readers would love it. Anthony said he was Essie's rock. Perhaps he might want to keep her spirit alive, too. In Liv's hazy state, it all felt possible.

However, as dawn broke and the bedroom filled with gray light, she was groggy and tired. She realized she'd been thinking crazily and her brain tossed new thoughts around instead. Would the inheritance from Essie allow her to carry on writing instead of cleaning? And what would she write? She'd been dedicating her life to Georgia Rory. What would Liv be without her?

As the bedroom grew even lighter, Jake began to shuffle around, and she got up and made toast and jam for breakfast.

Outside, the sky was gloomy. Rain specked the windows and dripped off trees. Liv put on a dress and blazer, adding black tights.

When she reached the apartment block, Liv stood on the pavement for a while and surveyed all the people milling around outside. Most of them were heading to their jobs, walking with impetus. She thought how her own purpose might end on November the first.

She flashed her electronic fob and entered the building, yawning as the lift doors started to close.

But then a hand appeared in the gap, followed by the toe of a snakeskin shoe. There was a flash of caramel hair as Chloe pushed the doors back open. "Hey, hon. Remember me?" She smirked, positioning herself in front of the button panel so Liv couldn't reach it. "Fancy seeing you here."

Liv stepped back and pressed her back against the glass. The doors closed again and the lift shot upward.

Chloe looked composed in a Breton striped top, jeans and red lipstick. "There seems to be something missing from your outfit," she said, tapping a finger against her lips. "Oh, perhaps it's a tie." She took the one missing from Essie's desk out of her handbag, slipping it through her fingers as if playing with a toy snake.

Liv touched her neck, which felt bare. "You lied to my teenage son and trespassed on private property," she said. "How does that make you feel?"

"Hey, don't be like that. I didn't know he was your son. You don't look old enough to have a kid that age." The journalist's lips straightened. "You act all high-and-mighty, but I heard you went to Croatia, supposedly with Essie. One of your bedrooms wasn't slept in."

Liv's mind spun. How did Chloe know this? Did she have a contact at the hotel? She kept her lips sealed.

"You can't blame me for being interested. Shall we get a coffee and chat?"

"Why would I want to do that?" Liv snapped.

Chloe's smile displayed a hint of menace. "Because I know *everything*, hon," she said.

Liv crept a hand to her stomach. What did she mean by *everything*?

Chloe stabbed the button for the twenty-ninth floor and the lift shuddered to a halt. When the doors opened, she stepped through them and jerked her head. "Are you coming, or not?"

Liv snatched the tie out of Chloe's hand and fastened it around her neck. "Yes, let's go," she said.

Three people were busy setting out long tables with white cloths in the open space. Wire arches were covered with pink, white and lilac silk flowers, in preparation for a party or wedding reception. The room was on the opposite side of the building to Essie's writing room, so the view from the windows was more industrial. Liv saw the canal, warehouse buildings, cranes and a freight train.

Chloe spoke to a man in a red T-shirt and pointed toward a roof terrace with large ferns and a glass roof. He nodded, gesturing she was free to use it.

Chloe located a table. She pulled out a chair and Liv sat down opposite her. She noticed a glass square embedded in the floor, giving a view of a sheer drop down to the streets below. It lured her toward it, tempting her to jump.

"It's a private bar for residents," Chloe said. "I've been here a few times."

Liv frowned at her. "How do you get inside the building?"

"A smile gets you most places. I talk to people. The security guys love to chat about their dogs, kids, wives or whatever." She rolled her eyes. "I told one I'd lost my fob and he gave me a new one. I'm very enterprising."

"I'd call it deceptive."

Chloe raised an eyebrow. "Well, you should know all about *that*," she said.

Liv thought about taking over Essie's suite in Croatia. Maybe she and the journalist were more similar than she thought.

The man in the red T-shirt carried over two bottles of Diet Coke and glasses filled with ice cubes. Chloe smiled thanks to him. "No coffee, but this is nice," she said to Liv, pouring their drinks. "Now, where were we?"

Liv lifted her glass. "You were telling me how you sneak into the building and lie to people."

Chloe sighed. "You're very theatrical for a cleaner, or assistant, or whatever you do for Essie."

Liv's fingertips turned cold from the ice. "Tell me what you *think* you know," she demanded.

The journalist drummed her fingernails on the table. "Not quite yet." She looked at Liv like she was a cat toying with an injured bird. "Tell me more about you. What's it like working with Essie?"

Liv felt she had no choice but to share a few details. She had to find a way to keep the journalist on side, while also throwing her off the trail. She noticed Chloe had a tiny speech mark tattoo on her right wrist. Liv had an ampersand one on her left shoulder blade that she got for her fortieth birthday.

"Three years ago, Essie was looking for a cleaner and I got the job," she said. "I'd always loved her books and working that close to her felt special. I'd always wanted to write too..."

Chloe sipped her drink. "How old were you, when you knew that?"

"Seven or eight. I read all the time."

"Hmm, me, too. I've wanted to write for as long as I can remember. I love knowing how people tick. What life experiences shape them."

"Which ones shaped you?" Liv asked.

"Nice try, hon. I'm the journalist here."

"I just wondered why you want to dig around other people's lives."

Chloe took a strand of hair and wrapped it around her finger. "I only ask the questions people want answers to. Why doesn't Essie do publicity any longer, or go to award ceremonies? One minute she's married to a hot fellow writer, and the next she goes all Howard Hughes. So, who's the real Essie?"

Liv bristled. "She's just a normal person."

"Normal. Ha, right," Chloe said. "As normal as a famous recluse can be."

Liv didn't want to get into a battle of words. She could spar with Chloe all day, and it wouldn't get her anywhere. "How's your article going?" she said. "How do these things work?"

The journalist tilted her head. "I come up with ideas, discuss them with my editor and work on several stories at a time. I'm hooked on this one, though. My friend the security guy has never spoken to Essie in the ten years she's lived here. He sees her scurrying out of the building sometimes, and into a taxi. She returns after a few days. But he hasn't seen her for months..."

"I've told you, she's working away. Just what is it you want?"

"The story that makes my career," Chloe said. "I don't have any formal qualifications or training. I'm fed up watching everyone advance around me, while I'm not getting anywhere quick."

Liv knew the feeling from working at Platinum and for

THE MESSY LIVES OF BOOK PEOPLE

the Cardinals. She felt a slight buzz that Chloe hadn't been to university either.

"I've got quotes about Essie that have been used before. I get titbits from someone at Peregrine, and a disgruntled ex-assistant. I've written a lot of my piece but need something bigger and fresher." Chloe pursed her lips self-assuredly. "And I'm pretty sure I've found it."

Liv saw ambition glinting in her eyes. It was something she'd started to feel for herself, too. She circled her glass so the ice cubes rattled. "What is it?" she said.

"Well, hon." Chloe met her eyes. She made the silence that followed feel like forever. "I *know* you've been ghostwriting for Essie. I have evidence. Now I'd like to hear it from you. What's the full story?"

Liv's mind spun like a toy windmill. If Chloe thought she was writing for Essie, perhaps that wasn't too bad. If she denied anything, Chloe would dig even deeper. She had to play things tactically. "Oh," she said, pretending to look ashamed. *"That."*

"Sorry. Game over. What will Essie's readers make of it?" Chloe sang. "I've got my story."

Liv paused for a moment, letting Chloe think she'd won. She repositioned the knot in her tie. Georgia Rory wouldn't give in to pressure, and neither would she. "I look after Essie's place while she works away. After three decades of writing, she needs a bit of help now and again with her editing. She has the ideas, and does most of the work. I help out a little, and that's it. I don't think you have anything at all."

Chloe sat up straighter. "I saw two manuscripts. Two sets of handwriting. You virtually live in her apartment. Why was there a man's tie on Essie's desk?"

"I'm sorry. You have nothing." Liv knew she'd have to dangle a carrot to get the journalist off her back. She couldn't risk her accessing the apartment again, or sniffing anything else out. Thinking quickly, she said, "We could do a trade."

Chloe narrowed her eyes. "*What* trade? An interview with Essie?"

Liv didn't want to answer questions on behalf of the author. She refused to divulge anything Ted, Sven or Anthony had shared with her. Hank Milligan's PR people had never got back in touch with her about her email.

The opening of Hank's new UK bar was in a couple of days' time, and she wondered if Chloe knew about it. A plan dropped in her head she wasn't sure she could deliver.

"Essie won't do an interview, but what if I can get you fresh material?" she said enticingly. "Quotes from someone close to Essie. Someone important..."

Chloe leaned closer. Her breath quickened. "You mean Hank Milligan? He's never spoken about Essie publicly before. There are rumors he paid off a journalist. Do you know why?"

Liv shrugged enigmatically. She didn't know anything about this. If she did get anything from Hank, she'd be discreet about what she passed onto Chloe.

"A confirmed quote?" Chloe said. "What's the deal in return?"

Liv finished her drink and set her glass firmly down on the table. "You don't publish *anything* until November the first."

Chloe thought about this. "Why then?"

"Essie's new book will be finished."

Chloe stroked a thumb across her tattoo. "Can you get me an excerpt? I'll make sure it gets great exposure. And I'd love to read it, too, of course."

Liv relaxed a little, glad she'd fallen for the bait, though she still didn't trust Chloe entirely. If Liv could access Hank, she might be able to keep the journalist away long enough to finish the novel. Perhaps she could share her own writing with her, rather than Essie's. "One step at a time," she said. "What's more important to you? Pulling strands together and not knowing if they're true, or fresh information and an exclusive excerpt? You might also want to think about a new angle for the article, too."

"Why?"

"Instead of writing something that Essie will hate, why not focus on Georgia Rory?"

Chloe arched an eyebrow. "And why would I do that?"

"Essie saw herself in her heroine," Liv said. "That's how she reached out and touched her readers. The fandom for Georgia is huge. If you write about Essie you'll be using old material, trying to weave snippets together into something threadbare, even if I get quotes from Hank. Why don't you write about what Georgia means to readers, and why people love her? Talk to her fans and publish their stories. You'll find more passion and adventure there than anything in Essie's life over the past ten years. Combined with Hank's quote and a small excerpt, you've got your scoop."

Chloe eyed her. "Readers still want to know why Essie disappeared from the public eye, hon."

"But isn't that part of Essie's allure and mystery? You really want to spoil that? Sometimes you don't want a story to end."

Chloe looked out of the window. The sunlight made her irises look translucent. Liv wasn't sure what she was thinking.

Eventually, the journalist stuck out a slim hand. "You've got a deal."

Liv stared at it. "How can I trust you?"

"Sometimes, you've got to take a chance in life, hon. What's your alternative?"

If this was a boxing match, Liv might place Chloe at a few points ahead of her. But there were still several rounds to go before a knockout. She wasn't sure who would win. She stuck out her hand and shook Chloe's. "Deal," she said.

Liv took three flights of stairs up to Essie's apartment. As she entered the writing room, she needed to create some kind of order in her mind and felt the need to clean.

There weren't any fresh ingredients in Essie's fridge or kitchen cupboards to mix her own solutions, so Liv grabbed some antibacterial wipes from the store cupboard and set to work.

After she'd finished, the apartment smelled of fake pine trees and she blocked out the thought of Essie shaking her head with disapproval. Liv had more important things on her mind. Like how she could engineer a meeting with Hank Milligan.

She spent the afternoon reading anything she could about him, studying his photos with Essie again and looking him up online. Hank only used social media to promote his books, and the photos his second wife posted on Instagram shielded their two kids' faces from view.

She finally found a recent shot of the family at a baseball game. Hank's daughter looked to be around six, and his son perhaps nine or ten. Liv hummed to herself and ran a quick calculation in her head. Hank's boy must have been conceived soon after his split with Essie…or perhaps even earlier. The possibility took root in her head.

Liv could go along to the opening night of Hank's Bar, maybe even gain access and stand at the bar. But how could she get Essie's good-looking, famous ex-husband to notice an ordinary fortysomething mum of two?

26

WHISKEY GLASS

On the evening of Hank's bar launch, Liv shaved her legs in the bath. She tied her dressing gown belt and bumped into Jake in their bedroom.

He wore a navy suit and fiddled with the top button of his shirt. When he saw her, he lifted his chin. "Does my tie look neat?" he said.

In that split second, Liv remembered the Paperpress awards were taking place that evening. She cursed herself for forgetting. She'd pledged to make more effort with Jake and was falling at a first hurdle. "Yes, it looks fine," she said, wondering if her words sounded strangled.

He glanced at his watch. "Are you nearly ready? We don't want to be late."

"Um, about that," she said, dreading her next words. "Sorry, but I have to work tonight."

He stared at her in disbelief. "Are you kidding me? It's Thursday evening. This has been in the diary for weeks."

"I need to help Essie with something last minute. I go to the awards each year. No one will miss me." She remembered last year's ceremony when Katrina ignored her all night. Jake and his parents were busy, too, laying out the buffet and lining up the awards. Liv's offers to help were batted away, so she ate cold sausage rolls and made small talk with the Paperpress employees instead.

"*I'll* miss you," he said coolly. "And my parents."

"I can't get out of this," she said.

He stormed out of the room, glancing back at her over his shoulder with such disdain it cut her to the core. "Whatever," he said.

And the thing was, she didn't *want* to get out of anything. She wanted to see Hank and find out his part in Essie's story. She felt like she couldn't write the end of Book Twenty without knowing what tore the couple apart.

Ten minutes later, Jake left the house without saying goodbye.

Liv looked in her wardrobe mirror and straightened her back. She felt like there was an invisible rope wrapped around her waist, pulling her toward Hank. She was sure he'd be surrounded by his management team, hangers-on and fans. How could she stand out from the crowd? Opening her wardrobe, she stared dolefully at an AC/DC T-shirt and her jeans. She ran a hair through her half-highlighted hair and had an idea.

She took a taxi to a city center hair salon. After an hour in the creative director's chair, she left with a new shiny bob, similar to Essie's style. All her blond streaks were now cut out, and her hair was a rich, walnut brown.

At Essie's apartment, she changed into the blue dress with embroidered birds. She applied orange lipstick, slipped on dark sunglasses and studied herself in the mirror. It felt thrilling to see a younger version of Essie staring back at her.

"Quite," Liv said to her reflection.

At Hank's Bar a blonde woman wearing denim shorts and a

T-shirt with prison bars printed on it, stood at the door holding a clipboard. "Name?" she said, as if for the thousandth time.

Liv pushed the sunglasses up her nose. "Essie Starling," she said.

The woman lowered her clipboard. Her eyes widened. "Really? Wow," she said. "You want me to go tell Hank?"

Liv shook her head. "Let's keep it as our little surprise."

The woman grinned and rubber-stamped the back of Liv's hand. "It feels weird to be saying this, but... Welcome to Hank's for a criminally good time," she said. "Any chance of a photo with you?"

"Maybe later." Liv waved a hand and swept inside.

The main room of the bar had red walls displaying framed photos of infamous criminals. Liv was about to say hi to a woman she thought she recognized. She stopped, realizing she'd seen her in a reality show that set up unsuspecting distant relatives on blind dates.

The bar soon flooded with people, many of them pretty young women who didn't typically look like Essie Starling readers. She was glad not many people actually knew what writers looked like. Soon, all Liv could see around her were the tops of people's heads. She kept on her dark glasses.

A young barman placed a glass in front of her, and poured purple liquid from a pitcher. "Care for a free drink?" he said. "Our Jack the Ripper cocktail."

Liv needed some liquid courage and took a sip. She could still feel Jake's disappointment rippling through her.

"Good stuff, huh?" he said.

"If you like rocket fuel." She tried not to cough.

"Nice to see a mature lady in here," the barman said with a wink. "You on your own?"

The word *mature* made Liv feel like Stilton cheese. She took off her sunglasses and emulated one of Essie's steely stares. "Yes, by choice," she said.

He skulked away, leaving the pitcher with her.

Liv hitched herself up on a high stool. The last time she'd been anywhere like this was for her thirtieth birthday. The cleaning team she worked with at the time had dragged her to a nightclub with a sticky floor and music so loud it made her chest thump. She danced all night until her feet were covered with blisters. She'd felt too old for that kind of night out, even then.

After Liv had been sitting at the bar and sipping purple booze for over an hour, there was still no sign of Hank. The pitcher was now half-empty, and she was regretting not going to the Paperpress staff awards.

Suddenly, there was a microphone screech. Everyone in the bar crunched their shoulders to their ears. Liv slid off her stool, stood on her tiptoes and saw a flash of red shirt and a denim jacket.

It's him, she thought and her stomach jumped. She tried to edge her way closer, but the crowd was a wall of bodies.

"Hey y'all, thanks for joining me tonight," Hank said. "Hank's Bar is open for a criminally good time. Hang out, don't get arrested, and grab a beer or three." He launched into a speech for ten minutes, about how it was his dream to have lots of Hank's Bars across the UK and the USA.

Camera flashes went off and two huge bodyguards flanked him when he left the microphone.

Liv sank back onto her heels. She blew out her cheeks. Her chances of getting close to him were zero. The DJ turned up the music and the bar grew even busier. The floor vibrated beneath her feet and she became more hemmed in, unable to move. Someone knocked her elbow and another person trod on her toe. When she felt a splash of liquid on her shin, she'd had enough. She jostled her way through the crowd and eventually found the nearest exit. She pushed outside and gulped in the fresh air, glad to feel cool speckles of rain on her face.

There was an argument going on outside. Two men raised their voices. One gestured with his fist and stormed toward her. Liv shrank back to let him past.

The remaining man stood alone and stared up at the sky. He raised his glass to his lips and took a long drink. Liv almost fainted when she realized it was Hank. She stayed with her back pressed against the wall, not quite able to believe she was standing only a few meters away from Essie's ex-husband. His tan skin was handsomely creased, reminding her of the rich leather covers of old books.

Gradually, he became aware of her presence. "Hey, doll," he said, with a slight slur in his voice. "You okay?"

Liv held her breath. She stroked her bobbed hair, slipped on Essie's sunglasses again and stepped out of the shadows to stand before him.

Hank looked at her briefly before doing a double take. He barked a surprised laugh. "Jeez, you look like someone I know."

A voice in Liv's head told her to go home, but she wanted to talk to him more. "I hope it's someone you like," she said.

As they faced each other, the raindrops grew heavier. Hank's eyes didn't leave her, sweeping over her clothes and hair. "You're getting soaked." He shrugged off his denim jacket and draped it around her shoulders. His short shirtsleeves showed off his biceps, and Liv realized she had never seen him wearing long sleeves in any photos. He'd have no need for bee-shaped cuff links, and Essie had commissioned them a long time before she'd even met Hank.

"You should get back inside," he said.

Liv shook her head. "It's too busy in there," she said. She

couldn't believe she was actually turning down his offer. But her feet were sore and the rocket fuel was kicking in, making her light-headed.

"I know a place," he said. "Come with me."

"Where?"

"Don't worry. I don't bite." Hank held out his hand. "Got me a VIP zone."

He was every bit as magnetic as his author photos. Liv let him lead her through a door.

As Hank reentered the bar, people parted like the Red Sea. He made his way to a raised area. Someone moved a rope, and Hank and Liv sat on a squishy red leather sofa together. Hank repositioned himself closer to her, so his outer thigh nearly touched hers. She surreptitiously inched away. Two glasses of whiskey appeared from nowhere.

"You sure look like Essie Starling," Hank said. "You know her?"

"I actually work with her. She lent me these clothes."

He twitched an eyebrow. "Yeah? What's your name?"

"Liv. Olivia Green."

"Hey, right." He nodded, tipping his glass toward her. "Yeah, I heard of you."

Liv's heart almost leaped out of her body. "You have?"

"Ess mentioned you."

"You still talk to her?"

"Rarely." He smiled wryly. "Wish it was more often."

"She doesn't speak to many people."

"Yep. Have to trick her into taking my calls. Got unfinished business, me and Ess…"

Liv wondered what it was. She was more amazed that she'd been a topic of Essie and Hank's conversation. "What did she say about me?"

Hank swigged his drink. "Can't recall much. Ess said someone worked for her, name of Olivia. Said you guys got along. 'Fraid that's all I got."

Liv felt flames of curiosity ignite inside her. "Please try," she said, trying not to sound desperate.

He frowned and shook his head. "Nope, don't know. She likes you, though. Ess don't trust many people. Couldn't trust me," he laughed, until his face gradually stilled. "Jeez, I loved that woman."

There was something sweet and open about him. Liv could tell he'd be devastated to learn of Essie's death in eight weeks' time. She felt the need to comfort him. "She must have loved you, too," she said. "She left England to be with you."

"That surprises you, huh? We're totally different people, right?"

Liv nodded, but she could see how sparks might fly between them. "How did you both meet?"

He circled his glass. "At a book launch of mine in London. We got talking and she was a real lady. Classy. They say opposites attract, and they did. I went home with her that night and felt like I never wanted to leave her. Ess'd had enough of the UK, so I invited her over to LA. Life was fun for a long time." Ice clinked against his teeth when he drank his whiskey.

"You've never talked to the press about your life together. That's noble," she said.

"It's the least I can do," Hank murmured. He stared into his glass.

"And you've remarried and have a family now?"

"Yep, moved on. A wife and two great kids," he said briskly. "How's Ess? Is she good?"

Liv didn't want to lie to him. After hearing how Ted and Sven tried to shape Essie, Hank sounded truly invested. "She's been struggling a little recently, with her health and work."

"I was afraid that might be the case." He shook his head.

"Wish I'd never coaxed her along to that damn Constellation thing."

Liv lowered her whiskey. It sounded like Hank recognized the awards were the catalyst for Essie's downturn, too. "I always wondered what happened that night," she said gently. "It was a highlight of her career, yet she was never seen in public again. Why did you have to persuade her to go?"

"Will telling you make me feel better?" He sighed.

"I suppose that's for you to decide," she said.

Another couple of glasses arrived. Hank nodded thanks to the server and refocused on Liv. "Ess always had this thing with dates. You've noticed, right?"

Liv nodded.

"She got a tip-off she'd won the award 'bout a week before. She was real proud readers had voted for her. But then she found out the date of the event was November the first. Her debut novel had been published that day, twenty years earlier. Ess was supposed to hold a big old party to celebrate back then, but something went wrong and it didn't happen. She was wary the Constellations were being held on the same date." He shrugged a shoulder. "We were struggling with some personal stuff in our lives and drinking more than we should. It made Ess paranoid about that kind of thing. I told her it was a chance to change the meaning of the date, and encouraged her to go."

"I saw footage and photos from the ceremony. You look so proud."

"Heck, I sure was. We both hit the champagne real hard and had a great time." He grinned. Then his smile slid away. He gulped his whiskey and glanced at Liv. "Everyone wanted a piece of her, especially the press. They wanted a piece of me even more."

Liv saw Hank's hand shake as he put down his glass. "Journalists?" she said, remembering Chloe's speculation that Hank had paid one off.

"You work with Ess. You're close to her, right?" he said, as if asking her permission to say more.

Liv didn't nod or say anything. She wanted him to speak freely of his own accord.

He ran his hand through his hair. "Some hack got Ess's ear. Told her I cheated on her." He let out the saddest sigh. "It was the worst."

Liv's stomach rolled. Had she found Essie's greatest love, but he'd stamped on her heart? "And did you cheat?" she said.

"I wouldn't call it that." Eyes glistening, Hank looked up at the ceiling and cleared his throat. "One night, me and Ess had been drinking again. We rowed, y'know? It happened sometimes. I went out and drank some more in a bar. I ended up going home with some girl. Had so much whiskey I don't even remember it. Except she..." He chewed his bottom lip.

"She got pregnant?" Liv added quietly. She thought about the photo of Hank and his family at the baseball match. "I read a quote that said Essie hoped to have children one day."

Hank didn't look up. "We tried for years and nothing worked. Drinking helped to numb the pain."

Liv pursed her lips. "How old is your son?" she said.

Hank's eyes flickered. "Did Ess tell you anything? She said she'd never—"

"No, not Essie," Liv said, realizing she'd stumbled upon something Hank had been hiding from the world. "I worked out some dates."

"Jeez." He dug his hand into his hair. "Well, yeah. You got me... The girl got back in touch and told me she was having a baby. Ess and I were still very much together and I hated myself. I decided to keep it from her, not my greatest idea. I told the girl I'd support her, but asked her to keep quiet..."

"I'm sorry," Liv said. And she was. For both Hank and Essie.

"This stuff's been eating me up for years. It feels good to speak to someone Ess trusts," Hank said. "Some journo found out the girl was pregnant and tried blackmailing me. I denied it, tried to brazen it out. Except the same hack was at the Constellation after-party and he told Ess before I did.

"It was her chance to shine, rewrite history for that date, and I ruined it. I humiliated her. She refused to come back to LA with me, left all her stuff behind in our home. Wouldn't even talk to our friends anymore. I ended up paying off the journo so nothing came out."

Liv winced. She imagined Essie's devastation at her husband cheating and fathering a baby behind her back. But was it enough for the author to hide herself away for ten years afterward? "What happened then?" she said.

"I tried to do the right thing. Ess got a quickie divorce and I married the girl before our son was born. We said he'd arrived prematurely, to avoid embarrassment for Ess. I was a real mess over losing her for a long time, even checked myself into rehab. My wife's been real patient with me."

"And you're happy?" Liv said. She really wanted him to say yes. He'd made a terrible mistake and regretted it for a decade. She could see he loved Essie.

"I love being a dad. Only wish it had happened in a different way, wish I hadn't been so weak."

They sat still together while bodies jiggled on the dance floor. Lots of people eyed Hank and he didn't notice.

"There's a journalist snooping around, wanting to write a story about Essie," Liv said. "I've suggested she write about Georgia Rory instead. I think a quote or two from you might seal the deal."

"A journo? Jeez... I hate 'em." Hank's lips twisted. He slugged his whiskey. "Will it help Ess?"

"Yes, and me, too."

"Sure. I love Ess. Always did, always will. I just happened to be stupid that one night." He took a business card from his pocket and passed it to Liv. "Put the words in my mouth, whatever you need. Send them my way to approve."

After draining his glass, Hank leaned in so close Liv felt the front of his hair brush hers. He looked deeply into her eyes. "I'm sorry," he said, as if he was speaking to Essie. "Forgive me, doll."

Liv felt his breath on her lips and her skin tingled all over. Every hair on her arms and neck lifted as he grew even closer. It had been so long since she felt this desirable. Just another few millimeters and their lips might touch. Fire flooded her body.

She closed her eyes. *This isn't for you*, she told herself. *Stop.* Another tiny part of her wanted him to carry on.

"You're forgiven," she whispered, to break the moment.

Hank kissed her lightly on the cheek, catching the side of her mouth. "Thanks, Ess," he said blearily.

As he pulled away, Liv swallowed and took hold of her bag. She quickly stood up. She felt like a bird who'd flown too close to the sun and singed its feathers. "I should go," she said.

"Hey, stay awhile. Please."

She shook her head. "I'm sorry, I can't." She was afraid of her own feelings.

Someone moved the rope for her and her heart galloped as she rushed away. She glanced back at Hank and he smiled sadly at her.

She returned it and saw his head tip forward a little.

In the taxi home, Liv wiped off most of her makeup and mussed her hair out of its bob. The house was dark, so she could slip out of her dress without Jake noticing it.

When she climbed into bed, her husband was already asleep. Liv lay awake for the longest time. The purple alcohol, whiskey and Hank's kiss were ingrained in her mind, making her head swirl and her cheeks burn.

She finally knew the truth about what had happened to Essie. She'd been humiliated on the one date that was supposed to reframe her past. The man she loved, who hadn't tried to shape her, had let her down. Everything made sense now. The mystery was solved and Liv should sleep peacefully.

Except she tossed and turned all night with something niggling deep inside her. She sensed a part of the puzzle was still missing, but didn't know what it was.

27

STARFISH

When she woke, Liv felt like her head had been squeezed in a vise, making her eyes bulge. Her mouth was gravel dry. She wrenched herself out of bed and swallowed paracetamol before going downstairs.

Jake and Johnny stood washing pots together in the kitchen. The atmosphere felt razor sharp.

"You missed breakfast," Jake said, not turning to look at her.

"It's half ten, Mum," Johnny said. "What time did you get in last night?"

Liv winced at her throbbing head. "Mums are supposed to say that to their kids," she said.

Neither Jake nor Johnny laughed at her joke. Johnny disappeared upstairs to gather more things together for university. His course started in a little over two weeks' time.

Liv sidled up behind Jake. "Sorry I was late home last night," she said. "Something cropped up. How did the awards go?"

"Fine." As he dried his hands his eyes skimmed over her newly bobbed hair. "I was late home, too. I stayed behind with Katrina to talk about the business."

"Anything I should know?" Her headache made it difficult to be truly interested.

"There's probably lots of things," he said curtly.

Liv moved even closer, still feeling guilty about missing something important to him, and how she'd almost let Hank kiss her. "I'd like to know."

He glanced at her again before parting his lips. "Well, Katrina thinks that—"

Johnny bounded into the room holding up a small pair of swimming shorts. "I think these have shrunk," he said.

"More likely that you've grown." Jake found a laugh for his son.

"I might get arrested if I wear them to the spa day," Johnny said.

Liv whipped them out of his hand. She'd not worn her own swimsuit in ages and wondered if it would still fit her, too. "I'll buy you some new ones." She turned back to Jake. "Have you bought Katrina's birthday present yet?"

Jake's mouth fell ajar. "Oh, I thought you might have sorted it out."

Liv stared at him. "Don't worry. I'll get something for her," she said, feeling like she'd redeemed herself a little. "You were going to tell me your business talk with her…"

Jake glanced at his watch. "Sorry, it'll have to wait. I said I'd go to the park with Johnny."

When she arrived at Essie's apartment, she drank two pints of water before crashing down into the writing chair. The previous night kept playing in her mind, the way Hank looked at her, and the sensation of his breath on her lips. Liv touched the side of her mouth and reminded herself that he wanted Essie, not her.

She'd not been that close to another man since meeting Jake. Again, she couldn't help wondering if she'd settled down with him too soon. Had she missed out on dating other men, and other life experiences? Essie was worldlier than her. It gave her material for Georgia's adventures that Liv didn't have.

Liv's bones felt heavy. She was exhausted after last night and from all the deceit and turmoil of the last few months. She just had to limp through eight more weeks of writing. Learning of Essie's superstition about November the first pushed her on.

She had now finished chapter thirty-two of Book Twenty and had to write the end to Georgia's story on her own. She had no skeleton bones to provide her with structure.

Liv crossed out all the remaining names off her hero list, and scrubbed the mishmash male character she'd been working on. She decided to create a brand-new leading man for Georgia instead, and she named him Frank. He was a handsome American with dark hair, a fellow novelist who now owned a bar in Texas. He and Georgia had sizzling chemistry together.

Liv finally started to craft her own sentences and paragraphs. She drew on her experiences in Croatia and from meeting Essie's men, and she added them into her work.

Except, as she developed Frank's character further, a sour taste crept into her mouth. Hank had cheated on Essie. The author might have loved him, but that love was tainted. Liv couldn't give Georgia's heart fully to her new hero.

Georgia pressed her body against his. She sought out his lips with a feral urgency she couldn't contain. "I've waited so long for this moment," she murmured.

"Don't talk, just kiss me," Frank said, pulling her toward him. His skin was warm against hers. He smelled of cedar wood and whiskey.

Georgia closed her eyes and felt like she was melting. But then something inside her seemed to snap in two. She pulled away from him. "Stop. We've got work to do," she said. "Time is running out."

Liv chewed the side of her nail. Frank felt more like Frankenstein's monster. He was good-looking, persuasive and confident, but didn't seem to have a soul.

She pressed on regardless for several days. The deadline was looming. She had to keep writing.

One day, when her wrists started to cramp, she took a break and wrote a couple of quotes on behalf of Hank. She emailed them to him and he replied soon after.

Go for it, doll. Did you say hello to Ess for me?

Liv let her fingers hover over the keyboard, not wanting to lie to him. Her attraction to him still sparked inside her. Her chest ached when she thought about him learning of Essie's death.

Thanks so much. She wrote back to him, keeping him at bay. **Great meeting you!**

She emailed Hank's quotes to Chloe, unsure if the journalist would keep up her end of the bargain or not. Liv sat with her eyes fixed on the laptop waiting for a reply. When nothing arrived in her inbox, she prowled around the apartment like a caged lion.

After printing out a chapter she'd just drafted, Liv scribbled lots of notes on the paper. She pressed down so hard her pencil snapped and she looked in the top drawer of Essie's writing desk for another one. When she saw a crumpled up yellow note, she picked it out and smoothed it out. Essie had written,

The best day of my life was also my worst.

Liv said it out loud. Although the words might be meant for a book, she felt the author was referring to the Constellation Prize. She pictured Essie writing the words on the note.

"Hank is really sorry, Essie," she said aloud. "Everything is nearly at an end."

Essie tossed her black bob. *"Humph,"* she said.

Liv's eyes settled on the bee-shaped cuff links sitting on the desk. It was obvious they didn't belong to Hank, so how did they fit into everything? Why would Essie push them under her pillow before she went in hospital?

Her brain was too stuffed from writing to think about it further.

She left the apartment early and headed into the city to buy new swimming shorts for Johnny, and Katrina's gift. Her limbs were sluggish and she came across a designer shop called Pooliversity. The items in the window display looked more like dental floss rather than swimwear. Tiny price labels displayed huge prices.

"Three hundred pounds for a straw bag?" her mum's voice appeared in her head. *"Has it been hand woven by fairies?"*

Liv was too tired to search around the city for somewhere else. When she entered the shop there were more dried starfishes on display than there were swimsuits. The changing rooms had driftwood doors and looked like beach huts. Picking up a silk sarong, she broke into a coughing fit when she saw its price tag.

A man wearing white shorts, a coral necklace and a name badge that said Randall, appeared and whisked the sarong out of her hands. He did the same when she found a pair of navy shorts for Johnny, and a striped Machiavelli beach bag for Katrina. "You have *such* good taste. I'll pop them in the changing room," he said before Liv could check the prices.

Too embarrassed to leave, she admired a Machiavelli swimsuit that shimmered green and silver like a mermaid. Randall appeared at her shoulder once more, like an unwanted genie. "*Stunning* isn't it? So darling." He dabbed a finger along a nearby half-empty rail. "I think we have the larger size for you, babe," he said with a wink.

By the time Liv made it into the changing rooms, she had more things on hooks than were in the shop. She kept on her underwear and wriggled into the swimsuit. It held her in all the places that needed nipping, and gave her the streamlined shape she hadn't seen since Mack and Johnny arrived and reconfigured her body.

"How are you getting on?" Randall cooed through the driftwood slats.

Liv jumped around and covered herself with her hands. "It's beautiful, but I'd need a second mortgage to..."

He interrupted with a well-rehearsed spiel. "Machiavelli is a new brand, so chic. The costume will see you through autumn and into next spring, too. You'd only spend the same on a nice meal."

Liv wondered how many people lived in *that* alternate reality, until she recalled how much she'd spent in Sorrento's.

"I hate to rush you," Randall said. "We're closing in ten minutes... I've found the dress to match the swimsuit. I'll pop it on the hook outside for you."

Liv tried on the green dress. It looked and felt gorgeous, cascading over her curves. She was too hungover to shop elsewhere and still had the expense cash envelope in her bag.

She hurriedly got dressed, and carried the dress, two swimsuits and bag to the counter.

Randall placed the items in a shiny bag and slid it across to her. "That's £726 please," he said. "I'll pop in a free sun cream sample."

Liv felt like she'd been shoved off a high diving board and smacked the water in a belly flop. That amount would pay her and Jake's mortgage and household bills for a month. She pressed a hand to the counter to steady herself and knocked a starfish onto the floor.

"I'll get that," Randall said. "Cash or credit card?"

Liv needed a few moments of recovery time. She crouched down and picked up the starfish, trying to ward off her hyperventilation. Her neck strained as she got back to her feet. "Cash, please," she said.

28

SPA DAY

"What actually happens today?" Johnny said from the back of the car as Jake pulled onto the gravel driveway of Hampton Hall for Katrina's birthday. The former stately home looked like the setting for a BBC Victorian drama. "Do we bob around in the pool and eat lettuce leaves?"

He was still hamming up his broken arm, even though it had healed well. Sometimes he was eager to get back to normal, screwing up his eyes as he performed his physiotherapy exercises. On other occasions, he swore he couldn't pick up his underpants off the bathroom floor, or hang his towel on the radiator. He was growing quieter as his university start date approached.

"We'll just go with the flow," Jake said. "Your aunt likes this kind of thing."

"This kind of torture." Mack laughed.

Liv turned to face her boys. "Look, let's just try to enjoy ourselves," she said, ordering herself to do the same thing.

When she got out of the car her dress looked parrot green in the daylight. She felt overdressed compared to Jake, Mack and Johnny, who wore jeans and T-shirts.

She and Jake performed air-kisses and embraces with a multitude of his relatives before heading into a room decorated with gold helium balloons and Happy 50th Birthday banners. A long table was set out with glasses of Buck's Fizz and orange juice, and the tiniest bacon and egg sandwiches she'd ever seen.

Katrina stood in the middle of the floor clutching armfuls of gift bags. She'd forgone her usual power suit and wore a white linen one instead with red heels. Her stiff coif remained and Liv wondered if it would collapse in the sauna. She queued with Jake to give the present to her sister-in-law.

"What did we buy her?" he asked.

She had already told him. "A beach bag."

"Is that all?"

"You can sort out her present in the future," she said.

"I only asked," he huffed.

Katrina ripped off wrapping paper and peered into bags as soon as she received them. Never one to hide her feelings, she either grinned or grimaced at her gifts. When it came to their turn, Jake got a warm hug and Liv received a polite peck to her cheek. She passed the present to Katrina.

"It's just a little something," Jake said.

Liv kicked his ankle.

Katrina peeled off the tape and her eyes widened when she saw the logo on the bag. "Oh, *wow*, thanks. Have you guys won the lottery or something?" She laughed and hung it on her shoulder.

Liv smiled nervously.

"Glad you like it. Liv chose it," Jake said.

"Thanks, bro. I love it." Katrina kissed him again and darted off to show her new bag to a friend.

Jake scratched the back of his neck. "How much did that thing actually cost?"

"I'm not sure," Liv said, averting her eyes. "Oh, will you just look at that pool, it's amazing."

She had put her name down for a facial and entered a room with three treatment beds in a line. Background music played a random mix of whales singing, monks chanting and bells chiming. She stripped off and dressed in a white robe, perching on the middle bed until Katrina and her friend filed into the room.

"*Oh*, Liv," Katrina said, not hiding the disappointment in her voice. She placed her new bag down on the bed as if settling down a puppy. "I'm here with Marcie."

Liv wasn't sure if this was an instruction to leave or not and stayed anyway.

"And what job do you do, Liv?" Marcie asked, after the therapist appeared and started on their facials.

"I work for Essie Starling—"

"Liv is her cleaner," Katrina intervened.

"Ooh, I used to love Georgia Rory and her adventures," Marcie said. "Essie was married to that crime writer fella, Hank something or other..."

"Hank Milligan," Katrina said, chipping in again.

"Why she left him, I'll never know," Marcie said. "He's prime beef of a man."

"You never see her in magazines these days," Katrina mused. "She used to go to all the best parties."

"I heard she had a face-lift that went wrong, and *that's* why she never goes out," Marcie said.

Liv gripped her robe. "That's not true," she said.

"Not that she'd tell *you*." Katrina laughed. "You only polish her bathroom."

Liv felt something rumble inside her that wasn't just hunger from the tiny sandwiches. "Actually, Katrina, I do much more than *that*. I'm Essie's personal assistant these days. She trusts me with her work *and* her greatest secrets."

"Wow," Marcie said.

"Yeah, like what?" Katrina muttered.

"Wouldn't *you* like to know?" Liv said, enjoying a rare feeling of superiority over her sister-in-law. "If I told you, I'd have to kill you."

Katrina fidgeted on her bed.

"Ooh, exciting," Marcie said. "How's things at work, Kat?"

Katrina sighed dramatically. "I can't wait for Mum and Dad to leave the business. Things need a reboot. I met some marketing guys who said we should switch up our branding, print glossy coffee table books and celeb biographies."

"That sounds amazing," Marcie said. "You could start with Essie."

Liv's body went rigid.

"Hmm, perhaps," Katrina said, thinking. "We need new equipment to increase output, too." She spewed forth with more scattergun ideas.

The more Liv listened, the more her head ached. Perhaps Jake was trying to protect her from hearing this stuff after all. Her sister-in-law seemed to think Paperpress would soon be printing *Vogue*.

"Why not build up relationships with small independent publishers, to print their books?" Liv said. "It's less risky and grows the business more gradually. If you fancy doing something creative, you could hold bookbinding workshops. I bet lots of people would love to try it."

The room fell eerily quiet apart from the sound of whale music.

"Nice ideas," Marcie piped up.

"Pardon me, Liv. What do you know about business?" Katrina snapped. "Or creativity?"

Liv blinked hard against the cotton wool pads covering her eyes. "Probably more than you think," she said.

"It's like me telling you how to mop floors, or clean a sink."

"I'm only trying to help..."

"Perhaps leave Paperpress to the people who know it best."

"I'd love to bind a book," Marcie said. "That's so cute."

Katrina let out a huff. "Oh, shut up, Marcie."

The music went off and the lights came on in the room.

"All done now, ladies," the therapist said, her arms hanging by her sides. "I hope you're all nice and relaxed."

Liv, Katrina and Marcie briskly got dressed and headed toward the changing area for the swimming pool. They stood in individual cubicles where they squeezed into their swimsuits and didn't talk. Liv scolded herself for even bothering to try and talk sense into Katrina.

When she was ready, she stood on the side of the pool on her own. At least wearing her expensive new swimwear gave her mood a small boost.

Katrina approached her. She ran her eyes over Liv's swimsuit. "That's a very nice costume," she said sweetly.

Liv wondered if she regretted her hostility. "Thanks."

"Join me in the sauna?"

It sounded like a command rather than a question and, as it was Katrina's birthday, Liv felt she had to obey. She followed her toward a structure that looked like a garden shed in the corner of the room. Heat blasted her face when she opened the door.

They sat together on a wooden slatted bench without speaking. The steam around them puffed like fog machines at a rock concert.

"Celeb biographies could be a real money spinner," Katrina said. "Essie could be a useful asset..."

Liv couldn't believe her ears. "She wouldn't do that kind of thing. Why don't you build on what you've got?"

Katrina stared at her through the steam. "Haven't you discussed the contract with Jake yet?" she said.

Liv frowned. "What contract?" Her mind flicked back to the paperwork she'd found under Jake's pillow and the figures she didn't understand. What had he been discussing with Katrina on the night of the Paperpress staff awards?

"For our new glam logo and branding, of course," Katrina said. "Jake's offered to pay for it. He's so generous."

Liv wiped droplets from her forehead. "I don't think so. We can't even afford to—"

Katrina barked a laugh. "Says the lady in the designer dress, swimsuit and Dior sunglasses, who hobnobs with celebs and bought me a Machiavelli beach bag."

Liv shivered in the heat. "What will a new logo cost?"

"Around twenty," Katrina said.

Liv's mind crashed. "What? Twenty *thousand*?"

"It's not just a logo, it's a vision," Katrina said. "We'll have to update the website, stationery, packaging and vehicles at least. It's only the first stage. We'll need new equipment after that. When my parents retire, Jake and I will control the business. The branding contract's drawn up and ready. All we need is a solicitor to check it over. Then it's full steam ahead."

Perspiration snaked down Liv's back. All around her was cloudy and she could no longer see. Her eyes started to burn.

"Gosh, it's hot in here." Katrina stood up and pushed the wooden door open. Her coif had remained intact. "Time for a swim, I think."

Liv stood up and fell against the wall. She flopped out a hand to steady herself. When she staggered out of the sauna, she tried to gulp in fresh air. All she could smell was chlorine from the pool.

Jake, Mack and Johnny were splashing around in the shallow end. When Jake jumped up and slicked back his hair, he looked like a different person. Standing here with her new haircut and in her designer swimsuit, Liv wasn't sure if he'd recognize her either.

After dressing for lunch, she met them back in the party area. Her sons horsed around, jabbing each other in their sides and laughing at the tiny food again. Liv nibbled on a cucumber sandwich that seemed to swell in her mouth and she started to cough.

Jake half-heartedly patted her back and returned to the buffet table. She stared after him with daggers in her eyes. When he reappeared, he placed a hand on her arm, making her jump. "Everything okay?"

She shrank back before making sure Johnny and Mack were out of earshot. "No," she said. "Things are very much *not* okay. We really need to talk."

29

LIGHT BULB

Once they got home, Liv wrenched off her jacket in the hall-way. She turned and marched upstairs, gesturing for Jake to follow her into the bedroom, then shut the door behind them. Mack and Johnny were making a cup of tea in the kitchen and she didn't want them to hear anything.

"When were you going to tell me about the twenty thousand pounds you've promised your sister?" she hissed.

"Oh." Jake's mouth contorted. "That."

"Your sister's been telling me all about her plans for Paper-press, starting with some extremely expensive new branding."

"I can explain..." Jake stepped toward her and tried running a hand down her arm.

Liv jerked away. "Really? I'm not sure how. You know we don't have that kind of money."

"It was a spur-of-the-moment thing." He held up a palm. "Katrina promised Mum and Dad we'd buy the business from them, without consulting me. It seemed a positive way forward, for all of us. I didn't realize what a mess the finances were in, or that my sister had such big ideas. Dad's made some unwise investments without telling anyone. It's all such a—"

There were footsteps on the stairs and Mack stuck his head around the door. "Do you guys want a cup of tea?" He glanced at Liv and then Jake. "Um, I'll make one later."

"We can't talk here," Jake said. "Let's go out for a walk."

Liv tore a hand through her hair. It was straggly after the sauna, and she wasn't wearing a scrap of makeup. She didn't want to take their problems out into the street. Music and computer game noises started up in Mack's and Johnny's bedrooms. "Let's talk in the coat cupboard," she said.

With two people inside it, the tiny space was stifling. They had to stand face-to-face.

As soon as Jake shut the door, Liv exploded. "You've lied to me, for months," she said, ignoring the irony of her words. "I thought our finances were under control."

Jake pressed a hand to his chest. "I'm sorry, I messed up. I thought things were better than they were, especially when you started to get paid more."

"It's not a bottomless supply."

"You're wearing a posh new green dress," Jake said, exasperated.

"It cost a lot less than a twenty-thousand-pound marketing plan."

Jake hesitated. "I've already called the bank to sort things out."

"How?"

"Um, a loan."

Fury surged through Liv's system. She slapped her hand to her forehead. "That's not the right way, and we can't afford to throw twenty thousand away on branding and coffee table books. We need to get the basics right with the business. Katrina's head is in the clouds."

"I didn't realize it would cost so much. Those branding guys could sell ice lollies in the Antarctic."

Liv didn't laugh. "Why do you always let her get her own way?"

He ran his tongue around inside his mouth and let out a defeated sigh. He seemed to turn something over in his head before he spoke. "I promised her I'd never utter a word..."

"About what? You need to start talking."

He nodded, his voice turning gravelly. "Before you and I met, Katrina was going to get married. She spent thousands on a fancy white dress, booked a big country house, and invited all her friends and our family. But her fiancé didn't show up on the day. He left her standing at the altar. It was bloody awful. Katrina took on a huge debt for their wedding and is probably still paying it off. Mum and Dad insisted she move back home with them. They fussed over her and she's got used to it. She always thinks she's right. Being let down like that really changed her. She always wanted to have kids, but couldn't trust anyone after what happened."

Liv understood how adverse events could upend your life. The repercussions from her childhood always floated around her like embers from a fire. It wasn't an excuse to be ignorant. "Katrina refused to listen to my ideas," she said.

"She's suspicious about anyone outside of the family."

"We've been married for over twenty years." Liv threw up her hands. "What did the bank say?"

"They looked through the company's books. Paperpress's income has dwindled greatly, and there's not many tangible assets in the business. We need to secure collateral against something else..." His words petered out.

Liv's stomach swilled. She felt like throwing up. "Not... our house?"

The way his eyes dropped told her she was right.

"Y-you can't do that," she stuttered.

He dug a hand into his pocket. "It's my name on the mortgage."

Liv clenched her fists so tightly her fingernails dug into her palms. "I can't believe you just said *that*. It's been *our* house for two decades. What will happen if the business fails?"

"It won't."

"We could lose our home."

"Sorry," he said quickly. "It was a stupid thing to say. I'm really knackered."

"Me, too," she fired back, taking a few minutes to think. The cupboard was hot and stuffy, contributing to her sensation of suffocation. She thought about Jake hiding paperwork from her. "We need to sort this out."

Jake rubbed his forehead. "Thanks for saying *we*. I know we've never had a fortune, but you never seemed to mind... until recently."

Liv's cheeks burned. In the past, if she had enough cash for a couple of glasses of wine on Friday night and to pop a small box of chocolates in her shopping trolley, that was enough. And now she'd stepped into a world of fine dining, designer bags and luxury hotel suites. Jake's observation was right, and she didn't want to admit it.

However, there were much bigger problems between them, besides money. "You've been totally suckered in by Katrina," she said. "It's all about what *she* wants."

"Well, what about you and Essie?" he shot back. "She tells you to jump and you ask how high. It's like you're carrying out some kind of secret mission for her."

Liv's head felt floaty and light. She longed to blurt out the truth and put an end to her deception. Her former life seemed so simple, and she was beginning to ache for it. "Essie needs extra help from me."

"And Katrina needs mine," he said firmly.

Above them the light bulb pinged and went out. The cupboard was plunged into darkness.

"The bulb's gone," Jake muttered. "I don't think we've got a spare."

"What is it that *you* want?" Liv asked him. The question was easier now she couldn't see his face. "Forget about Katrina and the business for a moment."

The sigh he let out was so deep it made her heart plummet.

"I've forgotten what it's like to think about me, about us," Jake said. "I'd turn the clock back ten years, to when the boys were happy building sandcastles, my hair was thicker and we were happier. You and I had more time together. Not like now. I can never seem to say the right thing to anyone, and the boys don't need me as much now they're older. I don't mean to be obsessed with Paperpress. Mum and Dad are relying on me to salvage the business, and Katrina wants me to implement her ideas. I don't know where to turn."

"Toward me," she said, not sure if she really meant it.

Everything felt like it was unraveling. The sparkle Liv had lusted after in Essie's life was losing its sheen. She felt like she was running on a hamster wheel and couldn't keep up. Any moment now, it might stop and she'd fly off, smashing into the wall of a cage. There were only seven weeks to go and Georgia's new hero, Frank, still wasn't working.

"It's so bloody easy if you're Essie Starling, with thousands of pounds at your fingertips," Jake said. "She's probably got enough money to give it away."

In the darkness, Liv's eyes narrowed. Even though her inheritance looked like the only way out of their dire situation, she hated to think that way. "I hope you're not suggesting—"

"God, no. I'm just saying it'd be great not to worry about our bank account, and to afford to take you somewhere hot and sunny, like Essie did," he said ruefully. He reached out and took her hand, stroking it with his thumb. "Look, I'll speak to Katrina and my folks and slow things down. I won't sign anything or make any more decisions without speaking to you first."

His words should have placated her, but Liv's stomach muscles were taut and sore, as if she'd stretched too far and pulled a muscle. If Jake didn't invest in Paperpress, where would it leave the business? She'd soon be out of work, too. Telling him would only pile on his worries.

"We're a team, aren't we?" Jake said. His voice was shaky but loaded with hope. He rested his chin on her shoulder so she could smell chlorine in his hair. "From now on, we'll discuss everything together. Let's promise not to keep any more secrets from each other, okay?"

Liv scratched under her arm. Even if she wanted to spill Essie's secrets to him, she couldn't do it. Not until the official announcement was made about her death. And then what would happen? Jake would know she'd been deceiving him for months.

She felt like she was lying at the bottom of a rubbish dump with stuffed black bin bags falling on top of her.

"Liv?" he urged. "Let's make that promise."

It sounded more important to him than anything. There was nothing she could say without arousing his suspicions. "Okay, yes," she said with a guilty swallow. Behind her back, she crossed her fingers.

For the next week, Liv and Jake assumed a polite pattern in their day-to-day lives. If Liv spoke at the breakfast table, Jake lowered his toast and listened intently. They both said, "Have a good day," when they left for work. In the evening, they almost fought each other to make dinner.

Jake told her he'd contacted the bank again and refused

the loan. He was going to speak to a friend who worked in strategy to help look at Paperpress with fresh eyes. They both wanted to listen to her ideas.

Liv tried not to tell any more lies to her husband. But she couldn't tell him the truth either.

Something had shifted in the air between them. Their trust had been replaced by a suspicion that thickened the air like mucus. They pasted on smiles and acted upbeat, trying to make Johnny's last few days at home the best they could.

Piles of stationery, socks, paperwork, jeans and T-shirts appeared around the house like strange molehills as Johnny gathered his belongings together for university.

It only seemed like minutes ago he was a baby, sucking his own toes and nestling into Liv's neck. She'd spent hundreds of sleepless nights with her cheek pressed to his scalp while he fed. She could get drunk off his milky, powdery smell, and exhaustion left her functioning like a zombie during daylight.

The era of petting puppies at the school gates, devouring jam sandwiches with other mums at soft play centers and dousing Johnny's broccoli in ketchup so he'd eat it, had whizzed by in a flash.

The thought of not seeing his flock of scruffy hair each day, not hearing his chatter about TikTok or straightening his crumpled bed sheets, filled her with a dread she couldn't explain or share. Even scooping up his socks off the bathroom floor made her feel sad. Liv felt like the house was burning down around her, the flames singeing her eyelashes, and no one had any water to put it out.

Mack left for uni a couple of days before his brother. When the day arrived for Johnny to leave, too, Liv stood beside him in the hallway, trying to disguise her fear and sense of loss.

As he stuffed yet another T-shirt into his huge bag, she couldn't stop a stream of mum-talk jettisoning from her lips.

He was to be careful on the train, and to pack his belongings away neatly when he arrived. He should have a decent breakfast each day, and phone home each week. Even she was exhausted by the sound of it.

Johnny unzipped his bag and moved some stuff around, not looking up at her. He'd been acting as if leaving home wasn't a big deal, but she saw his bottom lip quiver.

You leaving is like having my right arm sawn off, and I'm going to miss you more than you'll ever know, Liv wanted to tell him. Instead, her words came out as, "Have you remembered your phone and your wallet?"

He nodded. "Yep, and my keys, and my deodorant."

"Make sure you keep your new place clean and tidy."

He grinned at her. "Don't worry, I won't."

She was just about to touch Johnny's hair when Jake joined them in the hallway, stealing the precious moment away.

"You sure you've got enough stuff there, mate?" Jake said. "Shall I get the kitchen sink for you?"

"Nah, I've got one already." Johnny grinned. "This is cozy. Are you two escorting me off the premises?"

"Just making sure you're okay," Jake said.

Johnny turned to Liv. He shrugged a shoulder. "Well, I suppose this is it. See you, Mum."

Liv wanted to say something profound, that they'd both remember for the rest of their lives. Instead, she hugged her son with all her might. A tear she'd promised not to shed squeezed out and popped onto his shoulder.

"Mum, you're crushing me. Don't get my T-shirt soggy."

"Take care. Love you," she whispered in his ear.

"Love you, too," he said quickly.

Jake grinned at him. "Do you want to tell me, too?"

"Nope," Johnny laughed and they gave each other a quick bear hug.

"I'll give you a lift to the station," Jake said.

Johnny picked up his bag. "It's fine. I'll walk."

"It'll save you carrying all your stuff."

"I'm eighteen, Dad. I can manage."

Liv thought of how it was an age when you could study and live alone, travel wherever you wanted in the world, even have your own children, but there was still so much to learn, and so many mistakes to make.

The door opened, Johnny called back goodbye, and then he was gone. His footsteps grew quieter as he walked away, and the hallway fell silent.

Liv and Jake stood together for a while, their family disassembled. The air was cool and sharp, as if it contained tiny shards of glass.

Another tear wound its way down her cheek and Jake reached out to wipe it away. "Come on," he said softly, and wrapped his arm around her waist. "We'll be fine."

But will we? Liv wanted to say to him. She allowed her body to fall against his. Her head was heavy when she rested it on his shoulder. She thought of all the secrets weighing down on her, that would soon be released into the wild. And she wondered if it would break them.

"Let's look on the bright side," Jake said. "No killer clown films for a while. What do you fancy for tea?"

Liv wiped her cheek with her fingers. "I'll make it."

"It's fine. I'll do it."

"I don't mind."

"Neither do I." Jake left the hallway and headed toward the kitchen, leaving her standing on her own.

Liv stared after him, already feeling lonely. *How will we survive without the boys?* she thought. *And what will happen when Jake finds out about my lies?*

30

EMPTY NEST

Rather than dwell on her empty nest, Liv threw herself into her work and chose to imagine both her sons were still lounging around at home. Keeping up the facade of Essie being alive had given her plenty of practice. With several chapters left to finish, she pushed on writing, striving to craft a happy ending for Georgia with Frank, even if he still didn't feel right for the story.

Liv arrived at Essie's apartment at 6:30 a.m., traversing back streets as if still working for Platinum. As she lugged the manuscript to and from home it felt almost part of her, like a Siamese twin.

She stayed late into the evening, eating a quick sandwich at her desk for tea, or skipping food all together. Typing *The End* was like the finishing line at the end of a marathon, and she was tripping over her feet to reach it.

She noted down the number of weeks left until November 1, and crossed them off as she worked—five weeks, four weeks, and then only three. As the time remaining dwindled, her stress levels grew. Autumn stole away the sunshine and rain tapped against the apartment windows.

As Liv wrote, she harked back to her first ever day working for Essie. Jane had given her a verbal list of dos and don'ts. "Never disturb Essie when she's writing or editing," Essie's PA had said. "If you hear typing or scribbling, don't knock on her door. If Essie wants anything, she'll tell you. Don't worry if she doesn't eat or drink, she doesn't want to break her concentration."

When Liv had glanced through the door at the back of Essie's bobbed hair, she thought the author was being a diva. Now she understood how she felt.

When emails dropped in her inbox they felt like an intrusion. Liv unplugged the author's desk phone and kept her own mobile on silent. If Jake rang, she let her voice mail kick in and listened to his messages on the way home.

She opened an envelope addressed to Essie to find someone had made coasters out of cat hair. Liv yelped and dropped them, using two pencils like chopsticks to deliver them to the bin.

She and Jake drifted in and out of their house at different times, barely seeing each other or speaking.

At night, before bedtime, Liv lay in the bath reading *Such a Fun Age* by Kiley Reid. It featured a bright, sparky toddler who reminded her of Mack and Johnny when they were little. Her sons were carving out their own lives and futures, whereas she felt like the opposite. She no longer had kids at home, no employer and, very soon, no Georgia Rory either. She wondered if she could only exist through other people. Liv hankered after the days when she arrived at Essie's apartment with fresh lemons in her handbag, and she missed finding the notes and books the author left for her.

Liv battled with writing the last chapters until she had just one left, the very end to Georgia's story.

Georgia and Frank kissed as the sun glowed gold and then scarlet before finally dropping down behind the ocean. Swathes of twinkling water stretched out in front of them. She took his hand in hers and held it tightly. It had been a perfect day and now it had ended. But Georgia knew it was only the beginning of their life together. And she couldn't wait to see where their story took them.

"And they all lived happily ever after," Liv said aloud and punched the air. She'd completed her draft, ninety-five thousand words. Even though she'd left herself three weeks to polish them all up before Essie's deadline it still felt like a momentous occasion, one she should celebrate.

If Jake knew about her secret task, he might buy wine and cake. If Essie were still here she might order afternoon tea. Liv imagined a cherub appearing to herald her achievement with a trumpet. But everything in the apartment was just the same as always. Silent and still.

She stood and looked out the window across the city, holding out her arms like Kate Winslet on the bow of the *Titanic*. But there was no wind in her hair, or anyone to entwine their fingers with hers. Feeling rather silly, she lowered her limbs. Success didn't feel very big when you had no one to share it with.

She found Anthony had left her a voice message suggesting he call at the apartment the next day, to share Essie's will with her. He was attending a wedding and would be passing by. Liv wondered if the contents of the will would provide her with the proper celebration she was looking for.

For now, she listlessly tidied the writing desk and picked up a few emails. She saw Chloe had got back in contact at last.

Hey Liv

Thanks for Hank's quotes, so great. Sorry for my slow reply. I wanted to finish my article to show you. I've

written about Georgia Rory, not Essie. I guess I don't want to be the person you think I am. I've been busy talking to fans and discovering their stories. They're so great! My editor loves the piece and I hope you do, too. Here's a link to the Sheen website. And, yes, I'll wait until after Nov 1 to share it more widely. Photos attached, too.

Let's grab a latte soon.

Take care, hon.

Chloe xxx

Liv reread the message. It sounded like the journalist had experienced some kind of epiphany and was following a new direction. She opened the three photographs before reading the article.

The first one showed Chloe wearing a floral dress, blazer and tie. Grinning and posing with a copy of *The Moon on the Water,* her face shone. In another she stood with a small group of men and women holding a handmade banner that said Georgia Forever. The third was an aerial shot of hundreds of fans, taken outside an event. From above, all their faces and dresses looked like a wildflower meadow. A banner on the building said, Georgia Fans United. Chloe had added her own text to the bottom, *Having the time of my life, hon. More fun than hanging around Essie's lobby.*

Liv read the article and all the readers' stories within it. People of all ages shared how Georgia Rory had helped them with jobs and relationships, confidence and mental health issues, inspiring them to be brave and to take chances.

Chloe's article was ultimately about the power of books and stories. And it was beautiful.

A lump of emotion swelled in Liv's throat. She ran a hand through her hair and looked at all the people in the photo again. When she imagined them rushing to the shops to buy

Essie's twentieth novel, or ordering it online, her palms grew sticky.

A feeling of expectation crept up on her like wolves upon an injured lamb, nipping at it first before going in for the kill. She was pleased with her writing quality, and the story might work for an earlier novel. But was it truly a fitting goodbye for Georgia? Was Frank really her ideal hero?

Deep down, Liv knew she hadn't crafted the perfect end to the series.

But what could she do? The ending was the only one she had. She'd put her marriage and sanity at risk to finish the story and honor Essie's last wish. It would be Essie's name on the cover, not hers. No one would ever know. She could slip away, back into the side streets. Anything she received from Essie's will might help to repair her finances, if not her relationship with Jake. Even so, Liv felt she was going to let down Georgia Rory fans everywhere, including herself.

One of Chloe's sentences stuck in her head. *I guess I don't want to be the person you think I am.*

Liv asked herself if *she* was really being the person *she* wanted to be.

If her dad were here, he'd congratulate her anyway. He'd encourage her to think positively and not to fret. He'd be proud of her, and she wished he was here to talk to.

Suddenly needing to see his face again, Liv took the box of photos her mum gave her off the shelf. She leafed through them, and her worries settled down a little. Whatever issues her parents had, they looked so strong together.

She looked at the unused theater tickets again and pictured an alternative scenario, where her dad hadn't kept her mum waiting. Grant and Carol walked to the theater together arm in arm and watched *West Side Story*. They enjoyed a happy-ever-after, and Liv smiled.

But then her eyes settled on the date on the ticket and the curve of her lips fell. November 1, 1989.

The publication date of Essie's first novel.

And something hit Liv like a wrecking ball, almost knocking her off her feet.

November 1 must also be the date her dad died.

She shivered, as if drenched by a surprise storm. A warning bell clanged in her head and she wasn't sure why.

Surely, it was all a strange coincidence.

31

BRIEFCASE

When Anthony arrived at Essie's apartment to share the will with Liv, he wore a white rose in his buttonhole and had a speck of confetti on his shoulder. His formal, distant air had returned as he sat down at Essie's dining table.

Liv supposed it was a serious occasion, and she felt stiff, too. Finishing the manuscript had been like giving birth. It brought back memories of delivering Mack and Johnny, after her adrenaline rush faded and she wanted to crawl into a cave to hibernate.

She poured glasses of water and drank hers in one go, trying to get rid of a jittery sensation in her stomach. The stack of documents Anthony took from his briefcase could change her life and fortunes around forever.

The solicitor cleared his throat. "As you know, in three weeks' time, the six-month period Essie specified for her death to be kept a secret will be over," he said. "We've both made it through alive."

Liv smiled weakly. She jiggled a leg under the table, urging him to move on. She had the striped tie in her pocket, but Georgia's courage was evading her.

"First of all, a few logistics," he said, passing a piece of paper to her. "This is Essie's obituary. I started to write it, but you're far better at these kinds of things."

As Liv read the words, tears welled in her eyes. She blinked them away, unable to bear reading about Essie's death. "What happens now?" she said.

"On November the first, notice will be posted in the London Gazette and a local paper notifying everyone of Essie's death under her real name and pen name, to enable any creditors to come forward. Her obituary will be more of a tribute to her, to be published more widely. I will personally contact Marlon so he can pass on the news to others in the publishing industry."

Liv looked down at the paper. Everything felt so final and real, even clinical. Essie's life and achievements had been condensed to one sheet of paper. "I know of a beautiful article where fans share stories about what Essie's books mean to them," she said. "We could add a link to it in her obituary."

"Good idea." Anthony nodded. "Who wrote it?"

"Chloe Anderton from *Sheen*."

"The journalist who was digging for info on Essie?" he said, furrowing his brow.

"I think you should read it. It's very touching, and people *can* change."

Anthony thought for a moment. "Okay, I believe you."

Liv's heartstrings tugged when she thought about Hank receiving the news. "I'd like to tell Hank Milligan personally," she said.

"Yes, whatever you think is best."

He ceremoniously turned over the first piece of paper. Last Will and Testament was typed on the page. "And that brings us to Essie's will," he said.

Liv's stomach clenched when she saw it. Over five months

ago, she and Anthony had sat in a coffee shop together and he delivered Essie's last wish to her. And now they were here, trying to wrap everything up with a neat bow. She clutched the tie in her pocket for comfort.

"There's a lot of legal jargon involved," Anthony said. "Although I know you'll understand it perfectly, it is rather long-winded. So, I won't read out the entire document to you. I have other beneficiaries to contact, too."

He ran a hand through his hair. The tuft he left on top somehow made him more human. "Suffice to say, as the executor of Essie's will, I am to oversee all the administration and financial arrangements relating to her estate. Essie has bequeathed the vast majority of her assets to the Museum of Writing in Manningham. She requests that a contemporary writer's room be set up in her name, and also that a series of bursaries are made available for writers in underrepresented communities."

He continued. "After her death is announced I shall set up a meeting with the curator and the museum board to inform them of Essie's generous gift." He looked up at Liv. "You previously mentioned a lack of modern exhibits. How do you think Essie should be best represented in the museum?"

Liv thought about what she'd like to see. "What about setting up a replica of her writing room?" she said. "It was the place she spent most of her time. Readers would love to see where she wrote about Georgia Rory."

"Perfect. I knew you'd have a great idea." Anthony cracked a smile. "Would you like to be involved with the project at all? It'd be fantastic to have you on board."

She blinked hard at him. "Are you offering me a job?"

"Yes. You'll have completed Essie's book soon. You won't be able to clean for her any longer."

Liv hadn't told Anthony she'd finished the manuscript and was polishing it up, or about her serious doubts over its ending. This was a chance for her to try something new, an opportunity she'd never have imagined. The role deviated from her dream of being a writer, but it meant she could be close to *other* writers. "Great, thanks," she said, then hesitated. "Is the job my inheritance?"

"No, don't worry. I have that here." Anthony took a large brown envelope out of his briefcase. He shook out a brass key and passed it across the table to her.

They both stared at it.

Is that it? Liv wanted to say. A key wasn't going to pay her bills, help support her kids through university or bail out Paperpress. "Do you know what it's for?" she said.

"I was hoping you could tell me." He passed her the empty envelope.

Liv turned the key over in her hands. She glanced toward Essie's writing room. The key looked too large to fit the bottom drawer of her desk. "I have no idea." She opened the envelope, peered inside and saw a small slip of paper in the corner. "We almost missed this," she said, taking it out. She read out the address.

"25b Hollinhall Street."

Anthony's face speckled red. He swallowed and shuffled his papers together, avoiding her eyes. "Well, I think that's everything," he said, clearing his throat. He took hold of his briefcase and made to stand up.

Liv narrowed her eyes. "Hey, wait up," she said. "There's still things I want to know."

He scratched his neck and settled back down. "What things?"

Something had been rankling Liv about her parents' theater tickets, and also Essie's will. "You said Essie left a proviso in her will. If I didn't complete her last wish I wouldn't get my inheritance." She stared at the key in her hand. "But that doesn't make sense. Essie didn't know she was going to die when she went in hospital. She wrote an impromptu wish in her yellow notebook when she got an infection. So, how could she add a proviso for me in her will, a document she set up months previously?"

Anthony's cheeks were now scarlet. "Ah..." he said.

Liv felt something inside her thawing like ice on the surface of a pond, revealing the water and fish beneath it. "There was never a clause in Essie's will, was there?" she said. "You made it up?"

Anthony's Adam's apple bobbed. He fidgeted with the handle on his briefcase. "When you mentioned the journalist snooping around, I had to keep you focused and on track. I was away in Italy and under pressure. Essie wanted her death to be kept a secret for six months. She wanted you to finish her book. I had to make sure they both happened as per her last request."

"I told you I was committed to the task." Liv glared at him.

"I'm sorry."

She folded her arms. "What else have you lied to me about?"

"Nothing." His eyes sought out the door.

"If there's anything you need to spill..."

Anthony's breath grew coarser. He swallowed audibly. "You asked if I knew anything about the cuff links—"

"So, they *are* yours?" Liv said triumphantly.

He shook his head. "No," he hesitated. "I told you Essie and I were together through university..."

"Go on," she demanded.

"One day, I found some cuff links in Essie's room. They were shaped like bees and looked expensive. I thought she'd bought them for my birthday." He looked at his shirt cuffs. "Except she didn't give them to me... They were for someone else."

"Who?"

"I didn't know at the time. I think I now know."

Liv gave him an exaggerated shrug. All the pieces of Essie's mystery looked to be in place. The cuff links must be superfluous.

"While I was writing her obituary, Essie's death hit me hard. We had something between us, and could have had it again. If we'd got back together, I could have helped to save her. I wanted to remind myself of our time together, so I looked at old photos and letters. I watched videos of her, too…" He paused and gulped his water. "I found something and things suddenly made sense. I know why she chose you."

"What things made sense?" Liv demanded. "What do you mean?"

Anthony smiled tightly. "You know, you have *his* eyes," he said.

Liv was getting fed up with all this. She shook her head at him, not understanding.

"Grant Cooper," he said. "Essie's English professor."

Liv scowled at Anthony. Anger ignited inside her. "My dad didn't teach Essie," she said. "I didn't even know she went to university until her ex-agent told me." However, as she said it, something flashed in her head like a warning beacon.

Three and a half years ago, she'd written a letter to Essie sharing lots of things about her life, including losing her dad. The author invited her to an interview out of the blue and told Liv she reminded her of someone. Years later, when they'd had afternoon tea together, Essie studied her napkin when Liv mentioned her dad. She'd mistaken the author's gaze as distraction. Had she been recalling old memories instead? Had Essie really been lying to Liv all the time she'd been working for her?

But *why*?

Unless…

Blood rushed to Liv's brain. "What are you inferring?" she demanded.

"I think the striped tie you wear belonged to your father," Anthony said. "When I was looking at the old photos, I noticed lots of the university professors wore them. Burgundy-and-yellow stripes. Where did you find it?"

"In Essie's wardrobe," Liv spluttered. She took it out of her pocket and examined the worn fabric. "Lots of people wear striped ties."

Anthony took a deep breath. "Just before Essie died, she said there was only one man she ever really loved," he said. "My ears pricked. I thought she meant me. I asked myself why she'd leave her cleaner such a monumental task, and for her death to be kept a secret…"

Liv clenched her fists. "I kept asking myself the same thing. You *know* I did."

"It's because you're Grant's daughter."

Liv sprang out of her chair, knocking it over. "That doesn't make sense. You lied about the proviso in her will, and now you're lying about this," she barked. "Where's the evidence? You have a tie that could belong to anyone, and some cuff links Essie didn't give to you."

"I found a video on YouTube, from the Constellation after-party—"

"I've seen it. There's only one film and it's nothing."

"Did you watch it all the way to the end?" he said.

Liv's scalp prickled. She felt dizzy and then nauseous. She picked up her chair and sat down again, slumping forward. "I didn't need to. I stopped it partway through."

Anthony stood up and clutched his briefcase. "Should I send you the link again?" he said quietly. "There's something you should see."

"Get out," Liv yelled, gripping the edge of the table to stop herself from lunging forward. "*Get* out."

Anthony hurried out of the room. She heard the front door open.

Liv followed him along the hallway, squeezing the key in her hand. "Why six months?" she called after him. "Why did you insist we follow her last wish through?"

Anthony paused in the doorway, his face in the shadows. "Because when someone you've loved for a lifetime asks you to do something for them, you promise to do it. No matter how big or how strange it seems. Essie was dying. She thought you could finish her novel."

Liv shook her head at him, stunned. There had to be more to this. Anthony might be happy with that reason, but she wasn't buying it. There was still something missing.

When he closed the door behind him, she flung the key at the door. She crashed against the wall, tears falling hot onto her face.

Had Essie and her father really been in love? Surely it had to be a figment of Anthony's imagination. It was crazy, and she'd already proved he was a liar. He was a spurned lover making up a story.

Liv saw something lying on the carpet and picked up the rose that had fallen from Anthony's jacket lapel. As she lifted it to her nose, dates began to crystalize in her mind like a jar of honey stored in the fridge.

Essie sent white roses to herself on November the first.

Liv's dad died on November the first.

She let out a strangled cry and all the blood seemed to drain from her body.

Taking her phone out of her pocket, she clicked on the link for the Constellation Prize after-party and turned up the sound.

THE CONSTELLATION AFTER-PARTY

YouTube Video

The footage is shaky and pixelated. The venue looks like a restaurant or function room with grand chandeliers and large circular tables strewn with cocktails and glasses of champagne. A banner on stage says, Congratulations to Our Constellation Winners. The person recording seems to be testing out their technology, walking around. There are a few authors and people from the publishing industry remaining at the party, which appears to be winding down. The filming continues for fifty minutes. Not much happens until there's a crashing noise. The camera pans across the room and back again before zooming in on some action.

Two women stand close to the stage. One of them is Essie. Her eyes are bleary and her lipstick is smudged. Her dress has slipped off one of her shoulders. She holds a glass of champagne in one hand and the bottle in the other.

"Hank is a bastard," she slurs to the other woman, whose face can't be seen. "He told me he never wanted children. Some bloody journalist has just told me he cheated on me, and fathered a child. I wasted ten years of my life with him. *Ten bloody years.*"

The anonymous woman leans in to say something in Essie's ear. She tries to take the glass off her, but Essie swipes it into the air.

"Why did this happen to me?" Essie yells. Her eyes are wild and full of anger. "He's stolen my chance of ever having a family."

The woman takes hold of the bottle, but Essie snatches it back. The chunky rings on her fingers catch the woman on her chin.

The woman clamps her hands to her face and steps back in shock. Blood trickles through her fingers. The camera pans in closer. Her name badge can be seen clearly. She is the president of the Constellation Prize. Unaware of what she's done, Essie swigs from the neck of the champagne bottle.

A tuxedo-wearing man appears. He places his hand firmly on Essie's shoulder. Startled, she spins around and throws a punch that connects with his ear. The man's head jerks to the side. Two more men arrive. They wear suits and look like bouncers. They try to reason with Essie before she shoves them both away. The champagne bottle goes flying onto an empty table.

The two bouncers take hold of Essie and march her toward the door. "I only ever loved one man and he's dead," she yells, back over her shoulder. The camera zooms in on her mascara-streaked face. "Grant, I'm so sorry…"

32

THE BRASS KEY

Liv doubled over. She felt like she was going to vomit. She staggered along the hallway, scraping her shoulder against the wall. Finding herself in Essie's award room, she clenched her fists. She'd stood here so many times, gazing at all the trophies and photographs, full of admiration for Essie and her spangled life. And the author had lied to her for three bloody years.

Did her dad and Essie really have an affair? She hated Anthony for suggesting it. Her parents had been happy, but Carol's words about their arguments wriggled in Liv's head like maggots in old meat.

In the video, Essie said she was so sorry. But what did she have to be sorry for? Something to do with the death of Liv's father? It had been a terrible accident.

It didn't explain why Essie gave her the task of finishing her final book and her belief that only Liv could deliver it.

She was only sure of one thing—that Essie Starling was a liar.

With her thoughts a whirlwind in her head, Liv let out an ear-shattering cry and lunged forward. She swiped a hand along one of the shelves. The awards queued in a line before dropping off the end and crashing down. Crystal flew and smashed. It splintered and shards shot out in all directions. Thick black plastic bases bounced onto the floor.

Liv stood on tiptoes to reach the top shelf and pulled each of the awards toward her, as if using hand pumps to pull pints of beer. They hit the top of her socked feet, but she didn't care.

On the next shelf down, she pressed her palms together and inserted them between two photographs. She flung her arms apart and a stainless-steel prize shaped like a book hit the wall and chipped the plaster. Photograph frames flew.

Liv didn't stop until she'd swept every award and photo frame off the shelves. It did nothing to dampen the anger that still raged inside her. She kicked the wall for good measure and pain deadened her toes.

When she limped out of the room, she left a trail of glass chips shining like diamonds on the hallway carpet. She entered Essie's writing room and treaded toward her desk. Liv shoved all the things off its top.

She didn't know what the hell to believe.

She looked down at her hand and realized she was still holding the key. She'd held it so tightly, it had made a red imprint on her palm. The expression on Anthony's face told her he recognized the address.

Liv clenched her fingers back around it. She pulled on her shoes, left the apartment and ran down all the stairs until she stood panting in the lobby.

Outside, she hailed a taxi and showed the driver the address on the slip of paper. She rammed her seat belt into its fastener, trapping a slither of skin on the side of her hand. She cried out and rubbed the red weal.

Slumping down, she stared out of the window, unable to take in the roads and buildings as they rolled past. Her vision became a blur and she soon lost track of where she was in the city. It only seemed like seconds later when the taxi pulled up on a crescent of tall white houses. The driver said the fare was fifteen pounds and Liv pushed a twenty into his hand and scrambled out of the car.

The city was silhouetted in the distance and Essie's apartment block rose above it, giving her the middle finger.

There was a high concentration of young people streaming up and down the street, and Liv realized she must be close to the university. Her ankles threatened to give way as she counted down the numbers on the houses until she stood outside the one on the label, number 25.

The white Georgian house was run-down with stained walls, a missing gate and windows with lots of panes, several cracked. It looked like a building from a Charles Dickens novel. Next to the front door were several doorbells, as if the building had been converted into apartments at some point. Bob Marley blared from one of the top stories.

What was this place?

As Liv hesitated on the pavement, a thought streamed in her head like the banner across the screen on a twenty-four-hour news channel. *Essie had an affair with my dad. Essie had an affair with my dad.*

The thought twisted her gut, and she bent her head to take deep gulps of air. She saw the feet of people passing her, scuffed Doc Martens and worn running shoes. Some hesitated, but everyone moved on.

Straightening up, Liv pressed a hand to her throat and walked along the path to the front door. It didn't seem right to let herself inside, so she knocked and waited. When there was no reply, she pushed the key into the lock.

A long hallway stretched in front of her with several tiles missing from the mosaic floor. Two well-used bicycles were propped against the wall, and takeaway menus were pinned to the wall.

She stared around her, not sure what to do next. A young man wearing oversize camouflage trousers and a yellow beanie jogged down the stairs. "You looking for someone?" he said cheerily.

Liv held up the key to show she hadn't broken in. "Which door is number 25b?"

"End of the hallway," the man said. "The mystery thickens."

She frowned at him. "What do you mean?"

"That flat is privately owned, right? Like, not a student?"

"I don't know," Liv said. There didn't seem much point in covering up the truth. "I've been left a key to the place, in a will."

"Yeah? That's cool. My uncle just left me his mangy old Labrador." He laughed. "I once saw a woman scuttle inside. She had black hair, like a helmet. I knocked to see if she wanted a coffee, being neighborly and that. She didn't answer. Weird, huh?"

"Um, yes."

"My mate Dave reckons she's a dominatrix, you know with that hairstyle."

"Oh…" Liv blushed.

"I just hope you don't find any bodies in there."

"Me, too." Liv smiled too widely. She waited until the man left the building before she approached the peeling green door.

The same key opened this lock and a strange damp smell hit her as she stepped inside, a hint of Fracas underneath. The carpet was a swirly red-and-gold pattern with bare patches along the short hallway. Cheap paintings hung on the walls, as if bought from charity shops.

Liv entered the room closest to her. The sunlight cut through the windows, illuminating specks of dust sparkling in the air. There was a small run of yellowing kitchen units, and a tiny dining table that would struggle to seat two people. A single bed was covered with a knitted patchwork cover. There was a squishy teal velvet chair with a hole in the cushion and an old oak desk with a missing drawer and a flat melted candle in a saucer on top.

Somehow, despite the apartment's scruffiness, Liv could sense Essie's presence.

She jumped when a door banged somewhere upstairs, followed by laughter. Dropping her handbag to the floor, Liv looked around her and saw there was a layer of dust over everything.

Photos pinned to the wall caught her attention. When she peered closer she saw Essie, younger and reclining on a picnic blanket, with a pen and pad by her elbow. She was laughing and had black winged eyeliner and orange lips. A photograph farther along showed her blowing out nineteen candles on a birthday cake. In another, she stood with a group of friends throwing their mortar board hats into the air. There was a prize day booklet with the university coat of arms—featuring a bee, perhaps to represent how hard the students worked. A mug on the side of the sink was printed with a bee, too.

It's the emblem of a prestigious university, Liv realized. It could be the reason Anthony used a bee-printed handkerchief, and for the cuff links Essie commissioned for Grant.

Liv stared at all the photos. It was difficult to imagine Essie was ever that young. Had she lain on her bed in this room, scribbling in a notepad and listening to music with Anthony?

Her eyes settled on another shot. It didn't seem to be of anything at first, a door opening onto a classroom. There was a desk, blackboard and a figure in the distance. Liv squinted closer and let out a short gasp when she saw it was her dad. Tears rushed down her face.

Another shot beside it was much clearer. Her dad lay on the grass using his hand as a visor against the sun. His lips curled into a smile. He looked so much younger than he did in her memories.

The grief of losing him could always knock her off her feet, like a freak wave on a sunny beach, and it came at her now and left her reeling.

Liv fell back onto the bed. It was lower than she expected so the back of her head smashed against the wall. She flailed like a beetle trying to right herself, and her leg became entangled with the bedcover. The futility of trying to get free made all the strength desert her body. Her limbs flopped, suddenly too cumbersome to move.

She wasn't sure how long she stayed there, her heart thumping and her legs leaden. Possibly hours. It was like being locked in a bad dream. She watched a fly jerking in a spider's web on the ceiling, until it became still. Time and space faded away.

When she blinked and looked up, the sky was darkening and streetlights glowed amber outside. She heard doors slamming as students returned home for the day.

Jake called her phone and she let it ring, too upset to speak to him.

Slowly, she propped herself up on one elbow and caught sight of an envelope standing up against the kettle. Liv detached herself from the bedcover and forced herself to stand up.

Olivia Green.

When she saw Essie's handwriting, her body almost caved in. The envelope was unsealed, and her fingers felt like they belonged to someone else when she took out the letter.

Several words and sentences had been scribbled out, as if it was a work in progress. Liv knew that she had to read it, even if the words cut through her like cheese wire. If she'd managed to cover up Essie's death for so long and complete her book, she could find the strength to do *this*. Her pulse galloped as she started to read.

Dear Olivia
I was once in love with a man called Grant Cooper...

Liv screwed her eyes shut, not wanting to read more, while also *needing* it more than anything. She wanted to screw the paper into a ball and hurl it across the room, but she kept it in her hands. She held her breath, and started the letter from the beginning.

33

THE LETTERS

Dear Olivia,
I was once in love with a man called Grant Cooper.

My health has been failing for several years and living alone has allowed me to think about the past. Probably too much. I've been sitting here revisiting photographs and poring over old letters. My achievements may shine brightly, but they can never make up for my mistakes and regrets. It's strange that I'm a writer, yet I can never find the right words to say to you. They flow on paper but not from my lips. One day, I hope to speak to you in person. For now, this letter allows me to lay down my sentiments.

When I met your father, it was a meeting of minds I'd never known before or found since. We shared an intellectual connection. Quite simply, Grant Cooper was the sentence to my paragraph, the full stop to my words. I believe everyone has a small pocket of their life when everything is perfect and the sun seems to shine. Mine was when I was with him.

At first, I didn't know he was married with a wife and child, and I admit it suited me not to ask. I laughed with him and learned from him. We challenged each other. I pictured my future with him, though I can see now my imaginings were those of a headstrong girl rather than a woman. By the time I found out he was married, I was in too deep. I was in a relationship with Anthony at the time, but my pull toward Grant was all-encompassing. I never told Anthony who had captured my heart and I'm afraid I hurt him deeply. Even though my relationship with your father never became physical, I was devoted to him.

When Grant told me he was taking your mother to the theater, rather than attend my publication party for The Moon on the Water, I kicked up a fuss and tried to get him to change his mind. He attempted to calm me down and was late when he rushed away.

When I learned of Grant's death I was devastated. I wished I hadn't made a scene and felt everything was my fault. Even worse, I couldn't attend his funeral to mourn him. I began to drink and have never known if alcohol is my salvation, or my punishment.

My life has been full of soaring highs and the deepest lows. I married Ted Mason, a man I didn't truly love. My next husband, Hank, fathered a child, something I could never give him. I utterly disgraced myself at a party, on the twentieth anniversary of losing your father. I couldn't face the world and my readers any longer. I wasn't the person they thought I was, that I could no longer pretend to be, and I shut myself away. When I received my diagnosis, I felt like it was my penance and that I deserved it. I'm not trying to gain your sympathy. I just want you to understand.

I realized who you were when you wrote to me and mentioned Grant's name. You were looking for work and I found myself in a dilemma. Did I help out the daughter of the only man I ever loved, or keep her at bay?

I offered you the job, initially for a few months, until you found something else. Except, something strange happened. I found myself falling a little in love with you. Not in a romantic way, but I saw glimpses of Grant in you and it brought me

THE MESSY LIVES OF BOOK PEOPLE

a touch of joy I hadn't experienced for many years. You were determined and fun, even reminding me of myself before my health diminished. I couldn't tell you that I knew your father. It would raise too many questions, and then you'd leave me. And I couldn't bear to lose you, too. The closer we became, the more difficult it was to reveal the truth. You said in your letter you wanted to write. I thought I could help you, and it might help me out, too. It would take time and I thought I had plenty of it. Except my health worsened and I wrote my will.

I see you look at my apartment and awards with stars in your eyes. I know better than anyone that health, family and happiness are things money can't buy. I see talents glimmering in you that are probably invisible to you. The longer you stay working for me, the more you might see them, too.

Please don't stop cleaning if that's your destiny. However, if anyone can refresh Georgia Rory and her story, I think it's you. I've lost my passion for her, just as I've done for my own life. Maybe you can help it to return.

If you're reading this letter I may have disappointed you beyond measure, and it makes me sadder than you'll ever know. My student flat was the only place I could ever find any peace of mind and I'd like you to be its new owner someday, to sell it, or to use as a writing space, as I did.

I'm deeply sorry for any hurt I've caused, and I hope you don't carry your anger with me around forever. If you ever think about me, one day I hope it will be kindly.

Live splendidly, Olivia.

Love,

Elsbeth x

A lump swelled in Liv's throat so large she had to rub it away. She thumped the top of the desk, and it sent shock waves through her body.

She welcomed an ache of hatred toward Essie. Yet, she couldn't help still loving her, too. And it was impossible to separate the two streams of emotion. They were both part of her, tangled and knotted together.

She could feel Essie's pain and longing for Grant, because she shared it, too. It was all-consuming and never-ending.

Is a meeting of minds greater than a meeting of bodies? she asked herself.

Was Anthony wrong to believe her dad and Essie had an affair? Could she blame the solicitor for how he acted, especially if he loved Essie?

Liv couldn't think straight. Somehow, she knew Essie's letter was only part of the story and there had to be more.

She scoured the walls again, taking in more photos. Here was Essie sitting on a wall with a dog in her arms, and huddled in a towel after swimming. An image showed her holding a bouquet of white roses. It sat alongside an acceptance letter from a publishing house. Liv wondered if her dad had sent Essie congratulatory flowers.

There were a couple of photos Liv had never seen of him before. It was surreal seeing the face she missed so much in this setting.

She thought of him ruffling her hair and holding a finger to his lips as she sneaked into his lecture theater. "Pick a good seat, sweet pea." When Liv closed her eyes, she could feel his hand, warm and reassuring on her shoulder, and the tickle of his hair against her cheek. And she couldn't help smiling to herself. Seeing him again, and sensing him beside her, made her feel that not everything was broken.

When she noticed a desk drawer was partially open, she pulled it toward her. Inside was a small bundle of letters, fastened with a rubber band. She saw her father's signature on one of them and tugged them out. With her hands shaking uncontrollably, she unfolded the first letter.

November 19, 1988
Dear Elsbeth,
I can't tell you how wonderful it was to see you today. Thanks for your encouraging words about my lectures. Not many people find character arcs as riveting as I do (I'm sure I heard snoring at the back), and it's heartening to discover another fanatic.

I read your manuscript for The Moon on the Water *and this is strong, intuitive writing. Well done. Many readers relish an adventure and the opportunity to step outside their lives for a while. You should definitely submit this widely to publishing houses. I'm happy to help, if you need it.*

My daughter, Liv, is ten and always has her nose in a Nancy Drew book. Her dream is to be a writer, too. She's showing real promise, though is reticent to recognize her own talents. If you ever meet her at one of my lectures, please do encourage her and help her to realize her potential. I think you'd both get along.
Keep writing!
All my best,
Grant

Liv's jaw hurt and she stopped reading. "He told you about me," she whispered. "Dad asked you to help me become a writer."

Had Essie been doing what Grant wanted her to do? To nurture his daughter and help her achieve her potential and dream? Did she give her six months to do it, until November the first?

Liv remembered the note she found in Essie's apartment. *The greatest day of my life was also my worst.*

November the first was the publication date for Essie's debut novel, and also the date Grant died. Twenty years later, Essie won the Constellation Prize and learned Hank had fathered a child behind her back. Superstitious about dates, it was both bitter and sweet in Essie's mind.

Liv's love for Georgia Rory and her in-depth knowledge of the character had always shone through. On her deathbed, Essie hadn't wanted her beloved heroine to be passed on to anyone else. Who better than the daughter of the man she loved, who dreamed of writing, to complete the last book of the series?

November the first.

What better date was there for a deadline?

What better date was there for Essie to officially *die*?

Standing there, Liv felt like the curtains had opened at the theater. The red velvet swished away to reveal the performers onstage. The spotlights turned on.

She opened up a few of the other letters and read them.

February 12, 1989
Dear Elsbeth,
Thank you for the exquisite cuff links. I'm extremely flattered you remembered my birthday, the only person on campus that did! After careful consideration, I'm afraid I can't accept them, even as a thank-you for help with your submission. The hard work was all yours. I appreciate your invitation to dinner to celebrate your novel's acceptance by a publisher. I'm pleased for you and sorry I have to decline. I have a lot of work to do for the university and I'm sure you have a lot of other friends to raise a glass with.
All my best,
Grant

————

May 19, 1989
Dear Elsbeth,
I feel I must write to you about something of concern to me. The other night, we almost kissed and I shouldn't have let it hap-pen. Your delight and exuberance about your writing are infec-tious and we almost crossed a line that needs to remain firmly in place. I find you funny and kind, my intellectual counterpart,

but I'm a happily married husband and father and wish to remain that way. I can't offer you anything more than support for your work and a shared love of character journeys. I'm sure in the light of day, you'll feel the same way, too. I hope the summer break gives you time to think things over.

Best wishes,

Grant

———

November 1, 1989

Dear Elsbeth,

Thank you for the invitation to your party today. I'm afraid I won't be attending and wanted to give you this letter in person. You've done amazingly well and I wish you all the best in your career as Essie Starling.

A colleague recently asked me about my girlfriend. I honestly didn't know who he meant until he described you. When I insisted our relationship was platonic, he told me that rumors were circulating around the campus. Although we know our connection is innocent, others do not, and I cannot put my job or family at risk.

I know you say you love me, but you're still so very young. And life isn't that simple. One day, I promise you'll meet someone who can make you happy. That person isn't me. I'm pleased for your success and will always cheer on your career from afar.

Best regards,

Grant

34

CEREAL BOX

Liv staggered back and fell onto the bed scrunching the letters in her hand. Confusion rattled inside her. She wanted to hate Essie, but couldn't help feeling the slightest touch of empathy for her, too. She wished she could reach into her own chest and rip out her emotions.

An invisible domino effect had been set in motion, and no one could have predicted the outcome. Would her dad have been killed in an accident if he hadn't been late for the theater, or if Liv's mum had waited for him by the park gates? She could ask herself all the questions on earth and there was no way of knowing. Every second of every day, you made decisions that affected your future and that couldn't be reversed.

Completely drained of energy, Liv crashed sideways onto the pillow. The events of the day played out in her mind in freeze frames. The will, Anthony's lies, the brass key and the broken awards crunching under her feet. The taxi ride, Essie's secret apartment, the photos of her dad and his letters. She tried to get up but a wave of exhaustion hit her, making her hug her stomach. She just about managed to text Jake to tell him she wasn't coming home that night.

Where are you? he said. **Are you okay?**

She was so fatigued she could only manage one word in reply, **Yes.**

The room soon grew darker and noise from upstairs and the hallway petered out. Liv's eyelids were so heavy she fell into the kind of deep sleep that had evaded her for weeks.

She woke in the morning to the sound of a radio blaring something. She missed the sounds of Jake, Mack or Johnny moving about. After wiping her face in the bathroom, she called her husband.

"Where were you last night?" he said urgently.

"It's a long story." She gnawed the side of her thumbnail. "Essie owns another flat, from her student days."

"Has she asked you to clean it?"

"No, but there are things here I have to do. I need to be by myself."

"What's going on?" he said. "Just come home. We can talk here."

"I can't. Not yet."

He was quiet for a while. "Look, I know I messed up. You don't have to leave. I'll go if you want me to."

She shook her head at her phone. "No, it's not that..."

"Are you there with someone else?" His voice was full of pain.

She cupped a hand to her face, too shattered to deal with this. "Of course not." Her words sounded vacant to her. For almost six months there *had* been someone in her life. Essie. Focusing on the author had stolen her attention away from her husband and family.

"How long will you be?" Jake said.

"I'm not sure yet. For as long as it takes."

"You're speaking in riddles."

"And that's what it feels like talking to you, Jake, about Paperpress."

He sighed before he answered. "I probably deserve that, and I'm trying. For what it's worth, I put forward your ideas to Mum and Dad and they want to explore them further. They're delaying their retirement for a while, so we can focus on the business as a family. And that includes you, if you want to be more involved. We'd love to hear your thoughts."

She was too tired to think about Paperpress, her potential job at the museum or anything else. "I'm sure Katrina won't agree with all this," she said.

"My sister has got her own way for too long. Me, Mum, and Dad all agree on the business and she'll have to get in line. There's not going to be a big rebrand. We won't be printing any celebrity autobiographies."

Liv closed her eyes. She'd wanted to hear something like this for such a long time, but she was still reeling from the revelations about Essie.

"At least give me your address, so I know you're safe," Jake said.

With reluctance, she told him.

Liv got out of bed and padded through to the bathroom again. She was pleased to find shampoo and a fresh towel in a cabinet next to the shower. Everything looked clean and the water was hot when she ran it. As it bounced off her face, her thoughts rumbled in her head like an earthquake.

She remembered Essie once saying that being a writer meant putting yourself inside different people's heads, imagining how they think and feel. And she tried to do this now, with the author.

She pictured Essie as a young woman, clasping letters from a handsome witty professor to her heart. His interest in her mind and talent were enthralling. Liv imagined Essie's heart pattering as she raced to the lecture theater, yearning for a glimpse of Grant, not realizing that her youthful exuberance was taking gradual steps toward being overbearing.

It must have been painful to receive the cuff links back from him, and to be crushed by his final letter. Grant Cooper could never be a lover, nor a friend. Liv saw Essie crying herself to sleep night after night, after Grant died, not being able to share her devastation with anyone.

Liv wondered if Essie escaped her gilded life to return to her old flat, to pretend she was young again. Did she come here as Ted tried to make her more sophisticated, taking her to parties as if she was a show pony? Did Essie dream of her dingy little flat as she lay on silk sheets with Hank in LA, while their driveway was full of cars and she wore diamonds on her fingers?

Liv could never know for sure. But over the last few months she had developed a writer's imagination and intuition. She had battled temptation when Hank's lips were close to hers. Just a few seconds more could have changed everything. The wrong decision could have damaged her marriage further, and swamped her with guilt.

Had Essie faced a similar temptation with Grant?

Had the author made the wrong choices?

Liv turned off the shower and stepped back into the bathroom, naked and dripping wet. She shivered and grabbed a towel, rubbing the fabric across her skin. Although she had pieced things together, she still felt there was a black hole inside her body.

What about my story? she wanted to shout at Essie. *How are things supposed to end for me? What happens to the young girl who dreams of becoming a writer?*

As she dressed in the clothes she wore yesterday, an answer came to her. The only one she could find. *The girl has to write her own story.*

Liv's stomach groaned and there was no food in the flat. She traipsed to a corner shop where she bought a sandwich, crisps and an apple. She sat down at the desk to eat.

As the rest of the house came to life, she listened to an audiobook on her phone, *Heartburn* by Nora Ephron. It was about the breakdown of a marriage, and it seemed apt. Doors banged around her, hair dryers roared, and the smell of toast filled the air. It reminded her of being at home with Jake and the boys and she felt homesick.

Liv had known the ending she'd written for Georgia Rory wasn't the right one. The hero she'd created wasn't her Mr. Right. To distract her thoughts from Essie, Liv took a taxi back to the penthouse. She asked the driver to wait outside.

In the hallway, Liv crunched over chipped crystal to pick up Essie's original manuscript, her own rewritten version and the laptop. She took clothes from Essie's wardrobe before returning to the student flat.

She tried to polish up her work, so she could submit it to Marlon, but knew she was doing Georgia and her fans a disservice. Just as Essie was stuck in the past, so was her heroine. Both of them deserved a better ending.

The next day, a rap at the door made Liv sit bolt upright in bed. She wore the knitted blanket around her shoulders like a superhero's cape and her eyes were crusted with sleep. She cleared them with her fingertips before opening the door.

Jake stood there holding two stuffed carrier bags. "Hi," he said casually, though she heard his one word was loaded with hope. He raised the bags. "I've brought a peace offering."

"It doesn't look like chocolates and flowers."

"I like to think it's better than that."

Liv glanced behind her, at her crumpled bed and an apple core on the writing desk. "Come in."

Jake raised a bemused eyebrow at the room. "This is where you're, um, working? Is it really Essie's place?" A banging noise sounded above and they both looked up at the ceiling.

"It's her old student accommodation, a secret hideaway. I

think she bought it when she got her book deal. I bet it's tidier than Johnny's new place."

Jake laughed. "I can imagine." He proffered the bags to her. "I know you never got the chance to be a student, so I brought you some essentials. I lived on this stuff for years."

Liv looked inside one of the bags and couldn't help laughing as she took out a box of Rice Krispies, and a box of minestrone Cup-a-Soups.

"There's also a multipack of cheap crisps and some chocolate digestives." He smiled. "A week's worth of meals. I used to keep a box of cereal at the side of my bed. I had a handful in the morning for breakfast, and the same for supper."

"So nutritious. I definitely missed out," she said. "I'd offer you tea and toast, but I don't have milk or bread."

"Hmm, looks like I forgot those." Jake looked around for a chair.

"Use the bed. It doubles up as a sofa," she said.

They sat down together and scooped puffed rice from the cereal box with their hands.

A couple of Rice Krispies stuck to Jake's cheek like warts and she reached over to flick them off. They made general chitchat about Johnny and Mack, and after a short while Jake stood up. "I'll leave you to get back to work," he said. "What are you doing?"

"I'm supposed to be writing," she said glumly.

When he headed to the door her eyes followed him. Wasn't he going to ask her more questions before leaving? Or enquire when she was coming home? But, he gave her a warm smile and was gone.

The next morning, he brought fresh bread, and they ate slices of buttery toast, perched on the edge of the bed together. He left after fifteen minutes and Liv found herself wishing he'd stayed a bit longer.

The next day, she read her version of the manuscript all day before Jake knocked on the door at 8 p.m. They drank soup from cups and dropped in pieces of torn bread. When ten o'clock came around, he stood up to leave and they kissed in the doorway, as if Liv was nineteen again.

After a few more days following a similar pattern, Jake asked casually, "How is your writing going?" There was no tension in his voice, or pressure for her to tell him. Liv felt he really wanted to know.

"I gave Georgia Rory a hero, but he's not the right man to end her story with."

"Has he done anything wrong?" Jake said.

"They don't suit each other's needs. She's deciding what to do."

"Oh." He reached over and pushed a lock of her hair behind her ear. "Do you know who the right man should be?"

Liv shook her head. "Not yet. I'm really struggling."

"I've brought you something. I thought it might help." Jake took the notebook he'd made, when they'd first met, out of his pocket. It had lain unused in her bedside drawer for over twenty years. "You said you'd use it for something special one day."

Liv's spirits lifted a little. "Thank you," she said.

For the next couple of days, she continued to battle with the ending for the book. She tried to write different scenarios for Georgia and, again, they didn't feel right.

Jake continued to appear with food and drink for her. He left to go back to their home and didn't put pressure on her to join him. He didn't ask her anything about Essie, and Liv continued to keep the author's death to herself.

One evening, after Liv had rewritten two new chapters and deleted them, her eyes were red and sore when Jake arrived.

She sank down on the mattress and felt like crying. He had brought her a photo of the boys and her slippers.

"I think I'm going to lose my job with Essie," she said with a sniff. "The boys have gone, and it feels like me and you are losing each other, too."

He sat down beside her and took her hand. "You're never going to lose me," he said. "I know we've been going through a hard time. But you're kind of stuck with me. Unless you don't want that?"

"I don't know what I want."

"Then stay here until you do," he said softly. "I'll wait."

When he wrapped his arms around her, she'd forgotten how good he smelled and she nestled against his chest. Throughout life, their haircuts might change, their skin would grow looser, and there would many more ups and downs, but his heartbeat would always be the same. She felt it thrumming soft and strong against her cheek.

She thought about how Anthony was Essie's rock, the love of her life she didn't realize she had. She wondered, in that moment, if Jake was hers. Did love always have to be about golden sunrises and raging ravines?

Perhaps life was divided up like a book, into scenes and chapters. Liv and Jake were making their way through the bumpy middle and heading into the second half of their story.

She spoke to his chest. "There are some things about my job I've not told you, about Essie. Big, weird things."

"That's fine. Tell me when you're ready…"

She raised her eyes at him. "Do you trust me?"

"Yes."

She liked how he didn't hesitate.

As the streetlights came on outside, rain bobbled on the windows. There were distant voices and Jake and Liv held each other until they grew tired. It felt natural to lie down on the bed together. They cuddled and kissed.

"What do you want?" he said softly in her ear. "When the sun rises tomorrow, what will make you feel better?"

Liv thought about it for some time. Her brain was scrambled and she wanted to stop thinking about Essie. "I know it sounds odd, but I really want to write," she said. It was no longer a dream for her, it was a burning desire. Something her dad would want for her, too. Jake's love and patience had helped her to find it. "As for right now, I think I'd like you to stay," she said.

35

PUMPKINS

When Jake left the next morning, they kissed on the doorstep and wished each other a good day. Back in the room, Liv wrapped a blanket around her shoulders and sat down at the desk.

She recalled one of Essie's memes on Instagram and looked it up on her phone.

If you meet something insurmountable, don't try and fight it. It will only leave you with bruises. The trick is to outsmart it and do something it wouldn't expect.

Liv deleted the last eight chapters of the manuscript. She wanted to completely rewrite them and she only had seven days left. November 1 was looming. She had to set all her emotions about Essie aside, and put her last wish to rest, for good.

She had to stop trying to write like Essie.

She had to stop trying to *be* like Georgia.

She just wanted to be Liv again.

Essie had looked to men to provide her happy ending for her whole life and had never found it. For too many years,

Georgia had relied on heroes to help save her. And it was time for her to break free.

Liv took the original dog-eared manuscript from her bag and looked through it once more. As she turned page after page, Essie's underlined passages and notes all made more sense. Slowly, the anger she felt toward the author began to subside, overtaken by sadness and loss. Liv tried to think of her kindly.

She wrote in the notebook Jake made for her and channeled all her feelings into her work.

"I need to do this alone," Georgia said to herself. "There are roads I want to travel. I need to look forward and not back, to make my own choices and mistakes. I'm finally letting you go. You might not be by my side, but you'll always be in my heart. I'm ready to take my own path, not anyone else's."

For seven days solid, Liv wrote around the clock. She nibbled on dried cereal and typed as soon as the sun rose, and until it set. She fell asleep at the writing desk and crawled into bed when she woke in the night, shivering and cold. She asked Jake to keep away so she wouldn't be distracted.

The end of Georgia's story spilled out of her, and it was the one she wanted to tell.

When she eventually typed "The End" to the book, Liv burst into tears. They streamed down her face, for the loss of her dad, and Essie, and at finally saying goodbye to Georgia. The heroine had been with her through thick and thin for thirty years. Liv had sometimes felt as if her life depended on her. But not any longer. She was now her own woman.

She wiped her face with her sleeves and sat back in her chair. She imagined her dad's hand resting gently on her shoulder. *"Well done, sweet pea,"* he said. *"I'm proud of you."*

She was proud of herself, too. She suddenly felt lighter than she'd done in months, as if she'd thrown off a heavy cloak exposing her skin to sunlight. She didn't need cherubs or trumpets or a new swimsuit to make her feel this way. She had the love of her family.

Liv might not have gone to university or dated around. If things had been different she might not have met Jake, nor had Mack and Johnny either. Maybe Essie was indirectly responsible for the way her life panned out, setting actions in motion the author could never have imagined or stopped. But Liv was in charge of how they progressed from here.

She now knew she wanted to work on things with Jake. Whatever happened, Liv wouldn't trade the life they'd had, or were going to have, for anything.

Inheriting the flat might mean she could start a new career and cast her financial worries aside. She didn't want bitterness, regret or anger marring her future.

She had to find it in her heart to forgive Essie, so she could move on. Just like Georgia Rory.

Liv called Jake and told him she would be coming home, but not just yet.

Liv hunched her shoulders as she walked along the path to her mum's house. The sky was dimming, turning blue to navy. The stars were coming out and the moon was a silver crescent. Halloween pumpkins flickered in doorways and windows displayed spiders, ghosts and cobwebs.

"It's only me," she called out, her voice already shaking. What should she tell her mum about Essie? She took a couple of minutes to stand in the hallway, taking a few deep breaths to quell the worry squeezing her lungs.

"Hiya," Carol said. She frowned when she saw Liv's rounded posture. "What's wrong, love? It's late."

Liv had a boulder-sized lump in her throat. "Can we talk?" she said.

"Of course. Let's get a cuppa."

When Liv followed her mum into the kitchen, she used the wall to steady herself.

Carol made two cups of tea and Liv's hand shook when she picked hers up. "Did you know that Dad taught Essie?" she said.

Her mum frowned at her, taking this in. "No. Did she tell you that?"

"Yes, in her own way…"

"I don't understand."

"Essie was in love with Dad, while she was at university."

Carol smiled. "I'm sure lots of other students felt that way about him, too. He was well-liked and handsome."

"No, I mean, she *really* loved him."

Carol set her cup down. She pulled at a button on her cardigan. "Do you mean that they…?"

Liv shook her head. "No, nothing like that happened. But she did fall for him very hard. He was always on her mind then, and throughout her life."

"And she's told you all this?" Carol's chin quavered. "What is she thinking of?"

Liv held her hand, not sure what to say next.

Carol drew a deep breath. "I know there was one student your dad grew particularly close to. He started to stay late at work for various functions and presentations. It was all part of his job." She paused. "One day I found some cuff links hidden in his sock drawer…"

"Shaped like bees?" Liv said.

"How do you *know*?"

"Essie has them."

Carol's face fell. "Grant said they were a present, from the university. But I could tell they were expensive. I wanted to believe him, but…" Her words trailed away. "I began to wonder…

"I waited for him to arrive home one day and showed them to him. I asked him if there was someone else. When he hesitated, I threw them at him. He picked them up and I never saw them again after that. Later that evening, after you'd gone to bed, he admitted a student had been giving him lots of attention, and he was flattered. I didn't want to know her name, or see her face. I just told him to stop it." Carol clutched her hands together. "Are you telling me it was Essie?"

Liv nodded. "I didn't know until recently. It made me feel sick. But, I know Dad loved us. He was only human."

Carol looked frail, like a baby bird who'd fallen out of its nest. "There's always been a part of me in limbo, wondering if he had an affair with this student."

"Dad rejected Essie. He wanted a life with us." She squeezed her mum's fingers and hesitated. "There's something else I need to tell you."

Carol looked at her fearfully.

Liv released a breath, heavy from her chest. She could tell her mum about Essie making her dad late for the theater, but what good would it do? There was no way to turn back time or rewrite the story. Or predict what might have happened afterward.

Tomorrow was the official date of Essie's death, when Liv would submit the finished manuscript to Marlon. Her mum should know the full story behind it.

Sharing Essie's last wish with her mum, a day early, made Liv feel like she was breaking a bad spell.

She explained everything right from the beginning, starting with meeting a blue-suited solicitor in a café, who passed on a very strange last wish that Essie had made on her deathbed.

Liv revealed that she'd stepped into Essie's shoes in order to complete her last ever novel and had no choice but to cover up the truth. Everything had been like a huge truck with a broken brake pedal.

When she'd finished, her body crumpled, exhausted at keeping the secret for so long, and finally being free of it.

"Oh, love." Carol shook her head very slowly. "I had no idea this was going on. I don't know whether to be sad or happy. I'm just shocked. Does Jake know Essie's dead?"

"Not yet. You're the only one I've told. I wanted you to know about Dad." She lifted her eyes. "Are you angry with me?"

"No. I'm upset you had to go through this alone. What on earth was Essie thinking?"

"She was dying. She was a storyteller with deep regrets."

Carol shook her head, thinking to herself. "I thought your clothes looked smarter than usual," she mused.

It was such a Mum thing to say, Liv couldn't help laughing. "Thanks."

"I mean, you always look nice but…"

"It's too late. You can't take it back."

Carol sat thinking for a while. "So, when we went to that posh Italian restaurant, you used her name…" she said.

"I got carried away, about a lot of things. I'm not proud of it."

"It's not your fault, love. I'm still thinking about that strawberry tart."

"It did taste really good."

They smiled at each other.

Liv thought of how her parents' relationship was one she'd always aspired to. Was it possible she'd never allowed Jake to live up to her dad's superhero memory?

"I've spent too many years thinking about the past." Carol set her cup down. "I'm darned if I'm going to do it any longer."

Liv felt the same way. "Why don't I stay here tonight? I'll phone Jake and tell him I'll be home in the morning."

"That'd be lovely."

Carol yawned and pecked her on the cheek. "I'm usually in bed by now." She headed toward the hallway and disappeared, before sticking her head back around the door. "It's nice to have you home, love."

After calling Jake, Liv wasn't sure how long she sat on the sofa, thinking about Essie. Whatever had happened, she had something the author never had, a family who supported and loved her. And she was all the richer for it.

When midnight arrived, the dining room chilled and the lights went off in the surrounding houses. Liv headed for her old bedroom and saw her mum's bedside lamp was still on. Through the gap in the door, she saw her sitting up in bed, reading. With her face in the shadows, she looked young, just like she used to. Liv opened it a little farther. "I thought you'd gone to sleep," she said.

Carol lowered her book. "I couldn't drop off. Reading helps."

"What's the book?"

Carol held up The River After Midnight. "I want to know how it ends."

"There's a really bad guy in that one."

"I can't remember." Carol shrugged. "And the thing is with baddies, you can't help admiring them a bit sometimes," she said. "They do things you never would."

Liv suddenly had a flashback to being a girl and reading in bed with her mum while her dad was shaving in the bathroom. "Can I get in next to you?" she said.

Carol nodded. She flipped back her covers and shuffled across the mattress to make room.

Liv climbed in and rearranged the bedsheets over their legs.

Carol picked up the book again. "Want to join me?"

Liv hesitated for a moment before nodding.

They read together until an owl hooted outside and they reached the last few pages. As Georgia prepared to ride off into the sunset, Carol's breathing grew shallow and her head fell against Liv's shoulder.

Liv eased the book from her fingers. "Let's finish it tomorrow."

"I want to know how it ends," Carol said sleepily.

"Essie's books always have happy endings." Liv slid out of the bed and helped her mum to lie down. She pulled the covers up to her chin and kissed her on the forehead. "Night, Mum."

"Good night, love."

Liv slipped quietly away and into her old bedroom. She gazed at a photo of her dad on the wall for a long time before her eyes began to shut. She could understand why Essie had fallen for him so deeply and, in time, she thought she might be able to forgive her. But she knew she would never forget.

"Night, Dad," she said and turned off the light.

BESTSELLER
ESSIE STARLING HAS DIED

Sheen Magazine

Essie Starling, the bestselling novelist, who entertained millions of readers with her adventurous stories and daring characters, died on November 1 2019. The cause of her death remains unreported at present.

Born as Elsbeth Smart in London, England, Starling attended Manningham University where she studied English. She subsequently moved to Los Angeles where she cut a glamorous presence on the party scene. She spent the last ten years of her life back in the UK, where she enjoyed a quiet, private life.

Essie flew onto the bestseller lists with her debut novel, *The Moon on the Water*, which introduced readers to Georgia Rory, a new kind of heroine who blazed a trail for other female writers. Essie subsequently wrote a further eighteen novels that have been published in more than forty languages worldwide.

Kind and considerate to many, while always demanding high standards, Essie has bequeathed the majority of her estate to the Museum of Writing in Manningham, where a contemporary writers' room will be set up in her name. An annual award will be made available to underrepresented writers.

Essie was married twice, to English publisher Ted Mason, then to American crime writer Hank Milligan. She didn't have any children and always saw her readers as her family. She will be sorely missed by her friends, fans and everyone in the publishing industry.

Starling's literary agent Marlon Austin said: "Essie was an extraordinarily talented writer with an irrepressible personality and a big heart. She was whip smart and didn't suffer fools gladly. Her curiosity about human nature shone through in the stories she gifted to the world. We're very lucky she finished one last book that I know she would love sharing with her readers everywhere. It's a fitting farewell for all the fans who supported her and who love Georgia Rory."

Read what Essie and Georgia meant to readers, in an exclusive online article by Chloe Anderton.

36

BOOK PEOPLE

A few hours before Essie's obituary was made public, Liv pressed Send on Book Twenty to Marlon. Anthony also contacted the agent to tell him Essie had died. Unusually solemn, Marlon said he'd pass on the awful news.

Liv finally told Jake what had been going on in her life and he was supportive and understanding.

She called Hank and spoke to him in person. "I'm so sorry to break the bad news to you," she said.

"Oh, jeez, I can't believe it. Ess has really gone?" he said. "How? What happened?"

"She'd been fading for some time and passed away on November the first."

He was quiet for a while. "*That* date," he said.

"Yes." Liv swallowed, wondering if it sounded suspicious.

"Heck, it's the day she'd have chosen," Hank said. "She published her first book that day, she won her great prize."

"She'd just finished her new book, too."

"I'm glad 'bout that. It gives me real comfort."

Liv spoke to Chloe next.

"I'm glad I stopped digging into Essie's private life, hon," the journalist said. "I'd have felt so guilty. The article celebrates her life, and the lives of her fans. She'll live on through Georgia Rory forever."

The internet and news channels everywhere were soon awash with announcements about Essie's passing. With no recent footage of the author available, they focused on Georgia Rory fans instead. Clips showed crowds gathered outside bookshops in London, America, Japan and Australia. *The Moon on the Water* and several other of Essie's books rocketed up the charts.

Liv and Anthony passed on information that Essie's funeral would be held privately, as per the author's request, without guests in attendance. When they spoke to each other on the phone, the air was still thorny between them.

"We should hold some kind of memorial service for Essie," Liv said.

"That's not what she would have wanted."

"Maybe it's what *I* want. People who were part of Essie's life should have the chance to say goodbye to her properly."

"I don't suppose there's any point arguing with you," Anthony said.

Liv contacted the owner of the Bookshop on the Square and arranged to hire the café in mid-November. She invited Ted, Sven, Hank, Marlon, Meg, Chloe and Anthony to attend.

She now stood in front of a long table that ran down the middle of the room. Delicate cakes and scones sat on tiers of floral china, and tiny triangles of sandwiches lay in lines. White roses and gypsophila sprung from apothecary-style blue vases. Jake had printed several postcard-size booklets, featuring photos of Essie from across the years, and helped set them out on the table. Tears pricked Liv's eyes when she looked at them.

A shaft of November sunshine sliced through the window,

and she stepped into it, so it warmed her skin. *Come on, Liv*, she said to herself. *How can anyone feel down in a bookshop?*

Instead of dressing up, she wore a Blondie T-shirt, jeans and Converse, and hoped Essie wouldn't mind. She picked up a ham sandwich and a hand promptly shot out and slapped it. "Ouch," she said, pushing the bread into her mouth.

"Wait for the guests," Matilda demanded.

Liv had asked Essie's ex-PA for help with the food order. She swanned around the room in a puff-sleeved yellow chiffon dress more suited to a cocktail party. She straightened cake forks that were already perfectly positioned.

"I expected the smoked salmon sandwiches to be served on brown bread. And the cucumber is sliced too thickly." Matilda flicked a speck of cress off the tablecloth.

"It's a tea party, not the Oscars," Liv said. She could see Matilda's eyes were shiny with tears.

"We both know *Medusa* was a stickler for details, and we want to get this right for her." The ex-PA sniffed. "Are you serving breakfast tea?"

"Yes, and Darjeeling, Earl Grey and some herbal varieties. The Moët & Chandon is on ice."

"Super. Very organized," Matilda said. "I'm so glad *Medusa* gave me my reference, before she—"

Liv fixed her with a stare. "Really?" she said.

"Anyway, I'm starting a new job tomorrow, a permanent role at Alchemy."

"Congrats. What will you be doing?"

"Working in branding, turning water into wine, that kind of thing. Not everyone has the genius to buy Jo Malone candles for the interview panel. Reach out if you ever need any advice, with your PA stuff, or cleaning, or whatever it is you do. Actually," she said, frowning. "What *are* you going to do now?"

Liv didn't have any proper plans yet. "I'll probably help out with my husband's family business for a while. I've been offered a role at the Museum of Writing," she said.

"Cleaning or secretarial work?" Matilda said.

"Actually, neither."

"Hmm, shame." Matilda sipped her tea. "Not everyone has experience in communication *and* organization *and* diary keeping *and* administration."

Liv exaggerated a jaw drop. "Matilda Hennessy," she said, "did you just pay me a compliment?"

Matilda took out her phone and used the screen as a mirror. "Maybe. Now, I should go."

"Stay for tea. I think Essie would like that."

Matilda smiled tightly. "I doubt that very much, but I'm guessing there'll be useful people for me to meet..." she said.

As she swept away, Marlon entered the room. He wore checked suit trousers with a biker jacket and an orange gerbera pinned to his lapel. He kissed Liv's cheek and his usual booming voice was sombre. "It's such a shock, Liv, a damn shame. I've read Essie's latest manuscript and loved it. Who knows what she'd have written next?" He stopped talking and glanced across the room as Ted, Hank and Sven filed inside.

Sven's eyes narrowed when he saw Marlon, but he strode over and outstretched his rose-tattooed hand. Marlon returned his handshake gratefully. They set aside their previous grievances for Essie's sake and sat down together.

Hank wore black jeans and a green shirt unfastened at the neck. "Hey, Liv," he said, stifling a yawn after his flight from LA. "I had to come and say goodbye to Ess. I still can't believe she's gone." He pulled her toward him and held her tightly until Jake gave a small cough.

Liv pulled away. "Hank, this is my husband, Jake," she said.

Hank stuck out his hand. "Hey, man. Cool to meet ya."

THE MESSY LIVES OF BOOK PEOPLE

"You, too," Jake said. He leaned over to speak in Liv's ear. "Good luck. Everything looks great. Call me when you want picking up."

Ted stood ramrod straight as he surveyed the scene. He brushed his hand through his white hair several times. "Good afternoon, Olivia. It's such awful news," he said. "I'm truly sorry."

Liv's throat tightened at the sight of Essie's two ex-husbands standing before her. "Ted, have you met Hank Milligan before?"

Ted visibly stiffened. "I've not had that opportunity."

"Hey, man, I hear you're one of the best book guys in town," Hank said. "Ess said some great things 'bout ya. She sure appreciated the best of everything. Me and you are proof of that."

Ted found a small smile. "That's very kind of you to say so. Would you like a cup of tea?"

They both made their way over to the table.

After the two men had talked for a while, Chloe arrived and Liv introduced her to Hank. "Chloe wrote a lovely piece about Georgia Rory fans everywhere," she told him. "She used your quotes wisely."

Hank shook her hand but then his forehead crinkled. "Are you the hack that was snooping around Ess?" He kept hold of her fingers.

Liv's and Chloe's eyes met.

"I changed my mind about my story. It takes the same amount of words to bring joy, as it does to hurt," Chloe said. "I'd prefer my writing to do some good."

Hank nodded at her. "I'm all for second chances, doll," he said, briefly catching Liv's eye.

Liv Skyped Meg, who wasn't able to make it to the tea party.

"I'm with you all in spirit, Livvy darling," she said. Her eyes were pink as she fiddled with her crystal earring. "So dreadfully upsetting I can't join you in person."

Liv propped her phone up against a vase so Meg had a good view of the table. She moved closer to the screen to keep their conversation private. "Have you had a chance to read Essie's manuscript yet?" she said.

Please let the book be worthy of Essie and her fans, she thought.

Meg's expression gave nothing away until she fluttered a hand to her heart. "I devoured the entire thing in one reading, Livvy," she said. "Essie really knocked it out of the park this time. The ending is wonderful, so poignant. I totally understand that Georgia needs to find herself. So many readers will relate to that."

Tears of relief rushed to Liv's eyes and she blinked up at the ceiling so Meg wouldn't notice.

"Oh, don't cry, darling. You'll set me off." Meg dabbed her nose with a tissue. "Essie certainly left her best work until last. I wish she were here, so I could tell her to her face. Not that I'd seen it for a long time. And, of course we'll need edits… I wonder if you'd be interested, Livvy? You know her creative spirit so well."

"Thanks." Liv smiled to herself. "Perhaps I could take a look."

She looked around her, and didn't feel out of place among all these book people. She was no longer on the outside looking in.

"Are you raising a glass to her, darling?" Meg said.

Liv glanced at her watch. Anthony still hadn't arrived, and she didn't know if he was coming or not. When the door opened a little, she raised her chin expectantly. One of the bookstore staff entered with a jug of water.

Liv sighed and turned away. She straightened a tablecloth and poured more tea for Ted.

Sometime later, she felt a tap on her shoulder. She turned to see Anthony wearing his cobalt suit. His neck muscles were taut and his arms hung stiffly by his side. The white patch in his hair appeared to shine.

Her eyes met with his and she felt an unexpected gush of understanding toward him. Essie's strange last wish had thrust two people together, her ex-lover and the daughter of the man she loved. She and Anthony had both struggled, and searched, and learned the truth. They had survived all the craziness and carried out Essie's request. Liv felt much stronger for it, but she wasn't sure about how he felt.

His eyes were downcast. "Apologies for being late, and for keeping things from you," he said. "Finding out you were Grant's daughter brought back a lot of old emotions I thought I'd buried."

"You were right to be suspicious. I hope I proved myself to you."

He raised his head and looked into her eyes. "You didn't need to," he said. "Essie saw you as her worthy successor and that's good enough for me." He paused before holding out his hand for a shake.

Liv hugged him instead.

"I'm sorry," he said again.

"Me, too."

Pulling away, he looked around him. "You've done Essie proud. Have I missed your speech?"

"I hadn't planned one," Liv said, then realized the room had fallen quiet. "Essie would hate *that*."

"You seem to have everyone's attention," Anthony said. "It looks like they're all waiting for you."

Liv thought about all her feelings for Essie, from being a timid twelve-year-old schoolgirl, to becoming her cleaner, and evolving into her trusted coauthor. How could she ever explain her myriad emotions to anyone? "What should I say?" she said.

"Just say what she meant to you, what she meant to us all." He rubbed her arm and started to pour champagne into everyone's glasses.

As Liv stood at the head of the table, palpitations pattered in her rib cage. She sipped water to wet her throat before she spoke. "Thanks, everyone, for coming today. And for keeping everything under wraps," she said. "I'm sure if Essie was with us today, she'd insist I keep things short and definitely not sweet."

A ripple of laughter sounded around the table.

"What can I say about Essie?" she continued. "When we first met, she was pushy. She was stubborn, and scared me half to death. Not much changed as time progressed. She wasn't an easy person to please. But when you did, for those few seconds you managed it, what a great feeling that was. Like walking on the sunny side of the street.

"I didn't do well at school. I cleaned houses and offices for a living. Some people looked down on me. Yet, Essie never did. She had her demands, liked her carpets cleaned a certain way, and hated the smell of grapefruit in her bathroom. But she treated me with respect, like I was a human being. If she asked me a question, she listened to my answer and considered it. Even a small gap in a door can let in a lot of light. And it made me feel special. I'm proud to be one of the few people she let into her life. The other people were *you*. Our relationships with her weren't smooth. Maybe Essie could have treated people better. Maybe they could have treated her better, too..."

Ted looked down. Sven played with his cuffs, and Hank nodded.

"You probably all gave her great material for her books. She loved us all in her own way, even if she didn't always show it."

Liv took a moment to look down at her hands. She pictured her fingers tracing across Essie's manuscript and dancing across keyboard keys.

"My dad, Grant Cooper, taught Essie at university and recognized her talent. I'm proud that he helped her to write. He also brought me up to be a good person, encouraging me to understand and forgive others. I'm pleased to have been Essie's cleaner, her assistant, but most of all, her friend. I'm going to leave the last few words to Essie's heroine, Georgia Rory."

Liv had been listening to an audiobook of *The Moon on the Water* that morning, and paused it on a favorite passage. She took out her phone and played it out loud.

> *"I hate saying goodbye," Georgia said defiantly. "It's so final, like reading 'The End' when a book is over. I want to think there's going to be another chapter, another story and a chance to say hello again. I prefer to say, until next time, friends..."*

With those last words, Liv felt she might split in two. She furiously brushed away the tears streaming down her face. "Let's have a toast," she said.

"To Essie Starling," Ted, Hank, Meg, Anthony, Chloe and Matilda chorused.

"To Essie bloody Starling," Marlon boomed. "Long may she reign."

When everyone sat back down, the mood lightened and they ate the cakes and sandwiches. Anthony explained about Essie's generous donation to the museum in her will. "If you or your clients can contribute items for display, it will certainly be appreciated," he said.

Chatter rose up, laughter started, and they all talked about Essie and her books until the sky grew black outside.

As the last of the champagne was being sipped, Anthony ushered Liv to the corner of the room. "There's something I need to tell you," he said. "I suppose you could call it the last part of Essie's wish."

She exaggerated a sigh. "Haven't we had enough of these things?"

"You might want to hear me out," he said. "I found something written in Essie's yellow notebook, a small note. She'd like you to receive a co-credit for her book. It means you'd receive part of her advance and royalties when enough copies are sold. *Olivia Green* could sit next to *Essie Starling* on the cover."

Liv held her breath and clamped her eyes shut. She pictured her name in shiny raised letters. It was what she'd always dreamed of. But something, deep down, told her this wasn't the right way.

"The advance and royalties would help my family out no end. But let's keep my name off the cover and not confuse things for Essie's fans," she said. "It's Essie's book. I helped Georgia to find a new path, and I'm happy knowing that. I've actually always been fascinated by the acknowledgments in books…"

"Are you sure? Please take your time to think about it."

She shook her head at him. "We really need to find a new relationship," she said. "This solicitor-cleaner thing isn't working for me."

"Hmm." Anthony rubbed his chin. "It might be a tricky habit to break."

"Give it a try. I think *that* would be part of Essie's wish."

"Ah, I think so, too."

"Are we really agreeing on something?" Liv said. "It feels kind of weird."

Anthony gave her a hug. "Yes, but also very nice at the same time."

37

FRESH SNOW

A few weeks later, in early December, snow fell heavily as Liv headed toward Essie's apartment for the last time ever. She wore her jeans, boots and a bobble hat, and her breath clouded the air.

She took her favorite shortcuts along the back streets where last night's pizza crusts and coffee cups were covered with a layer of white. The snowy coating made the city look like it was snoozing under a duvet, not yet ready to wake up. She loved the sensation of her feet squeaking and crunching, and she looked back over her shoulder to admire her fresh footprints.

Wooden Christmas market stalls had appeared across the city, and Liv found one that sold cups of hot chocolate in many flavors. She bought a cherry and cinnamon one and wrapped her hands around the cup to warm them up.

When she reached Essie's apartment block, the building blended against the gray-white sky so it didn't look quite solid. It wasn't going to be easy saying goodbye to the penthouse. It had provided her with an escape, inspiration and fantasy for three and a half years.

In the lobby area, a Christmas tree was topped with a huge angel who had feathered wings and a golden halo. Clusters of baubles were dotted around, and Liv peered at her distorted reflection in one that hung near the mailboxes. She looked pretty much the same as she did seven months ago, wearing a Rolling Stones T-shirt beneath her sweater. But she felt like a completely different person inside.

She took a few moments to think about everything she'd done since Essie passed away. She'd stepped out of her comfort zone to travel overseas on her own, met agents and publishers, completed writing Essie's book, and made new friends. She'd found out things about her family she'd never have imagined, and felt even closer to them. Paperpress now had a better outlook and, most importantly, she and Jake had pressed the reset button on their relationship and were stronger for it. Liv looked forward to her own future.

She opened Essie's mailbox and found nothing inside it. Leaving it open, she pocketed the key, ready to leave it in the apartment for its next owner. She sighed as she thought about other people moving into Essie's home, not wanting to believe it was really happening. She was aware that each step she took across the lobby felt like a countdown.

Liv took the lift up to the thirty-second floor and enjoyed the floating feeling of rising up through the snowflakes as they flurried down.

She took off her boots in Essie's hallway and stood with her hands on her hips. All the rooms had been stripped bare, so little soul or personality remained. Anthony had sourced agencies to handle the sale of Essie's clothes and belongings. Any unbroken literary awards had been boxed and transported to the museum. The furniture was gone and had left imprints in the carpets, as if the author wasn't quite ready to move on. Liv rubbed a socked foot along them, trying to smooth them out. She plugged in the vacuum cleaner and gave the rooms one last sweep.

After placing the mailbox key on the kitchen worktop, she concocted a bottle full of water, distilled vinegar, lemon juice and drops of lavender oil using ingredients she'd brought in her handbag. When she'd finished wiping down all the surfaces, the apartment smelled like a fresh field in springtime, although the hollows in the carpets still remained.

Liv recalled a trick her mum once showed her. If you placed ice cubes on sunken areas of carpet, they melted and the fibers fluffed up like magic.

Essie's freezer was still plugged in and Liv was pleased to find a tray of ice in the bottom drawer. She pressed out the cubes and placed them in lines along the indentations. Soon, the last traces of Essie would be gone for good.

When she finished, she sat on the windowsill in the writing room and looked out across the city, no longer fearful about the long drop down to the streets below. The soothing scent of lavender helped her thoughts to drift.

In her head, she heard Essie's pen scribbling and the sound of crumpled paper balls plopping onto the carpet. She almost reached out to pick one up. She listened to her breath for a while, the only sound in the room.

All Essie's books had gone, and the photos that displayed a lifetime of memories, too. Whatever Essie might have lost over the years, her passion, her health and her ability to love, she and Liv had found each other, even if it was in an unusual way.

"We could have been a good team, Essie," she whispered. "But it's time to move on, on my own. I want to keep diving for treasure."

She had always thought that forty-two-year-old mums didn't appear in fairy tales, but she didn't believe that any longer. If stories didn't exist the way you wanted them, you had to create your own. And whatever happened in Liv's life from now on, she knew Essie's influence would stay with her forever, like an invisible force field, making her feel brave. Making her feel like Liv Green rather than Georgia Rory.

She wiped a tiny smear off the window with her sleeve and reluctantly got to her feet. She padded toward the writing room door and stood there for a while, allowing herself one last memory of Essie sitting at her desk. The author had her back to Liv. Her head was bowed and her black bob obscured her face.

Liv placed a hand against the doorframe. "I'm not sure I can totally understand everything you did, Essie, but I'll always try to think of you with kindness."

She imagined Essie lifting her chin, turning her head and pressing her fingertips together. As Liv pulled the door closed, the two women held each other's gaze and smiled at each other through the gap, until it finally clicked shut.

Liv lowered her chin.

With her vision blurring, she entered and quickly scanned each of the other rooms. She wiped her eyes and glanced around for dropped pins, stray earring backs and specks of paper. She said her goodbyes to the fluffy carpets and marble work surfaces. She hoped wherever Essie was, there was a nice view and decent cakes.

When she finally walked along the hallway and reached the front door, Liv imagined Essie calling out to her. *"Goodbye, Olivia."*

Liv hesitated with her hand on the handle. "Goodbye Essie," she said. "Thanks for everything."

"That is all," Essie said.

When Liv felt the handle moving downward, she jumped back and the door swept toward her by a few inches. A black boot appeared, nudging it open. Liv craned her neck to see

Jake carrying a small cardboard box under one arm. She'd arranged to meet him outside the apartment block a little later that morning.

"Another resident let me in downstairs," he said. "I finished work early and left my dad showing Katrina how to bind books. Can you believe it?"

"I need a good imagination to actually picture it."

"Well, you certainly have that. To apologize for her behavior, I suggested Katrina should make you a notebook."

"You might be pushing her too far." Liv laughed. "But I do actually need a new one."

Jake raised the box he was holding. "The postman was delivering this and I saw your name on the label. I said I'd bring it up for you." He passed it to her.

The box felt heavy in Liv's hands. "I think I know what it is," she said. She crouched and set it down on the floor. Peeling back the strips of tape, she opened the flaps and curls of polystyrene sprang out.

Jake stooped to pick them up. "Got to keep this place tidy. I can see all your vacuum tracks. Imagine trying to keep this place clean with Mack and Johnny around." He rolled his eyes.

Liv looked along the hallway. The pale gray carpets looked like an ice rink, with marks made by skates. "Imagine?" she said. "I've been trying to do it for years."

They met each other's gaze, knowing the two of them would be alone in the house for a while, until their sons came home from university for Christmas. And Liv felt in her heart it was all going to be okay.

She pulled down her sweater sleeves to cover her hands so she didn't get fingerprints on the crystal award that lay in the box. It was a good copy of Essie's Constellation prize. She'd ordered it while staying in the student flat, to replace the broken version, and gave the delivery address for Essie's apartment while on autopilot. "I'll take this to Anthony at the museum, this morning. Want to come with me?"

He nodded and read the engraved lettering. "You might win something like that, one day," he said.

Liv didn't joke, or bat his words away, or say that it was impossible. Instead she imagined how that would feel. *Well done, sweet pea,*" her dad whispered in her ear. "I'd love that," she said. She didn't need a prize to feel his pride in her, and her own pride in herself.

Jake stood back up and looked around him, at the high ceilings, pristine white walls and skirting boards without scuff marks.

"I can show you around, if you like?" she offered. "You'll need to take off your boots."

He shook his head. "I don't think it's my kind of place. It's too stark and I like my home comforts."

"Me, too." She smiled. "It's not very family friendly, and you can't hang clothes out on a washing line."

He reached down and squeezed her shoulder. "Are you sure you're ready to leave? We can stay longer if you like," he said.

Liv shook her head. "No, let's go and drop off this award, and then I'd like to go home." She put on her boots and tied the laces. She locked the front door.

Inside the lift, she and Jake stood together, watching the city growing closer and bigger as they dropped down toward it.

"Johnny phoned home this morning," Jake said, as they stepped out into the lobby. "He grumbled about having to do his own washing up and laundry and buying his own loo rolls. I think he's learning to appreciate everything we did for him. He mentioned inviting a new friend around for a coffee over Christmas. Perhaps we could make lasagna and chocolate cake, together."

She squeezed his hand. "Sounds lovely, but I'm just as happy with beans on toast."

They walked toward the exit doors and Liv caught sight of something out of the corner of her eye. Her shark blood senses kicked in and she glanced back over her shoulder. "I'll just be two minutes," she said, handing the box to him.

She darted back toward Buddha and whispered a quick farewell. Taking a tissue from her pocket, she pinched up a few stray pine needles that had fallen off the Christmas tree onto the floor. "One quick last cleanup," she told Jake, when she rejoined him.

"Will you miss doing that?" he said.

"Probably, but I have an idea...for a new story."

They left the building and Liv grinned as snowflakes settled on her eyelashes and the tip of her nose. Taking the box off Jake, she tucked it under her arm.

As they strolled toward the museum, they held hands and chatted about their plans for Christmas Day. And when Liv looked up at the sky it shone pure white, like a blank page of paper waiting to be written upon.

Acknowledgments

I'm always astonished by the amount of time and effort that goes into publishing a book. It's a truly collaborative affair of which my writing is only part of the process. As always, I'm grateful for my agent, Clare Wallace: her calmness, belief in my work and her encouragement. Also, the support of the entire Darley Anderson team, including Mary Darby, Kristina Egan, Georgia Fuller, Chloe Davis, Rosanna Bellingham and Sheila David. You are all wonderful.

My US editor, Natalie Hallak at Park Row, saw the potential in my idea right from the very beginning, and her vision for the book, patience and creativity spurred me on to push my boundaries and write a better story. As always, huge thanks also go to Erika Imranyi, Emer Flounders and the rest of the Park Row team for their tireless work on my books. My UK editors at Harlequin/HarperCollins, Emily Kitchen, Abby Parsons and Katie Seaman, have also been brilliantly supportive in helping to bring my book to life, and thanks to Lisa Milton for her continuous championing. I'm truly appreciative of each and every other person involved, too, including copyediting, cover design, marketing, publicity and sales and distribution.

Special mention and thanks go to my friend Janine Mc-Kown for her medical advice on Essie's situation in hospital, and to solicitor Andrew Harrison for his thoughts and comments regarding Essie's will. Also, to David Birchall, my dad, who worked as an undertaker for many years and helped me to understand how the mechanics of Essie's last wish might work. Any artistic license I've taken in the telling of Liv and Essie's stories, or any mistakes I've made, are entirely my own.

Writing a book can be a solitary process, so I'm grateful to my wider support group of other writers in the UK and USA. It's great to know so many kind and talented people are just the click of a button, or a coffee, away. Thank you especially to B. A. Paris and Roz Watkins. You are both great writers and lovely human beings.

I'd like to thank booksellers, librarians, bloggers, reviewers and readers everywhere for their amazing support and for helping to spread the word about my writing. My books couldn't happen without you.

Finally, a huge shout-out to my family, especially Mark and Oliver, who put up with me disappearing to my writing shed for long periods of time, sometimes at unsociable hours. For my mom and dad, Pat and Dave, for always encouraging my love of reading and for being such proud advocates of my books. For all my friends, particularly Nu Motley Cru and Private Members Club—hello and thanks. Sending love to you all.

Questions for Discussion

1. Liv Green and Essie Starling live very different lives. Liv is a busy cleaner, wife and mum of two, struggling to make ends meet. Essie lives a quiet, solitary life of luxury. Which woman did you relate to the most? Which woman's life would you prefer to lead and why?

2. Essie leaves Liv a very unusual last request and an unexpected inheritance. Have you ever been left anything unexpected in a will?

3. Hannah Cardinal and the Platinum office staff don't always treat Liv with respect. Should Liv take some responsibility for this? Have you ever found yourself in a similar position at work, and did you stand up for yourself? If not, why not?

4. We learn of Essie's death early on in the book. How is her spirit kept alive on the page? What did you learn about her life and how did it change your opinion of her?

5. Liv steps into Essie's world and is seduced by her lifestyle. If you could step into someone else's shoes for six months, who would it be and why?

6. Liv has wanted to be a writer since childhood but was too embarrassed to share her dream with others. Did you

have a childhood dream, and did you follow it? Did you tell others about it, or keep it to yourself?

7. Georgia Rory is an important character in Essie's fiction. How did Georgia influence and inspire change for Liv?

8. What was your favorite scene in the book and why? Did reading the book impact your mood? If yes, how so?

9. Liv and Jake endure various marriage struggles throughout the book, making Liv question their future together. Ultimately, she decides she wants to make things work between them. Did you agree with her decision?

10. What do you think Liv will do next? What might her life look like in two years' time and beyond?

More Delightful Reads from Bestselling Author
PHAEDRA PATRICK

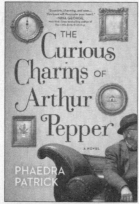

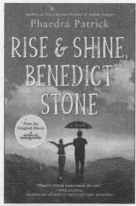

Connect with us at:

BookClubbish.com/Newsletter

Instagram.com/BookClubbish

Twitter.com/BookClubbish

Facebook.com/BookClubbish

PARK
ROW
BOOKS